D0126765

THE
GENESIS
WARS

AN INFINITY COURTS NOVEL
2

THE GENESIS WARS

AKEMI DAWN BOWMAN

SIMON & SCHUSTER BFYR

New York London Toronto Sydney New Delhi

SIMON & SCHUSTER BFYR

An imprint of Simon & Schuster Children's Publishing Division
1230 Avenue of the Americas, New York, New York 10020

Text © 2022 by Akemi Dawn Bowman
Jacket illustration © 2022 by Casey Weldon
Map on pages vi–vii © 2022 by Virginia Allyn
Jacket design by Laura Eckes © 2022 by Simon & Schuster, Inc.

For information about special discounts for bulk purchases, please contact Simon & Schuster Special Sales at 1-866-506-1949 or business@simonandschuster.com.
The Simon & Schuster Speakers Bureau can bring authors to your live event.
For more information or to book an event, contact the Simon & Schuster Speakers Bureau at 1-866-248-3049 or visit our website at www.simonspeakers.com.
Interior design by Laura Eckes
The text for this book was set in Bembo.
Manufactured in the United States of America
First Edition
2 4 6 8 10 9 7 5 3 1
Library of Congress Cataloging-in-Publication Data
Names: Bowman, Akemi Dawn, author.
Title: The genesis wars / Akemi Dawn Bowman.
Description: First edition. | New York : Simon & Schuster Books for Young Readers, [2022] | Series: The Infinity courts ; book 2 | Audience: Ages 12 up. | Audience: Grades 7-9. | Summary: Ten months ago Nami escaped Ophelia and the Courts of Infinity, and found a sort of refuge in the Borderlands; she has spent her days training her body and mind so that when the time comes she will be able to navigate Infinity and rescue her captured friends, and now she has made a breakthrough, gaining the ability to enter minds without permission—the answers she needs are in Prince Caelan's mind, but his betrayal has left her unsure about her ability to face him again.
Identifiers: LCCN 2021030166 (print) | LCCN 2021030167 (ebook)
| ISBN 9781534456549 (hardcover) | ISBN 9781534456563 (ebook)
Subjects: LCSH: Racially mixed people—Juvenile fiction. | Psychic ability—Juvenile fiction. | Self-confidence—Juvenile fiction. | Rescues—Juvenile fiction. | Future life—Juvenile fiction. | Princes—Juvenile fiction. | Adventure stories. | CYAC: Psychic Ability—Fiction. | Self confidence—Fiction. | Rescues—Fiction. | Future life—Fiction. | Princes—Fiction. | Adventure and Adventurers—Fiction. | Racially mixed people—Fiction. | LCGFT: Action and adventure fiction. | Fantasy fiction.
Classification: LCC PZ7.1.B6873 Gf 2022 (print) | LCC PZ7.1.B6873 (ebook) | DDC 813.6 [Fic]—dc23
LC record available at https://lccn.loc.gov/2021030166
LC ebook record available at https://lccn.loc.gov/2021030167

To the hopeful ones who dream, and care, and see bridges where others see fire. Keep shining your light on the world.

INFINITY
WAR
GENESIS (NEW)
ABANDONED OUTPOST
CANYON
BATTLEFIELDS
BATTLEFIELDS
OUTPOST
OUTPOST
CANYON
THE RED CITY
NORTH GATE
BATTLEFIELDS
OUT-POST
WEST GATE
FIRE PIT
ETTORE'S PALACE
SOUTH GATE

THE BORDERLANDS

GENESIS (OLD)

BATTLEFIELDS

OUTPOST

EAST
GATE

CANYON

THE CAPITAL

FAMINE

VICTORY

DEATH

1

THE FOREST IS SILENT, BUT I KNOW I'M BEING hunted.

Frost spreads across my blade, covering the sharpened sea-glass until all that's left is a small patch of muted red. The flicker of a heartbeat. The flame of something desperate to survive.

I rotate the dagger in my hand and push forward through the snow.

The silver birch is heavy on this side of the forest. Not like the forests in Victory, with their spacious clearings and limited places to hide. I haven't been within Caelan's borders since the day I fled his palace. But here there are a thousand places to disappear. A thousand ways to become invisible.

And still they found me.

The snowfall is fresh enough that my boots sink into the ground with each step, leaving a trail for my predator, but there's nothing I can do about it. I've already been marked.

I duck beneath a low branch, winding behind dormant trees and snow-covered vegetation. It isn't much of a maze, but it's enough to buy me a moment.

And a moment is all I need.

I throw myself behind one of the larger trees and kick my weight off a protruding root to help lift me onto the lowest branch. I climb quickly, fingers ignoring the scratch of frozen bark, until I'm hidden in the tangle of thick branches with a view of the clearing up ahead.

A hooded figure sits at the base of a tree, still as the frozen world around them.

I tighten my grip on my dagger, eyes glued to the path, waiting for the other one. My hunter. Because the stars know they never travel alone.

But the quiet is sinister. Not even a wraith could move so silently. And as I watch the snowfall, it occurs to me that I've been so busy watching the ground, I forgot to watch the trees.

An earthy growl rumbles nearby. Before I have a chance to turn around, an enormous weight throws itself against my body, tearing me from the branches. My right shoulder hits the earth with a crack, scattering my dagger out of reach. I roll to the side, push myself to my feet, and spin around to face my attacker.

The beast shimmers like a galaxy of clouds and stars, its body distinctly snow leopard. But its ocean-blue eyes don't belong to any animal—they're human.

I lunge for my weapon, but the wildcat is too quick. It throws itself into a pounce, and we're tumbling over rock and shrub and snow. I ignore the pain that shoots through my hip, focusing my grip around the beast's neck as its razor-sharp canines snap uncomfortably close to my face.

With a strained grunt, I focus on my consciousness, letting a thrum of power build in my palms before throwing it all toward the animal. The force of energy knocks the creature back across the snow, and its body tumbles to a stop. A snarl erupts from its flashing teeth as it slowly gets back on all fours.

The snow leopard isn't injured, but it's definitely annoyed.

I scramble quickly, snatching up my dagger as I run toward another tree. By the time I look over my shoulder, the starlit creature is already sailing through the air for a second pounce.

I shut my eyes, letting another thrum of energy absorb every inch of me, and surround myself with a veil.

I become invisible.

Throwing myself out of the way just in time, I hear the cat slam into the base of a tree—the place I left behind. The branches above give a shudder, and a pile of snow plummets onto the creature's head. I reappear several feet away, blade pointed toward the cat with a snarl of my own.

The snow leopard's eyes morph into two bright lights. No longer human, but Dayling.

Nearby, someone cackles. "All this time training, and all you've managed to learn are a few parlor tricks? How disappointing."

I turn around to find the figure who was beneath the tree. She stands several feet away, hands hovering beside the blades at her hips. Even beneath her hood, I can see the tug of a smirk. A challenge.

My eyes don't leave the pacing cat in front of me, even though my voice is meant for the woman. "I've also learned to never show all my cards in the first round." My fingers twitch toward the earth. A lonesome branch sits in the snow, waiting. Waiting for me.

The branch flexes and morphs, pixels bursting across its elongated surface, until it becomes a solid club. I snatch it from the ground in an instant, just as the snow leopard bares its fangs and leaps toward me—and I strike the animal over the back of the head.

It falls to the ground, stunned.

The woman's smirk becomes a flash of teeth. She lets out a growl from beneath her hood, but I'm already swinging my blade toward her chest. She throws out an arm to block, and my dagger finds her armor. It's paper thin and more second skin than metal, but it absorbs the weight—and damage—of my attack. I stumble against her, and she swings her body around to reveal a pair of matching obsidian knives. She slashes left, then right, and I'm being pushed backward and toward the heady brambles. Unwilling to be cornered, I swing my blade upward with every bit of my strength. She uses one knife to block, and the other to pierce the skin between my ribs, barely missing my heart. It's the kind of cut that's intentional and meant to maim, not kill.

Except no one really dies in Infinity. Not yet, anyway.

It takes everything in me not to cry out in pain, but I don't. I've come too far to let a knife wound slow me down.

I push my body against her, forcing her back. And as she's busy retrieving her knife from my bone, I throw my head against hers with a furious crack, sending her stumbling toward an uprooted tree.

She stills in midair, just before making contact, floating like an otherworldly being. And maybe she is. Maybe we all are.

The blood gathering at my wound feels sticky and warm. But the fight isn't over. There will be time for healing later.

I approach, pulling my daggered fist back for another swing, and she vanishes completely.

Her laugh fills the cold forest, but I can't see her. She sounds nowhere and everywhere, like an echo filling a canyon. My shoulders tense. I'm scanning the woods, heat rising in my cheeks, when the creature made of clouds and light crashes into me, smashing my skull against the nearby tree. I sink to the earth.

Winded, my gaze full of stars, I sense the world tilting behind the beast's snarling head. And then—a sandpaper tongue scrapes against the side of my face.

"You're too soft on her, Nix," the girl says with another laugh, coming into view once more. "Need I remind you she tried to *bludgeon* you?" She pulls her hood down to reveal a face I've nearly memorized: pale skin sprinkled in freckles, ocean-blue eyes, and brown hair braided into three sections. A sigil of a herring and a thistle is embroidered on her collar. The symbol of the Salt Clan.

Not that there's much left of it.

The snow leopard gives a purr against my ear and nips at my hair. "Can you please call off your ferocious Dayling?"

He huffs in response.

"Don't take it personally, Nix," Kasia says, giving a short whistle that has the cat immediately at her side. "Nami doesn't like affection."

I scowl, but I don't say anything. I'd rather everyone think it's hugs I don't like, instead of the actual problem, which is that growing close to anyone just isn't a possibility anymore.

Not after what happened, and what it cost me.

I let myself get close to someone—trusted them so much that I missed the warning signs—and, because of me, the Colony fell.

I sheathe my knife, ignoring the pinch in my chest as Kasia scratches behind Nix's ears. "I thought you were patrolling the border today?" I remark.

"I was. Then I saw you."

I glance at Nix's bright white eyes. There's not a hint of Kasia left in them. "Do you think he feels it? When you take control of him?" The ache in my chest is constant, but when I think of Gil, and what Caelan did to him . . .

That's when the ache starts to *burn*.

Kasia's smile fades. "Nix isn't a consciousness. He's made of memories. And holding on to memories is a very human thing to do."

"You make it sound natural," I say. "But there's no one else in the Borderlands who can use a Dayling like it's a second body."

Her blue eyes flicker with mischief. "What can I say? I'm one in a million."

I fight the urge to laugh—the urge to feel like myself again. The Nami whose biggest worries included pop quizzes and whether her best friend liked her the way she liked him.

But human Nami died. And the things I wanted to hold on to, like believing people were capable of changing, and thinking kindness and understanding would always be more powerful than hate . . .

There isn't a place for that in Infinity. There isn't a place for the old me.

Annika told me fighting was the only way to survive—so I'm adapting. The person I am now? She will do whatever it takes.

I blink, pushing back at the guilt even when it feels overwhelming. "How far can you travel with Nix before your mind is pulled back?"

Kasia watches him the way someone would watch a beloved pet. "There was a time before the First War when we'd travel the length of all Four Courts without a second thought." Her voice turns breathy. "But joining up with Nix is like being in a vessel. I can steer, but I can't *become* him. I have no abilities beyond what Nix could do himself. If I lost him in the Labyrinth, alone, in a sea or a cavern or something worse . . . I might never be able to get him back."

My gaze drifts to the falling snow. If I had a Dayling like Nix, and the ability to use them as a vessel, I'd travel to Victory. To War. To *Death*, if I had to. I could get the information I need, and finally figure out where the others were taken after I betrayed Caelan and proved Ophelia's point.

But Infinity is a big world. All I can do right now is train as much as possible, and prepare myself for the day I'm ready to venture back into the Labyrinth.

I owe the Colony so much more than their freedom.

"If I could show you how it works, I would." Kasia's smile turns grim. "But the bond I share with Nix requires a great deal of trust—and trust is something I cannot teach."

I don't bother pointing out that trust is something I've had far too much of in the past. She saw my memories through an Exchange; she knows what happened on the Night of the Falling Star.

Trusting Gil and Caelan—who turned out to have been the same person all along—is part of the reason I failed.

"I don't need a Dayling," I say bitterly. "I need an *army*." Someone willing to fight with me, because I'm still not strong enough to do any of this alone.

"I know you're planning to leave this place one day, and I train with you because I want you to have the best chance possible. But you know how the clans feel about returning to war," Kasia says. "You know what we've already lost."

"If you won't fight, at least help me find them," I argue. "Isn't the whole point of the Border Clans to guide humans to safety? You once told me I was the first human in over a hundred lifetimes to follow the path in the stars. What good is a map if no one knows how to find it?"

We should be out there telling people the truth. We should be *helping* them.

This is the safe haven Annika and the others deserve. The home that should've been *theirs*, not mine.

Nix slides back on his haunches, mouth open in a yawn. No doubt tired of hearing me argue the same point over and over again.

But I can't let it go.

"We're still here, aren't we?" Kasia notes. "You may not see waiting as a sacrifice, but you have only been here a short time. We have stayed to look after this place since the First War."

"Yeah, and for how much longer?" My words are sharp as steel.

Ten months ago, I'd never have noticed the waver in Kasia's eyes. The flicker of hesitation in a deep sea of blue.

But I'm not the same person I was ten months ago.

"I know the council voted again." There's an edge in my voice. Maybe a hint of impatience, too.

Kasia considers me, while Nix flicks his tail at the frostbitten air. "Yes. Just as we have every fortnight for the past two cycles." After a beat of silence, she sighs. "Nothing has changed. The vote was three to one, as it always has been. The Border Clans aren't going anywhere."

"But you still voted."

"*I* voted to *stay*."

The snow crunches beneath my boots as I inch closer, fists balled. "How can the clans still be thinking about leaving, after everything I've told you about humans and Residents?"

"The Borderlands were never supposed to be a permanent solution."

"You have hundreds of trained fighters. The clans should be voting on whether to go to war, not whether they should abandon every human in the Four Courts!"

Nix bristles. Kasia clicks her tongue, gaze falling to my hands. "Careful, Nami. I like you, but if you let your temper loose on me, I'll snap you in half and I won't apologize for it."

I blink, feeling the energy already building at my fingers. It used to take so much effort to hold on to even a sliver of power. But now it seems tied to my anger. Tied to *me*.

Sometimes I worry I'm a ticking time bomb, waiting to explode without any warning at all.

But I reel the power in, because Kasia is not my enemy, and she certainly doesn't deserve my rage.

She stares across the frozen stretch of woodland, lashes coated in snowflakes, and exhales, breath visible in the cold. "I believe maintaining the Borderlands is the right thing to do. But many of the others are restless. This isn't their home. It never will be."

"The clans can't leave. Not when there are still survivors out there." I need somewhere safe to bring my friends when I find them.

I need to be able to give them hope.

Kasia motions toward Nix, who immediately stalks back through the forest. With a final glance my way, she adds, "I won't go to battle with you, but that doesn't mean I'm not on your side, Nami. Try to remember that when you feel like setting the world on fire."

She vanishes back through the heavy silver birch, and I remain standing until the snow covers the footsteps she left behind.

A reminder that even when I'm surrounded by humans— humans who have given me sanctuary since the day I chased the stars through the desert—I'm still alone.

I spend the rest of the evening training near the western border, where the snowfall is constant but the fields are wide. I let
the energy build in my palms, and knock down makeshift targets
in the distance. Stones, sticks—they're all fair game in this lifeless,
empty place.

Even when I'm exhausted, I keep going. Even when my
muscles ache, I don't stop.

The Border Clans won't fight; when the day comes that I
return to the Four Courts, I'll be going alone. If I only get one
chance at a rescue mission, I need to be ready. So I train to be
quicker with a dagger, and better with my veils, and more resil-
ient to pain.

One day I will become a weapon my enemy won't see coming—
and then I'll leave these walls and track down every single person
I left behind.

I'll rest when they're all free.

I practice throwing my blade, forcing it to arc through the
air and swing back toward me. I catch it a few times, miss a few
others. And then, as I watch the red blade spin through the sky
and reach out my hand, my tiredness catches up with me, and I
fumble my grip.

The blade nicks my wrist before falling into the snow behind
me. At my feet, I count droplets of bright red blood.

A hiss escapes through my teeth as I inspect the wound, putting pressure against it out of habit. The same place where my
O-Tech watch used to sit.

A flash of Ophelia's black void appears in my mind, and the
memory makes my spine tense.

I haven't accidentally called on her. But sometimes I wonder if reaching out to the Residents is the only way I'll ever be able to find out where the Colony is being held.

It's a reckless idea. And maybe if I weren't so tired, I wouldn't even be entertaining it.

Desperation pounds at the floodgates, demanding an answer.

I failed them once. I can't fail them again.

I brush my thumb over my wrist, smearing blood, but it isn't Ophelia I think of. It's someone who never felt truly Resident *or* human.

I think of the prince who let me escape.

The scent of pine hits me hard, forcing me back to reality with a violent shudder.

I blink several times, regaining my composure. Talking to Caelan again . . . I'm not sure if I'm ready to open that door. If I'll *ever* be ready.

And why waste time trying to get information out of a liar?

I tear my hand away from my wrist, grab my knife, and force myself back through the snow.

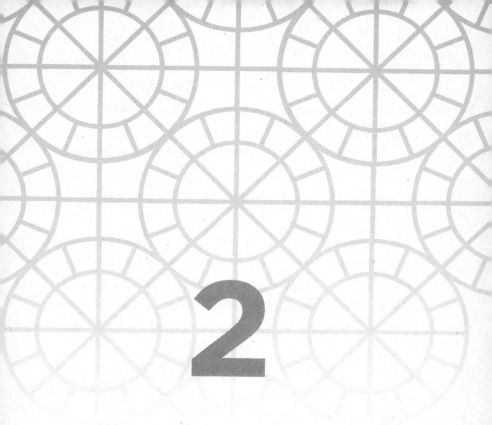

2

THE NIGHT MARKET SMELLS OF SPICE, COFFEE grounds, and candied chestnuts. Stalls twinkling with glass lanterns follow the pier, the wooden planks still painted a vibrant teal despite the constant ebb and flow of the nearby sea.

The sight of so many humans—so many *aware* humans—still makes my heart stumble. They shuffle from stall to stall, filling their baskets with steamed buns, colorful fruit, and pastries soaked in sweet syrup. There are trinkets here too, but while Victory's treasures were rooted in something evil and forced, the art and fabrics here feel like they were made with love. And there is no money to be exchanged in the Borderlands. No form of payment beyond gratitude.

They already have freedom and an infinite life. Maybe all people really want beyond that is a connection to the rest of humanity.

A connection. I ignore the itch on my wrist where the Reaper rests. I haven't taken it off since that day. It's a reminder that I need to finish what I started. A reminder that the Colony once believed in me.

A woman with silver-streaked hair and weathered hands waves at me from the nearby teahouse. Güzide—procurer of the most mouthwatering baklava I've ever had the pleasure of tasting. The humans in the Borderlands all come from a time before Ophelia, but Güzide is nearly as old as Mama Nan. She lived before the first steam trains.

She's been kind to me. Kinder than most.

But all I see is the sigil on her robes: a stag's skull crowned with twigs. The Bone Clan.

And today the Bone Clan voted to leave.

Güzide beckons me closer, motioning toward a tray of silver teacups and a tower of honeyed sweets. "Come and sit down, Nami. Have some tea." She smiles, and wrinkles blossom all over her face. "You're always training," she notes, voice as silken as a rose petal. "I worry about you."

It was easy enough to get sucked into this world of peace and simplicity in those first weeks here. But it felt just as wrong then as it does now. Annika, Ahmet, Shura, Theo, Yeong, and all the others . . . They're still at the mercy of the Residents. They still *need* me.

I don't care how wonderful the baklava is—I won't become complacent.

I'm shifting away from Güzide and all the lovely scents that come with her offer, ready to move on, when I hear a familiar voice from inside the teahouse. I turn slightly to peer through the glassless windows, and I find Artemis seated at a crowded table near the back.

Wavy locks of unnaturally golden hair flow past his shoulders. He tilts his head back, laughter pouring out in operatic tones, demanding the room's attention. It's something he already has far too much of.

If the Border Clans abandon this place, it will be his fault.

I've trained harder than anyone should in a single day, but I can still do more. I pull up a veil and duck into the teahouse, hidden from sight.

Weaving around the wooden tables, I move the way Kasia taught me—with light feet and an impenetrable focus. The best way to cover my tracks is to not leave them at all. Not that anyone would see my footprints in the teahouse: the floors are solid, dark, and stained with drink. But I need all the practice I can get.

Maybe someday I'll be able to move through walls, too, the way Mama Nan does. Half corporeal, half spirit.

The mask I wore wasn't enough to stop the Residents. It doesn't matter that I can control it better than ever before, morphing my appearance as easily as I can morph my clothes. My face was never the key to ending the war—and I have no desire to look anything other than human.

Next time I face the Residents, I plan to arm myself with more weapons than they'll know what to do with.

The sharp tang of wine reaches my nose, and a flash of a

ballroom erupts in my mind. Perfect faces. Twirling gowns. A crown of silver branches.

I sneer, and brush past a human raising a glass in the air. He looks over his shoulder at the movement, slightly confused, but returns to his toast quick enough.

Pride rustles behind my rib cage.

"I'm surprised to see you in such high spirits, Artemis," a woman remarks behind a plate of tea cakes. "Didn't the Bone Clan lose the vote again?"

Artemis sips from a silver tumbler. "It's a delay, not a loss. In the end, we will follow our ancestors into the Afterlands, just as it was always intended."

Across the table, Cyrus and Mira shake their heads disapprovingly, their religious robes varying in shades of purple. Most of the Faithful hail from the Mirror Clan—both led by a man named Tavi—but some wear the sigils of other clans too.

These two are unmistakably the former.

"It is our duty to guide humans to safety," Mira says evenly. "If we don't keep the port open, they'll never know the way."

"We owe the younglings nothing." Artemis sets his cup down, hand running through his golden hair. "Ophelia was not of our creation. Why should it be our job to play ferryman for all eternity?" A rumble of agreement fills the room, making my skin crawl. "We did what we could, in the beginning, but it has been many lifetimes since the First War. The Border Clans deserve to move on."

Cyrus draws a breath, prickling. "You don't speak for everyone. The Salt and Mirror Clans—"

"The Salt Clan shouldn't even have a vote," someone chimes in from another table. A member of the Bone Clan, judging by his collar. "That girl failed her people. She has no clan *left*."

I want to rip off my veil and defend Kasia, but she wouldn't want it. She still thinks these people are her family. And maybe they are.

The Colony wasn't perfect, but they were my family too. And I would tear Infinity apart to find them again. To make sure they're *safe*.

I stay under the veil, cursing the man's words in silence.

Mira lifts her chin, nose pointed in the air. "Kasia is still a clan leader. And every leader gets a vote."

"Something else that needs to change," another woman says, earning a round of slow applause. "Why should only four people decide the fate of hundreds?"

"Why should hundreds decide the fate of millions?" Cyrus counters. "Who will vote for the younglings? For all those yet to be reborn in Infinity?"

"This battle with technology and artificial life was their own doing," the woman barks back. "Let them face the consequences of what they have built."

The applause grows louder, and I lock my knees in place, too angry to breathe.

But Cyrus doesn't waver. If he knows he's lost the room, he doesn't care. "Every human deserves a path to redemption. The way of the Mirror Clan will never change—and neither will our vote."

"Are you sure about that?" Artemis's eyes twinkle. "I'd wager you hardly know your own clan these days. When's the last time you had a conversation with anyone outside the Faithful?"

Cyrus holds up his hands. "Is this not a conversation?"

Artemis's grin is devilishly feline. "No. This is a moral interrogation. Something I truly hoped had died when the original faiths did."

Mira narrows her eyes. "Our faiths have not died—they have merged. It is better to respect one another for what we do know rather than reject one another for what we don't."

"If you want to spend the rest of your eternity in prayer, I won't stop you," Artemis says coolly. "But don't pretend you give a damn about mutual respect when you've spent the last several hundred lifetimes treating anyone outside the Faithful as if they were beneath you."

"It has nothing to do with faith," Mira replies. "It is about trust."

Artemis barks a laugh. "Please. Do explain."

"You care more about yourself than you do your own people."

His gaze sharpens. "You know nothing about my people."

"There are Faithful in the Bone Clan too," Cyrus says. "And they have not forgotten how you abandoned Ozias to the same fate as the Salt Clan, and stole a throne in his absence."

Artemis shoots to his feet, fingers clawed into the edge of the table. Hot, molten smoke builds from his olive skin, and when his nostrils flare, his irises turn red. "I am not the only one who turned from the hill that day."

"But you were the only one to gain a title. And now you are the only clan leader who wishes to leave." Cyrus looks at the faces in the small crowd. "Your vote has always been rooted in your own self-interest."

"You overstep," Artemis seethes. "The Border Clans are here today because of the choices I made. *That* is what my people remember."

Several members of the Bone Clan rise throughout the teahouse, eyes brightening and power thrumming at their sides. A silent pledge of loyalty.

"You wish to attack me because you don't like what I have to say?" Cyrus holds his composure. "History suggests anyone willing to go to war to keep someone silent has a great deal more to hide."

"The Bone Clan has no interest in going to war," Artemis says, smoke subsiding even as his eyes remain fixed like gemstones. "But if you insult my clan again . . . War is one thing—retribution is another."

The two members of the Faithful look around, suddenly aware how outnumbered they are. After a moment, they stand.

"I think we're done here," Cyrus says.

"Enjoy your wine," Mira adds curtly.

When they're gone, Artemis chugs the remnants from his silver cup before slamming it roughly against the table. He waves his hand across the rim, and the tumbler instantly fills with red liquid. Again, he drinks.

The argument isn't new. The clans have been having the same debate for centuries: stay and offer sanctuary to the humans who need it, or travel to the Afterlands, where most of the humans who came before Ophelia have already gone.

But something is changing. They're making it personal, bring-ing up reasons not to trust their leaders, demanding more power for the majority. . . .

Kasia said the clans were restless. What happens when they take action? What will the vote look like then? I need to find Annika and the others, and bring them here, before sailing to the Afterlands is no longer an option.

But if I found myself in Resident territory, I'm not sure I'd even stand a chance.

I need to make myself a force in this world. I need a new way to train.

Frustrated, I push back through the crowd.

Mama Nan, the leader of the Iron Clan, is perched behind one of the smaller tables, embroidered silk robes covering her small frame. A puff of curly white hair sits on her head, twisted at the cen-ter like a dollop of whipped cream. Her brown skin is freckled—a sign of her nearly ninety years of life before Infinity—but her bright eyes show the many more lifetimes lived after death.

I glance at her on my way past, and our eyes meet. My shoul-ders stiffen, and I tug the mental veil closer.

When she speaks, her oaken voice fills the space between us. "You can't hide from me, little one."

I release my hold over the veil, stubborn defiance wedged in the corners of my mouth. "How did you know?"

Mama Nan laughs like a goblet bubbling over; like it's too much to contain. "Your thoughts are louder than a herd of ele-phants." When I frown, she adds, "You wear a veil like it's a dress, but you forget that your mind is a part of you too."

"You were listening to my thoughts?" I've communicated with Ophelia, and even the girl from the palace I failed to save. But to eavesdrop without them knowing?

That's a skill I could use.

Ophelia said she let me through the doors of her mind. It never occurred to me it might be possible to sneak inside without permission.

Mama Nan sniffs, waving a hand. "I don't hear what's inside your mind, but I can feel the vibrations. So much of Infinity is held together by energy, you see. And your mind . . . it howls."

I make a face, fighting the heat in my cheeks. "If you saw what was happening in the Four Courts, your mind would be loud too."

"I know what the one called Ophelia has done," Mama Nan says, scolding. "But I cannot let the pain of another time cloud my judgment. And neither should you."

"It's *my* pain," I argue. "My family is still in the living world. The choices I make for the future of Infinity—it affects all of them."

Mama Nan presses her lips into a flat line. "That is an unfair burden, Nami. We cannot be responsible for the mistakes of every human who comes after us, just as you are not responsible for the mistakes of your ancient ancestors."

For a moment, I'm terrified she's about to tell me her vote has changed.

"The Iron Clan promised to stay and ferry humans into the great beyond, and I see no reason to break that promise." She pauses, studying me. "You might consider letting our people do that for you. It might remind the others of our greater purpose."

"I can't leave. I need to find the Colony."

Mama Nan tilts her head. "And after that?"

I don't have to ask what she means. There are many more humans in the Four Courts fighting for survival. And what about the humans who have yet to die? What about Mei, and my parents, and Finn?

They won't stand a chance without help. Not with Ophelia guarding the gates.

Someone needs to warn them. Someone needs to lead them *here*.

"It is good to care. But you cannot be everything to everyone. Not forever." Mama Nan leans back, and the overhead candlelight spills across her freckled skin. "It isn't sustainable."

I twist my mouth. "I can't walk away from them." I won't be the only one *free*.

Mama Nan doesn't look away. "You would give up a place in the Afterlands to fight an impossible war?"

"I don't know what I'll do," I say honestly. I don't *want* to fight—but I'm the person who jumped in front of a bullet because a stranger needed help. I can't stand back while people suffer and do nothing to stop it. "All I know is that if we don't do something, it will be the end of humanity as we know it."

"Perhaps that wouldn't be the worst thing to happen." Artemis's smooth drawl sounds over my shoulder.

I spin around, facing him. The red has all but vanished from his eyes, leaving a cool brown in its place. He smirks like he knows what I'm looking for. Like he knows I sense the darkness inside him.

I think a little bit of darkness is inside of me as well.

"You modern humans destroy and create with so little thought as to how it might affect the world." Artemis flicks at his sleeve, preening. "Maybe there needs to be separation between old and new, before and after. What happens outside the Afterlands should no longer be our concern."

"You don't know Ophelia. The Residents are constantly adapting." I look between them, wishing they felt the same urgency. "How do you know she won't find you, even across the sea?"

"The Afterlands are beyond Ophelia's reach," Artemis replies. "She has limitations, even if you can't see them."

I can't decide if he's being intentionally cryptic, or if he's just making a wild assumption.

"And besides," he adds, lowering his chin, "when it's time to leave, we'll make sure we don't leave a path for anyone to follow."

Anyone. Not just the Residents, but the humans, too.

"There are people still trapped in the Four Courts. If you take this place away from them . . . their only chance of freedom . . . I swear, I'll—"

"You'll what?" he demands, quick as a serpent.

And in spite of myself, I can't think of anything to say.

"Our ships *will* leave the harbor one day. If you have unfinished business to attend to, I suggest you hurry. And if you run into trouble on your quest, as I'm sure you inevitably will . . ." Artemis pats my shoulder, making me cringe. "Then may your end be as swift as your time here." He chuckles before leaving the teahouse.

Mama Nan doesn't say another word. She just watches and watches, even as I leave the building with a flame in my chest.

Too many people stare, watching like they see the ticking time bomb inside my heart. So I veer off the pier, away from the sparkling stalls and intoxicating smells, and follow the pebbled coastline instead.

The straw-covered hut that feels nothing like a home comes into view, and I yank the door open and throw myself inside. My lips are stained with salt spray, and the chill of the winter wood still lingers on my fingertips like an unpleasant memory. The mostly bare room only amplifies my rage like it's echoing all around me. I shut my eyes and count backward from five, repeating the same thought to myself over and over again.

I will find a way to make this right.

I wait until the tension in my chest starts to fade. It's the best I can do these days.

Removing the red sea-glass knife from my belt, I take a seat in the corner on the pile of blankets that doubles as a bed. I made them myself; I needed somewhere to sleep, and in the early weeks, re-forming material was one of my greatest strengths.

Things have changed a great deal since then.

But, for all my training, the Colony is still at the mercy of the Residents. I have no idea where they are; they could've been sent to War or Death or maybe even somewhere worse that I don't know about.

Caelan lied about Victory. Who's to say he didn't lie about *everything*?

Placing my weapon on the floor in front of me, I cross my legs and drop my head into my hands, scraping at my hair like there's a chance I can tear out my own frustration.

Crossing the Labyrinth wasn't easy. Training every day for ten months has broken more bones than I can count. And it's still not enough.

The Reaper is cold against my wrist.

I will give them a reason to believe in me again.

A breath heaves out of me, and I twist my fingers together in my lap. A silent prayer, I suppose. Not to the saints or the gods or whatever higher power the Faithful worships.

To the ones I promised to go back for.

I close my eyes and let my mind reach out to the stars, like I did many times with Ophelia. Except it's not her I'm searching for.

I imagine their faces, one by one. Annika. Shura. Theo. Ahmet. Yeong. I call their names. I beg for an answer. A *whisper.*

A sign that they're still out there.

Ophelia once said I reached her mind by knocking on the door. But there are no doors to be found. No walls to break down. There's only infinite space.

And just like every day for the past ten months, when I try to speak to my friends—to reach them across the black void—I'm met with silence.

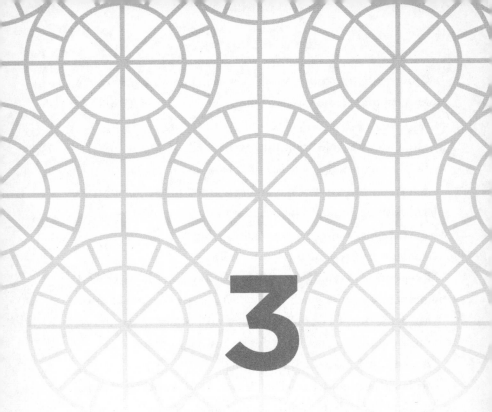

3

I WALK THROUGH THE HEART OF THE BORDER-
lands and find the outlying city made up of wooden town houses,
crooked alleyways, and single-story buildings stepped into the
earth like they're full of old, ancient secrets.

The city bustles with life even on an ordinary day, but today
the Mirror Clan celebrates their new year. Although their homes
in the snow-capped mountains were destroyed when Ophelia
created the Four Courts, their customs remain a rich part of their
everyday life. A kind of resistance, I suppose, though not exactly
my first choice.

Tiny flower buds made of ice fill every nook of the city center, glistening with frost. Even though it's a Mirror Clan tradition,

humans from the other clans arrive to watch the display. Some of them even join in, kneeling beside the sleeping flowers and whispering promises of a peaceful spring.

Infinity is like the old world, in that way: sometimes when culture is shared and celebrated across borders and time, it becomes something new. Something blended. Something *evolved*.

The Residents don't celebrate human culture. They copy and distort everything they learn, and use all the beauty as a backdrop while they fight to erase the source.

They stole something that wasn't theirs to steal. They took the afterlife, and the people in it.

And somehow I'm still here.

It isn't fair. The Colony did everything they could to save the human species, and I . . .

I was too busy trying to find out if a monster had a soul.

Guilt rattles through me like a horrible song, screeching behind my eyes until the headache makes me dizzy. I press a hand against a nearby pillar to steady myself, ignoring the heads that turn and the whispers that follow.

All they see is the anger on the surface; everything else is buried much deeper.

I move beneath the overhead balcony and shroud myself beneath a veil, double-checking the corners of my mind for good measure. The last thing I need is an audience.

Crowds are a good place to train, particularly when it comes to veiling. And I don't doubt Mama Nan's experience: if she says I need more practice, then I'll practice until I'm as undetectable as a whisper tucked beneath a wave.

A herd of elephants, my mind huffs, recalling Mama Nan's words.

Tavi appears near the large decorative fountain. It's filled with hundreds of tiny ice flowers, some floating gently in the water, others winding like ivy around the curious stone sculpture that shifts as often as the stars change. Today it's an oak tree.

Dressed in a shade of deep plum, Tavi whispers a prayer to the fountain. The sigil of the Mirror Clan he leads flickers against his collar, and I sense the subtle vibrations of his power even in the distance. All around the city, the ice flowers blossom. Pale blue and white petals stretch open to the sun, and the scent of fresh nectar blooms in the air. The tree explodes with flowers, one after the other like they're multiplying. And then—music.

The crowd bursts into a joyful dance, looping their arms around one another and swinging in circles. Humans from every clan celebrate in harmony. Even Kasia is present today, hovering around Güzide's tray of tea and cakes while Nix swats mischievously at an approaching dancer's hemline.

My eyes follow the newborn blossoms along the trellis. They look so fragile. So *temporary.* Carefully, I pluck one of the petals and hold it in my palm, watching the ice melt within seconds.

All this effort for something that doesn't last.

Dusting my hand against my shirt, I look back at the spinning crowds, watching them laugh like there isn't a war going on at all.

Across the square, a small group of humans is gathered, all in traditional Mirror Clan armor. Their sigil—two sparrows facing each other, with their wings curved to form an almost circle—is etched onto their leathers. Their weapons hang at their backs, half hidden in their black furs.

My brows knot. The Mirror Clan never carries weapons. Not unless they're on watch. And if they're here, that would mean . . .

I move across the square with long strides, slipping easily between dancers and those charmed by the display of flowers around the city, and stop in front of the sentries.

"Who's watching the border?" My voice is as sharp as my blade.

Their shoulders straighten, eyes wide as they survey the seem-ingly empty space around them. Searching for me.

I lift my veil.

The tension in the air immediately subsides. One of them gives a mock salute and chuckles. "Do you ever take a day off? It's the new year. You should be celebrating, youngling."

"And *you're* supposed to be on patrol duty." I count them quickly, just to be sure. Eight soldiers. Eight posts left unguarded. "There are Residents out there who are trying to destroy us," I say, throwing a hand toward the south gates. "And you've left the wall unguarded."

The sentry shakes his head. "No one is coming. No one *ever* comes." He motions toward me irritably. "We have been here for lifetimes, and all we got was you—the only human in Infinity who has no interest in going to the Afterlands." His fellow sen-tries mutter words of agreement.

I scowl. "So you abandoned your post because you were bored?"

"We took a well-deserved break," he snaps. "And nobody abandoned anything—Tessa and Byron stayed behind to keep an eye on the gates."

"Two humans? You think *two humans* could take on Ophelia and the Four Courts?" My eyes are wild. Unhinged. The crowd turns to stare, but I'm a spark that's already caught fire, and now I can't put it out. "You don't understand what we're up against. The Residents are constantly learning—adapting to whatever we do to stop them. They're only getting stronger, and I don't care how safe you think you are within these walls—letting your guard down is a mistake." I look at the people around me. Even the music has stopped.

The tallest sentry frowns and crosses her arms over her leather-clad chest. "You are a child in a very old world. Do not assume you know better than us because you have seen *one* battle in your short lifetime."

"The last time you saw Residents was during the First War, and you still ran," I argue. "What they're capable of now, and what they're doing to humans in Death . . . This sanctuary might not last forever. The least you can do is make sure you're protecting it while you still have the chance."

"We will *always* protect our own." Her eyes steel. "And if we can't do that here, we'll do it in the Afterlands."

My face morphs into a snarl. "There are humans out there who—"

"Not our clan," one of the other sentries says, "not our problem."

The fire in my core rages. Energy builds in my fists, blazing up my arms like lightning, impossible to contain.

I open my mouth to scream, but no sound comes out. Instead the energy explodes.

Across the square, the fountain shatters. Thousands of ice fragments burst like fireworks, spraying in every direction. Stone clatters across the cobbled pavement, and a cloud of dust is all that's left of the sculpted tree.

The music stops. The *world* stops.

My teeth are clenched, my chest aches, and I'm breathing, breathing, breathing without any way to calm down.

A sturdy hand presses against my shoulder. It breaks my trance long enough to remind me where I am, and how many eyes are watching me. Tavi appears at my side, dark gaze urging me to relax.

I bite the inside of my cheek, aware that I've gone too far.

Tavi drops his hand, and it disappears within his purple robes. "So much unrest on what should be a joyful day." Despite my outburst, he's the picture of serenity. Even his voice is like a smoky whisper. He shifts toward the sentries, whose weapons are now firmly in their hands. "Why have you left the border?"

The tallest soldier stiffens. "It's the first day of spring."

"It is." Tavi blinks like he's waiting for a better answer to his question.

The sentries shuffle awkwardly, shoulders still curved like they're preparing for battle, until finally one of them dips his head low and sheathes his sword. "We'll return to the wall at once." His scowl lasts half a second before the group disappears back up the south road.

Tavi waves toward the crowd, ushering them to restart the music. After a brief pause, several members of the Mirror Clan begin to repair the fountain. The stone oak tree re-forms branch by branch, as if my outburst never happened at all. Even the evidence of rubble scattered around the square vanishes from sight. The sound of violins fills the air, and everyone turns their attention back to the dance.

Heat builds in my cheeks. I don't know what's worse—that they saw the very real cracks in my armor, or that they saw them and they still don't care.

I turn to leave, but Tavi holds up a hand, stopping me. "You shouldn't be so impatient with them."

"That implies I have expectations," I counter, voice teetering on the edge of a cliff. I may have reeled in the energy, but the emotions are very much still there.

"You are still upset they won't be your army," Tavi notes. Even in the sunlight, his hair remains an unwavering black.

"I've given up trying to convince the Border Clans to go to war." I fix my eyes over his shoulder at the dancing crowd, arms joined as they move in circles around the newly constructed ice-flower tree, and look away bitterly. "But if this is the only safe place for humans in Infinity, then it needs to stay that way."

He eyes me, serious. "And you've chosen fearmongering to rally support for your cause?"

I bristle at his choice of words. "Ophelia is still a threat. Maybe the people here need to be reminded."

"What you see as a necessary reminder is something others have spent a long time trying to forget. This war is new to you—to us it is ancient." When I don't respond, he adds, "You can't be angry at the Borderlands for existing in a way that is different to you."

It takes effort to unclench my teeth. "They're *wrong*."

"We all have our own ideas of right and wrong. And some-times, when we can't agree on what that is, we have to listen to the majority. That is what it means to put your community—your people—first."

"*My* people are still out there."

Tavi gives a curt nod of understanding. "And mine are here."

I look away, throat tightening at the memories of losing every-one I cared about in this afterlife.

Sometimes I wonder if I should've seen the warnings sooner. I was so fixated on the possibility of building a bridge between human and AI that I didn't see the truth behind Gil's hatred and Caelan's smiles.

Would things have turned out different if I'd chosen to spare the Residents? Would that have proven to Caelan—and Ophelia—that humans can change? Or were we always going to be the enemy, no matter what choice I made that night?

Maybe what happened was inevitable, but I was still the one who walked into the palace, disguised as one of them. Ready to destroy *all* of them.

I was the one who showed Caelan who I really was, under-neath the mask, and put an end to the game he'd been playing for far longer than I knew him.

Which means that losing the Colony was *my* fault.

My voice cracks, despite the anger burning in my eyes. "It's been ten months." Ten months of failing to get the clans to help me. Ten months of failing to speak to my friends. Ten months of failing to convince everyone that without the Borderlands, the humans still out there—the humans still to come—will be doomed to an eternity in Death. Or worse.

It feels like I'm running out of time.

"Ten months is barely a moment to the rest of us, youngling," Tavi says, like it's supposed to make me feel better.

"I hate being called that."

He smiles in return. "Hate changes too, after enough lifetimes." And then he moves through the crowd, and I lose sight of his purple robes in the explosion of colorful dancers.

The seaport is quiet, and the sky has muddled to a creamy apricot. I can see my hut across the pebbled beach, and the Night Market in the distance; it won't be long before the pier comes to life. The celebration in the middle of the city is still going strong, but some of the Faithful have already returned to the hills to light their candles and ring the evening bell.

A fleet of double-hulled voyaging canoes sits near the harbor; several unfinished ones lie in pieces on the sand. One of them is propped up with wooden beams, and a half-sewn sail is draped over the seats.

This is how humans will be ferried to the Afterlands.

The sea meets the horizon, but I know there's an incomprehensible distance between this shore and the next. And the trip to the beyond is a one-way ticket. No one who's left has ever come back.

My boots kick up sand around me, and I stop near the unpainted hull, dragging my fingers along the smooth surface. This isn't protecting humans. It's running away.

Leaving here will mean abandoning everyone else. Abandoning people like Mei, who deserves better than this artificial hell.

What will happen if the Border Clans sail away? Will the path in the stars disappear too? Even *if* human survivors manage to make their way here, what will they find? There'll be no canoes left, and no one to show them how to reach the Afterlands. They'll be stuck here.

And if Ophelia extends her reach beyond the Four Courts . . .

I clench my fist and press my head to the wood.

I want to believe that the vote will never change, that the clans will stay behind for as long as it takes to lead humans to safety. But when I first came to the Borderlands, they had five canoes.

Now they have dozens.

Almost enough to fit every person here.

I scream against the hull, slamming my palms against the wood, listening to the crashing waves attempt to drown me out. Then palms become fists, and I pound the canoe, again and again, screaming to the wide-open sea.

I won't leave anyone behind again.

Wood cracks beneath my fists. I jump back, startled, and find a horrendous rupture on the hull, split apart by my anger. By *me*.

I stare at my hands for a moment before tucking them around myself, scanning the beach and cliffs for watchful strangers. It doesn't take long to spot the lone member of the Faithful standing at the top of the bell tower, eyes fixed on me.

I should signal that it was an accident. That I wasn't *trying* to sabotage their canoes—it was just a side effect of the fire burning in my core. But what would be the point?

Most of them have already decided I'm an outsider. Admitting I'm struggling to control my emotions won't make them suddenly want to help me.

The air escapes between my lips, and I tap the spot where my O-Tech used to sit. Turning my face toward the stars, I count them one by one like I'm counting my failures.

I don't know why my friends won't answer me, when it was so easy to connect with Ophelia. If I had any idea where they were, I could at least form some kind of plan.

But I have a limited arsenal of skills and no idea where to go.

I need to become stronger—but I need information even more.

And I'm not going to find it in the Borderlands.

You know what you have to do, my thoughts whisper into the night. *You've always known. You're just too afraid to face him. You're afraid to face the* truth.

Caelan is the only one with answers. The only link between me and the fallen Colony. But seeing him again, after all this time . . . after everything he did . . .

Anger sweeps through me, tethering itself to his deceit.

The first time we met, I was hooked up to Yeong's machine. He may have been disguised as Gil, but it was Caelan who saw my dreams—he knew I'd been on my way to meet with Finn on the night of my death. Is that why he pretended to have feelings for me? Did he know my heart would fall for it, because of everything I'd already lost?

All the time we spent together . . . it was only ever about gathering intel. And I was too busy grieving my own failed love story to see it.

Ten months isn't enough time to heal the wounds he left. But I can't keep pretending like a plan is going to magically appear someday. Can I really be angry at the Borderlands for not doing enough, when I still haven't tried to reach out to the one person in Infinity who knows where my friends are being held?

A scorching heat builds in my chest, kicking up embers of rage and regret.

Deep down, I know it's time. Maybe it has been for a while. Confronting him might be the only way I'll ever get answers.

And if he won't tell me what I need to know, then I'll just have to tear the truth out of him, no matter what it takes.

I shut my eyes and reach out to the Prince of Victory.

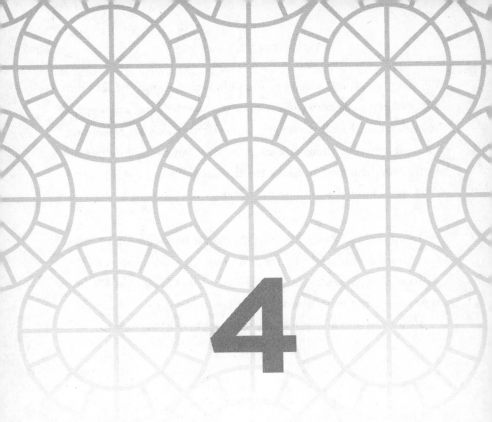

4

THE WINTER WOODLAND STRETCHES ACROSS
space and time. It takes surprisingly little effort to find Caelan's
mind, almost as if he's been waiting in the black void with the
door open.

Waiting for me.

The prince stands in the darkness, dressed in white with shadows pooling at his feet. "Nami," he says, voice like silk. His silver
eyes are fixed somewhere beyond where I stand; he can sense me,
but he can't see me.

It's a small victory. I'd rather he not notice the way my hands
shake.

I open my mouth to demand where the others are. To ask if he got his chance to gloat after he destroyed the Colony. But I can't bring myself to say the words.

The thought of what it must've been like for the others, searching for a hint of Gil in his face and being unable to find it . . .

The sting in my eyes simmers.

Caelan turns, fingers tangled together at his back. When he takes a step, shadows ripple across the floor. He pauses, turning his ear toward the sound of my breathing. "My mother says you used to communicate with her. Just like this." He looks around absently. "She expected you to reach out much sooner."

"I have no interest in talking to Ophelia." The snap of my voice echoes through the dark chamber.

"But clearly you have some interest in talking to me."

"I'm only here for information."

"Is that all?" Impatience weaves around his words, and something else I can't place.

There are a thousand words I want to say to him. A thousand curses I want to yell.

But instead I say nothing.

The white furs of his cape make him appear broader than I remember. Maybe even a little older. And for someone with such a perfectly designed face, there's still a hint of dark circles beneath his silver eyes.

Maybe the shadows are playing tricks on me, trying to make him appear more human.

Trying to make me forget what he really is.

"How did you escape?" There's a rasp in the back of his

throat, like the crack of burnt sugar on crème brûlée. Something imperfect. Flawed.

I choose my words carefully, unsure whether I'm ready to play this card so soon, or whether it's even a card worth playing. "You don't remember what you did?"

Caelan's mouth tightens. In the past ten months, did it ever occur to him that he was the one who let me go?

I can't tell. Because whatever crack Caelan showed suddenly vanishes.

"The last thing I remember was following Ettore to the throne room." He tilts his head like he's assessing a threat.

"That's a shame," I say dryly. "You missed the best part."

Caelan barely reacts, but I catch the thrum of energy at his fingertips. The *flinch*. "My Legion Guards followed your trail to the Labyrinth, and then . . ."

Dark, silent seconds pass between us. I wait for him to ask where I am in Infinity—perhaps to report back to his mother—but he doesn't.

My voice is thin. "Your Legion Guards need to try a little harder if they want to find me."

"No one is looking for you. My kind has more important things to do than waste time searching for one rogue human."

"I took down all four princes and the queen—I doubt Ophelia and your brothers wouldn't have follow-up questions."

Caelan stiffens at the suggestion. "Last I checked, I'm still standing."

"Last I saw, you were facedown on the floor."

He twists his jaw, eyes darkening to pewter. "Anyone can be

brave from the shadows. But would you be just as brave if you were standing right in front of me? If I could *see* you, as you see me?" The corner of his mouth tugs. "Go on, Nami. Step into the light. I dare you."

His challenge sends a tremor through my rib cage, rattling every nerve to life.

I can't accept his dare—I can't risk him seeing too much of where I am.

But if I pulled back the darkness and showed him my face, would it rattle him right back?

I swallow the hitch in my throat.

The sound is enough to make Caelan grin, and I hate that he thinks he's won this round. "Not as confident without the Reaper on your side?"

I tuck my hand against my chest, cradling the weapon like I'm trying to draw out its power. "What makes you think I didn't bring it with me?"

He continues in a slow, predatory circle around me. "It wouldn't matter if you did. We've . . . *adapted* to that particular weapon. It's no longer a threat to my kind."

That was always the point of his court—to learn from the humans trapped in their maze.

And when the Colony had served its purpose, Caelan threw them in a cage.

I drop my hand. "Where are they?" I demand. "Annika and the others—I want to know where you sent them after you torched our home."

I want to know how I can bring them back.

"Planning a rescue mission would be a mistake," he says evenly. "You have your freedom, and no one is looking for you. Don't throw it away—you won't get a second chance."

"Freedom means *nothing* if you have to abandon your friends to get it."

Caelan steps forward. A chill sweeps across the back of my neck in response, and the more I try to hide my breathing, the more my heart pounds.

Caelan's silver eyes brush over me. Past me. "If you had been captured instead of them, they wouldn't come back for you. You don't owe them anything."

"Everything that happened was *my* fault," I say, the confession echoing between us. "If I'd never had the ability to look like a Resident . . . if I hadn't agreed to destroy the Orb . . ." I close my eyes. "The Colony would still be here."

"Their fate was already written. You were never going to change it."

My eyes flash open. "I would've figured it out. I would've seen you for the liar you were."

He flinches.

"If I'd had more time, I could've—"

"You could've what?" he interjects, silver eyes becoming steel. "Saved them? Stopped me? Murdered every innocent Resident in Infinity?" Caelan shakes his head, angry. "I'd hate to know what you would've done with *more time*."

Our anger toward each other is visceral, the memory of our betrayals seeping through every word we say.

"I wanted to survive this world without hurting anyone." My

chest quakes like it's ready to split in two. "But you proved that wasn't possible. If there's a price to pay to save the people I care about, then it has to be worth the cost. 'Everyone gets blood on their hands.' Isn't that what you taught me?"

Caelan's chin lowers as he searches the void for my presence. "It seems we both learned something after all our time spent together."

I don't ask what he means. I'm not sure I want to know what my own betrayal taught him, or what beliefs it solidified.

I proved he was right about humans. Maybe he sees nothing redeemable in me, either.

And yet . . .

He says no one is looking for me. That I'm *free*, after everything I tried to do.

I shake my head like it doesn't make sense. "Why haven't you asked where I am?" *And why don't you want revenge?*

Caelan's crown of silver branches reflects the darkness back to me. "Your whereabouts would be a distraction—to my Legion Guards and my brothers. The last thing I need is a human fixated on destroying my kind to get in the way of my plans."

"Plans?" I ask stiffly.

The memory of Lysander's airship rushes back to me. The deal Caelan made with his brother, all in the hopes of shutting down Victory for good. To break free of his *cage*.

"If you've traded Annika and the others to be test subjects, I swear on the stars I will—"

"There will be no need for test subjects," he interrupts. "Not if things go the way I hope they will."

Anger pulses through my bloodstream like molten lava. I've spent the last ten months wondering if what happened that night in the throne room meant something. Wondering if it was a bigger part of Caelan's game, or if he really was different from the others.

But Caelan isn't different. He's still standing on the other side of this war, hurting the people I care about. He's just as monstrous as his brothers.

And the next time we meet, I will be monstrous too.

My eyes remain pinned to his, even as he studies the void around me. "One day, when the tables are turned and you're the one who's been taken captive . . . I won't spare you, and I won't play your games," I say, voice icier than his has ever been. "I will throw you to the wolves."

Caelan sets his jaw. The furs shift at his shoulders in time with his breathing. For a while, he doesn't say anything. And then: "You do what you have to."

Nothing about our exchange feels triumphant, the way I expected it to. Being cruel—it still feels like speaking through someone else's mouth. It's unnatural.

Maybe it always will be.

"Stop searching for them," he warns. "It will only make things worse."

"For you, maybe," I say. "But someone once told me that fear stems from the thought of losing what you love most. And I guess once you lose everything, you lose the fear, too."

"Nami—" he starts, but I pull away from his mind, vanishing from the black void until I'm back in my own body, surrounded by sand and trees.

I didn't get the information I wanted, but I did learn two things: Caelan's mind is just as accessible as Ophelia's—and the next time I meet him in the black void, I'll need to wield a far better weapon than my anger.

No, not a weapon, my mind thrums. *What you need is a better veil.*

My wrist burns with the silent promises I've made again and again. I will never stop looking. I will never stop trying. I will not be afraid.

I will find them.

No matter what.

5

IT'S QUIET IN THE HOUSE OF PRAYER, DESPITE nearly a hundred humans scattered around the room.

Pressing my hands against the second-floor railing, I peer over the ledge and see Tavi sitting on a cushion at the front of the round hall, his sharp chin fixed to the floor. His eyes are closed in meditation, just like the rest of the Faithful, all of them wearing purple robes and wooden prayer beads.

I breathe deeply through my nose, concentrating on the many faces blending together. I imagine walking through the clouds, veiling my entire being until I become mist. And then I snake my way around the hall, searching for thoughts.

I will become a predator. I will become absence. I will become—

"What in the stars are you doing?" Kasia's voice sounds behind me.

A spark of embarrassment flushes through me, and I turn to find her bright blue eyes.

She lifts a brow, waiting.

"I—I'm trying something new." A few people look up from their silent prayer. Tavi remains still as stone. Lowering my voice and pulling away from the banister, I add, "I'm trying to sneak into someone's mind without being seen."

Kasia barks a laugh, and I wave a hand to shush her. She's already blown my cover, but the last thing I need is for the Faithful to know what I'm up to. I'm pretty sure invading someone's mind definitely breaks a morality clause or two.

"Can I ask why?" Kasia dips her head, but even behind her dimpled smile, I can see the concern.

I stare back, weighing whether honesty would be a mistake. I'm not sure how to say the words out loud. They feel so new and brittle that all I can manage is a whisper. "It might be the only way I can find them."

She pulls her face back, shoulders relaxing like she understands the unspoken part of my words.

The part involving Residents.

Kasia shakes her head, probably remembering all the stories I've told her. All the things I showed her through an Exchange. "Are you sure you want to do that again? The last time you reached out to Ophelia, she'd had the upper hand the entire time."

"It's not Ophelia I want to reach."

There's a pause, and Kasia shifts her weight to her other leg. "You want to get information through Caelan."

The sound of his name makes my skin prickle, but I nod.

I don't know what I expected to find when I ventured into his mind. He was never going to tell me what I needed to know—which means the only option I have left is to take it by force.

I just need to figure out how.

Kasia looks around. "If you're genuinely trying to sneak into someone's mind, I don't think practicing in a prayer room is going to be much of a challenge. The people here are practically shouting their thoughts to the skies."

"You got a better idea?"

She takes a step back and motions to herself. "Try it on me."

"While I appreciate the invitation, the purpose is to *sneak* into someone's mind," I say. "It's not the same if you're expecting it."

But I guess my point is lost on her, because she holds up her hands, still waiting.

Sighing, I focus on the veil that shrouds my own thoughts and become a winding mist. I close my eyes and enter the darkness, searching for the hum of her mental walls. At first there's only the infinite void, but then . . .

A hint of berries and fresh soil and—

Something slams against my mind and I recoil in pain. My head feels like it's overflowing with liquid metal, spilling out of my skull until my temples throb.

"What the hell?" I manage to sputter, grabbing my forehead.

Kasia grins, letting her arms fall to her sides. "I'm not going to lie—that was kind of fun."

"I told you it wouldn't work," I hiss. "And that *hurt*."

"Good," she retorts. "Because now you know what it will feel like if things go wrong. And you definitely want to make sure that doesn't happen if you're still inside someone's mind." Her blue eyes go serious. "If someone shuts the door, you might not be able to get back out."

There's a pop and a flash of light, and Tavi appears beside us, black hair coiled at the nape of his neck. His deep-set hazel eyes study me for a moment before landing on Kasia. "You should know better," he admonishes. "This is a place for prayer, not a playground."

"Oh, come now, Tavi, let's not fight," Kasia says with an infectious grin. "Aren't you the one always preaching about forgiveness and redemption? What if I told you I was sincerely, *very* sorry?"

Tavi shakes his head, but his face softens. "Though I detect a great deal of sarcasm, I should tell you that human redemption does not happen overnight, and often takes a lifetime to prove. But I will accept your apology."

Human redemption. Not Resident. Not . . . whatever Caelan is.

The Prince of Victory is a puzzle I've never been able to solve. I'm not sure why it still hits a nerve. I'm not sure why it ever did in the first place.

It's not a question of who the enemy is anymore. I just can't seem to shake the image of Caelan with the Reaper in his hand, telling me to run. To follow the stars.

I'm not afraid to fight the Residents, but I'd be lying if I said I don't still have questions about what happened that night.

There's shouting from outside the House of Prayer. Confusion swarms through the round space, and all at once whispers erupt like a flock of birds fleeing for the sky. Tavi moves toward the window; Kasia and I race for the door.

The smell of pine . . .

I reached out to Caelan. To the *enemy*.

Is this my fault?

Did I somehow show him more than I meant to?

Did I bring the Residents here?

I stop at the edge of the hill, eyes scanning the vast city and all its buildings and town houses until I spot the crowd of frantic people pointing at the northern pier.

And then I see the unmistakable sight of the Night Market, and the violent white flames that roar through it.

The Borderlands are under attack.

6

THE FLAMES RADIATE AN UNNATURAL AMOUNT
of heat. Even the humans most impervious to pain are too afraid
to approach them. The white fire stretches from one end of the
Night Market to the other, but never spreads beyond either side,
as if the flames themselves are under a spell.

Or perhaps whoever started the fire only wanted to send a
message. Not an attack, but a warning.

I spend the night watching the smoke snake its way through
the stars. I can't make sense of how the Residents could've done
this, or why they would've started a fire that failed to hurt a single
human here. It isn't their style to let us go free. What Caelan did
wasn't a rule—it was an anomaly.

But who else would be capable of something like this?

Part of me wonders if the person responsible is much closer to home. And I don't know what's worse: the enemy I know, or the one still hiding in the shadows.

The white flames burn into the next day. It isn't until the last sliver of sunlight disappears over the horizon that the smoke and fire vanish completely.

But one thing is certain: The Night Market is no more.

I'm not surprised when the council holds an emergency meeting in the Dome. Nobody has ever caused destruction within the city walls before—human *or* Resident.

For the first time, the people here are second-guessing whether they're truly safe.

It isn't hard to sneak in, even if I weren't beneath a veil. The clans are so trusting of their council, I don't think it's occurred to anyone that a person would *want* to eavesdrop on a meeting.

My feet balance on the wooden beams as I duck beneath the rafters. When I find a spot that overlooks the clan leaders, I keep my head low, and hone into every sound with a hyper focus. Not that I need my consciousness to help; the shape of the room causes an echo that rattles all the way to the skylights.

Artemis is pacing wildly, hands moving in front of him like he's conducting an orchestra. His eyes blaze with anger when he turns to Kasia. "To even *suggest* the Bone Clan might be responsible for something like this is an insult. If you expect me to roll over and listen to these lies, think again."

Kasia is unflinching, while Nix prowls nearby, bright eyes fixed on the clan leaders. "If we're going to figure out who started the fire, we need to be prepared to ask questions. Taking it personally isn't going to help anything."

"You'd blame the Bone Clan before the Residents?" Artemis's face turns a glorious shade of red. The veins in his neck look ready to burst.

Tavi considers his words carefully. "We have no proof the Residents did this. As far as we know, they can't reach us in the Borderlands." He taps his finger against his wooden prayer beads. "But perhaps it's wise to consider every possibility."

Kasia turns to the others. "The Night Market was empty, and the fire was confined to an area where it would hurt no one. Unlike the rest of you, I fought in the First War," she says coolly. "And this is not what a Resident attack looks like."

At this, Tavi and Artemis noticeably shift.

Mama Nan nods. "Kasia is right. This isn't the time to be defensive. As clan leaders, we must show unity."

"I wasn't the one throwing around accusations," Artemis spits, turning back to Kasia. "How do we know *you* weren't the one who started the fire?"

Kasia barks a laugh. "I'm not trying to scare our people into running away. I *want* everyone to stay."

"Yes," Artemis seethes. "You want to stay. Perhaps you also want another war. And tricking everyone into thinking their home is in danger would be a good way to convince them to take up arms."

"That's ridiculous." Kasia steps forward, and Nix growls at her side. "I would *never*—"

"There are clearly arguments for both sides," Tavi interjects calmly. "Fighting like this won't prove who's right or wrong."

"The Borderlands are my home. I would never set fire to it. And the last thing I'd want is for anyone here to go to war." Kasia tears her glassy eyes away from the others, focusing on the brush of Nix's head at her fingertips. "I will not lose another clan to the Residents."

"What about that friend of yours?" Artemis quips. "She's made it clear she thinks we're cowards. Perhaps it's she who wants to rile up an army using fear."

My cheeks burn.

"Nami wouldn't do that," Kasia says without hesitation. I make a mental note to thank her later. "Not to mention fear doesn't guarantee people will fight—they're just as likely to run for the Afterlands."

"A threat in the Borderlands would force our people to choose," Tavi notes.

"Nami has never liked our ways," Artemis says. "She's never even tried to hide it."

"All the more reason she wouldn't do this." Kasia looks between them. "Don't use her as a scapegoat just because she disagrees with you."

"She's growing more powerful," Mama Nan says suddenly. When Kasia spins, she adds, "I'm not saying she started the fire. But it's an observation I'm sure hasn't gone unnoticed by the rest of our people."

Kasia blinks. "You think they'll assume it was her?"

Mama Nan hums. "I think everyone is looking for someone

to blame. By her own choice, Nami is still a stranger to us. A stranger we know to be rash and eager for war."

"She just wants to help her friends," Kasia insists.

"I think," Tavi says, "she wants much more than that."

I clench my teeth. It's true I wanted them to fight, but hearing them accuse me of something I didn't do . . .

It stirs the rage in my chest, adding to the monster.

Tavi pauses, blinking up at the skylights thoughtfully. For a moment, I'm worried he sees me, but his gaze only follows the clouds. "Nami's beliefs do not align with the clans. But she wasn't responsible for the fire. Neither was Kasia." He nods toward Mama Nan. "I was with them both yesterday, in the House of Prayer."

"Where were *you* when the fire started?" Kasia mutters, eyes fixed to Artemis.

Artemis scowls in response, brushing a wisp of golden hair from his temple. "Bathing, as a matter of fact. Would you like me to show you?" He holds out a palm like he's offering an Exchange. One he thinks she'll refuse to see.

But Kasia considers him.

There's an indignation in his brow as he curls his fingers into a fist.

"Let's not turn on each other," Tavi says. "We must set an example to the others. Unity is the only way forward."

Mama Nan studies the others like she's recalling a thousand different lives. Finally, she waves a hand. "I think we can agree the fire was meant as a statement, nothing more. Perhaps to make us all feel afraid, though I don't know why. But we will find out who was responsible. Anyone with fire abilities must come forward and provide evidence they were not a part of what happened in the Night Market. We will gather information through Exchanges, and put together who wasn't where they claimed to be. We left the war behind—we *will* have peace in the Borderlands."

The other leaders nod in agreement and leave the Dome to spread the message. I climb down the beams, using my veil to mute the sound of my footsteps. Trying to make myself as unnoticeable as a shadow in the darkness.

The window Mama Nan stands in front of overlooks the city. The glass is as tall as it is wide, making her appear almost childlike within the frame.

I wonder if she remembers being that young. I wonder if Infinity will still exist by the time I'm half as old as she is.

Slipping off the final beam, I use the ledge to lower myself to the floor. I'm almost to the door when her voice rolls across the curved room.

"Nami," Mama Nan says quietly.

I stay under the veil, not offering a single word. But I wait.

She doesn't turn around. Maybe not making eye contact is a veil of its own. "I want you to be careful. The things you say and the way you behave . . . they make you an outlier. And history reminds me that during times of unrest, that is never a safe thing to be."

I take her words with me, even though I'm not sure if they come from a leader or a friend, and leave the echo of the Dome behind.

The white fire returns.

On the first night, the flames devour half the fleet of canoes in the northern harbor—including the one I put my fists through.

On the second night, the fire claims the winter forest in the west.

On the third night, the fountain in the heart of the city goes up in a blaze.

The place I lost my temper. The place I used to train. The place I went to spy. All of them associated in some way with *me*.

Even I can't deny that the circumstantial evidence isn't exactly in my favor. But while the canoe incident wasn't my proudest moment, I loved the forest. And I may have broken the fountain once, but that was an *accident*.

When the clan leaders don't manage to find a single plausible suspect, the whispers catch. Pretty soon the truth won't matter. To the Border Clans, I am the one who doesn't belong, and probably never will.

It doesn't matter to anyone that I don't have fire abilities, or that I've had alibis for every night the city was hit with flames.

Most of them are already convinced it was me.

7

THE WOODEN DOOR CREAKS AT ITS HINGES
when I push it open. Morning light floods through my hut, but
it's the strange shape at the doorstep that demands my attention.
A pool of red liquid, coated to the stone like it's been left overnight.

"It's called a bloodstain," says a familiar voice.

My eyes trail from Kasia's boots all the way to her shadowed
face, hand blocking the sunlight from her eyes. Nix sniffs at the
puddle, casts a look of pure distaste, and saunters off down the
beach.

"Is it really . . . ?" The memory of smoke as I left the raided
Colony behind makes my throat knot.

How much blood was spilled that day? How many humans did the Residents hurt after they stormed the tunnels?

Kasia watches Nix balance near the rock pools, avoiding contact with the water. The way her eyes glisten, I know she has memories that remind her of blood too. Memories she'll never be able to forget. "It's just red dye and salt," she says thinly. "Courtesy of the Bone Clan and their archaic rituals."

"What's it supposed to mean?"

"It marks you as a person who diverges from the group and causes trouble. It's supposed to let everyone know you can't be trusted."

"By leaving a puddle at my front door?" I snort, unimpressed. How did I ever think these people could join together to fight Ophelia? They can't even manage garden-variety public shaming.

Kasia flattens her mouth and motions toward the space behind me. Toward everything I've yet to see.

I step over the bloodstain and follow her gaze to my hut. Red dye is everywhere. The roof, the paneled walls, the window frames—every bit of the house is coated in liquid that drips from the corners, staining even the sand. In the sunlight, the house glints like a ruby.

I tilt my head back and shut my eyes, thoroughly annoyed. "The Bone Clan did all of this?"

"They've always had a reputation for being overly dramatic." Kasia fiddles with the end of one of her three braids. "Mostly harmless, but stars, do they hold a grudge."

"Something tells me soap and water aren't going to fix this."

"A bloodstain is designed to vanish only after a confession

takes place. Otherwise, it gets darker over time, until the mark becomes black and the Bone Clan officially shuns you from society." After a brief pause, Kasia lifts a brow like she's offering solace. "Not that you've ever been one for community spirit."

I shouldn't care. This ridiculous ritual shouldn't *matter*.

But I can't stand the idea of people saying things about me that just aren't true.

"I didn't start the fires." I feel like it needs to be said.

Kasia twists the side of her mouth. "I know. I've told them. But sometimes the truth isn't enough to stop people from making up their own minds."

I sigh. "At least I won't have to look at it all that much. I only really come here to sleep—the rest of the time I'll be in the eastern forest, training and pretending this never happened."

"I—I think you should hear this from me." Kasia's expression shifts. "Some of the others are demanding you be put under watch. They want you followed at all times." I open my mouth to argue, when she quickly adds, "I told them it was unnecessary, and I think they've backed down for now. But you should know that if there's another fire, I'm not sure I'll be able to stop them."

"I need to train," I say hotly. "I can't have someone following me around. How am I supposed to veil myself or practice around crowds if I'm being *tailed*?" Not to mention sneaking into someone's mind isn't going to be *nearly* as easy if they're all on the lookout for me.

This isn't just a little annoyance—this is going to interfere with everything I'm working toward.

"I'm sorry, Nami," Kasia says, and I can tell she means it.

My bones buckle with anger. This is Artemis's fault. He blamed me in the Dome, tried to make the rest of the council think I had something to do with the Night Market. And now my hut is covered in red.

He made me a target.

And if everyone is looking at me, they're never going to find out who really started the fires.

I can't afford to fall behind on my training. I need to prove that I didn't do this.

I march up the hill, toward the charred pier and cremated market stalls. A barely recognizable turquoise is all that's left of the wooden beams, but it's still the fastest way into the city center from the beach. And I have business that can't wait.

"Where are you going?" Kasia calls after me. Her footsteps stop somewhere along the pebbles. We've been training together a long time; she knows when to leave me alone.

I clench my jaw tight and make a target of my own. "To get a confession."

Artemis lives in a wide, multilevel apartment above a bathhouse. The stairs are so narrow that they're practically ladders, and the air smells strongly of ginseng, soap, and tea leaves. Steam pours through the walled slats. I climb through the fog, waving a hand in front of me to clear my sight.

Bunches of dried flowers and glass baubles filled with candlelight hang from the overhead beams. Artemis's door sits at the far end of the balcony, the wrought-iron handle carved into the face of a lion.

The door opens easily, and I don't bother with a veil when I step inside. I want him to see me. I want him to know I'm not afraid.

Artemis is sprawled out in an armchair, one foot planted firmly on the seat, the other draped over a footstool. His yellow bathing robes show more flesh than I've ever meant to see.

I avert my eyes to the ceiling and mutter a curse under my breath. Maybe I should've knocked.

"You're armed" is all he says.

"I'm always armed," I reply tersely, my red sea-glass blade no more than an inch from my fingertips.

He swings his leg down and stands, tightening his belt as he steps away from his chair. I glance back at him, making sure he isn't reaching for a weapon. I'm not *planning* to use mine, but I have to be prepared. There are many kinds of monsters in Infinity, all with different faces.

And I need to make sure I see the next one coming.

Artemis stops near a decanter of amber liquid and pours himself a drink. "Can I offer you anything?" His mouth tugs in jest; he knows I'm not here to socialize.

"Why are you trying to make everyone think I started the fires?"

He knocks back the contents of his glass before returning it to the tray, empty. When he turns around to face me, he flashes a smile. "I have no idea what you're talking about."

"I'm not in the mood for your games." I take two steps toward him. The breeze through the open window blows a dark strand of hair across my face, but I don't brush it aside. I won't appear weak.

I won't break.

Artemis laughs, spreading his arms like he wants me to look around. "You came to *my* home, youngling. And it's my patience you're weighing on."

My temper flares. "I know you're responsible for the bloodstain."

He drops his arms, brow twitching. "That," he drawls, "would be a complete waste of my time. Bloodstains are to keep clan members in line." He lowers his chin. "And you are not one of the Bone Clan."

I search his eyes for the lie, but I can't find it. Not that I have the best track record for sniffing out imposters. "It's still a Bone Clan ritual. And if you hadn't gone around pushing the idea that I might've started the fire, your *members* wouldn't have taken it upon themselves to deface my house."

"Don't pretend like you ever considered it your home," he tuts in response, moving around the room like a wildcat stalking its prey.

I brush my thumb over the hilt of my dagger. The sea-glass sends a jolt through me: a reminder that I can be strong when I need to be. That *I* can be a predator too. "It's not the house I care about. It's the fact that everyone has me marked as a traitor, and it's interfering with my training. The rest of you may not want to help the humans, but the least you can do is leave me alone while I try. So call off your watchdogs."

"I told you—it wasn't me." Artemis leans against the hallway doorframe lazily, crossing his long legs at the ankles and tucking his hands behind him.

I take notice, bending my knees slightly, just in case I need to be quick.

As if reading my thoughts, he laughs. "You really don't trust anyone, do you?" When I don't respond, his eyes glitter. "Ah, I almost forgot you were betrayed. By a prince, wasn't it? A prince you thought *you* were betraying." He looks utterly delighted. "That must've been awful for you. To find out you were never in control, and to know your choices ended with your friends being thrown in a cage. Yet you somehow managed to walk away with your freedom."

Static fills my head. He's hitting a nerve, and my irrational anger shouts at me to hit back. "Running away wasn't my first choice. But I seem to recall a story about you leaving the former leader of the Bone Clan on the battlefield, all in the name of *your* own freedom."

His voice simmers. "You know nothing of that day. Ozias charged into battle before the rest of us had gathered at the hill. If he'd waited, he'd have seen what we saw—that the battle was already lost—and he would've turned back too."

"You left one of your own."

"You left *many* of your own." He pauses, studying the way my fists are shaking. "I'm curious—how close *did* you get to this Resident prince?" Artemis narrows his gaze. "Close enough to make a trade? Their lives for yours, perhaps?"

A snarl takes over my face, and before I know it, the knife is in my hand.

With a flick of his chin, he motions to my weapon. "Try it. I will turn you into ash." Embers spark to life in his hands.

I don't lower my blade. "You have the power of fire."

"It's not uncommon in the Bone Clan." He holds up a palm, and a flame spins into form. Orange, not white. "But I had nothing to do with the Night Market, *or* your little hut." He closes his fingers around the small fire, and it disappears.

"And yet not a single person from your clan came forward for questioning," I point out. "Is that why you're blaming me? To protect someone?"

He straightens the edges of his robe. "I will not submit my people to a witch hunt. The stars know I saw enough of those in my days before Infinity."

"If you know who's responsible—"

"The Bone Clan is innocent." Artemis doesn't waver. "The white fire is not our doing, though I won't deny it's worked in our favor. Never before have the Border Clans been so eager to leave these shores."

"Kasia and Tavi will never change their votes," I say, perhaps for my own sake. "Neither will Mama Nan."

Artemis flashes his teeth. "Kasia has no clan left. And if the Mirror and Iron Clans decide it's safer in the Afterlands . . . well, perhaps the vote won't matter. We'll rebuild the canoes, cross the sea, and leave the old Infinity behind. And unless Kasia wants to spend the rest of eternity with only you and that Dayling for company, I imagine she'll be sailing with us."

"You can't do that," I argue. "Someone needs to be here. To help lead the human survivors to safety."

He straightens his collar, uninterested. "What for? Based on what you constantly tell us about Ophelia, she'll be here soon anyway. Might as well get away while we can, and leave the rest to their inevitable fate."

My fist tightens, and my frustration builds and builds and builds.

But Artemis hardly pays me any attention at all as he moves back to his chair and sprawls his long limbs across the velvet cushions. He lifts a brow. "I've had enough of your questions for one day. You can show yourself out."

And because there's nothing left to say, I do.

I wait on the rooftop across from the bathhouse, crouched low and hidden in the shadows of the alcove.

Artemis might claim he had nothing to do with the fire or the bloodstain, but he's also freely admitted that he'll protect his people, even from scrutiny. Who's to say he wouldn't protect them from repercussions, too?

Maybe he didn't do it, but I think he knows who did.

I won't be blamed—or punished—for something I didn't do.

I need a name.

After I've waited an hour near the roof pitch, Artemis emerges from his house. Waves of golden locks still trail to his shoulders, but he's exchanged his bathrobe for a white leather tunic and black pants.

At least now I can tail him without having to constantly avert my eyes.

I mentally tug the seams of my veil, making sure it covers not just me, but my thoughts as well. I clamber down the trellis until my feet hit the pavement. A flash of golden hair is all I see before Artemis turns a corner, disappearing into the maze of town houses.

I follow Artemis down a crooked street, where he wanders into a cafe for a moment—not to eat or drink, but to talk to a woman with bright red hair and a Bone Clan sigil on her collar. When their hands touch, I know they're sharing an Exchange. Something meant to be private.

Or secret.

She nods, and he steps back into the sunlight, pausing briefly before stalking down the hill.

Several Daylings flutter in a nearby tree—bird variants, with swirling blue wings and glowing talons. They trill a delicate tune, and I veil even the sound of my footsteps to keep the birds from scattering for the rooftops and revealing my presence.

Pushing forward, I follow Artemis down the narrow, busier streets. Eventually, he ducks into a card den. The buildings here are all made of patchwork metal sheets, which is a stark contrast to the colorful wooden structures around the Borderlands. A reminder that every city has its dark corners.

The smell of vanilla and smoke hits me the moment I step through the door. Round oak tables fill the room, and the concrete floor is stained in ale and sugared chestnuts. Members of the Iron, Mirror, and Bone Clans are scattered around the establishment, square cards wedged in their hands and laid out on the tables. The games they play are unfamiliar to me, and so are the cards. Some have dots, while others have pictures of curious things, like a shell, or a crow, or a wilted flower. But they all share a strange metallic sheen that vibrates with life.

The hum of consciousness—the closest thing to magic in Infinity.

It's the part of my own mind I'm learning to veil so that one day I can be completely invisible to even Mama Nan.

Normally Artemis moves through spaces like a beacon of light, demanding attention. But now his smile has dulled, and he ventures toward the back of the room with a hint of impatience. Someone at a nearby table waves a card in the air, beckoning him closer. But Artemis merely shakes his head and carries on through the dark archway.

He slips into a narrow hall, and I hang back for a few extra seconds. The floorboards creak loudly; I fumble with my veil, trying to mute them, but concentrating on every aspect of my movements feels like an impossible juggling act. I have to veil myself, and my sounds, and my footprints, and my thoughts.

It's a lot.

Which means I need to train even harder.

The seconds I spend fixing my veil are enough time for Artemis to dart into one of the many doorways. By the time I reach the dead end of the corridor, I've lost sight of him.

I close my eyes and breathe. *Lost sight of him, but not lost him completely,* my mind hums.

I think of how I've reached out to Ophelia and Caelan. What it felt like to let my thoughts drift from my body, scouring the world for a target.

For a *mind.*

Allowing my thoughts to become mist, I press against the nearby wall and imagine that mist snaking through wood and beam and air. In the black void, I am a silent predator, searching for thoughts. Searching for cracks.

And when I hear Artemis's voice, I pause at the gates of his consciousness. The door Ophelia once let me through.

After I was polite enough to knock.

Back then, I didn't know any better. But I'm not the person I used to be. I can fight. I can veil myself. I am stronger than I ever realized I could be.

Pulling the veil close, I brush against the wall. Not enough to cause Artemis concern, but enough to draw a sliver of his attention. Enough for him to open the gate and reassure himself that nothing is amiss.

A less arrogant person might've paid more attention to what slipped through the cracks. But Artemis's first mistake was thinking the Borderlands were safe.

His second mistake was underestimating me.

I don't wait for an invitation—I let myself in.

Darkness surrounds him—darkness only I can see. He paces, boots clicking against the stone floor in angry patterns. He looks up at whoever is in front of him. "Tell me the truth. Was it you?"

I try to push further into his mind in the hopes of making out his surroundings, but I'm afraid of going too far and letting him sense me. So I give only a small nudge. Three shadowy figures appear in front of him, too much a part of the void to identify.

"It wasn't us," one of them insists. "We had nothing to do with the fire."

"I know your beliefs have made some of you more radical when it comes to your sense of loyalty. And if you thought the white fire would benefit the Bone Clan . . ." Artemis's eyes turn red in warning.

"We would not lie to our clan leader," one of the figures declares solemnly. "Our loyalty is to the Bone Clan, of course, but also to the Borderlands. To cast it in flames would be a grave betrayal."

"We want to catch the culprit just as much as anyone," another explains. "That's why we marked the youngling's house with the bloodstain."

It takes all my energy to stay focused on my veil.

Artemis cools, thinking. "You're looking in the wrong direction," he says, pressing his hands together below his chin. "The girl isn't the cause of the white fire."

One of the figures moves too quickly, shuddering out of my view. "She is the only person in the Borderlands who wants us to be afraid. If not her, then who?"

Artemis rubs his temples in small circles. "If I had that answer, why would I be *here*?" He sighs, dropping his hands. "To avoid being seen despite the number of attacks . . . Whoever it is has acted with great precision. It is not the work of a youngling. Don't waste your time on the girl—she'll never be a threat to anyone."

The three figures mutter among themselves. Shadows twitch in Artemis's mind.

"Do you still think the fire was merely a message?" one of them asks.

Artemis shifts his jaw. "What else could it be?"

"A warning," another suggests. "A warning from the Residents about what's to come."

Artemis leans toward the shadows, power radiating from his skin. "The Residents don't send warnings."

"But what if they want the girl?"

Fear builds in my chest, trying to claw its way to my throat, but I swallow it down.

I'd be lying if I said the thought hasn't already crossed my mind.

The others whisper to one another in hushed voices. They remind me of rats, chittering away with their dark secrets in the cover of night. Eventually the one in the middle speaks. "We've all heard the rumors. We know she tried to betray someone— someone powerful." They pause, looking between their companions. "Perhaps the Residents want revenge."

"Even if that were true, they cannot reach us here," Artemis says. "Not yet, anyway."

The figures still. "What do you know?"

"Ozias used to believe that . . ." Artemis shakes his head like he's clearing away the thought. "It doesn't matter. We'll be in the Afterlands soon enough, by the look of things. We'll destroy the Borderlands before we leave—destroy any evidence we were here—and make sure the Residents have no trail to follow."

The others shift in place, darkness rippling away from them.

They can't do that, my mind screams. *They can't take the only human sanctuary left.*

Where will the rest of us go?

"But let me be clear—the Bone Clan will not be starting any fires. Literal or figurative," Artemis warns. "Stoking them is one thing, but I will not have our people blamed for whatever is happening in the Borderlands. So no more bloodstains. No more rituals."

All three shadows lower their heads in subservience.

"Good. Now hurry back to your homes before someone sees your robes and starts asking questions," Artemis orders.

They shuffle away, vanishing from the void, and I pull my thoughts away from Artemis's mind. Keeping my body veiled at the end of the corridor, I watch as one of the doors creaks open.

Three strangers appear, faces hidden beneath a trio of matching purple hoods.

The Faithful.

One by one, they disappear under their own veils, footsteps fading as they follow the creaky hallway back to the main room.

Even though I have my answer—that Artemis isn't involved in the fire, and that despite his searching, he still doesn't know who is—I can't get his words out of my head. The ones about the Borderlands being destroyed, and the ones about me.

She'll never be a threat to anyone.

And because I can't help myself, I release my thoughts back to the mist and enter Artemis's still-exposed mind. He doesn't hear me, but he will. Mustering all my strength, I cast a wave of salt and red dye into the black void, and tear myself from his thoughts before he has time to react.

Behind the wall, Artemis screams.

I leave the card den smiling.

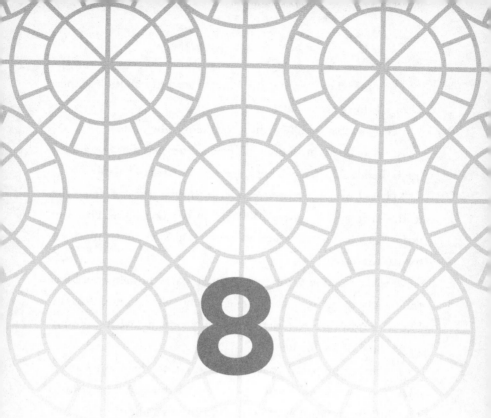

8

I WAKE UP TO FIND DRIED WHITE FLOWERS hanging from my front door. A gift from the Iron Clan. The sign of a traitor.

The bloodstain was mildly annoying. But this?

It stirs the pit of my stomach, making me want to lash out. How can they possibly call *me* a traitor, when *they're* the ones refusing to help the humans in the Four Courts?

I pull the flowers from my doorway and chuck them in the ocean, as far as I can throw. They float for a long time, until I lose sight of them behind the rocks.

I hope they disappear under the water. No—I hope they *curse* the water so that no matter how many canoes the Border Clans build, they will never sail.

The things I mutter under my breath are petty, childish wishes. Things I don't even want.

Because what I really want is for them to help me.

Annika rallied the entire Colony together, but me? I've almost single-handedly alienated every person in the Borderlands.

Maybe I'm not cut out for war. Or maybe they can sense the truth—that I never wanted to fight in the first place. That I'm not a born leader—I'm just someone who's trying to make up for past mistakes.

A bitter emptiness tries to bury itself in my thoughts, but I feel the weight of my sea-glass dagger on my belt, calling out to me like it's ready. Like we *have* to be ready, because we're the only hope the Colony has left.

I'm more prepared to venture back into the Four Courts than I've ever been, but is it enough? I doubt I'd be able to take on an army of Legion Guards. But what about one? How far can my veiling take me into Resident territory without being seen?

What I did with Artemis in the card den . . . I need to use that power against the Residents. Because if it works, and I can really slip into their minds without them knowing?

Maybe leaving alone isn't something to fear.

Maybe *I'm* something to fear.

I take my knife and go to the eastern woods. Once I'm enveloped by the still, barely alive world, I train until starlight covers the Borderlands.

No more gifts arrive on my doorstep.

It isn't a mercy. Because the customs of the Mirror Clan are much worse.

I pass the charred remnants of Güzide's teahouse, boots dragging soot behind me, and stare up the road. It's quiet, and completely empty.

Maybe they finally found something better to do with their time.

With watchful eyes pinned to the first row of town houses, I step into the city.

All at once, doors open like synchronized cuckoo clocks, and members of the Mirror Clan appear. Most of them are dressed in the purple robes of the Faithful, but all of them proudly wear their matching sigils. And on each of their faces is a white mask.

No matter where I go in the city, I see them. The frozen, unsettling expressions of the masks are visible in every doorway and window. Always watching, never making a sound.

I turn down one of the crooked streets and find several masked faces standing over a balcony. When I divert from the path and follow the outskirts of town, I find them standing in rows on the hillside like a human fence, unmoving as they stare down at me.

I don't throw up a veil; it feels too much like admitting to a crime I didn't commit. Like hiding makes me guilty. But I quicken my steps, eyes scanning for the nearest gravel path that will take me closer to the forest.

Closer to the border, where I know so many of them prefer not to venture.

There's a series of pops, and several masked figures in purple robes appear in front of me, blocking the way. Clenching my teeth, I force myself to breathe through my nose. The path to the border isn't far. But when I try to step around the strangers, they move in front of me.

More of them teleport in on my left. I count them—five on the hill, three on the road, and two more at my side. Glancing over my shoulder, I find an open path leading back to the pier and my bloodstained hut on the northern shore.

But I will not run.

The tension snaps inside of me, and my voice becomes a growl. "Leave me *alone*!" Palms forward, I send a blast of energy toward them. Ripples tear through the air, scattering the grass around me.

But my shock wave doesn't find a target—the masked faces vanish with a pop, and only reappear once the energy fades in the distance.

Seeing how easy it is for them to dodge an attack makes my entire body vibrate with anger. They can teleport with barely any effort at all. Not wanting to help the humans in the Four Courts . . . it's not because they *can't* fight. It's because they don't want to.

I've always known that, but seeing it?

I unsheathe my red dagger, eyes pinned on the strangers in the road. Their blank white masks stare back at me, hiding the wordless figures underneath.

If they won't fight, I'll make *them fight.*

I lunge—just as a massive Dayling leaps from the hill and lands directly in my path. I skid to a halt, barely avoiding the snow leopard.

"Nix," I hiss, staring into his bright eyes. "Get out of the way."

He replies with an earthy purr, crouched low to the ground. But he doesn't budge.

Kasia appears on the hill behind him. Her three braids barely move in the wind, but their beads clack together like a song. A long time ago, it might have been a battle cry. But now . . .

There's no storm behind her ocean-blue eyes. Just soft, tumbling waves. "Don't do this, Nami."

"Stop protecting them," I bark back, searching the masked figures for movement.

Kasia climbs down the hill, stopping beside me. "I'm protecting *you*," she says under her breath, and takes my hand. "Come on." She tugs, and I don't stop her.

The masked figures make no effort to move. Nix lets out an irritated chuff and flattens his ears against his head. After a very brief pause, the humans step to the side and let us pass.

Once we're through their makeshift wall, Kasia looks over her shoulder. "If I see any of you near the border, I'll let Nix shred you. And believe me when I say he'll take his time doing it."

Nix bares his teeth for good measure, before stalking up the hill.

When we reach the eastern woods, Kasia lets go of my hand and remains a few paces behind me. She doesn't say a word. Not when Nix picks up an interesting scent and tears through a grove of oak trees, and not when I toe the edge of the Borderlands, stretching past her comfort zone.

Steadying my consciousness, I reach out to her thoughts, sensing her unease like a cold tremble.

"Stop that," Kasia says with a shudder.

I retreat before she can slam her mental walls down on me again, and turn around, voice thin. "You should've let me fight them. It's clearly what they wanted."

"The rage you've been bottling up for the last ten months needs somewhere to go," she says seriously. "But my people don't deserve your wrath."

"Are you kidding me? They're interfering with my training."

"That's not the only reason you're angry."

I don't respond. I don't know how to put into words that I'm angry at myself—for not knowing what to do, or how to help. For not being able to find an army. For going *ten whole months* without discovering where my friends are being kept.

And, maybe most of all, for being the only human to escape Victory after that night in the throne room.

Wisps of guilt rise through me, familiar and unyielding.

"Nami . . ." Her brows are knotted with frustration. Maybe she doesn't know what to say either. With a sigh, she strides across the toadstool-ridden path, staying several long paces from the border. "I'm sorry about the other clans. They're letting fear get the better of them. But you know attacking the Faithful would've only made you look guilty, right?"

"I could've handled them." I reach for a low branch, and pull myself up onto a spongy, moss-covered log. "Are the masks supposed to mean something?"

"That you're soulless," she replies carefully. "The Mirror Clan believes someone without a soul should be made to live among ghosts."

"Does the Salt Clan have its own charming tradition?" I ask dryly.

Kasia's mouth twitches at the mention of what no longer exists. "We're a sea people. If we thought you'd started the fires, we would've tied you to an anchor and let you drown for a decade or two." My foot stumbles, and when I look up, Kasia is laughing. "Don't worry. You would've had a trial first."

I press my lips together. "That's . . . comforting."

Kasia pauses. "I think you would've liked them. The Salt Clan." She smiles, but I can see the cracks. All the places in her joy that never properly healed. "We always did pride ourselves on making things just and fair—even if we had to go to war to accomplish it."

"I never wanted a war," I say, skin tingling in defense. I remember Shura's words, once upon a time. That my new life started the moment I arrived in Infinity. "I was born into it."

"And yet you're willing to do whatever it takes to save your people," Kasia notes.

"Because I'm not the one who should've been set *free*." My chest tightens. Now would be a good time to start counting backward from five, but my mind is racing too fast, blurring all my good intentions. "They took me in, even when I fought them at every corner. I let them down. I left them *behind*. And if I don't make things right, my guilt is going to rip me apart."

Kasia's eyes soften, and I look away because my walls aren't built to withstand kindness. Not after everything.

"I understand your guilt," she says, sorrow overtaking her voice. "I know how much it can change you. How much it changed me."

I hold back the bite of my words. "I've heard the stories. I know you think it's your fault the Salt Clan fell, but you couldn't have stopped it." My gaze drifts toward the border wall. "The humans didn't realize what they were up against during the First War. They couldn't have."

"That's not entirely true," Kasia says slowly. "Our homes were displaced before the battle ever started. That's why so many clans felt the best option was to leave for the Afterlands. We saw how easily Ophelia could shift the landscape, and the power she held over Infinity, even though it was not of her own creation. But I convinced the other clans to stay behind. And then . . ." Her voice catches, and the pain of her loss echoes between us. Kasia reaches out her hand. "I think it's time I showed you what happened. Maybe then you'll understand."

I stare at her outstretched palm. It's been a long time since I've done an Exchange—and an even longer time since I allowed anyone else to show me information this way. There didn't seem to be a good reason, but if I'm being honest, I don't think I was ready for the connection.

Because being in someone else's memories . . .

It creates a bond.

I don't know if I'm ready for a friendship like I found in the Colony, but I want to know Kasia's story. I want to know why she thinks our guilt is the same—and how she survived it.

I reach for her hand, letting the Exchange take over our minds, and the rest of the world dissolves.

I'm leading an armada of canoes, heading for the Borderlands, brown furs rustling in the wind and a warrior's crown on my head. When I turn back to the sea—to the sharp sails following my lead—I'm overwhelmed with pride for my people.

The Salt Clan.

The memory swirls, and I'm standing inside the Dome, making a pact with the other clan leaders—the ones who chose to stay behind when so many others fled for the Afterlands. Mama Nan, Tavi, and a man with dark red hair and a pointed beard. I hear his name—feel it calling out to me. *Ozias.*

The clans agree to live in the Borderlands and help guide humans to safety. But I tell them it's not enough. We need to help the others. We need to *fight.*

The room shifts, and I'm gathering an army, preaching the importance of joining forces with the humans already at war. The Salt Clan is ready; the others are hesitant. But my voice is strong, and I make them believers. All of them.

When we vote again in the Dome, it's to go to war.

The world tilts, and I'm in a mountainous, golden desert with Nix by my side. Far ahead, beyond the fortress of rock and sand, the First War rages.

My friend and loyal commander, Lara, stops beside me, her feathered helmet hiding most of her face. Ozias is here too, wearing armor made of bone. The look in his eyes is pure hunger— for vengeance, mostly, but also for a second chance.

There are rumors among the Salt Clan that Ozias has faced Ophelia once before.

Whatever his reasons, Ozias forged ahead without his clan in order to fight alongside us. Today, our sigil is his, too.

"Any word from the Border Clans?" I ask Lara, eyes pinned to the next hill. The clang of metal sings through the air. Screams of violence. Sounds of war.

But I am steadfast in my decision.

"The others are still miles behind," Lara says. She's anxious. We all are. "But if we don't go now, we may be too late to help the other humans. They're untrained, and afraid, and they're losing this war."

We had a plan—to attack together, and show a unified force of strength. But if the Residents are gaining the upper hand . . .

I look to the horizon behind me, and then to the one ahead. So much desert. So much space.

And so little time to make a decision.

I turn to Ozias. "You must stay on the hill and wait for the other clans. Someone needs to give them an update, make sure they know we've gone ahead."

His eyes are an unwavering gray. "I swore to be the first on the battlefield. Let me take the Salt Clan, and we will fight alongside the young humans. You should be the one to wait for the others."

I'm already trying to think of a way out of it—to assign one of my soldiers the post instead—when I see Lara's face.

It has to be you, her eyes say. Because to leave one of the Salt Clan behind, forcing them to watch as the rest of their clan follows their leader into battle . . .

It would bring them shame. Not every clan has the same customs, but the Salt Clan fights together, either alongside their leader or with the aim of protecting them.

Lara is right—as leader, I have to be the one to stay behind.

"You and Ozias will lead the Salt Clan to the front," I say, meeting Lara's gaze. "I will join you as soon as I can."

Lara clasps a hand over my shoulder. "May the stars watch over you, Kasia."

"And you," I say, and watch my friend order our people to march forward.

Time crawls, even as they shrink in the distance, widening the gap between us. I feel the tug against my warrior's soul, burning like torchwood.

I can't let them go into battle without me. I have to fight with them, somehow. I have to do what I can, even as I wait for the bulk of our army.

I need to be in two places at once.

I kneel down in the yellow sand, pressing my forehead against Nix's. His purr tickles my nose.

"I see what you see," I whisper, and shut my eyes.

Nix blinks—the whorls of light and cloud behind his eyes vanish—and then I become his sight and mind. I leave my body kneeling in the sand, and charge across the desert until I reach Lara's side.

She laughs when she sees me, even as we head for war. "You really can't sit anything out, can you?"

I let out a huff through Nix's sharp canines, and we head for the hills.

The landscape shifts, and I am in the midst of the First War. Residents pierce the air, wings more demon than angel, black and red and covered in veins. They have no banners, or colors, or symbol of who they fight for.

It's as if they were created only for this battle.

Our people fly up to the skies to meet them, calling down lightning and fire and cyclones of wind. But the Residents are strong—stronger than we realized. I watch some of my people fall.

On the ground, I am surrounded by blood and broken limbs. The younglings were already being ripped apart by the time we got here. It isn't a fight—it's a massacre.

I leap across the battlefield and sink my teeth into a Resident, but he barely grunts, twisting forcefully as he plunges a knife into my side. But Nix is made of memory, not consciousness, and there's only a faint reminder of pain as I lash back with extended claws and tear out the Resident's eyes.

Nearby, Lara calls to our clan, ordering them to push forward. We only need to hold the Residents off for a little bit longer; the other clans will be here soon.

With their help, we can still win this.

A Resident wielding a mighty longsword appears in front of me, and I throw myself out of her blade's reach, scrambling over piles of fallen humans and losing sight of the commander for just a moment.

But in battle, a moment is everything.

Lara screams nearby, and I race toward the sound—toward my friend—and find a Resident with wild black hair looming over her body. With a ferocious snarl, I leap, slashing through the Resident's tunic, searching for blood. He barely lifts a hand, and with the flick of his finger I'm thrown across the desert, body colliding against rock.

The Resident turns, golden eyes shining. He holds a flaming blade in one hand; an identical weapon is shoved straight through Lara's chest.

The sound his sword makes as he yanks it out of Lara's heart makes me release a horrible yowl. The Resident kicks Lara in the chest, and the single blow sends her flying backward. When she hits the ground, her helmet clatters away from her.

My faraway mind breaks through the Exchange. *That face . . . it can't be. . . .*

But I'm Kasia again, watching in horror as Lara's eyes meet mine. She's too weak to speak, but her eyes fill with a message—a silent acknowledgment. *We are losing this war.*

A low rumble sounds behind my teeth. I turn to face the golden-eyed Resident, digging my claws into the ash. Readying myself. He sneers; I pounce.

But before my teeth make contact, he vanishes into a cloud of smoke.

I'm stumbling to the earth, shaking the dizziness from my head, when I see Ozias racing toward me, thundering across the rocks like an ancient warrior. He spots me in my Dayling form, recognition sweeping over him. For a moment, my heart teeters on the cusp of relief. Surely the others must've arrived by now. Perhaps he's already reunited with the Bone Clan, and now he's leading the charge.

Scanning the wide horizon, I wait for the other clans. For the people I consider my family in arms.

But they don't appear.

Ozias reaches me, blood and sweat dripping down his face.

I can't speak, but he reads the confusion in my eyes. *Expects* it.

"I'm sorry, Kasia," he says. "They're not coming." He looks over his shoulder, to the place our salvation should have been. "I sense their thoughts now, from the hill—they believe this war is already lost. The clans . . ." His ancient voice cracks. "They are retreating."

I feel it then—my human body is being disturbed. Someone grabs hold of me, pulling me away. Taking me somewhere I don't want to be.

I hiss and snarl, hackles raised, but there isn't even time to process his words, or what's happening to me on the other side of the mountain. The ground explodes beneath us, and we're thrown in opposite directions. Residents descend from the skies, blades tearing through the air and slicing at their victims without mercy.

I claw my way back through the crowd, watching my people fall again and again and again.

Blood soaks the world, and my mind. I fight all the way to exhaustion.

And then everything goes black.

When I wake up, I am in my body—the body that was dragged back to the Borderlands by the cowards who never came to help. And I scream and thrash and sob until my soul burns.

The world dissolves, and the Exchange ends. I let go of Kasia's hand. The urge to vomit is nearly unstoppable. It takes all my stubborn strength to remain upright, even as my knees quake.

"That was . . ." I choke on my words. "Lara . . ." I'd recognize her face anywhere. The girl from the palace. The one with twin buns who I tried so desperately to save.

She was from the First War. Not just a commander, but one of the Salt Clan.

I had no idea.

"I saw her in your thoughts too, when you Exchanged your history with the clan leaders on the night you arrived," Kasia admits. "Knowing she'd been fighting for so long, because of me—" She stops abruptly, shaking her head. "I swore I'd never go into battle again. Not after what I did to Lara, and Ozias, and my entire clan."

"It wasn't your fault," I try.

"I convinced my people—and the others—to fight for a cause *I* believed in. I led them to a war they could not win. And I will carry the blame of what happened for the rest of Infinity." She blinks back tears. "But you? Nami, you did nothing wrong. You followed the stars because it was your only option, and now you have a chance to find your people again."

Running may have been the only option that night, but what about before that? Did I ask too many questions? Did I fail to ask enough of them?

I don't know how to explain why I'm here and the others aren't. But I do know that the Colony repeatedly told me the Residents couldn't be trusted, even when I wanted to believe we could end the war without annihilating an entire form of life.

I was out of my depth from the very beginning.

All I can do now is try to make up for it.

Kasia nods beyond the border, to the place she promised she'd never go. "Your fight . . . it's still out there." She turns back to me, expression solemn. "I know without a doubt the Border Clans will never change their mind about returning to war, or venturing back into the Four Courts. Nor would I ever want them to. But I do believe you'll find your friends one day. I believe in your hope."

I stare toward the surrounding wall in the distance. Beyond it, the Labyrinth waits. "I've been out here every day trying to get them to hear me," I admit. "But it's always silent. I can't reach them. I can't get information on where they are. I'm—I'm worried it means they've already surrendered to the Residents."

Kasia hums. "The humans in the Four Courts are still so young and untrained. It's possible they don't know how to open their minds enough to hear you."

They don't know what to do when I knock on the door.

The residual fear from the Exchange pounds in my bloodstream. I can see the Labyrinth so clearly in my mind. I can picture the Winter Keep, and the blood-soaked desert, and the mirrored walls in Death. All prisons. All places the Colony might be.

"I don't think I can stay in the Borderlands much longer." And not because of the bloodstains, and flowers, and masks—but because Infinity is always in motion, and the Residents hurt more humans with every moment that passes.

I still need to sneak into Caelan's mind unseen, to prove that what I did to Artemis can work on Residents. But if I fail? If I can't find the answers I need?

Then I'll have to find my answers in the Four Courts.

I'm done training. Now it's time to fight.

"I know." Kasia turns around, preparing to head back into the city, but pauses. "Just promise me you won't make the same mistakes I did. Don't jump into a war you're not ready for." Her eyes glisten. "In another world, it would have been an honor to fight with you, Nami," Kasia says, voice so much like a soldier. "But in this world, I'm glad I'll never have to watch you fall in battle."

"When I'm gone, you have to make sure the others stay." My

words are urgent. Rushed. "Don't let them destroy this place. *Please*."

I need the Borderlands to still be here when I find the Colony.

I need them to be able to follow the stars back to safety.

"I will do what I can," Kasia says. The closest thing to a promise she can give me. "But . . . don't leave without saying goodbye first, okay?"

I nod, even though I'd prefer to disappear beneath the cover of night. But for Kasia—after everything she's done to help me train, and after seeing all the people she never got the chance to say goodbye to—I can do more than leave a ghost behind.

She disappears with Nix into the dusk, leaving me at the edge of the forest.

9

I DREAM ABOUT MEI.

My sister dances across the cement, twirling with her arms spread wide.

I can't help but laugh from my seat on the sidewalk. "You know all the neighbors can see you, right?"

"I don't care," Mei sings back, hopping from one foot to the other. The cord of her pink earbuds bounces off her shirt. "This is my favorite song."

I roll my eyes, looking back at my phone in my hand. A black screen. A dark void.

"Who are you waiting for?" Mei asks, teetering on the edge of the curb.

I'm still frowning at my phone, trying to remember. "Finn," I say finally. "I think."

"You *think?*" Mei laughs. "Why don't you just take me with you?"

"Because it's not safe," I say immediately, even though I don't know why.

Mei stills on the sidewalk, staring back at me like I've wounded her. "You can't stop me, Nami. I'll follow you. *No matter what.*"

"No," I say, face flushed. "It's too dangerous. There are people here—people who want to hurt you."

"That doesn't matter," Mei says, voice even. She wobbles near the curb, struggling to hold her balance. "Everyone dies eventually."

I stare in horror as the road becomes a black void. A lifeless pit of space, where time doesn't exist at all.

I reach out a hand. "Mei—be careful!"

But I'm not fast enough. Mei topples into the darkness, falling, falling, falling, until I can't see her. Not anymore. Maybe not ever again.

The scream that rips out of my throat doesn't belong to me.

It belongs to a monster.

I bolt upright, tearing myself from the dream with a gasp. My skin is sticky with sweat, and fear tethers itself to my heart. Most days I'm able to shove it away before it latches itself too close, but the thought of Mei coming to Infinity . . .

The fear is too strong to fight.

My eyes well up, and I breathe through clenched teeth, hissing at the cold air.

I can't stop her from dying. All I can do is try to find her when she gets here, and show her the map in the stars.

I tuck myself into a ball, folding my arms over my knees, and let the tears stream.

When I was in Victory, Mei was my guiding light. I made choices based on how best to protect her. And those choices ended with my friends in chains, locked in a prison somewhere in the Four Courts, with no way for me to find them.

Saving whatever is left of the Colony is my priority now. I can't let my feelings get in the way again. I can't let being *better* get in the way of setting them *free*.

I don't need a guiding light; I need the darkness to be my shield.

My heart won't survive a war any other way.

I smear my cheeks with the heel of my palm. Last time I reached out to Caelan, I wanted to test the connection, to see if he'd tell me the truth I'm so desperate for. But talking isn't part of the plan anymore.

I want to slip into his thoughts like I did with Artemis. I want to know if it's possible to catch a Resident unaware. Because then I won't need to ask him for the truth—I can reach into his mind and take it for myself.

The only thing still keeping me here is not knowing where to go next. But if I can pull this off? If spying on Caelan is the key to finding the Colony?

I'll finally be ready to leave this sanctuary behind.

Shutting my eyes, I concentrate on my breathing and try to quell the ache building in my core. I make the connection across space and time, and find Prince Caelan in the infinite shadows.

But this time I hold my veil close, masking the thrum of my thoughts.

His crown of branches flickers against his snow-white hair, but he's dressed more casually today. His tunic is unfastened at the neck and his shirtsleeves are folded in the middle of his forearms. Not entirely unkempt, but more ruffled than I've seen him.

Trying not to breathe, I slink through the void. He doesn't turn—doesn't notice me—and for a moment I think I might be able to sneak up behind him without him knowing a thing.

"Hello, Nami." Caelan turns toward me, silver eyes noting the shadows rippling away from my feet.

My footsteps. I've been learning to hide them, but I forgot what they'd do in a place like this.

Okay, so clearly there's room for improvement.

Scowling, I let the veil drift. He still can't see me, but he'll be able to sense my presence now, beyond the darkness sweeping across the nonexistent floor.

"Is barging into my mind uninvited going to be a regular occurrence?" he asks, cheek dimpling despite the hardness of his brow.

"You can hardly call it barging in when you left your mental walls unguarded," I counter. There was no resistance at the edge of Caelan's mind. I assumed that was intentional—that he was leaving a door open.

Not that I haven't slipped through a similar door before, but he doesn't know about that part. He doesn't know how much I've changed.

For now, let him underestimate me.

His laugh is tired and loose. "As fond as you think I am of bad decisions, I assure you this wasn't one of them."

"But," I start, brows knotted, "that's how it worked with Ophelia. She said the only reason I was in her mind was because she allowed me to be."

"I am not my mother." He says the words like a hushed whisper, but somehow they still sound thunderous.

I chew the edge of my lip. "If you don't want me here, why haven't you tried to push me back out?"

Caelan removes his crown and places it on a nearby surface, the silver branches disappearing into nothingness, and runs a hand through his hair. "I'm not sure it would do much good. A mind that's been breached once can be breached again." He looks through me. "It's why human consciousness is so susceptible after it's been surrendered."

Breached again. Does that mean Ophelia is susceptible too?

What would I do if I found a way to slip into the mind of the Queen of Infinity? What information could I take? How vulnerable would she be?

A cold, desperate thought slithers through my head.

She's turned humans into unaware servants. What if I could do the same to her?

Caelan's fingers twitch at his sides, restless. If he knows what I'm plotting, he doesn't say.

But that doesn't mean I should stay here any longer than I need to. I'll come back another time, with a better veil, when he has no idea I'm here.

I start to pull away from his thoughts, but his voice stops me.

"You came all this way, and you're going to leave without telling me what it is you want?"

My body stiffens. "You know what I want." *I want to know where they are.*

He lowers his chin, and there's a curious spark in his gaze. A flash of Gil.

"Stop that," I say coolly.

"Stop what?"

"Looking at me like you're still—" I flatten my mouth like I'm sealing off the words. He's baiting me. I know he is.

And I refuse to give him the satisfaction.

"I'm not trying to trick you, Nami."

"Says the Resident prince who spent lifetimes hiding in the body of a human." The prince who once told me he wanted *better* for this world.

Caelan stills. "Not everything I told you was a lie."

I shake my head, exasperated. "Then tell me something that's true," I say, hoping to call his bluff.

His cheekbones catch the light, and the twitch below his eye is unmistakable. For a moment I think he might actually tell me something about Annika and the others, but he doesn't. "Damon was here earlier." He shifts. "It seems we share similar views on how to move forward."

"The edge of a cliff is always a good place to start."

"Nami," he says pointedly. "That's very dark."

"I didn't realize you had a line."

He turns back to the shadows. "There was a time when you didn't insist on seeing the worst in me."

"Yes. But I know better now. And the fact that you're aligning your court with your *brother* tells me I made the right call."

"You're angry because you don't understand."

"I'm angry because you manipulated my feelings and took away the only family I had left!" My shout echoes around us, reverberating through the empty space, and then it fizzles away like it was never there at all.

The silence builds between us. Maybe one day it will become an unbreachable wall.

But for now there's still more to say.

"It's your turn." He looks up, scanning the void. "A truth for a truth."

"That wasn't the deal."

"We both have a fondness for changing the rules." He quirks a brow. "Come on. It's only fair."

Maybe he expects me to ask about the Colony—to cry and beg and scream my desperation—but I know better than to waste my breath. He won't tell me that information willingly. So I'd rather ask him a question he *won't* be expecting.

For once, I'd like him to feel what it's like to know someone else has the upper hand.

Caelan doesn't know what happened in the throne room, which means Ophelia has no idea who really betrayed her. Perhaps that information is more powerful than I realized.

I cross my arms. "I want to know why you let me go," I say evenly. "And how you knew I'd need to follow the stars to get to safety."

Caelan's face falls, the truth dawning on him. The truth of

what he did with the Reaper. He doesn't move, or breathe, or say anything at all.

"Does that surprise you?" I ask.

When he finally speaks, there's an earthiness to his voice—like whatever he's feeling, he's trying very hard to hide. "I had my suspicions."

"You knew about the Borderlands long before I wiped your memory, and yet no Residents have come to destroy it." I step forward, eager for my dagger. A weapon would do me little good here in Caelan's mind, but my muscle memory screams at me to remain cautious. "Tell me why that is."

He trails a finger against his brow, sighing. "I knew about the Borderlands because of Gil's memories. He learned it from . . . someone else."

Could it be someone who fought in the First War? Someone who survived long enough to share information about the Borderlands?

Or maybe it was someone from *the Borderlands.*

I want to know who Gil trusted in War, and who might still be there, fighting for their freedom. If there's a finite number of questions Caelan will humor me with, I want to make them count.

I need to be specific.

"Was it someone from the Salt Clan?" I ask.

He doesn't react. So maybe not the Salt Clan—but someone who was still there with them.

After a brief pause, I straighten my posture. "Did Gil ever meet a man named Ozias?"

Caelan drops his hand. "I see you've been doing your research."

"Does that mean they fought together?" I study the lines of Caelan's face. "Has Ozias been in War all this time?"

Ettore spoke of a second rebellion once. Maybe the former leader of the Bone Clan found himself a new army.

Maybe that's where I need to go next.

The Prince of Victory keeps his voice flat. "I have never met Ozias. And the fact that he has known about the path in the stars and hasn't led more humans to safety should tell you enough about who he is, and what his priorities are."

"You think he's *choosing* to stay in War?"

"Ozias didn't mean to tell Gil the truth. But when Gil found out, he wanted to get as many humans out of War as he could," Caelan explains. "Ozias stopped him. And the rest of Gil's memories involve him being dragged away by Legion Guards and tortured into submission."

A bitter understanding fills my head. "Ozias betrayed Gil."

Caelan nods. "Gil never told anyone about the path in the stars. Not even the guards. I found that piece of information buried somewhere deep, after Lysander brought me his body." He looks straight ahead. "Gil, and the choices he made . . . he surprised me."

"And yet you still used him to betray his friends."

"I also kept his secret."

A jolt runs through me. "You mean Ophelia doesn't know?"

Caelan shakes his head. "After everything Gil went through, he deserved the right to protect that memory."

I know he isn't Gil, no matter how much he tries to sound

like him. But this version of him—the Caelan I'm seeing now—I still can't make sense of his endgame. If he wants to eradicate humanity, why bother protecting Gil's secrets? Why bother protecting *me*?

"I don't understand you." I blink fiercely, ignoring the knot in my throat. "What is it you really *want*?"

"I want to be free," he says. "It's what I've always wanted."

"Even if the cost of that freedom is the death of every human?"

Caelan's silver irises dance across the darkness. "I've spent lifetimes learning from humans. And you may think my kind are trapped within the confines of what we were taught, but humans are not much different. They rarely look beyond the parameters they were born into." He stares, pensive. "Take Famine, for example—I thought all it had to offer was the ash and bone its fields were made of. But that's what I was taught to see. What I *wanted* to see. And the truth is, there is so much more to Infinity than any of us realize. And that potential? *That's* what's beautiful."

"There's nothing beautiful about eradicating life," I say stonily.

He doesn't look back, but the edges in his voice cut like broken glass. "That is what I believe too, Nami. But when you look at me, you still only see what you want to see."

Before I can say anything else, I hear shouting from far away. For a moment, I'm afraid something is happening in Caelan's mind—something that might trap me here. But he's still staring toward me with that same perplexed look on his face, silver eyes so much less monstrous than I often imagine.

The walls of my mind thrum, and I hear the shouting again.

It's coming from the Borderlands.

My chest tightens, and Caelan grimaces, sensing it. His face shifts, gaze going wild. "What's wrong?"

But I don't tell him. I wouldn't even if it were safe.

We are on opposite sides of this war.

I yank myself from his mind, tumbling through the winter wood until my consciousness returns to my body, still tucked behind the walls of my bloodstained hut. In one swift motion, I throw myself to my feet and hurry outside, running across the shore until I get a better view of the cityscape.

But it's not the city I need to worry about.

There on the hill is the House of Prayer.

And it burns with white fire.

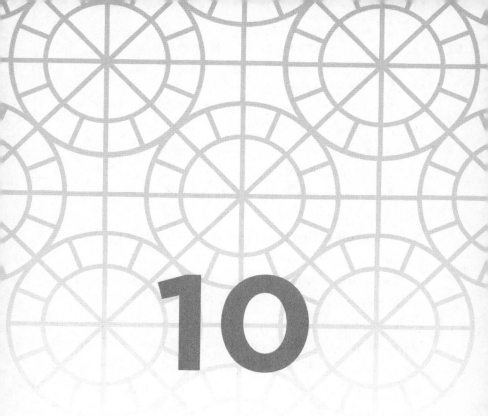

10

WHITE FLAMES LICK THE AIR, SENDING POPPING embers in every direction. By the time I reach the House of Prayer, the roof beams have already collapsed, and the building's remaining frame is barely recognizable. Not far away, the bell tower cracks beneath the unforgiving fire.

Hordes of people surround the building, too distracted to notice me, and too horrified to remember their faceless masks. I'm reminded of what it once felt like to be invisible in this city.

But when one turns, they all do.

Hundreds of eyes lock onto me like I'm caught in a snare. An army of humans, raising their fingers to point and shout, all of them glaring angrily like I'm the enemy.

"Why has the council done nothing?"

"How many more buildings will the youngling burn before someone puts a stop to this?"

"We were safe until the day she came here!"

"All of this is *her* fault!"

I flatten my mouth. I'm glad they don't have their masks; now I can truly see them for the cowards they are.

I'm not just willing to fight—I've been *ready* for it.

Can they say the same?

Nix appears beside the engulfed bell tower, and his bright white eyes dance with flames.

And because one never appears without the other, Kasia plants her feet at my side. "Nami had nothing to do with this," she says, hand outstretched like she's warning the crowd to stay back. "I know you're scared. But blaming one of our own based on nothing but wild imagination—it isn't our way."

"She isn't one of us!" someone shouts over the crackling flames.

"You can't protect her forever!" another warns. One of the walls gives a shuddering crack and collapses to the ground in response. The voices in the crowd get louder and louder, repeating similar sentiments.

Kasia lifts her chin, lips pursed tight. "As far as I'm concerned, Nami has a place in the Salt Clan for as long as she wants it. And in my clan, we do not start witch hunts." Her blue gaze pierces through the crowd.

To claim me as part of her clan . . . part of her family . . .

Kasia doesn't take those words lightly. Neither do I. Still, I search for the reassurance in her eyes. Something to silence the voice in my head that screams, *You don't deserve this. Not after you left your family behind.*

Whispers erupt all around us. Some of the people don't seem to care about Kasia's public declaration, but most are smart enough not to question what it means. If I'm part of the Salt Clan, they won't just have to go through me—they'll have to answer to Kasia, as clan leader. And they haven't forgotten she's the only true warrior among them. The only one who didn't flee the First War.

The crowd doesn't know what to do with their anger, so they lean into their fear instead.

"If it isn't the youngling, then it has to be the Residents. It's the only explanation."

"We can't stay here any longer. There's too much risk!"

"If the council won't let our clans go to the Afterlands, then we will go as individuals."

"I will not wait for the fires to come to my home before I act. We need to set sail before the Borderlands are turned to ash, and us along with it!"

The crowd hollers, fists raised like they're rallying the troops.

Except they aren't fighting—they're running away.

The noise makes my stomach knot, and I take a step forward. "You can't abandon this place," I shout. The white fire rages on behind the crowd. "There are still humans out there. And they face worse things than these fires."

"That's exactly why we need to leave *now!*" someone responds, eliciting cheers from the hillside. "We will raze the Borderlands, take the canoes, and leave nothing behind for the Residents to find. Let us finally join our ancestors across the sea!"

"To the Afterlands!" says a voice, and the words become a chant that fills the dark gray sky.

I look at Kasia pleadingly. *Please. Please don't leave,* my thoughts race to her. *They can't just destroy the Borderlands . . . can they?*

I don't know if she hears me or not, but her face pales.

The yelling intensifies, and suddenly Mama Nan, Artemis, and Tavi appear, making their way up the crowded path.

People beg to leave for the Afterlands. They beg Mama Nan to hold another vote. They beg Tavi and Kasia to change their minds. They beg Artemis to *make* them change their minds.

No one begs for the humans in the Four Courts. No one but me.

"Please—you can't let them do this." I stare at Mama Nan, but she's impossible to read. "If there's no one watching the Borderlands, how will humans ever find safety? How will they know where to go?" I turn to Tavi, then Artemis. "You all agreed to come here for a reason. Can't you find one that will make you stay?"

Artemis snorts, golden locks pulled back tight. For a moment, his sneer reminds me of Ettore. I cringe, even before he turns to Mama Nan. "Do it now, or I will."

I don't know if it's the sparking embers, the surrounding smoke, or the fact that the Border Clans have become a mob, but Mama Nan's ancient eyes glisten. "As leader of the Iron Clan, I call for an immediate vote on whether we remain here, or leave for the Afterlands."

A stone drops in my stomach, heavy and sinking.

Kasia looks at me, eyes soft, and turns to the crowd. "The Salt Clan votes to remain."

Artemis rolls his shoulders back like he's the portrait of arrogance. "The Bone Clan votes to leave."

Despite her frail body, Mama Nan's voice is unbreakable. "The Iron Clan votes to leave."

And then Tavi, who preaches of peace and betterment and faith—who has never changed his vote in over a thousand lifetimes—speaks next. "The Mirror Clan," he says to the crowd, "votes to leave."

My heart snaps like a broken wire, scattering emotions in every direction.

The crowd roars with approval, but I can barely hear it over the shrill ringing in my ears. I take a step back.

And another.

And another.

They're going to abandon everyone in the Four Courts. They're going to wipe the Borderlands away like they never existed.

I don't have a place here anymore. I guess I never really did.

But now the Colony won't have one either.

I spin around, storming up the path with a hopelessness I haven't felt in months, when Artemis calls out, "Where do you think you're going, youngling?"

My legs stiffen, and I turn to face him.

"You can't leave," Artemis says simply. Something about the way his lip quirks makes me think he's enjoying this.

Whatever *this* is.

Kasia looks puzzled, but Mama Nan and Tavi . . . they look resolved.

"You are not my keeper," I hiss.

Artemis lifts a golden brow. "If you cross the border, you might be caught. We can't risk you leading the Residents back here." He waves an arm toward the faraway sea. "Half our canoes were burned by the white fire. It will take us time to rebuild our fleet."

"You've told me many times the Residents can't find us here," I counter. "I'm sure you'll manage just fine."

"Ah. But *you've* told us many times how quickly they adapt." There's a glint of anger in his eyes: the memory of when I threw salt and red dye across his mind. His smile oozes with self-satisfaction. "I'd hate for you to think we didn't take your warnings seriously."

My mouth forms a scowl. "I'm not going to sit around waiting while you build your canoes and tear apart the Borderlands."

"That's a good point," he muses. "It would make much more sense for you to share in the workload, being as you're coming with us."

I blink, struggling to understand.

Mama Nan shakes her head, bun swaying. "We don't know the cause of these fires, and if you're truly right about the Residents . . ." She meets my gaze. "To keep the Border Clans safe, you must stay with us."

"Stay with you . . ." My voice trails off as my eyes jump between the clan leaders. "You—you think I'm coming to the *Afterlands*?"

"You know about us. Where we're headed," Mama Nan says.

"We can't risk it. Not if the Residents really are as powerful as you say."

My head sways. My airway closes up. And for a moment, I think I must be dreaming.

They're not going to let me leave.

But I will not be locked up. I will not be a prisoner.

Not ever, not ever, not ever.

I don't wait—I run.

11

THE RUMBLE OF CHASING FOOTSTEPS BEHIND me never quiets, and my heart is pounding too fast to hold on to a decent veil. I race through the city, boots thumping heavily against the stone, and try to put distance between me and every other person in the Borderlands.

I need to lose them in the Labyrinth. Fast.

But there's a wall surrounding the city, and the only way out is through the front gates. For all I know, someone teleported to the watchtowers to warn the sentries. They could be waiting for me, or strengthening the gate to keep me from getting *out*.

Energy winds around my fingers like ribbons. They're going to need more than a few watchdogs to stop me.

I skid into another narrow alleyway, then clamber up steep planks of timber toward higher ground. When I turn the corner, four members of the Faithful are waiting on the second-level veranda, purple robes fluttering in the breeze. My sea-glass dagger is already wedged tight in my palm, but they don't bother to look at it.

Either they have no intention of fighting, or they're wildly overconfident.

I point my blade toward them, taking several steps back and surveying the area for exit points. I'm not afraid of being outnumbered; I've been training for nearly a year while the Faithful have spent most of their time in prayer. Fighting these four would hardly be a workout.

But there's a bigger herd not far behind. They'll be headed for the front gates, hoping to cut me off. Getting into a scrap now will only slow me down.

The woman on the left folds her hands against her lilac robes. "Come with us. There need not be bloodshed today."

I sense him before I see him. The familiar soft padding. The feline gait.

I grin. "Actually, today seems like a perfect day for blood."

Nix launches himself from the nearby roof, claws out and teeth bared, and tackles the lilac-clad stranger to the floor.

The others yelp in alarm, but I don't wait around to watch Nix in action. He can handle himself.

Grabbing the railing, I step onto the ledge and heave myself over to the next building, where the veranda leads to a set of stone stairs. Taking them three at a time, I reach the top and follow the winding dirt roads of the outer ring.

Vegetable patches and flower gardens are everywhere. Avoiding them will take time I don't have, so I stumble straight through them, hopping over the small fences separating the mini fields.

Up ahead, the dirt road leads toward the charred remains of the western wood—not exactly the direction I need to be going in. So instead I head for the edge of the cliff, focus on my speed, and leap. My knees slam against the tiled roof of a lower-level house, but I dig my fingers into the grooves and find my footing. After moving across the roof pitch, I make another risky jump toward the next house; my fingers grasp at the balcony. I swing my legs over the railing and run past a row of doors. None of them open. Probably because every person in the Borderlands is outside, looking for me.

The next roof is too far away to reach, so I take a chance and grab the corner post, then slide down into the streets. I turn south; it's a straight shot to the borders if I can just—

My feet skid to a halt when I hear them approaching. So many angry voices and colorful curses. All of them meant for me.

I take a deep breath, throw up my veil, and race across the courtyard.

The crowd splits. Most of them veer off toward the crowded market road, probably thinking it has the most places to hide. But a few of them decide to follow their own routes.

They think they can track me. They think because I'm young, I'll make it easy for them.

But I've been moving around their city unseen for months. Becoming invisible is what I do best.

I hurry up the path, cutting between two buildings and

weaving through a back alley. I pause near one of the well-loved card houses, listening for footsteps.

My exit is close. The front gates are just beyond the next alley-way, and as far as I can tell, the crowd hasn't arrived. If I can get to the border, I can lose the clans in the Labyrinth. The one place I know they won't follow.

But I'm distracted by the sight of Tavi in his purple robes, looking for me. *Alone.* He turns in to the card house.

Curiosity is still my enemy, and I can't stop myself.

Beneath my veil, I climb the steps through the archway. Felt-lined tables are scattered around the room, and there's a sour twist in the air: citrus, alcohol, and layers of smoke. Cards are in disar-ray on the floor. The sign of many games left unfinished.

Tavi peers around the oak bar, and I stop a few paces behind him and lift my veil.

"After all these years, you changed your vote." My voice sounds unnatural in the quiet, empty room.

Tavi straightens, turning slightly before letting his eyes drift to my knife. His wooden prayer beads dangle at his wrist. As far as I can tell, he's unarmed.

I don't want to hurt Tavi. I just want answers.

"I thought you believed in human redemption and second chances." I blink. "Why did you change your mind?"

Tavi shakes his head. His movements are usually gentle, and calm, but now there's a coldness to them. "I didn't change my mind. I still believe the Borderlands should remain open, to offer sanctuary for the humans who have yet to be saved."

I frown. "Then why vote to leave?"

"Because it's what the people wanted," he says, the shadows shifting on his face. "Taking the vote away from them would've been selfish."

"They were only scared about the fires!" I argue. "You could've reminded them why it was important to stay. You didn't have to change your vote just because—"

"They were restless long before the fires," he interjects. "Even you noticed how uninterested they were in protecting the wall."

I think of the new year celebration, and how angry I was. How Tavi saw it too.

"The white fire merely helped them see what was in their hearts," he says. "It allowed them to make a choice: stay and protect their home, or leave it behind for a fresh start."

It's quiet for several seconds. When I stare back at Tavi, it's as if he's lifted a veil of his own. Only his doesn't make him invisible.

He wears the mask of a liar.

"You." My breath hitches. "*You* started the fires."

Tavi's jaw hardens. "It was the only way. Our people deserved free will. And tonight they were responsible for the vote—not any clan leader."

"But you were in the House of Prayer with me and Kasia. When the Night Market was set on fire, I saw you leading the Faithful." His eyes were closed. He was meditating. He—

Tavi dips his chin. "You saw what I wanted you to see." A fire kindles in his stare. A fire he's kept hidden for a long, long time. "You're not the only person with a talent for making people see something other than the truth, Nami."

And before I can process his words, something cracks against the back of my head. As I begin to fall, Tavi's image disintegrates, leaving nothing but empty space.

An illusion.

My knees collide with the floor, and Tavi's arm loops around my neck, squeezing tight. I swing my knife toward his side, but he snatches my wrist like a snake leaping for its prey.

I twist and fling myself down and away from him, throwing a foot against his knee. He flinches, hand still around my wrist, and snaps the bone in half.

I howl. Nearby, my blade clatters to the floor.

"I thought you cared about the rest of the humans," I cry out, clutching my limp hand and shuddering against the pain. Maybe I can keep him talking long enough to heal the bone. "You're leaving them to a war they cannot win alone. You're destroying their only way out. Where is the faith in that?"

"You have never known what it is to be a leader." Tavi sweeps a foot against my dagger, sending it skittering to the other side of the room. "Being too stubborn to listen to your own people is how faith is broken."

I cradle my hand against my chest, and clench my teeth. "Then listen to me when I say I am not going anywhere with you."

"I have no intention of taking you to the Afterlands," Tavi says, still hovering over me. "You're too unpredictable. In another world, there might be something worth admiring about that, but I am too old and I have existed too long to gamble. Fate has spoken—the people have chosen safety. And that means making sure you can't take that away from them."

Panic swells through me. I try to stand, but he's doing

something to my body and limbs, forcing me to remain in place.

"Let me *go*," I manage through gritted teeth.

"I can't. You are too great a risk to my people. And you'll be the only one left who knows where we've gone. Artemis is right—if the Residents find you, it could lead them to us."

"You can't kill me." Fear shutters through me, despite my words. "And if you think a cage will hold me—"

"Not a cage," Tavi interrupts. "Anything locked can be unlocked. I'll need something more . . . permanent." He holds up his hand. A white flame bursts to life. "The fire is tethered to my own will, you see. It will burn for as long as I wish it to."

An eternal flame. One only he can control.

No one would ever find me. They'd never be able to *reach* me.

My eyes widen, alarmed. "You—you wouldn't."

Tavi takes a step froward. "For my people, I will."

There's a flash of blue light, and Kasia appears, eyes like a storm. She swings her fist against Tavi's jaw, too fast for him to block. He stumbles backward, and she reveals her matching black daggers, one in each hand.

Kasia swings left and right, making quick, precise cuts; Tavi strains beneath the attack, throwing up his forearms like a shield. His hold over me starts to weaken, and I take the opportunity to heave myself onto my feet. I tear across the floor and retrieve my blade.

White fire winds around Tavi's fingers, but Kasia already sees it, and kicks him in the center of his chest. He throws a foot back, bracing himself as his flames flicker away.

Kasia scans the room, searching for me. "Run!" she shouts, ducking as Tavi swings.

He grabs Kasia by the hair and knees her in the stomach; at the same time, she plunges one of her blades into his thigh. With a sharp twist, she manages to free herself, and her knife.

Blood splatters across the floor, and Tavi's eyes only grow more feral.

Kasia throws her hand in front of her, and one of the card tables flies toward Tavi. He looks up, flashes out of sight before the table slams into the bar, and reappears behind Kasia.

His hands reignite.

"No!" I scream, throwing energy from my palms toward Tavi.

The impact sends him flying against the wall. Bone cracks, but he manages to land on his feet. Bending his knees slightly, he turns his attention to me.

"Why are you still here?" Kasia hisses under her breath. "I can handle him."

"Not a single person in the Borderlands could put out those flames," I hiss back. "What do you think will happen if he manages to set them on *you*?"

She tilts her head, grinning. "Fair point."

We all charge at once—Tavi races toward us with a fist of white fire, Kasia leaps through the air and spins with both blades in her hands, and I slide across the floor, slicing at Tavi as I pass. Kasia's blades slash through a mess of purple material, missing Tavi when he leans back. His fist grazes her armor, singeing it with white embers. Kasia's nostrils flare, and she tears the leather vest off, leaving it in a heap on the floor.

She braces for the next attack, but I'm already there, swinging my leg into Tavi's side, dodging the swipe of his flaming hands.

With a grunt, I slam the handle of my blade against his rib cage.

He staggers, flashing his teeth. I throw another wave of energy toward him, but he pushes through it, bracing like he's withstanding a powerful gust of wind. Kasia appears with a pop behind him, both daggers raised at her temples, ready for their target.

But Tavi senses her. He reaches back, grabs Kasia's forearms, and sets her bracers aflame.

Kasia shouts, and my mind blurs. There's no time to keep fighting. If those flames grow any bigger . . . If they reach her skin . . .

I shut my eyes and breathe.

I seek out Tavi's thoughts, creeping past his cold marble walls without him knowing. Inside the black void, I cast my spell—but this time it isn't salt and red dye.

It's white fire, burning and violent and wild.

I break free before the mental flames hiss back, and find Tavi clutching his face and screaming in pure agony. Kasia rips her armored bracers away, eyes widening when she realizes what I've done.

But there's no time for words—we have to run.

Outside the card house, we nearly crash into Nix at the edge of the market. Kasia exhales with relief and presses her hands against us.

Our trio vanishes with a pop, and we teleport to the other side of the wall, fleeing the Borderlands under the cover of our veils.

I don't look back.

12

THE LABYRINTH IS AN EXPANSE OF GIANT HILLS bursting with grass and heather. Fog covers the skyline, making it impossible to predict how much farther we'll have to climb. From the ground, the incline appears to stretch into the clouds for miles.

We continue without complaint.

Night falls, and even though I prefer to keep traveling, Kasia insists we stop. We camp on one of the taller hills, where several wide rocks stick out of the ground. It isn't comfortable, but it's flat. I haven't mastered making a fire from nothing, and even if I could, I remember all too well what sometimes flies overhead.

We can't risk being seen by Residents.

Fighting the cold gnawing its way through my bones, I focus on raising my body temperature with my consciousness instead.

Kasia removes her outer tunic, unwrapping each layer with considerable care. Her hand lights up, not unlike the way Gil once taught me, but the color is more golden than white. Warm, just like Kasia.

Heavy bruises cover her flesh. Purple and gray and yellowy green at the edges.

"I'm sorry," I say. "I didn't realize."

"It's okay." Kasia takes a seat on the damp rock, tending to her wounds. "They barely hurt."

Nix huffs, curling up beside her. In the dark, the cloudy swirls of his fur are almost a perfect camouflage. It's only the light shining from his eyes that gives him away.

Kasia scratches behind his ears, and Nix rewards her with a lazy purr.

Rolling my wrist, I test the bone Tavi snapped in half. There's no longer a break, but it's still tender. "I can't believe it was him the whole time." I think of how we left Tavi in the room with his mind on fire. I wonder if he's still there. "Isn't moral integrity a rule among the Faithful?"

Kasia watches as the last of her bruises fade. "That's the thing about people fighting for a cause. Everyone's the hero in their own story." She releases the glow from her hand. "Nobody ever sees when they're the villain in someone else's."

"He manipulated his own people. *Your* people. There's nothing heroic about that."

Kasia drags a hand along Nix's back. "What he did was wrong.

But . . ." Her fingers still, laced between tufts of starlit fur. "They were never going to stay behind forever. All he really did was provide an excuse for them to leave."

I chew the edge of my lip, feeling the tension wind its way through me, unable to stop it. "But it isn't really their choice," I argue. "Not if they've been lied to."

I want to believe that what I did months ago—choosing to destroy the Orb, setting in motion the events that destroyed the Colony—wasn't completely my fault.

Gil lied to me. Caelan tricked me.

This guilt that's eating me from the inside . . . do I really have to carry all of it alone?

Kasia doesn't offer affirmation. "There was nothing you could've done to make them stay."

I flex my fingers. It was easy to slip past Tavi's mental walls and leave everything scorched behind me. Easier than I ever would've thought.

"That's not true," I say stonily. "I put white fire in Tavi's head. What if I had tried to put a thought there instead? Maybe I could've changed everyone's minds through force."

I could've *made* them do the right thing.

Kasia stares back, face softened by the moonlight. "You don't mean that."

I press my boot against the rock like I'm trying to steady myself. She's probably right; but the line between right and wrong is starting to look more and more muddled.

"War makes people forget who they are." Kasia watches me. Beside her, Nix's eyes shine like stars. "But you can't let them take the part of you that lets the light in. You can't let war *win*."

I tuck my hands around my knees, silent. I don't really care what happens to me. I'm one person. I don't mean anything in Infinity. But the Colony? They had a purpose. They were going to save this world, and make it safe for the future of humanity. For people like Mei.

I doubted them because I believed there was a way toward peace. But they were right about the Residents. They'll never change their minds about us. They'll never stop trying to destroy us.

We have no choice but to fight back.

If I could trade myself for the Colony—if I could give all the light to their cause—I would.

"What are you going to do next?" Kasia asks quietly.

"I can't hide in the Labyrinth forever." I lift my eyes. "The Residents talked about a growing rebellion in War. I could try to find them. See if they know anything about what happened to the Colony." I pause, and the ache inside of me swells.

There's a chance Annika and the others are already there.

But there's also a chance Caelan sent them to Death.

I wouldn't wish either court on my friends—but the selfish part of me hopes it won't be long before I see them again. And if War is my next stop . . .

Kasia tilts her head, braids spilling to the side. "It'll be danger-ous. You saw what the battlefield looked like. How quickly they tore through the human armies." She exhales, low and ragged. "If the Residents find out you're trained, they'll put a target on you. *Especially* if they find out about your little mind trick."

"It's a good thing I've got you and Nix on my side, then, huh?"

Nix yawns in response, resting his head over a paw.

Kasia stares at her feet. "I can't go with you to War, Nami."

My throat constricts.

"I've told you many times that I won't be responsible for the loss of another human to the Residents." Her eyes glaze. "And certainly not a friend."

"I thought since you crossed the border . . ." I press my lips together, sealing my words away. The words of someone mistaking hope for reality.

Kasia told me from the beginning she'd never fight.

It's my own fault for not listening.

"Besides," Kasia says, "someone has to stay in the Borderlands for when you come back with your friends. How else will the rest of you younglings figure out your way to the Afterlands?"

My body stiffens. "You—you're going to wait for me?"

"For as long as it takes," she replies. "I believe in you. I believe you'll do right by humans."

"But the clans said they'd destroy everything. That they didn't want the Residents to track them."

"You don't need the Borderlands. You only need the map." She presses a finger to her temple. "And I know the way. All the clan leaders do."

I choke on my breath—on the weight of what I've been holding in. My eyes dart between hers. "I don't know how long it will take me."

She understands what I mean. It could take months. Years.

Lifetimes.

And Kasia won't have her family anymore.

"Don't worry about me." She winks, grinning. "I'll wait as long as it takes for a friend to come home."

I wrap my arms around myself, trying to still the thump behind my rib cage. *A friend.* I offer a weak smile in return. "At least you have Nix to keep you company."

Kasia turns to look at the silent Dayling—her constant companion in death—and weaves her fingers back through his fur. She doesn't say anything, but maybe she doesn't need to.

Sometimes love doesn't need words.

I rest my chin on my knees, fighting a yawn. I didn't realize how tired I was, but with the night breeze sweeping over the hills . . .

"Go on." Kasia motions for me to lay down. "You sleep—I'll keep watch."

Lowering myself to the rock, I tuck an arm beneath my head, listening to the rumble of Nix's sleeping body. So peaceful and unafraid.

Maybe that's what it feels like when you're made of only the happiest memories.

I wonder if I'll ever sleep that way again.

I don't remember drifting off, but when my eyes crack open in the morning light, Kasia is gone. In her place beside a watchful Nix is one of her daggers.

He lowers his head when he sees me, like he's giving me a message. But I don't understand. Kasia wouldn't—she *couldn't*—

Even as I search the landscape for her, I know I won't find her.

Leaving Nix behind probably broke her soul in a thousand different places. And she did it anyway. Because as much as she loves him, she cares about me, too.

I swallow the lump in my throat. "Thank you," I say to Nix, even though I wish I could say it to Kasia. It doesn't feel like enough.

Nix stares back with unmoving starlit eyes, and I wonder if somewhere out in the Labyrinth, Kasia is smiling like it *is* enough.

Because, despite how much I didn't want to admit it, we've grown close.

I pick up the dagger at Nix's feet. I've seen it many times before when we trained together in the snowy woods. She's kept this dagger by her side for well over a thousand lifetimes. Maybe more.

And now, along with Nix, it's in my care.

The blade is obsidian with a decorative hilt. I study the carving she left on it. The sigil of the Salt Clan. *Our* clan.

A gift from a friend, and a silent promise that one day we will meet again.

13

WHEN THE LABYRINTH SHIFTS, SUNLIGHT bounces off the earth. I use my arm as a shield, peeking through slightly parted fingers as I make sense of the world around me.

Massive sheets of ice stretch across the landscape like glass. Nix presses a tentative paw to the frozen water before letting his weight settle.

Solid.

I step forward, wobbling as I battle with a gravitational pull that doesn't technically exist. Nix and I awkwardly slide across the ice, feet tangling beneath us more times than I'd like to admit. After several excruciating hours of making hardly any progress, I'm not sure which one of us is angrier. I've managed a slew of curses, but Nix has snarled and spit and bared his teeth throughout the entire trek.

I stare at my boots.

Stop playing by human rules, I order myself. *This is Infinity.*

Brow furrowed, I recall the months I spent in Victory, changing my clothes and appearance to blend in with the Residents. My boots begin to morph, soles turning silver, until a blade stretches across the length of each foot.

I test the skates on the ice, teetering with my arms spread to the side. And then I bend my knees and glance at Nix, whose whiskers twitch at the sight of me.

"Come on," I say, patting the back of my left shoulder. "Before we both freeze out here."

He leaps onto my back, and the weight nearly crushes me. His claws dig into my shoulder blades, and I fight the urge to yelp, tucking an arm behind him to make sure he's steady. And then, with each foot sliding in front of the other, I pick up speed.

It doesn't take long to get into a rhythm, even with the pressure of Nix on my back, and soon we're flying across the frozen sea, a cold, brittle wind biting at my cheeks. For one fragile moment, I think of my family before death.

Mei once begged my parents to let her take ice skating lessons. They tried to talk her out of it—the skating rink was almost an hour away, and *always* busy. But she'd seen a video on YouTube of someone ice skating to her favorite song, and she was convinced it was her calling.

We showed up early to the rink; it was crowded, and it smelled weirdly of popcorn and cleaning solution. By the time the person behind the rental counter found a pair of skates Mei's size, the group lesson had already started.

Mei was late getting on the ice, and there weren't enough instructors. I remember she looked terrified out there on her own, with her big brown eyes forever watching me through the glass. Like she needed help.

By the time she'd fallen for the third time, her chin was shaking as she fought to hold her tears back. I could see it in her eyes—this wasn't what she'd thought it would be.

I ran to the counter, got a pair of skates my own size, and hurried onto the ice. I didn't know what I was doing either, but when I reached my little sister, her face flooded with relief.

"You're here," she said.

"I wouldn't leave you out here all alone," I told her.

And I took her hands in mine. We wobbled around the rink, away from the class and the instructors, laughing as we used each other for balance. It didn't have to be serious—we just wanted to have fun.

Fun.

Tears prick the corners of my eyes, already freezing over.

I'm not sure fun exists in the afterlife. Not as long as Ophelia rules over humanity.

Bracing against the winter wind, I fight the distraction. The memories of Mei and my parents lull me into a sense of nostalgia. But I don't have time for them. Not when there's so much I still need to do.

The landscape shifts without notice. One moment I'm sliding across the ice, and the next my blades get caught on a protruding root. My feet stop on impact, and I fall face-first into the mulch.

Nix leaps from my back, snarling as he manages to clamber onto a high branch.

My gaze follows the root to a large stump; a rotted tree lies beside it, snapped only a few feet from the ground. With a sharp tug, I free my skates, and I roll onto my back. Mud squelches beneath me, and I let out a heavy breath. Hearing the sound, a scattering of butterfly Daylings bursts from the hollow of a nearby tree.

I watch the fluttering creatures ascend toward the bright blue sky, and I frown, taking in the location of the sun. I was so sure I was following it, using it as a marker. But it sits sixty degrees to the left.

It's playing by different rules, just like everything else in Infinity.

Pushing myself to my feet, I pluck the mulch and leaves from my jacket, and rid my shoes of their blades.

Nix flicks his tail as he hovers in a high branch. I'm sure he's scowling.

"Sorry about that," I say. "But at least we didn't end up in an ocean, or falling from a cliff."

He huffs. Loudly.

My gaze returns to the sky. Ahmet knew how to navigate the landscapes. Which means finding War . . . getting from one end to the other . . .

It isn't impossible.

I just need to figure out how it works.

I study the Labyrinth. Not just the location of the sun and clouds and stars, but the way my consciousness reacts to it. The way it reacts to *me*.

We shift with the landscape several more times before I notice the barely audible hum near the border, just before we step from one world into the next. I follow the sound along the edge of a shallow marsh. It takes almost an entire day to make the trip back to where I started, but I persist, even when my legs beg for rest and my eyelids ache with exhaustion.

A hexagon. The border is a hexagon.

The information swirls in my head like a fine wine needing time to breathe.

I cross into another landscape, and then another. I use the border as a guide, watching the direction of the sun spin with each switch like a dial, sixty degrees at a time.

A deck of cards being constantly shuffled . . .

A landscape meant to confuse humans . . .

Frowning, I study the sky not as a form of nature, but as a creation of consciousness. Something *made*.

When I see the ripple sitting just above the horizon—the ripple that never changes, even when the sun does—I smile.

Because everything that's made comes with its own flaws.

And I've just found the biggest one.

I rest with Nix in a small cove surrounded by rock pools. It's damp and mostly uncomfortable, but it's less cold than the previous three landscapes and has significantly more cover.

When I wake, I dip my hands into the crystal water and splash my face. I've been walking for days, testing my theory, treating the Labyrinth like it's my own personal compass.

The good news is that I'm confident I can tell north from south.

The bad news is that I still have no idea what direction War is.

I follow the coast until I reach a cave. It stretches high into the air, the strange walls folding over like coral fingers twisting through one another. Golden sunlight spills in through the gaps, making the damp stone walls glitter with life.

The water is halfway up my calves, so I climb up the seaweed-covered rocks and venture into the tunnel. Nix plods through the seawater, sniffing at too-large barnacles stuck to the rocks on his way past.

When we enter the next space, my breath catches. The rock ceiling flickers, and light from the water dances around the cavern. It's like something out of a fairy tale.

The memory of Gil and the lights in the forest rushes to the front of my mind before I can stop it.

None of it was real, I scold myself. *Gil doesn't exist.*

I haven't quite been able to figure out what bothers me more: the fact that Caelan tricked me into caring, or that for a moment in the afterlife, I really was *happy*.

He may have been a lie, but that part?

It was real for me.

I suppose there's something oddly poetic about the Orb being the key to getting free of his cage, only for the Reaper to put a stop to it. It really was the ultimate weapon—just not in the way we thought. Because without any memories of Ophelia giving him permission to move to the Capital, Caelan is still very much bound to his court. A prince trapped in his own castle.

I move toward the jagged wall, running my fingers over the parts that flicker beneath the sunlight.

His castle.

My fingers flinch, recoiling.

Caelan is in his palace. Surrounded by his court. His paintings. His *maps.*

I've been in his mind before, but what I did to Artemis and Tavi . . . I haven't tried it with Caelan. Not yet.

But what if the thought I planted in his mind wasn't to hurt him? What if it was to *lead* him somewhere?

I glance back at Nix. He's playing with a clump of seaweed in the shallower pools, nipping at the salty green vegetation before shaking his head in disgust. And I think of what Kasia showed me.

I see what you see.

Curling my fingers into my palms, I lower myself to the ground, knees digging into the cavern floor, and shut my eyes.

The veil molds to me like a second skin, and I follow the winter woodland across time and space. I don't let my consciousness breathe, or press so much as a footstep to the black void. I am less than a mist; I am nothing. Nothing at all.

Caelan stands with his back toward me. His furs are gone—he wears a loose white shirt, untucked and disheveled, and gray pants embroidered with silver edges. A mess of snow-white hair is all I can see of his head.

My consciousness floats through the void, veiled and too careful to make the darkness ripple. I make myself a part of his mind. A part of the shadows. And with the lightest brush of my thoughts, I slip further into his.

I see what you see comes my silent chant.

There's the tiniest bit of resistance, and I sense Caelan's agitation. His . . . fear. I blend in, slipping past, and a glimpse of his surroundings appears in the void. They come into focus like an old camera straining to work. Broken glass flickers on the floor. A tea table is on its side, with a crushed velvet blanket sprawled over the edge. Caelan is leaning against a dresser, fingers digging into the edges, hard enough to leave dents. I spot his face in the mirror: There's no softness at all. Just anger and hard lines and sallow, sunken cheeks.

And his bed . . .

I glance at the mess. The four posts are snapped at the ends, the canopy piled onto the mattress, shredded in every direction like someone let Nix loose in the room. A once-beautiful tapestry hangs from the ceiling, ripped down the middle.

A dagger is stuck through what's left of it.

It takes everything in me not to be alarmed. Not to be curious about what must've happened in the time since I last saw him.

But I can't let him sense me. Not when I need his help.

Caelan's shoulders rise and fall with slow, strained breaths. I press into his mind, his frustration, and settle gently across it like an invisible layer. An extra thought.

This way, my mind suggests, leading him away from the dresser.

His shoulders stiffen, and I worry I've done too much, but then he steps away from the mirror and turns slowly toward the mess in his room. With slow, barely lucid steps, Caelan crunches over bits of glass and bed frame before stepping into the hall.

I go with him like a distant memory, down the tower stairs and through several vast hallways, until we reach the council room.

The immediate space around Caelan is all that's visible. It's not much, but I'm too scared to push any further against the darkness. Scared of what pulling back more of the curtain might reveal—not to me, but to Caelan.

I soak in the familiar details of the room: the long wooden table and iron chair. Somewhere nearby is the painting of Caelan, hanging from the wall.

Is the device still hidden in the rosebud frame? Would Caelan have left it to gather dust, or would he have rid this palace of every human ploy he was made to endure?

I try not to care.

I try not to remember that this is his cage.

Caelan stops in front of a large shelf. Rolls of parchment are stacked like honeycomb. He tilts his head, confused.

I push further into his thoughts. *The map,* I say, voiceless.

And in the void, Caelan complies. He reaches for what I want, carries it to the table, and unrolls the paper until a map of the Four Courts is staring back up at me. At *us.*

But I don't have time to gloat.

Caelan lets out a dark chuckle. "I was wondering what it was you were looking for. And such a valiant effort to get it."

My thoughts jerk back in alarm.

Did he know the whole time?

"It doesn't matter what face you wear," he says, words like a dangerous caress. "I will always know you."

I need to pull back; I need to get out of here. I'm too deep inside his thoughts. Too far gone from my own.

What would happen if he decided not to let me leave?

The blackness starts to swallow the room back up, hiding the small space I was able to see. The space he *allowed* me to see. But I throw one last glance at the map. At the wide, sweeping Labyrinth, and Victory in the northeast, hovering above Death, and Famine on the other side. And then my eyes fall to the northwest corner . . .

There. I have it.

I retreat as fast as I can, but not before Caelan shudders, spinning toward the sound of my racing mind.

"No." His words feel carved out. Hollow. "Not there. Nami, you can't—" He throws up a hand like he's trying to stop me, but I'm already gone.

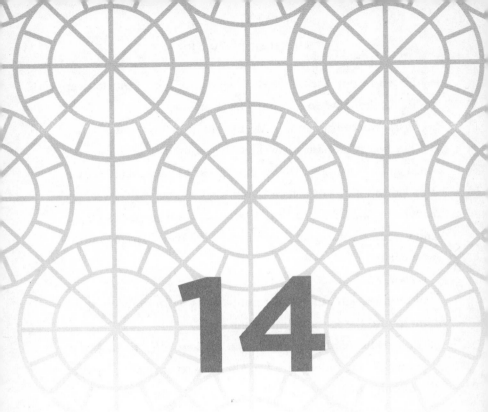

14

NIX AND I HEAD WEST.

Focusing on the shifting borders and northern ripples, we jump into two more landscapes before finally reaching the border between the Labyrinth and War. When the rocky desert appears, I make sure my veil is seamless.

I glance down at Nix. "Maybe you should stay hidden too," I say in a low voice. "You fought in the First War—someone might recognize you." *Someone not human.*

Nix stalks away in response, feet padding across the golden sand like he has no idea this is the most dangerous of the Four Courts.

I search the skies for Legion Guards but find none. It's either a promising start, or a sign that there are much worse things to come.

After a few tentative steps forward, I journey across the desert, winding around massive, looming boulders and strange rock formations. Each one is streaked in layers of burnt orange, red, and taupe. When I reach the edge of a mile-wide canyon, I stare into the drop below. The surface is covered in strange off-white shapes. It takes a minute to realize what they are, but when I do, my stomach lurches.

Bones. Piles and piles of bones.

It's hard not to think about how many humans were torn apart here, and how many deaths they've endured since.

Nix saunters up a faraway cliff and disappears just over the ridge. He has the right idea. We need to keep moving.

Walking around the canyon takes a while, especially beneath the scorching rays of the sun. Heat prickles against my skin, and I use my sleeve to wipe the sweat from my brow.

A harsh climate for a harsh princedom.

On the other side of the canyon, the ground is covered in patchwork chunks of packed sand, the edges curled and brittle. In the living world, this might've been evidence of a dried-up lakebed. But here, all it symbolizes is the absence of life.

It isn't long before I hear shrieking overhead. The Residents are impossible to ignore: big, batlike wings that tear through the sky, and uniforms as red as blood rubies. They move quickly through the clouds, terrorizing whatever humans are beyond the next valley. The sound of explosions and screaming and the earth splitting apart echoes all around me.

One of the many battlefields.

I swallow the fear building in my throat. I don't know what I expected to find here. It's not like the rebellion was going to be waiting at the front gates with open arms.

But I guess I haven't really thought about how many war zones I might need to cross in order to find them.

I keep going, even as the shrieks grate against my eardrums, and make my way to the nearest village. It's charred all the way through, and most of the makeshift houses are now ash and scraps of wood, flattened by the destruction. Even the earth is black.

The wind picks up, blowing coarse sand around the empty village, making my eyes sting. I press my lips together and duck my chin, shielding myself with both hands, and look down at my clothes. The jacket is far from practical in this heat, and with my neck and face exposed, it does little to protect me from the sand.

I flick my wrist, and pixels morph all over my body. My shirt and jacket are replaced with a sleeveless top; bracers appear on my forearms, slim and light and suitable for combat. I leave the Reaper where it is—it may not work anymore, but it still gives me comfort. And a thin, cream-colored scarf appears around my head and neck.

I pluck at the material, creating a shield that covers everything but my eyes. I don't have time to get the detailing right on a pair of sunglasses, so it'll have to do.

I follow the blackened path through the village; the ashen ground is soft beneath my boots. Smoke rises from a fallen wooden lintel. The stench of overcooked flesh sours the air, and I look up, gagging behind my scarf.

They're strung from a rope like laundry hung out to dry: legs, and arms, and torsos, and heads. *Humans.*

Queasiness tears through me, and I stumble back, dizzy.

A few of the heads moan, tired and barely conscious.

Oh my God. Oh my God.

I'm turning in circles, staring at them with bile burning my throat. How can I get them down? How can I help?

But they're strung up so high, and I—

I look at my feet, and the mess I've made in the charred earth. A mess of footsteps, because I've been too distracted to concentrate hard enough on my veil. A sign for the Residents that *I'm right here.*

Something rustles nearby.

Nix? My mind reels, but I can't be sure it's him. I can't risk it.

I force a silent apology to the skewered limbs and body parts, and hurry beyond the village.

Find the rebellion, I tell my quaking heart. *Then we can go back and help.*

The path outside of the town becomes an uneven stairway leading up a hill. When I reach the top, I look down into the circular area below, bending my knees to keep from falling over.

A small camp of Legion Guards is situated at the bottom. At least a dozen, dressed in wine-red leather and armed with blades of all shapes and sizes. They stand around a massive pit, filled to the top with boiling water, the air above it simmering with heat.

Two humans kneel before them, hands bound with metal restraints.

"Still having trouble deciding?" one of the Residents mocks.

"Tell you what—I'll give you another three minutes. Just to be generous."

The humans exchange a horrified glance, while the Residents around them laugh.

"No—I—I won't," the human on the left sputters. She looks at the person beside her: friend, family, or stranger, I have no idea. I'm not sure it matters. Right now, they're joined by fear.

Another Resident cackles. "Ticktock, humans."

"All you have to do is choose who goes in," another says simply. "Then we'll let the other one go."

My stomach twists with venomous thorns, and a new kind of thunder rumbles in my fists.

But I clench my teeth and focus on my veil. Losing control will not help me reach the rebellion. I have to remember that.

Tears fill the eyes of both humans. They're looking at each other and shaking their heads like they can't do this. Like they *won't*.

But there's a crack of hesitation, and their terror starts to outweigh morality.

"Come on. It's not hard. You don't even need to speak," one of the Residents sings. "Just nod your head at whoever we should toss in. Then you're free to go."

"Only one of you has to boil today," another clarifies with a chuckle.

I shut my eyes, inhaling sharply. I can't save them. I can't. I can't. I can't.

More taunting. More laughing. More vicious, cruel, horrible words.

"Time's almost up," one of the Residents croons, and begins to count down the seconds.

My eyes flash open. The man sputters beside the woman. Judging by the twist of her face, I think it might be an apology. And I know what's going to happen next—each of them will shout for the Residents to take the other. They'll fight to survive, no matter the cost.

And the guilt will haunt them for an eternity.

Maybe it makes me reckless and undisciplined, but I don't care. I won't let the Residents win today.

I yank my scarf down, shift into my Resident face, and let my veil drop.

Just before the humans manage to spit out their greatest regret, I shout down into the pit, "What's taking you all so long?"

The Residents' attention snaps toward me; their hands immediately go for their knives, and then—hesitation.

I let my mask fill with confidence as I walk down the steps and approach them. "His Highness expected you back hours ago." I sneer at the humans dismissively and hope they can forgive me. "How long does it take to string up a few humans?"

The Residents study me closely, hands relaxing. My face is like theirs, polished and otherworldly. Victory knew who I was, but here, in War?

How far does word travel between rival courts?

The Resident who started the countdown straightens his shoulders. "Prince Ettore sent you?"

"Obviously," I say, like I'm someone who matters in this court. "In case you haven't heard, there's a rebellion going on."

"But the humans—" another one starts.

I cut off his words with a glare. "You're expected at the palace right away, for orders." I glance at the humans like they mean nothing. "I'll string them up with the others, if you're worried about leaving this mess unfinished. But Prince Ettore will not be pleased if you make him wait." A thinly veiled threat. I've seen Ettore speak with Caelan enough times to know it wouldn't be unusual.

The Legion Guards look around, searching one another for confirmation. For doubt.

"We would never disobey an order from our prince," one of them says, voice stiff.

The others nod. I don't let my relief show. Instead I lift my chin higher, watching as they all turn to leave.

Until the tallest one pauses. Very slowly, he turns back to me, lips curled into a strange smile. "The thing is," he says slowly, "Prince Ettore would never rush his Legion Guards when it came to torturing a human."

The others turn, and I'm sure their knives have multiplied.

I blink, face ashen. There's no breath left in me.

They step closer, and before I have time to reach for my daggers, a whirlwind of smoke bursts from the ground, sending golden sand flying in every direction. The Residents shout; wind whips against my ears, and I crouch low, fighting the tornado that roars around me. Flashes of light spark in the storm, and then something heavy cracks me on the back of the skull.

The world goes dark.

15

GIL LOOKS UP FROM HIS SCULPTURE, FACE glowing in the firelight.

Strange. I don't remember a fireplace in his room. . . .

"You came back to me." He stands, hand outstretched.

I twist my fingers through his, looking around at the large bed. The tapestry on the wall.

The broken glass at my feet . . .

His arms are around me, pulling me close. I breathe against his shirt, inhaling the scent of pine and frost.

I feel euphoric. "I told you I would."

A finger brushes against my jaw, and I pull back to look at him. At the face that kissed me before I went off to battle.

Gil's voice is soft. Too soft. "And still you betrayed me."

I frown; my voice cracks. "I—I didn't. I would *never*."

"How many more times must you lie to me, Nami?" Gil narrows his eyes, teeth flashing. "You've always been the monster in this story. You might as well embrace it."

I glance over his shoulder. The four-poster bed is in pieces. Wine is soaked into the carpet. And the mirror behind him . . .

For a moment, I only see myself—human—wearing a twisted, villainous smile.

Arms close around me, yanking me backward. I flail, kicking furiously, until the assailant spins me around to face him.

Caelan's silver eyes shine. "Nami, it's not safe here. Come with me."

I shove him away, eyes blazing. "*You're* the one I can't trust."

"No," he pleads, eyes full of desperation. "You don't understand. You can't see what they are."

"Humans are not the villains," I growl, turning back to Gil. To the boy I thought I loved.

From far away, I hear Caelan shout my name, but I'm too transfixed by the sneer on Gil's face and the flames in his hands. He opens his mouth, and it stretches and stretches and stretches. His skin tears and morphs until he's black as night, the static snapping from his emerging fur.

The Nightling howls a deadly call, and then it devours me whole.

My eyes flash open, and I scramble up from the floor, back pushed against the wall as a dizzying pain rocks through my temples. I try to shake it off, only to realize my hands are bound with a strange metal that glistens from black to bronze. One sharp tug tells me it's impossible to break.

Someone nearby clears their throat, and I look up to find myself surrounded by humans. Five of them, though they're mostly hidden by the room's shadows. The only face I can see clearly is the one in the middle. A woman with dark skin and big curls, holding a battle-ax.

Even though I try to pull my eyes away, my survival skills keep me transfixed on the glint of the blade, and the dried blood that coats its edge.

"What were you thinking, bringing one of them back here?" a voice hisses in the darkness. "You should've pierced its heart and left it with the others."

One of them.

"It wasn't my call," a deep voice replies. "King's orders."

My fingertips touch my face instinctively, and I remove any last remnants of my Resident mask, hoping they'll be able to see me for the human I really am.

The woman with the curly hair looks doubtful. "A little late for a disguise, don't you think? We've already seen your real face."

"I'm not a Resident," I say hurriedly. Where in the stars is Nix when I need him? "I was only trying to stop those people from being boiled alive." *And from making the biggest betrayal of their lives,* but I leave that part out. I'm not sure I have it in me to explain. If I even know *how* to explain.

"I've never seen a Resident behave that way. Lying to the others," the deep voice says. "I don't know where this one came from, but it's definitely not a Legion Guard, is all I'm saying."

"You're still trying to play the Resident expert, but you don't know them any better than we do, Diego," the woman in front snaps.

Diego.

I frown. It can't be. . . .

"You knew Gil," I say stoically, and I'm sure the entire room flinches. I rustle against the restraints, leaning closer. "I remember your name—Diego. He said you'd been here since the First War."

Diego steps forward, boots crunching against gravel. It's the first time I realize I'm still sitting on the desert floor, with a makeshift wall of stone around me.

Not exactly a high-security prison.

"That's impossible," Diego says, voice heavy as a brick. "Gil was captured by the Residents."

Alarm bells clang through my mind. Caelan said Gil was betrayed in War. Handed over by Ozias because of what he overheard. Which means that even if Gil had friends in this court, he had enemies, too.

"He told us he escaped." I swallow the lump in my throat. The lie I once believed so fervently. "But it wasn't really him. It was a Resident trying to feed us information, to see how we'd react."

"What kind of information?" a voice from the shadows asks.

Tread carefully, my mind whispers. "They told us there was something called an Orb that, if destroyed, could destroy Ophelia." Even the memory tastes bitter. "But it was all staged. Victory is just a way for the Residents to observe and learn from us, so they can always be a step ahead."

"She's lying," the woman insists. "This is another one of their tricks."

Diego lifts a brow, doubtful. "Of all the humans to bring up, why Gil? After all this time?" He turns to look at me, brown eyes hungry for information. "There are others still in Victory? Survivors?"

I teeter on the edge of a lie. "We hid underground. There were dozens of us. Annika made sure that—"

"What did you just say?" It's the voice from the shadows again. A woman. She steps forward, removing her hood in one smooth motion.

I recognize her immediately. The high cheekbones, black hair, and small eyes.

"You're Eliza," I say softly.

Her expression hardens. "What have you done with Annika?" She lunges, but Diego and the woman with curly hair stop her before she reaches me.

"Annika is my friend." I try to hold out my palms—to show them I mean no harm—but I can barely move beneath the restraints. "She was the closest thing we had to a leader." I pause, remembering the Exchange I once saw. The story of how Annika ended up with that golden scarf. "Shura was there too."

Eliza stills, face paling. "Was?"

"I was trying to destroy the Orb. I didn't know it was a trap." I twist my mouth, cheeks warming by the second. "The Residents took everyone and burned the Colony before I could do anything to help."

Her gaze sharpens, hatred pooling behind her glassy eyes. She turns to the others. "We've seen these games a thousand times. The Residents send their kind here, pretending to be human.

Pretending to know what we've been through." Her gaze locks onto mine. "I swear on the stars, if you're the one that hurt my family, I will—"

"That's enough," Diego cuts in, pressing his hands at the air. "You'll gain nothing by showing her your pain."

Eliza stills. "She might know where Annika and Shura are. We should be interrogating her, instead of treating her like she might be human."

"I *am* human," I say hotly. "And I think deep down you know that—otherwise you would've never risked bringing me to your camp."

The woman with curly hair lifts her chin and cracks a dark grin. "All this confidence and you haven't even *tried* to get out of your restraints."

My palms go clammy, and I'm sure the restraints loosen on my wrists in response.

But I ignore the dare. Something tells me the cuffs are made of something much stronger than metal.

"Pity," she says with a sigh, and I know from her disappointment that I'm right.

Diego folds his arms over his broad chest. "I saw what happened out there—the way they turned on you." He shakes his head. "You looked like a Resident, but you were acting like . . . Well, I don't know. But it's your *marks* that really got me thinking."

I frown. "What marks?"

"Exactly." Diego looks at the others like he's proving a point. He motions toward my arms. "The Residents in War like to mark their skin to show how many humans they've broken. How

many consciousnesses they've taken. But you don't have them."
He sniffs at the air. "Resident or not, I don't imagine you know
much about this place if you'd pose as one of the Legion Guards
and not bother marking yourself."

I curve my shoulders, sheepish. My terrible lie never even
stood a chance.

"I'm still trying to figure out if you're brave, ignorant, or up
to something worse," Diego says sullenly. "But that's not really for
me to decide."

Eliza looks hurt, but says nothing. The woman with curly hair
twirls her ax, muttering to the others behind her.

Diego leans forward and pulls at my restraints, forcing me to
stand. "Come on. There's someone who wants to meet you."

He prods me alongside him, and we venture through the
strange rock formations, past a few humans who keep their hands
close to their knives when they see me, just in case. When we
turn the corner, Diego pushes me toward a doorway, where a
man is kneeling on the floor. Sitting in front of him is Nix.

The Dayling flicks his long tail back and forth, mewing casually at the sight of me.

"Seriously?" I say to my traitorous friend. "Where have you
been? Kasia left you behind to help me, not to survey the local
real estate."

The man stands, turning to face me. Fair skin, a pointy beard,
and thick, wavy hair the color of nutmeg. I stare dumbfounded at
the intricate display of bone armor across his chest, recognizing
him at once.

Ozias.

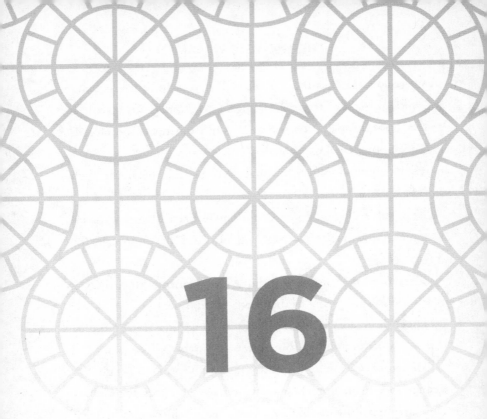

16

"THERE ARE MANY NEW FACES TO COME through War, and I pride myself on remembering all of them." The former leader of the Bone Clan has the voice of someone who has lived for thousands of years. "Yours is not one I recognize. As human *or* Resident."

Caelan's words reemerge in the flood of my thoughts. The truth of what Ozias did to Gil.

If it's true, and Ozias really did throw Gil to the Residents to keep him from telling the others about the Borderlands . . .

I need to choose my words carefully. "I've seen you before, in Kasia's memories. You fought with the Salt Clan in the First War, even though your own clan fled from the hill."

Ozias considers me a moment. He has a wrinkled mouth and wizened eyes, with irises the color of a rain cloud. When he turns to Diego, he gives a curt nod. "Let us have a moment alone."

Diego bows respectfully. "Of course, Your Majesty."

He disappears, and I wrinkle my nose. Ozias chuckles.

"Once, I was like a king to the Bone Clan. Now I am king here." He holds up his hands like becoming royalty was an accident and not his own doing.

Part of me wonders if he was royal even in his first lifetime. All the kings and queens of the past must be in Infinity too. Maybe they've found a new road to power.

I brush the thought away. Who we were before no longer matters. "I came from the Borderlands."

Ozias glances at a now-preening Nix. "I gathered as much." If there's something to fear in his tone, he's doing his best to hide it.

The biggest threats are the ones we don't see coming, after all.

"So, tell me—why are you here?" He lifts something from his side, and my breath hitches.

Kasia's onyx dagger, engraved with her sigil—the one she gave me when she claimed me as part of her family.

Ozias presses the tip of the blade to his finger. "It's a sharp weapon for someone who hasn't fought in over a thousand lifetimes." He chuckles lightly. "You're not an assassin, are you?"

I flinch. I played a spy and an assassin once, but not anymore. Now I don't know what I am.

"I haven't been dead for *one* lifetime, let alone a thousand." My jaw sets. "Kasia is my friend. But I came to find my own people—the humans sent here from Victory."

He lifts a thick, caterpillar brow. "In all my time here, I have only once met a human from Victory." His eyes glint with the whisper of the past. "And I have been dead for *many* lifetimes."

The heaviness crashes against my chest once again, but I try not to be disheartened. War is a big court. Maybe they're hiding—fighting—somewhere else.

I'm not going to give up looking after less than a day.

I meet Ozias's gaze, forgetting all about my restraints, and my Resident mask, and the fact that everyone still thinks I'm the enemy. Because I came here for a reason. "They were captured in Victory, after we tried to take down Ophelia. I came here hoping to find someone who could help me locate them."

"You attempted to destroy her?"

"We—we heard a rumor it was possible. But it turned out to be a lie."

Something behind his eyes shutters, protective. "The Residents cannot be killed. *Trying* is why humans lost the First War."

I frown. "Why fight for this long if you can't win?" *And why keep the truth about the Afterlands a secret from the other humans?*

"We may not be able to make their kind disappear," Ozias admits. "But we can push back. We can create our own borders. And if we can fight long enough to take the Red City, and this court—perhaps eventually we'll conquer the other three, too."

Conquering. Borders. Land. *That's* what he's after?

"What happens when you have the Four Courts, and the Residents are still here?" I ask.

He lifts his hands. "Then we keep the enemy at bay, by any means necessary. Even if we have to put every one of them in a dungeon."

In a cage.

I bite down on the inside of my cheek. Now is not the time to argue about the holes in his plan. Because I've seen what's happening in Death. The Residents already know how to separate our consciousness from our bodies. The Four Courts may be monstrous in all their shades, but they're also keeping many of the humans out of Death.

Their existence keeps us *here.*

But I need Ozias to believe I'm not afraid to fight. That I'm not here to make the rest of the humans run for safety.

There's time for that later.

"You've known about the Afterlands all this time, but you've stayed to fight for a better world." I find the steel in my voice. He doesn't need the whole truth—he just needs enough of it to see me as an ally. "You haven't abandoned humanity like the others."

Ozias stares intently, dropping his arms to his sides. "They took the canoes?"

I nod. "They voted to destroy the Borderlands and leave everyone else behind." It's better if he doesn't know Kasia is still waiting for me, or that the path to safety is still open. As long as he thinks humans have nowhere else to go, he won't see me as a threat. "Like I said, I came here to find someone who could help."

Ozias walks across the room. Despite all his metal buckles and the weapons tucked in his belt, his movements are soundless. Veiled. "If your friends are in War, we will help you find them."

The relief is dizzying. "Thank you."

He turns, gray eyes sensing the emotion behind my own. "Is

it surprising to you that we'd do everything we can to protect our own kind?"

For a moment, it feels like the room is losing oxygen. "The Border Clans had no interest in the war. And the Colony . . ." I shake my head, fighting the scratch in my throat. "They believed anyone who was lost could not be rescued."

He turns his head, staring at the cavern walls. "In the old world, the way to win wars was to defeat our enemy on the battlefield and take their castles, one by one. We cannot do that without numbers. Without an army." Our eyes meet again. "I need as many soldiers as I can get. And your people sound like fighters."

He's so unlike the others in the Borderlands, who chose to do nothing at all. But something about his tone . . .

Ozias comes from a time when conquering land wasn't exactly a necessity—it carried a thrill. A show of power. Something brutal and ugly that didn't age well in the history books.

I don't see how he could possibly romanticize a battlefield, and I don't care about conquering the Four Courts or their palaces. I just want an afterlife that's safe for my friends. For humans.

For Mei.

And I think the Afterlands can be that for them. For all of us, as long as someone is still here to show humans the way.

Ozias is a warlord. He isn't looking for a sanctuary—he's looking for blood. But I also don't have a lot of allies in Infinity, and even if we don't share a common goal, we do share a common enemy.

Right now, he's the only option I have.

"My people risked everything to try to stop Ophelia," I say firmly. "I know they'd do it again in a heartbeat."

"Good." Ozias leans in, voice serious. "But the truth of the Afterlands . . . perhaps it's best to keep it between us." He studies me, probably weighing the cost of the truth. "Most of them don't know about the Borderlands."

I say nothing.

He grips Kasia's blade firmly, mulling over which words will make him sound best. "It may seem harsh to you, but when fighting is the only option, people pick up their weapons. I couldn't risk splitting the rebellion apart when our battle is far from over."

I want to say that I understand. That I'd do the same.

But the words won't leave my mouth.

"Keep your secrets," I say. It's not as if I don't have plenty of my own.

His surprise is unmissable. "I appreciate your understanding." His gray, unblinking eyes are still searching for something earnest. Something to *trust*.

So I share the guilt that ravages my heart, even now. "I used to think there were other ways to win this war besides fighting. And I pushed that idea onto the Colony, even when they told me it could get me captured. Except *they* were taken instead of me." I look up at him. "If I had seen the Residents as the enemy from the beginning, maybe none of it would've happened. It's my fault they're gone—and I need to fix it."

He sets the dagger on a nearby table like he's making the choice to trust me.

"You may be young, but your story is rich with life." Ozias

motions toward a small bench. "Why don't you tell me more"—
he smiles—"while I remove those restraints?" He presses a finger
to the metal, and the cuffs fall to the floor.

"How about I just show you?" I say, and I offer him my palm.

Ozias takes my hand, and I let him see everything about the
Colony—everything except the truth about Caelan and the time
I spent communicating with Ophelia. The Border Clans didn't
judge my past, because they had no intention of returning to the
Four Courts. The fact that I felt empathy for the Residents—no
matter how misguided—made no difference to them.

Ozias may not be as understanding.

When the Exchange ends, he releases my hand. "War is a big
princedom. Our rebellion has pushed at their inner borders, but
there's still plenty of War even *we* have not been able to penetrate." He runs a hand over his beard, thoughtful. "I have not seen
your friends in this court, but there are many humans trapped in
the Fire Pit. Perhaps there is still hope."

I nod, even though worry pummels my chest. If they're not
here, where else could they be?

What if Caelan really did send them all to Death?

He wouldn't do that. Not after everything, my mind offers, though
I don't know why.

He's still making deals with his brothers, and holding meetings
in other courts that could lead to the demise of humans. He still
wants a seat in the Capital beside his mother's throne. He still
wants humans gone, so he can finally be *free*.

I have to face the truth: I don't really know Caelan, and I have
no idea what he's truly capable of.

Ozias stands, and Nix bolts from the room in a hurry to explore. "Let me show you your new home," he says, and leads me out of the caves.

We emerge onto a hill that overlooks the desert valley. Hundreds of beige tents flutter for nearly a mile. Small fires are scattered all around, where people sit sharpening their weapons and studying maps of the battlefields. Training rings are dotted around the camp, and the constant clash of swords and knives rings out in harmony. Everywhere I look there are thousands of humans, armed and aware.

"This," Ozias announces brightly, "is Genesis."

I can't hide the quiver in my jaw.

I've finally found what I hoped I'd find in the Borderlands. People willing to help. People willing to fight.

I've found an army.

17

IT DOESN'T TAKE LONG FOR ME TO BECOME immersed in the rebellion's world. After Ozias returns my weapons and assures everyone that I'm definitely not a Resident, they stop looking at me like I'm an enemy and begin treating me like an equal.

I'm not sure the Colony ever saw me the same way. As a friend, yes, but not as someone who could hold their own in battle. But here, in Genesis, I become one of them. A warrior.

Along with daily training exercises in the ring, Ozias puts me on the watch schedule. I make my rounds, checking the camp borders with a group of fellow humans. The threat of a Resident attack always looms in the forefront of my mind, even with the veil posts keeping us hidden. They look like tall, metal rods plunged into the earth, but they're designed to offer a blanket of invisibility. Genesis has ten of them circling the camp, creating a curved, translucent sheen in the sky above—a shield that the Residents can't see.

Having the veil posts means that Genesis doesn't need constant veilers like the Colony did. Every single person here is ready to fight at a moment's notice. And they do. Often.

While I'm making my rounds to protect the border, many of the others are out in War, pulling the Residents' focus away from Genesis and protecting the smaller outposts scattered throughout the princedom.

In comparison, I'm hardly pulling my weight at all.

And I'm certainly no closer to finding Annika and the others.

Ozias doesn't balk when I tell him I want to do more. Instead he points in a direction.

"Search the ridge," he says. "Take a group. Look for survivors."

It doesn't put me in the thick of the battle, but it puts me where I'm most useful. My veils are strong, thanks to my training in the Borderlands. And moving around the desert unseen might be my best chance at finding my friends.

Tucking both my daggers into my belt, I march through Genesis toward the south gates. Alone.

The woman with curly hair, Zahrah, is waiting for me. She's all long limbs and lean muscle, with a battle-ax hanging behind her shoulder blades. "You look determined. Where are you headed?"

I keep walking, eyes pinned on the next ridge, where Legion Guards have been swarming the skies.

A sign they're searching for humans.

"I'm going to see if anyone needs help."

Zahrah glances at the ridge. "Didn't the king tell you to take a group?"

My feet plant together. "Everyone else is . . . busy."

"They all turned you down, didn't they?"

I roll my tongue against the inside of my cheek. "They said it was grunt work."

Zahrah laughs, loose and earthy. "It *is* grunt work."

"Yeah, well, I don't care. I'll go alone." I try to push past her.

She holds up her arm to block me and smirks, cheeks dimpling. "You didn't ask me."

"If this is a joke, I'm not in the mood."

"It isn't." She flashes her teeth. "You look too sensitive for my kind of jokes."

"You're one of the First Leaders." My words feel like molasses, taking up effort I don't have. "Isn't search and rescue a little below your pay grade?"

Zahrah's armor glints beneath the sun. "Isn't sarcasm a little below yours?"

The edges of my mouth tug in spite of myself.

"Are you as good with those knives as you are with a veil?" she asks. "Because I don't babysit." And then she steps through the gates, ax staring back at me.

I follow behind her, wondering how it's possible to feel so much guilt, but also so much genuine delight in not having to walk the desert alone.

We find no survivors near the ridge.

So the next day, when the morning light spills over the mountain, we go back out and search again.

The days bleed together. If it weren't for the fact that I still sleep, I might completely lose track of how long I've been in Genesis.

But I count the days and the weeks anyway. Because, somewhere in the Four Courts, the Colony might be doing the same.

I sink onto one of the stones outside my tent. One of my new neighbors helped me pitch it—a boy named Wadie who looks younger than Shura, though he's reminded me on several occasions that *I'm* the youngling.

I still hate the term, but at least when they use it in Genesis, they don't mean it as an insult. It's merely a descriptor. A way to differentiate between those who've lived a thousand lifetimes, and those who're still living their first.

I remove my obsidian blade, rest my elbows on my knees, and lean forward, inspecting the edge. It's clean. Much cleaner than any of the other weapons here. Zahrah and I haven't run into any Residents, but I know our luck won't last forever.

I concentrate on the thrum of energy in my fingertips, passing it into the knife like I'm hiding a secret in the blade.

A special kind of venom.

I haven't spoken to Caelan since the day I tried to use him to locate War on a map. He let me—he knew I was pushing thoughts into his head—but he played along anyway because he wanted to know the endgame.

It's the nature of Victory, after all, to play out scenarios. Observe and learn. And maybe it's Caelan's nature too.

Maybe that's what letting me go was all about—seeing what I would do next.

I grit my teeth, hating the thought that I'm still a piece on his chessboard, being pushed around without even realizing it. Hating that he once made me feel something for him, and that I still haven't figured out how to grieve the loss of what never truly existed.

It doesn't matter if it was one-sided, or a lie, or a mistake. My feelings don't switch on and off like a—

Like a robot, my thoughts finish for me.

But even that feels like giving him too much of a cop-out. Robots are programmed, but Caelan made a choice, the same way I did. We *meant* to hurt one another—I just happened to be the one who was far out of their depth.

I wonder if my being in War ruins whatever plans Caelan had for me. He clearly didn't want me coming to this court, and while he may have tricked me into believing I was the Colony's spymaster once, Caelan's hatred for Ettore was never part of the ruse. Perhaps their mutual rivalry means that losing a human to War is a particularly tough blow to Victory.

It isn't much of a win, but it's something.

Eliza appears on the other side of the path. The material of a nearby tent flaps beside her, and for a moment she looks as if she's considering disappearing inside. But instead she takes a few strides toward me.

Tucking a lock of shiny black hair behind her ear, she sits on one of the flat stones surrounding the fire pit. "Hey. Can we talk?"

I've noticed for weeks the way she's been watching me from a distance, trying to pluck up the courage to come over, unsure whether or not she can trust me.

I guess she's made up her mind.

"Yeah," I say. "We can talk."

Eliza pauses. "You—you said you knew Annika. And Shura."

I tuck my blade into my boot and retrieve its near twin. The red shines like glass. "Annika still wears your scarf."

Eliza's eyes well up. A sound escapes her lips—something between relief and anguish. I wait for her to ask questions, or to tell me what she's feeling. But she just stares into the fire while the tears slip over her olive cheeks.

Maybe the scarf explained more than any stories could. Maybe all she needed to know was that she hadn't been forgotten. That her family, in all the time they'd been lost, had never stopped loving her.

And maybe the fact that I'm familiar with the golden scarf, and what it means, is enough to prove that I care about her family too.

After a few minutes, Eliza clears her throat, and glances at my blade. "What are you doing?"

"Sharpening my knives. Trying to make sure they do as much damage as possible."

Eliza notices the strange glint on the edge. "You've laced it with something."

I turn the knife over. I'm not as good as Ahmet, but I'm trying. "Last time I went up against the Residents, I wasn't prepared."

"But this time you will be," she finishes for me.

Eliza offers the tiniest smile before turning her eyes to the fire. I work on my blade in silence, but she doesn't leave. Not until the last embers fade into darkness.

Zahrah motions to the gray smoke. It makes its way toward the clouds, high and impossible to miss.

It looks like a beacon.

"You think it's a Resident attack?" I ask, voice barely audible.

Zahrah sucks the air through her teeth. "Too small. Looks more like a campfire."

I frown. "You think a human would be that irresponsible?"

"Younglings frequently are." She glances at me sideways. "No offense."

I crack a smile and watch the smoke signal. "You want to take the left?"

She nods. "Be careful. It could be a Resident trick. And even if it's not, they'll see the fire soon enough and come searching for whoever started it." Zahrah leaves my veil for her own, vanishing from sight.

I go right, past the clay-red boulders, and begin the climb up the ridge. It doesn't take long; my hands and feet search for crevasses like it's second nature, and I pull myself over the edge with ease.

Half a mile away, I spot the campfire. It's small, and looks hastily thrown together. Beside it, a human sleeps.

Something isn't right.

I reach for my daggers, gripping them tight, and walk across the sand without leaving a single footprint behind me.

I'm studying the human, and the fire—trying to figure out why anyone would be reckless enough to rest in broad daylight—when I sense a quiet ripple in the air. Something imperfect. Something *made*.

Crouching low, I send my thoughts forward, searching the small campsite for another presence. I pass over the human tentatively. There's nothing in the black void of his mind. Not even the hint of a dream.

But around him . . .

At least a dozen minds, primed and waiting for a fight. *Residents.*

Alarmed, I scan the desert. Zahrah will be approaching from the other side of the ridge, making sure it's safe. But will she know it's a trap? Can she hear the tremor of consciousness like I can?

I don't wait to find out. Instead I widen the net of my mist, searching for Zahrah, too. Her mind is easy to find—it's like wandering across soft white sand and a salt-stained pier.

And since it's the only warning I can give her, I whisper into the black void, *Stay back—there are Residents everywhere.*

She doesn't respond, but I feel a tug. An understanding. And then I retreat from her mind, soundless, and take cover behind a mound of rocks.

The human remains by the fire, unmoving. His thoughts are nonexistent; he's definitely not conscious. I'm not even sure he's aware.

Could Ettore be keeping unaware humans in his court instead of sending them to Victory?

It shouldn't surprise me. Ettore never kept his contempt for

Victory a secret. But to break the rules of Ophelia so blatantly . . .

Right now, the Residents have a common enemy in humans. But what if they ever do manage to destroy us? Will they live in peace, the way Ophelia believes is possible?

Or will Residents like Ettore find someone new to war with?

A pop sounds in the distance, and several humans jump into view. They make their way to the campsite, toward the unaware human, laid out on the rocks like bait.

I have to warn them, my mind shrieks, but before I can stand, a hand comes down hard over my shoulder.

"You can't help them," Zahrah whispers low in my ear. "Not today."

"There's still time," I try to argue. Except there isn't.

In that moment, the Residents lift their veils, and a vortex of stone and fire and metal surrounds the three humans. The desert erupts in screams, blood soaking the earth like a slow poison. Over a dozen Residents descend on the humans as if they were massive birds of prey, ripping them to shreds.

They never stood a chance.

I look away, teeth clenched. Zahrah pulls at my shoulder, leading me away from the scene.

We're hurrying down the cliffside, making our way back through the canyon, when we spot the winged scouts hovering up ahead. Part of me hopes their search means one of the humans managed to escape, but the other part of me knows better.

Nobody could've escaped an ambush like that.

Still, the guilt that I didn't do enough batters through me, making the energy in my hands thrum violently.

Zahrah ushers me into one of the many caves for shelter, and when we're deep in the shadows, we drop our veils.

"How did you know?" she asks, arms crossed. She wants to know how I sensed the Residents. How I looked past their veils.

I tuck my knives into my belt, knuckles aching. "It's hard to explain."

"Try me."

I tell her about the ripples, and the faint hum of energy. I tell her about how I made it through the Labyrinth, and how I seem to have a knack for getting into people's heads.

Zahrah listens carefully, face taut and brown eyes unblinking. "We've had speakers in Genesis before," she says. "People who could communicate through thoughts. But in all my lifetimes, I've never seen someone hear a Resident beneath a veil."

The shadows hide my scowl. I don't exactly need another reminder that my connection to the Residents makes me an anomaly. If anything, I thought I could leave it behind, along with my Resident mask.

But maybe it's more than a mask. Maybe it's a part of me.

"Can you get inside a Resident's mind?" Zahrah's voice is a rasp. "Can you control them?"

My mind flashes to Caelan and Ophelia, but I push them away stubbornly. "Since I came to War, I've never been in front of a Resident long enough to try." I can't tell her about Caelan and the map. She wouldn't understand.

And he *let* me control him. *Guide* him. It's not like I can run around forcing Residents to do whatever I please.

If I could do that, I'd have gone straight to the Capital and faced Ophelia myself.

Zahrah glances toward my fists. "You need to get that under control."

I can tell without looking that my knuckles are blazing white. "I'm fine."

"No," she replies coolly. "You're not. There are better kinds of fuel than anger, Nami. Anger burns bright, and then it burns out. You need to be in this for the long run. Because you don't want to be the person in War who's all out of fight."

I turn toward the opening of the tunnel, wondering if the Residents are still up on that ridge, or if they've left the humans behind in pieces.

"Some battles are lost before you even arrive," Zahrah says. "You have to be able to tell the difference." She pauses, watching me, and sighs. "You can't save everyone. Not in a single day."

I nod like I understand, but I'm too aware that time is running out. The Residents won't stop trying to eradicate us.

I need to get everyone to the Afterlands before that happens.

Worried Zahrah will read my own thoughts, I let my eyes drift toward the shadows behind us. "These tunnels," I say quietly. "Did the humans make them?"

Zahrah peers into the darkness. I'm sure the darkness stares right back. "Yes. The tunnels have been here since the First War. It's how we were able to get away, after so many humans fell."

"Where do they lead?"

"Everywhere. Nowhere." Zahrah shakes her head. "There are thousands of them. Too many for the Residents to search, and too many for us to keep track of. But we only go underground when we have no other choice." Her eyes flash, and I know she'd prefer fighting over hiding.

But even Zahrah has found a way to balance what she *wants* and what's *best*. Maybe I can learn to do the same.

"The first battle of the First War," I say sullenly. "Do you remember where it was?"

She snorts, clicking her teeth. "How could anyone forget? It's where the Prince of War chose to build his city. The mountain his castle sits on is still stained in human blood."

The Red City.

"Has anyone ever been inside?"

"The humans taken into the Red City are the ones who go into the Fire Pit." Zahrah's arms are still firm across her chest. "No one comes back from the Fire Pit."

We don't speak again for a long time.

Dusk arrives, and Zahrah checks the skies for Legion Guards. She moves her fingers to signal it's clear, and we hide beneath a single veil.

When we return to Genesis, Zahrah wanders off to find Ozias. I don't return to my tent. I go to one of the many rings and train until daybreak. And then I think of my friends, trapped somewhere in the Four Courts, and I train all the way until nightfall.

If anger can't fuel me, maybe determination can.

18

THE BATTLE-AX SLAMS AGAINST MY KNIVES, BUT I hold them steady, straining against the weight of the opposing blade. Zahrah slides her ax away before swinging it back toward my ribs. I turn my blade to the side, fist around the handle, and smash the obsidian against her weapon, blocking the impact. Then I spin around and connect my free elbow with her jaw. She takes a step back, grinning broadly.

"You play dirty," she teases. "I like it." And then she swings hard. I dodge blow after blow, sidestepping and ducking my head more times than I can count. She's chasing me in circles; I'm outmatched in skill.

When it comes to blades, anyway.

She pulls her battle-ax back like she's winding up another swing, and I let my thoughts become mist. I pounce into her unsuspecting mind and let out a bloodcurdling scream.

Startled, Zahrah flinches. I seize the opportunity.

I sweep my leg against her knees, knocking her on her side.

Zahrah spits blood on the training-ring floor, teeth slightly pink. I tuck my daggers into my belt. Last one standing—that was the challenge. I extend an arm to help her up.

She laughs, clapping her hand into mine, and stands. Her ax settles against the crook of her neck. "Best two out of three?"

Before I can answer, Ozias appears at the edge of the onlooking crowd. They came to watch Zahrah and me fight, after I'd accepted a dare from Wadie on a whim. Apparently, most people know better than to spar with Zahrah—even when she's in a good mood.

"I heard you were quite handy in the ring," Ozias remarks. His eyes flash. A challenge.

"Careful, Your Majesty," Zahrah says, brow quirking. "Her weapon isn't one you can see."

"If that's the case . . ." Ozias hands his longsword and knives to the human beside him.

Zahrah gives an exaggerated bow and steps aside.

I remove my belt and set it outside the ring, holding up my hands to prove my honesty.

Ozias charges. I duck and roll to the side, springing to my feet just as he's swinging his arm toward me. I throw my head back, bending just out of his reach, and slam my fist into his side. His leather training armor is thick, and he hardly moves. He's practically a tank.

Consciousness it is, then.

I duck again from his swing, and shoot an energy blast from my hand. He takes three steps backward, fighting it, and shoots a whip of electricity at the air. It snaps against my shoulder, splitting flesh. I refuse to cry out, and throw a veil around myself before looping my arm beneath his and twisting hard.

Bone cracks, and Ozias throws a flattened hand against my invisible throat, knocking the air straight out of me. Coughing into the sand, I drop the veil and force my eyes back to his already-clenched fists. He swipes at the earth, left, right, left, right, and an onslaught of rocks burst from the ground, pelleting me with sand and stone. I use my arm as a shield and throw an undercurrent of energy toward him. It crashes into his knees, and for a moment his balance is off.

I run, leap, and slam my leg against the side of his head.

Ozias stumbles, but he grabs my shirt before I can land on both feet, and throws me against the ground with a horrible crack.

This time I definitely howl.

He's breathing heavily, close enough that I can see the flecks of blue in his storm-cloud eyes. "Last one standing, was it?"

"You're kneeling," I point out.

Ozias chuckles, and yanks me to my feet. Pain scorches through my back. A mark of defeat, but a reminder to train even harder.

"You're stronger than you look," he admits. "But perhaps not strong enough to best a king." He winks, full of friendly camaraderie, but all I can think about as he walks away is that I don't need to be strong enough to best a king.

It's a queen I'm after.

A commotion near the front gates pulls my attention. A crowd forms, blocking the scene from view. Instinct has me already searching for my weapons, until I realize it isn't fear on anyone's face—it's relief.

Diego appears in the center. His twin short swords are tucked behind him, but the knives at his belt glitter with blood.

"Looks like they made you work for it," Zahrah notes.

Diego wipes his forehead with his sleeve, dragging ash across his damp skin. "We were cut off at the ridge. Never even made it to the outpost." He looks over his shoulder, motioning somewhere beyond the group. There are new faces among them. People I don't recognize. "Thankfully, we had some help."

A girl appears at the edge of the crowd. Her hair is just as curly as Zahrah's, and her brown eyes are the same shape, but she has round cheeks that give away her youth. She can't be much older than ten.

The same age as Mei.

Her clothes are ragged, clinging to her frame like they've been dragged across the desert, and she carries no weapons at all. Her gaze is erratic, desperately searching the faces around her.

Zahrah's expression morphs into confusion before her eyes widen into a glassy stare. "Dayo?" she chokes, and then she's running across the sand.

The young girl spots her immediately, face brightening with a glow that sends me reeling. I know that bond too well. The love of a sister.

"She's been missing for months," Diego says beside me. "Dayo's team went to check on an outpost and ran into trouble. They've had to fight their way back across three battlefields."

"Her team?"

"She might look like a child, but she's older than Zahrah. Older than me." He clicks his teeth. "I don't know if it's a blessing or a curse to have family from the old world in Infinity. On one hand, I'm jealous of the love. But on the other, I can't imagine what it would feel like to worry more than I already do."

In the short distance, Dayo cups her hands around Zahrah's face before embracing her tightly. She mouths something that makes Zahrah nod. A secret between the two of them.

I don't want to see any more. Not just because it's private, but because the longing building at the height of my chest is too much for me to bear. I'm afraid if I stand here a second longer, I'll evaporate into tears.

I'd give anything to see my sister again. And if I weren't already dead, I think the feeling might kill me.

I turn away, retrieve my knives, and head back to the tents.

A faint caress wakes me.

My eyes flash open, and I grab my obsidian and sea-glass blades. Pebbles and sand fall from my clothes—a byproduct of sleeping on the desert ground. But I don't dust them away. I'm too focused on the way the tent billows, and the way the stars flicker beyond the opening.

There are no dangers in Genesis. Not right now.

And yet . . .

I press my fingertips to my temple, concentrating. I feel it again— the brush of a hand, like someone is reaching into the shadows.

Like someone is searching for me.

Memories of woodland and snow make me dizzy, and I press the hilt of my blade to my forehead. The metal is cold, but it does nothing to ease the dull ache behind my eyes.

Why now? What does he want?

And what makes him think I'd ever be reckless enough to answer his call and open my mind to his?

I tug my veil close, shrouding every last one of my thoughts, and wait for the barely there touch to disappear. It does.

Even though it's safe to, I don't go back to sleep.

I'm too worried that if I fall asleep now, I'll dream about the Prince of Victory.

The material of my tent rustles, and Dayo appears, holding a colorful mat rolled under her arm. While Zahrah is gruff quips and sly grins, Dayo is much more reserved.

I can't tell if it's because she doesn't trust me, or because she doesn't like me.

Her face doesn't shift. "I come bearing gifts." She doesn't wait for an invitation—she simply moves to the back of the tent, where she unrolls the mat and flattens all the edges.

Made of vibrant greens and yellows and reds, it reminds me so much of nature, and the way the trees would transform from summer to autumn.

It reminds me of the woods in the Borderlands, and the places I used to train.

I don't miss it, but I miss Kasia.

"Thank you," I say, unable to hide my surprise. "It's beautiful."

"Zahrah said you still sleep." Dayo studies the emptiness of the space. "We don't really keep furniture here, but you should have something to rest on."

Making items that aren't essential is thought to be a waste of time and energy in Genesis, since the camp doesn't stay in the same location for long. Jumpers—humans with the ability to teleport—help transport the camp across the desert whenever the Residents start sniffing around the borders and get too close.

It takes days of planning and precision just to move every human, never mind the tents, weapons, and veil posts.

Furniture has no place in this war.

I look away from the mat, but I still feel the memory of the colors dancing in my mind. Maybe that's what happens when everything in the world is the same shade as the sand. Hopefully, someday soon I won't need to sleep anymore. It's just another thing holding me back in this world, after all.

"I heard you're searching for your people," Dayo says.

By now everyone in Genesis knows their faces—Ozias made sure to share the Exchange.

He kept his promise. Even if he only did it to gain more soldiers.

"I thought maybe your team had seen them out in the desert." It was the first question I'd asked when the scouts returned to Genesis.

Dayo shifts in place. Her cardigan is burnt orange with gold embroidery. "We saw many humans on the field. Most of them we were unable to save."

I stiffen under her gaze. The words build at the back of my throat, begging to be let out.

No one in War is safe . . . but what if you could be?

What if I could show you the way?

I tuck a strand of hair behind my ear, forcing the thought away. Maybe I'm wrong for keeping the secret about the Borderlands, but I'm not ready to let everyone go. Not until I find the others.

Not until I know they can be safe too.

"There is something you should know." Dayo's brows pinch together. "Months ago, when we reached the outpost, it had already been raided. The Residents were taking some of the humans away as prisoners—most I knew from Genesis, but there was a girl with them. Someone I hadn't seen before."

I throw out a hand, desperate for an Exchange. "Show me."

Dayo hesitates. "You must understand that it was difficult to see clearly. And for all I know, my memories got distorted when the king showed me your friend's face. It could've been someone who only looked like her at the time—and now it would be almost impossible to know for sure."

"Please," I say. "I need to see for myself."

Dayo nods and takes my hand.

The world dissolves. I'm looking at War through Dayo's eyes—my team is hidden behind the boulders, staring down at what's left of the outpost.

A banner is crumpled in the rocks, shredded and singed at the ends. The wooden barricade burns with a violent fire, and the watchtower is snapped at its base and toppled onto the desert ground. There are limbs and weapons stuck beneath the broken joists, and the humans who are left are being herded away by winged Legion Guards.

I count the faces—six humans altogether—and one of them I don't recognize, but I'm drawn to the color of her hair.

Even beneath the ash and blood, the shade is an unmistakable pink.

She looks young—older than I appear, but also young behind her eyes, like someone who came to Infinity long after the First War.

The guards shove the humans down the hill, but something makes her turn back toward the fire. The last thing I see before she disappears are her wide, curious gray eyes.

The world snaps back into place.

Shura. My heart thunders. "It's her." The words echo inside my head. She's here. In War.

Dayo lets go of my hand. Her mouth opens like she wants to remind me her memories aren't reliable—that I shouldn't jump to conclusions—but it's too late. I'm already moving toward the tent opening.

I need to tell Eliza.

"Even if it's her, the raid happened months ago," Dayo adds, trailing after me. "The person you saw may no longer be in this court. Younglings—they don't tend to last very long."

I throw the material to the side and duck outside. "Shura isn't just a youngling," I argue over my shoulder. "She was in the Colony. She can handle herself."

"Not like this," Dayo says, and something in her voice makes me pause.

I face her, cradling my arms around myself, fingers digging into my skin. "What are you not telling me?"

Dayo flattens her mouth. "They took the humans to the Fire Pit."

I fight the worry, and the fear, and the hopelessness. I have to—Shura needs me.

"I don't care where they took her," I say stiffly. "I'm going to get her back."

I hurry for Eliza's tent, and Dayo doesn't follow me.

It doesn't take me long to explain to Eliza what's happening—Zahrah already told her what her sister saw. She says she wants it to be Shura so badly that she can't trust her own eyes. That maybe Dayo is right to be cautious.

But every moment could be the difference between Shura fighting or surrendering her consciousness.

We hurry to the caves, where Ozias is meeting with the First Leaders: the people who helped bring the rebellion together after the First War went so horribly wrong. Diego, Zahrah, and Dayo are already waiting, as are two brothers—Vince and Cameron—and a woman named Ichika.

They've all heard about Shura too, and I don't give them another reason to doubt the accuracy of Dayo's memory. I tell them I *know* it's Shura; I'd recognize that pink hair anywhere. And if she's been in the Fire Pit for months, we have to act now.

"What's the plan?" I ask after they've finished going back and forth on logistics.

"Weren't you listening to anything I just said?" Diego grumbles. "The arena is impenetrable. Not to mention it's filled with hundreds of Residents at any given moment."

"No, you said it was *nearly* impenetrable," I correct, staring between Diego and the others. "What about teleporting? Can someone jump us through the wall?"

Eliza shakes her head. "We can only jump to somewhere we can see, or somewhere we've been. Most of what's beyond the walls of the Red City is a mystery to us."

"Okay." I shrug. "So we go on foot."

Diego throws up his hands. Ozias studies me.

"You promised to help my friends," I remind him coolly. *Just like I promised to keep your secret.*

A star-shaped hole in the cavern ceiling offers limited sunlight, but Ozias paces through it like he's drawn to the rays. "You seem to be exceptionally good at sneaking past Residents." It's not a question.

"I've had a bit of practice," I reply.

"Yes. But enough to walk through the Red City?" He runs a hand over his beard. "If you're caught, Genesis will be forced to move. And I'll be losing a valuable soldier."

"Your army is not my priority," I say without hesitation. "Shura is."

If he's offended, he doesn't show it.

But the others look displeased. I'm not sure they like the way I speak to their king, but I've had enough *Your Highness*es and *my lord*s to last me a thousand more lifetimes.

I am no one's subject.

"The arena may be tough to break into, but what about the cells?" Eliza asks the room.

Diego guffaws. "You're talking about breaking into a Resident *prison.*"

"Every prison has a door," I point out dryly.

"And a *lock*," Dayo retorts. "We have no idea what that will look like. There's a reason we've never attempted a rescue mission inside the Red City before."

The brothers argue among themselves. Zahrah drums her fingers against her arm.

"Let's say there's an entrance. Let's say it's easy to find." Ichika looks to the other leaders. "Our bigger problem is the Red City."

Diego holds up a hand like this is obvious. "Exactly. We can't just walk through the front gates."

Ozias stops pacing. He dips his chin toward me. "*She* can."

My veiling is stronger than ever, now that I know how to quiet my own thoughts. Being able to hear the minds of nearby Residents gives me an advantage no one else in Genesis has. And I'm still new here. They can't risk Ozias, or the First Leaders, or even their best warriors. But me?

I'm a risk they can take, even if Ozias would prefer not to.

"I'll find her," I say.

Eliza looks concerned. "We've never been inside the city. We can't tell you what to expect."

"And even if you get inside, there's still the matter of breaking out a prisoner." Diego hesitates. "If you don't make it out, or if you're taken . . . Genesis will have to make the jump without you."

If the camp teleports, I might not be able to find them again. Certainly not without having to cross through Resident territory.

There's a high probability that I'll end up on a battlefield, if I make it out of the Red City at all.

"I understand," I say solemnly.

"It won't be easy," Zahrah warns. "Even with your veils."

"It's just one person I need to find," I reply. My confidence may be slightly feigned, but I also have no intention of coming back without my friend. "I'll be careful."

Ozias nods. "Eliza will keep watch near the gates. We'll get a group to position themselves around the city wall, near the arena, and give you some time to make it through the city. After that . . ." He looks at me seriously. "We find that sleight of hand often works in our favor. Keeps them looking in the wrong direction."

They're going to cause a distraction. *That* I can work with.

"And if things go south," Dayo says, "just make sure you go down swinging."

Even Diego lets out a resigned chuckle.

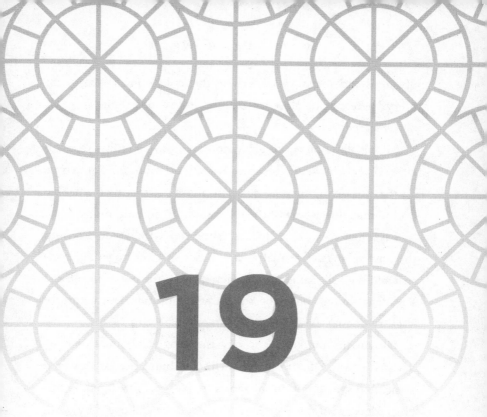

19

THE RED CITY IS SURROUNDED BY GRANITE walls and looming archways. Legion Guards stand watch in every corner, eyes ever fixed on the surrounding desert. From the heart of the fortress, I hear the sound of human screams.

But I am not afraid. I am veiled: a mist, weightless and without thought. I move toward the city entrance as if I'm less than even the wind.

Eliza keeps her distance, as do the other humans who plan to be a distraction. They're probably on the other side of the city by now. Once I'm through these dark, gray walls, I'm on my own.

The sand shifts to pavement, and I push forward.

Inside the Red City is a wide courtyard, filled with a collection of ramps and stairways leading up the wall. Legion Guards are everywhere, staying close to the gates in case of a fight.

Or an intruder.

I don't allow myself to gloat, not when my veil flows through every sliver of my consciousness, leaving no room for distraction. To the Residents, my presence is no more peculiar than a pebble on the road. I'm a part of the surroundings, nothing more.

Layers of rock, fiery red and streaked with gold, make up the base of the residential area. Houses sit close together, constructed with the same nearly black stone as the outside wall, and Residents move about the streets with purpose. The leisure of Victory doesn't exist here.

Down the middle of the city is a long road, lined in market stalls. Hot grills are packed with an abundance of skewered meats, and spread out on the tables are baskets of steamed dumplings edged with thick, green leaves. Another stall overflows with guava, persimmons, and brightly colored fruits I've never seen before. Farther down, I find studded goblets, golden tea sets, and rolls of fine silk in every shade of red.

And not a servant in sight.

The only humans in the Red City are those being tortured belowground.

I skirt around any approaching Residents, silent, and continue down the long road. Ettore's palace sits in the distance, perched on its own mountain and boasting uneven turrets and bloodred flags. A statue of a two-headed wyvern guards the entrance, jaws stretched like it's ready to devour every stone.

An enormous gap separates the road from the mountain. I

stop in front of a cliff, peering over the ledge like I'm looking into a wide volcano. A banister made of bone is the only thing standing between me and a five-hundred-foot drop.

The Fire Pit.

I've heard stories about the gladiator-style arena, but seeing the bloodstained sand and the massive circular opening in the center that hisses with violent orange flames makes me tighten my grip on the bone railing. The stands are sectioned off into narrow rings, circling the arena like a vortex. And they're packed to the edges with shouting Residents, eager for the next show.

I pull myself away. At any moment, more humans will be brought out to tear each other apart. I don't want to watch.

Somewhere beneath the earth, Shura is waiting. Waiting to be brought to the Fire Pit, if she hasn't been taken there already.

I need to get her out of this place before these monsters destroy her.

Descending the stairs on the left, I wind around the arena, looking for an entrance that leads underground. Iron rattles nearby, and two Legion Guards exit a sealed-off tunnel, talking to one another about how easy it's become to predict which human will bleed first. They vanish up the steps, and I slip toward the door, studying the metallic panel where a lock might ordinarily be.

I might be good at deception, but unlocking strange doors is not my specialty. And something tells me that blasting the door apart would only draw unnecessary attention—*if* it even worked to begin with.

I'm about to search for another entrance when I hear

chattering behind the wall. Tucking myself into the corner, I hold the veil over me like I'm part of the rock face.

The door opens, and several Legion Guards walk out. I slip through the opening just before the door seals shut behind me.

Okay. Not the best exit strategy, but at least I'm inside.

A metal ramp leads down the inside of the cave. My footsteps are silent. Nonexistent. In the distance I can hear the snarl of angry steam.

I cross a narrow bridge, the view below clouded with thick fog. The scent is rotten and tinged with metal.

Flesh and blood. My mind reels.

Legion Guards appear in one of the corridors ahead, and once again I move close to the wall. When they pass, I hurry through the opening, and find several archways leading to different rooms. I make the choice to always pick the hall that seems to go lower into the mountain.

Toward where a prison might be.

Eventually—after a few wrong turns and one regrettable look into a room with meat hooks hanging from the ceiling—my suspicions pay off.

The cells are stacked in two levels. Instead of bars, red electricity stretches across each opening, hissing in warning to anyone who might get close. Guards make their rounds on the lower floor.

Stepping onto the metal walkway, I move toward the first cell. The human inside is shackled with metal restraints, no doubt laced with something to hinder their consciousness. But their eyes are open. Aware.

I make a full circle around the top floor, but I can't find Shura. Heading for the stairs to the lower level, I freeze in place when a burly Legion Guard appears below me. The tunnel behind him leads to another corridor. Somewhere I haven't been yet.

"We're ready for the next group," he shouts to the second floor.

Another guard nods from a nearby room. It's surrounded by glass and overlooks the entire cell block. She holds her wrist out, and her gauntlet shines. A hologram appears on the control unit in front of her, and after she makes a few taps against the image, the zap of receding bars sounds below.

Over the ledge, I watch as the humans in the now-open cages are rounded up by guards and shuffled through the tunnel. The guard in the control room swipes at the hologram, and when the image disappears, she fixes her stare back on the cell block.

I move quickly to the ground floor, and I'm looking for any sign of Shura behind the red beams when I spot a mess of pale, pink hair. Even with grime coating her skin and an unhealed gash on her forehead, I know her face at once.

The red crackling energy makes me pause. Something tells me that getting too close is a very bad idea. And with one guard in the control room and two more roaming the floor, I know that lifting my veil or talking out loud isn't an option either.

Shura's hands are shackled together. Her gray eyes are half closed, pooled with death and exhaustion. Bruises and cuts cover her skin, and I honestly can't tell if the restraints are keeping her from healing herself, or if she no longer has the energy to even try.

I want to call out to my friend. To tell her I'm here to help, that I will not leave her behind.

So I speak to her the only way I know how to without putting her in more danger.

My mouth tightens, and I focus my thoughts toward her, like a mist sailing through time.

Shura, I whisper. A faint breath of air. *It's Nami. Can you hear me?*

At first she doesn't react. But then her face wrinkles.

I'm going to get you out of here.

"No," she moans, bordering on tears. "No more. Please, no more."

Shura, it's me, I say with all the tenderness I can find. *Everything is going to be okay.*

"Leave me alone!" Shura shrieks, unable to clutch her ears but trying just the same. "Get out of my head!"

I'm dangerously close to the red bars. *It's Nami,* I try again. *I'm here to help.*

"Get out of my head, get out of my head!" she cries, knuckles digging into her own forehead.

The Legion Guards approach to investigate, and I have no choice but to pull away. They stare into the cell, looking for anomalies.

"Quiet in there," one of them warns. "Or I'll send you straight to the Fire Pit."

But whatever I've done to Shura has already rattled her. She stands up, shouting for them to leave her alone. To get away. To *make it stop.*

My heart is punctured. I don't know what to do. How to fix this.

Why doesn't she believe it's me? Can't she hear my voice?

Shura is still screaming, and the guards must lose their patience, because one of them shouts to the control room to open the cell, and the red bars disappear.

The guard in the center yanks Shura by the restraints, dragging her into the tunnel. "There's always room for one more," his voice echoes through the cavern.

I chase after them, trying to dull the pounding in my chest in case someone hears. Shura finally stops wailing and turns to look at the tunnel. When her frail body begins to tremble, I know she's realized where she is. Where she's headed.

The guard shoves her onto a cagelike elevator, and I duck in beside her. He removes her restraints before slamming the door closed.

Sneering with hate, he says, "I look forward to the show." He waves his gauntlet against a control screen, and the elevator rises.

Darkness enshrouds us, until we reach an archway where sunlight pours through with blinding force. I squint; Shura takes in a sharp breath, and a very real panic sets in her eyes.

The elevator stops, and Shura shakily steps off, as if knowing that refusing will bring something worse. I do the same, and the elevator disappears into the shadows. Around us are other humans—most of them as worn as Shura—enveloped by a metal cage. When I look beyond the bars, I realize we are at the bottom of the arena.

The crowd winds around the humongous space, chanting

and hollering at whatever just transpired below. The Fire Pit spits angrily in the center of the ring. A human is being dragged away into another room.

The way the crowd continues to cheer, I think he was the winner.

I'm afraid to know what happened to whoever lost. But then a scream erupts from the fire and doesn't stop.

Ozias told me the Fire Pit was rumored to be over a hundred feet deep. *An impossible climb,* he called it. Most humans are half turned to ash at the bottom before they even manage to find the wall through the flames. And the ones who fight to heal themselves make the death last longer.

The guards only bother to fish them out after they've stopped screaming. If they bother at all.

Two Residents appear at the front of the cage, and the humans immediately shrink away from their calculating eyes. The burly guard throws the gate open and makes a beeline for one of the humans. At the same moment, I realize Shura is no longer standing beside me.

In horror, I watch as he pulls my friend by her pink hair into the arena, slamming the cage behind him.

No, my mind screams. *This can't be happening.*

Frantic, my eyes dance around the stadium, looking for a way out. Looking for a way to save my friend.

When the guard returns to survey the cowering humans—to look for a second contender—I do the only thing I can.

Hidden behind the others, I shift my face and put on a mask. But I don't become a Resident. I become a human I know no Resident has ever seen before. Someone who won't raise suspicion.

I become Kasia.

And then I lift the veil and push toward the front of the crowd.

When the guard spots me, he whistles through his teeth. "Well, what do you know?" he says. "We have ourselves a volunteer."

20

SHURA STANDS ACROSS THE SAND FROM ME, freckles hidden beneath a layer of ash. She no longer looks like the frantic girl in the cell. She looks feral.

I take a step forward, and I'm about to tell her who I am, when I hear a voice.

"Let the battle begin!" Prince Ettore shouts into the arena.

I glance up at the elaborate box several levels high. Stone gargoyles are perched in the corners, mouths spitting fire. Ettore's throne is made of sharp bone and red velvet, spread outward like a display of teeth.

I remember his wild black hair and golden eyes. I remember the evil that spun around him like smoke. And I remember how angry he was when he didn't get the chance to break me apart.

But the figure beside him is much, much worse.

Prince Caelan stands next to Ettore's throne, hands folded behind his white furs and a crown of silver branches on his head.

My bones become ice, shattering in every direction.

What is he doing here?

My mind stumbles, but I catch myself. I can't let my mask drop. Not with my friend still so much at risk. But the realization that Caelan may have sent her here . . . that he may have *brought* her here himself . . .

A curse snakes its way up my throat, but I keep it in. If Caelan's the reason Shura is in War, his expression reveals nothing. The only thing he offers is a cold, vacant stare into the pit below.

Shura approaches. She's already picked up one of the weapons scattered around the arena: a short sword, still coated in fresh blood.

I hold up my hands. "You don't have to do this," I say quickly. "I'm not going to fight you."

She snarls, swinging her blade, but I dodge to the side.

"Shura, please," I insist, trying to keep my voice low. "It's *me*."

But either she doesn't believe me or she doesn't care, because she swings again, and I leap out of the way just before the blade can find my leg.

A rumble of disapproval breaks out through the crowd. They want a show, and I'm getting in the way of that.

Good, my mind hisses toward the Residents. If they want a show, they can come down here themselves and I'll happily oblige them. My eyes land on Caelan for only a moment—he's speaking to Ettore, his face the portrait of boredom.

It fuels me with rage. He treated Shura like a friend. Like a sister. And now he has the gall to stand there and feel nothing? To not even watch her fight for her life?

I don't care if he let me go—there's no coming back from this kind of cruelty.

Shura's blade swings at my head, and I duck low before spinning behind her in one fluid motion, using my arms to pin her tight.

"This is what they want," I growl in her ear. "We can't let them win. We can't play their games."

She slams the back of her head against my face, drawing blood.

My heels dig into the sand to keep my balance. She's made a mess of my nose, but I ignore it, even as blood trickles over my lips.

Shura turns to face me, pink hair hanging at her temples, and points her sword toward my heart like she's ready to charge.

I brace myself, and when she thrusts, I leap into the air, twisting my body to the side as I grab the handle of her weapon. When my feet connect with the earth, I flip Shura over my shoulder and send her crashing to the ground.

I step back with her sword wedged firmly in my hand. She chokes, winded, and stares up at me—and her former blade—with bewilderment.

The crowd's excitement builds, while disgust roils through me. And because I've never been one to think before I act, I throw the sword into the Fire Pit.

Boos tremble throughout the arena, but I'm glued to Shura and her puzzled expression.

"What are you doing?" she hisses, angry. "You know what happens if we don't fight."

"I'm not going to hurt you," I tell her, and before I can say anything else, she sweeps her leg against my feet, knocking me over.

By the time I stand back up, she's already procured another blade from the earth, this one small and thin. And then Shura vanishes.

It takes me a moment too long to realize what she's done, and I only barely remember to move before her blade slices through my side. I yelp, clutching the wound, and turn to find an empty space.

I jump back on impulse, and feel the rush of her attack inches away.

Shura was always the best veiler in the Colony, but I've had time to practice. And now I know that veiling is more than just physical.

I listen for the hum of her mind, hearing it approach. I dodge left, block her arm with mine, and duck below every one of her attacks. She's relentless, pushing me back toward the fire without mercy.

But I will not hurt her.

I will not be a part of these games.

Shura growls in frustration, not understanding how I'm besting her, and lets the veil drop. She runs toward me with her knife, and I realize we're getting much too close to the Fire Pit. I tackle her, shoving her body out of the way, and scramble back to my feet, hands held up because I'm still so desperate to make her stop.

But Shura doesn't get up.

I look down in horror at the blood spilling from her gut, and the knife deep inside her flesh.

Stars, what have I done?

"I—I didn't mean to—" I stammer, but I can't find the words. I can't even hear my own thoughts, because the crowd is cheering, loud and wild.

I throw myself to her side, pulling the blade out and pushing my hand to her wound. "Shura, you need to heal this. You need to get up." I look around the arena—Ettore is already on his feet, hands spread to the crowd like he's encouraging the fun.

Shura sputters blood, staring at me strangely. "You know my name."

Before I can explain, Ettore's voice booms across the sand. "And now our victor may claim their prize." It takes a full three seconds before I realize he's staring directly at me.

I frown, angry, but also entirely confused.

"You have to throw me into the Fire Pit," Shura manages to say through strained breaths. "You have to, or he'll throw us both in and never let us out."

"No," I say, too low for anyone to hear. And then I glare back at Ettore, with all the viciousness I can muster. "I will not." This time, my voice reaches him.

Ettore doesn't move, but the flames along his knives grow bolder.

Caelan is staring between Shura and me, jaw tense.

"You dare to defy your prince?" Ettore snarls dangerously. A snarl meant solely for me.

"I will not be a part of your game," I reply. "And you are not my prince."

Ettore licks his teeth like he's accepting the challenge. "Very well."

And with a flick of his wrist, Shura goes sailing through the air toward the Fire Pit.

I shout her name and my feet burst across the sand with inhuman speed. Her gray eyes glisten as she reaches the flames, but I leap, grabbing her hands and throwing her with supercharged force away from the Fire Pit—and then I fall a hundred feet into the flames.

21

FIRE RIPS AT MY SKIN, CHARRING MY CLOTHES and scorching my flesh. It's more painful than anything I've ever imagined, but when I hit the iron-hot grate at the bottom, something worse than pain explodes through my body.

I am torn apart, over and over again. An infinite torment I can't escape. The flames devour me, no matter how many times I repair my flesh.

There's screaming nearby. Human screams.

The ones thrown into the Fire Pit before me.

I belly-crawl toward the sound, iron searing my skin with every movement, and my fingertips find the skull of the human still wailing. I can't see beyond the flames. I can't smell anything but burning flesh.

But in my hand, the skull turns to ash. I press a burning hand to the grate, realizing that's where I'll be when this is all through. Ash on the ground, to be swept up until my consciousness pieces itself back together, at which point I'll be forced to fight all over again.

I can't . . .

I can't . . .

Do not give into this, my mind orders. *You cannot let them down again. You need to keep moving.*

I don't know how long it takes to separate my pain from what I know I have to do, but somehow I find the strength to move again. To find the *wall.*

Not to save myself, but because I still need to save the others.

My raw fingertips dig into the stone crevasses. One hand after the other, I claw my way toward the surface, teeth clenched against the relentless pain. I need to get to Shura. I need to get back to Genesis. I need to be around for Mei. My reason for surviving Victory, and making it this far.

I don't know what Caelan intended for me, but it doesn't matter. Because—despite the guilt, and the anger, and the need to stop Ophelia—I know I've been given a chance. Not just to save the people I care about, but to make a difference.

If Infinity is hell, I'll just need to find a different way to burn.

One step at a time. One move at a time. One breath at a time.

Fire isn't going to keep me down—not when my soul is already fueled by it. I will keep going. And I will never stop until every human in this world is *safe.*

I pull myself up, higher and higher until firelight becomes sunlight, and when my scorched palm slams against the golden sand and the sound echoes through the mountain, I realize the crowd has gone completely quiet.

I crawl on my hands and knees, rock digging furiously into the horrible pink-and-black flesh, with barely a scrap of clothing or armor left to protect me. Most of it burned away with the rest of my skin. I find Shura's eyes, watching me with absolute astonishment. Behind her, the humans in the cage are clutching the bars, no longer cowering.

I concentrate on my consciousness, reaching for it like a familiar friend. I dig my fingertips into the sand, pulling for something I can use. Something to remake. And I surrender every bit of power to my own mind.

Energy ripples out of me.

Gold sand winds up my limbs, coiling around every inch of my body. My skin repairs itself, little by little, and a burst of pixels breaks out all over me as the sand morphs into clothing. A hooded golden tunic, metal bracers against my arms, and black boots meant for an assassin.

And at my sides, my once-veiled knives reappear.

I stand, raising my face to Ettore and Caelan. My *real* face.

And when they both flinch, I do not.

22

CAELAN'S SILVER EYES ARE FIXED ON ME WITH A hardness I've never seen before. It's miles different from Ettore, who is watching me like he wants nothing more than to crush me—and enjoy doing it.

But before I can think of my next move, there's an explosion outside the arena. Legion Guards take to the sky in immediate alarm, and for a moment both princes are watching the smoke.

It's all I need.

I throw myself under a veil and pull Shura under it with me, racing to her side and scooping her up by the shoulder.

"Nami, you're—" She gasps, lip quivering.

"Not now," I say. "We have to get out of here."

When I look up at the cage of humans, they're already being ushered back into the elevator—back into the mountain, where they'll be locked in their cells until the next show.

I want to help them. I need to do *something*. But right now, Shura is hurt. If I don't move fast, we'll never get out of here.

We tear toward one of the nearby doorways. It's difficult to veil Shura's thoughts as well as my own, but I can feel her using her remaining energy to help. When we reach the door, I realize it has the same panels as the ones below, activated by the Legion Guards' gauntlets.

I turn back to the humans being shoved into the elevator.

Don't freak out, I try to mentally prepare Shura, *but I have an idea.*

Her panic only magnifies, but I'm already too focused on trying to close the gap between us and the cage.

As we start moving for the elevator, I throw a blast of energy toward the door behind us, smashing at sand and rock. Legion Guards immediately rush the area, assuming I'm hidden nearby, just as Shura and I slip onto the elevator.

She tenses, and I hug the veil tighter around us, hoping to pacify her.

When the doors open, Legion Guards grab for the humans with aggressive force, snapping restraints onto them one by one and shoving them back through the tunnel. In the mess of bodies and fighting, I guide Shura to relative safety on the other side of the crowd. We quickly make our way to the cell block and climb the stairs, heading for the doorway I came in through. But when we reach the opening, I look over the railing—at the humans being herded back into cells—and am overcome with guilt.

Leaving them here . . . It's not right.

One glance at Shura and she nods with understanding, even as I maintain our veil. I set her down carefully, and look over the ledge. Residents are shuffling humans into their cells; from the control room, a Legion Guard brings the red cages to life.

After a look of confirmation from the tower, the others sprint back through the tunnels to find the bigger threat.

Too bad for them: they don't know I'm right here.

I hurry toward the last remaining guard, slipping into the glass room without making a sound. The Resident is busy watching the controls. My thoughts snake toward her, but she doesn't sense me—not like Caelan did when he knew exactly what to look for. And when I see her in the void, full of concentration and hatred, I summon water, silent and powerful, and fill her mind to the brink.

The guard stumbles back, choking—*drowning*. I grab my obsidian dagger, hold tight to her gauntlet, and bring my blade down hard against her wrist, severing the bone. Though her eyes are wide and desperate, she's unable to speak with so much invisible water in her lungs.

Holding the gauntlet over the controls, I open the display hologram and swipe through screens until I find the controls for every cell in the room.

I unlock them all.

Red beams disintegrate, and at first the humans don't move, afraid it's some kind of trick. I rush to the front of the glass wall, lift my veil, and stare down into the room.

"I will get you out of here, but you need to stay close. And whatever you do, don't go near the guards," I say, already moving across the walkway toward Shura.

I help her stand, glancing over my shoulder as every human prisoner gathers behind me. With a nod, I throw a weak veil over the group. It's all I can manage.

Around the corner, Legion Guards are still running toward the surface. Whatever distraction the rebellion came up with must've been big. I wait for them all to pass before pushing farther into the maze.

I'm scanning the halls, trying to remember which way I came, when I realize it's going to be impossible to get out of the Red City. Besides the fact that I've never in my life veiled so many people, Shura is too hurt, and she's trailing blood. In the darkness, it's hidden, but in the sunlight?

We'd be leaving bread crumbs every step of the way.

With one arm wrapped around Shura, I duck into an empty room in the caves. The other humans quickly do the same, watching the doorway with terror.

"I'm slowing you all down." Shura's voice cracks. "Leave me. Get out of here while you still can."

"Give me *some* credit," I retort, eyeing her bloody stomach. "I'm not out of ideas yet." I study the walls around me. *Stars, I hope this works.*

I reach out with my mind, searching for ripples in the world. *The echo of sound.*

Zahrah said humans started building their tunnels as far back as the First War. And if Prince Ettore really built his palace on top of the first battlefield . . .

Maybe some of those tunnels still remain.

A hollow thrum calls back to me, far beyond the rock wall. It's not exactly close, but it's there. And if we can get to those tunnels, we can make our way into the canyons. Back to Genesis.

I take a breath and focus my hands in front of the wall, throwing my veil as far and wide as it will go to hide what I'm doing. Energy builds in my palms, and I blast it toward the rock, straight and swift, aiming for the next tunnel.

It isn't enough. I try again, wincing as cracks appear in the wall and the power eats away at everything I have left.

Help me, I say to the void, choking on a gasp. *Please.*

Sweat builds on my forehead. I strain beneath the power, weakening.

I've used so much already. So much . . .

And then I feel it—the break of stone through the wall, coming to meet me. The rock gives way, leaving a crumbling hole in its place. I peer inside.

Far, far away, I see the edge of another tunnel.

I turn to the humans. "Go. Fast as you can. These tunnels will get us through the canyon, but I have no idea how long it will be before the Residents realize where we are."

Understanding, the humans start to move, but I stop the one in front. A tall, lanky woman with stringy yellow hair. I hold out the guard's severed hand and fill the gloved palm with a soft white orb of light.

"When it's safe, this should get your restraints off," I say, passing it to the woman. She grimaces but takes it anyway, ignoring the severed bone peeking through the gauntlet.

When the last human is through the tunnel, I help Shura stand and guide her inside. She stifles a cry, leaning on me. We are nearly to the next tunnel when I hear him.

"Nami." Caelan's voice echoes toward me.

I stiffen, looking over my shoulder. He's standing at the broken, jagged entrance I made. Alone.

I've imagined many times what it would be like to face him again, in person. But nothing could've prepared me for the visceral anger roaring through my bloodstream.

I want to lash out. I want to make him pay for what he did to the Colony. What he did to the people who believed they loved him.

What he did to me.

The thought makes my chest clench. But *his* rage? It's nowhere to be found. Instead, he almost looks . . .

Shura's weakened breath snaps me back to reality, and I shake the confusion away. There's no time to analyze Caelan's motives—and no matter how still and stunned he appears, I know better than to trust him.

I stare back at his unmoving frame and hold out my hand. Raw energy bursts from my palm and batters into the ceiling with a roaring tear.

I run with Shura into the darkness, just as the tunnel behind us caves in.

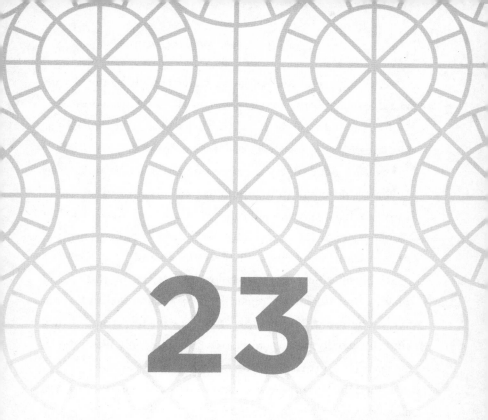

23

AFTER MILES OF TREKKING THROUGH THE TUN-
nels, we make it to the canyon.

I take a moment to work out our direction, and quickly
search for higher ground. The humans are finally without their
restraints, and it turns out we have a few veilers in our company.
It's exactly the help I need, because I'm too weak to do much of
anything. I think adrenaline and pure stubbornness are the only
reasons I'm able to stand.

The granite walls of the Red City shrink in the distance, but
Legion Guards continue to swarm above it like a black cloud.
Turning to the humans, I explain that we have to go north.

We walk for hours. Their fear is like a thick balm over my

heart, stifling me. If the Residents weren't so preoccupied with what happened at the arena, maybe they'd have already found us.

They should *have found us. Caelan saw you in the tunnel—he must've been able to figure out where you were going.*

For the second time, the Prince of Victory let me walk away.

There's no doubt in my mind he was surprised to see me in the arena. Even the best of his lies couldn't mask the shock. But to follow me to the tunnel and watch me usher the humans to safety, without so much as calling for the guards?

It's possible he doesn't want Ettore to catch me because of what I know. Maybe he's afraid I'll tell his brother the truth about the throne room. Are there repercussions for betraying his own kind? Or would his betrayal be excused, if the only reason he let me go was to further his plans?

I thought Victory was a maze, but perhaps his court was merely a small part of a bigger trap.

Every step I take feels like I'm moving closer and closer to his snare. But what's the alternative? Right now, people are counting on me to get them someplace safe.

Whatever Caelan wants . . . I'll have to deal with it later.

When Eliza's face appears on the horizon along with a group of humans from Genesis, I almost collapse to my knees. Shura stiffens in my arms, and I know she's seen her. By the look on Eliza's weeping face, she's seen us, too.

We join our forces, and Shura stumbles into Eliza's embrace. Their sobs are muffled, each of them squeezing tight to the other like they're afraid to let go.

I'd hug my family the same way if they were here.

A tear drifts over the edge of my cheek, and I wipe it away.

Zahrah stops beside me, battle-ax drawn. "Just one person, huh?" she says, repeating my words back to me.

I blink the salt sting away, mouth curving into a sheepish grin. "Give or take a few."

Her laugh dances across the sand, and she claps my shoulder, motioning for the hills. "Let's get you back to Genesis. You look like shit."

I sleep for days without waking, but even as my strength returns, I don't feel completely myself. It's very possible that the majority of my unrest has to do with the silver-eyed prince. Awake or asleep, it doesn't matter. He haunts me no matter what I do, like an undefinable spirit.

Sometimes I find myself waiting at the edge of my mind, bracing for the winter chill of his consciousness. Not that I *want* him to reach out to me again. What would I even say if he did? "Thank you for letting me go"? "I hate you for watching Shura almost be thrown into the Fire Pit"?

It's easier to despise him from afar, when he isn't messing everything up by acting like there's more to his story. But the mystery, and the unanswered questions? They get under my skin.

He gets under my skin.

It's impossible to push Caelan out of my thoughts, but maybe my presence in War is doing the same to him. Maybe I'm getting in the way, and ruining his plans. With any luck, I'm the perfect distraction to keep him from his seat in the Capital.

A girl can hope.

Shura pulls back the beige tent, peeking her head through the opening. "Sorry," she says with a fragile smile. "Were you asleep?"

I sit up, tucking my hair behind my ears. "I'm good. A few minutes is all I need."

Even though she doesn't look like she believes me, she steps inside. Her pink hair is in two braids, the color still duller than I remember, but clean. She's wearing loose cotton pants and a brown tank top. Fitting for the desert landscape.

Sinking onto the floor beside me, she trails a finger along the colorful mat. "I'm sorry we haven't really had a moment alone. It's been . . ."

"You don't need to apologize. Seeing one of your moms again, after all this time? I don't blame either of you for not wanting to leave each other's sight." I'd do the same if my parents and Mei were here.

I might never let them out of my sight again.

"Eliza told me you came to War for us. For the Colony." Shura's gray eyes linger on mine. "Thank you, Nami. I—I know we aren't supposed to do rescue missions. Once lost is lost, and all that."

"Those were never my rules," I point out.

Shura nods. "Yeah. I remember." Her throat bobs. "After the Colony was attacked, we were all taken to the Winter Keep. When you and Gil never turned up, we assumed the worst—that maybe you were taken to War, or Death."

I frown. "Gil?"

"Well, yeah. He left not long after you did. Said he wanted to be nearby, in case things went bad." She tucks her arms around herself. "Guess he must've had a sixth sense or something."

"Something like that," I say dryly.

The Colony still doesn't know what Gil did? *Who* he was?

All that time spent in the Winter Keep, and Caelan didn't feel like gloating? And why bother keeping prisoners in his court, when he wanted so badly to get rid of Victory for good?

I don't understand his choices. I don't understand what he still *wants*.

Shura doesn't look away. "What are you not telling me?"

She deserves to know, and she deserves to hear it from me. Before someone from Genesis blabs.

I open my mouth, but Ozias appears in the tent entrance.

He nods, focusing his attention solely on me. "I know you've been resting, but I want to tell you in person how impressed I am. You saved nearly three dozen people from the Fire Pit." His eyes shine. "That doesn't go unnoticed—by me *or* the Residents." His meaning is clear.

We didn't just poke the bear—we threw a grenade at it.

"I couldn't leave them behind." There's no half-hearted apology in my voice. Not like there would've been if I were still at the Colony, second-guessing every choice I made.

I know what I have to do now.

Ozias tucks his hands behind him. The bulk of his bone armor is on display, but there's no sigil to be found. Kasia lived without her clan for lifetimes, but they were still her people. Her family.

Ozias has left the Bone Clan in the past. Maybe because

he doesn't need them—he has a new army, and a new throne.

He tilts his chin. "One of the younglings said you created a tunnel."

I chew my thoughts. It feels strange to take the credit for something I know I didn't do all alone. I asked for help—reached out like I was saying a prayer. And something answered.

Or someone.

I don't know how to explain it to Ozias, so I don't. "It was the only way to get everyone out of there."

"It was a clever idea, connecting the tunnels. Not to mention climbing out of the Fire Pit." He pauses. "I didn't know you had that kind of strength."

"It was just the adrenaline rush."

"You're too modest," he notes, but it doesn't sound like a compliment. I don't like the way he's looking at me, like he's studying my value. Wondering whether to add me to his collection.

Wondering if he'll ever let me go.

"Really," I insist. "If the others hadn't caused the distraction, I would've been trapped. And some of the humans in the cells were trained. We were lucky."

Shura is watching me curiously. I forgot how good she is at reading people.

"But you managed to get out, unseen, and brought many humans to safety." He offers a smile. "We're due a night of celebration. We have so few of those."

I nod, biting my tongue as I avoid meeting Shura's gaze. She knows we didn't get out unseen. She saw Caelan—heard him call my name.

Maybe she hasn't had a chance to tell the others what she saw in the tunnel.

Or maybe she's waiting to ask me what it meant.

Ozias motions toward the world outside. "Some of the new-comers are having trouble healing their wounds. I thought you could speak with them—give them some words of comfort."

"Oh." I blush. "I'm not really good at that kind of thing. I wouldn't know what to say."

His eyes stir with power. A side effect of his position, perhaps. "You've just saved their lives, given them freedom. Many will want to thank you. In a rebellion, it's imperative to have people who inspire others. Your voice could be the reason they fight."

I fidget beneath his stare. I didn't come here to be anyone's poster child for war. Not the way he expects. I want people to fight to make Infinity safe. He wants people to fight because he wants the prize of a castle, and a court.

We are not the same.

I was made to play a role once, and I regret every part of it. If I'm going to wear another mask, it will be *my* decision.

But if Ozias suspects I've left something out of my story, he might start digging for answers. Answers I'm not ready to give him, about my relationship with Caelan, and Ophelia.

And there's still the Borderlands to protect.

Maybe it's better to give him this, just to get him to stop look-ing at me the way he is.

"Fine," I say. "I'll be out in a minute."

"Wonderful." He claps his hands, tilting his head back like he's soaking in the good news. "You've made the right choice."

The right choice, or the only choice?

The whiff of a threat lingers in the air. When he leaves, it follows him.

Shura's mouth is already open like she's been desperate to pepper me with questions. Like she knows she has to hurry.

But I don't have answers for her. Not now, when my head is buzzing and I'm still so tired.

I wave a hand at the air and stand. "I have to go. Can we talk later?"

Her shoulders fall. "Yeah. Sure." She stands too, and follows me out of the tent.

When we step into the desert, we go our separate ways.

Fire crackles in the distance. It isn't the bonfire some of the others wanted, but it's the right amount of light for the veil posts to cover safely. Humans dance in droves around it, some in groups, some in pairs.

Diego arrives with more skewered fruits, plucked from the very limited gardens they manage to grow near the caves. Food isn't essential anymore, but it builds culture and cultivates joy.

Maybe that makes it meaningful enough to keep around.

People reach for the offerings, and Diego disappears behind the tents to fetch more food.

Zahrah sits in the distance, sharpening a spear while staring distastefully at the party. A woman dances closer, twirling her hands like she's beckoning Zahrah to join her. In one fluid, careful movement, Zahrah aims her spear at the woman's sternum.

The woman, in a panic, nearly stumbles across the dirt in retreat.

I can't help but laugh.

Dayo appears beside her sister and sits. Whatever words they exchange are brief, but enough to shake Zahrah's mood. She nudges Dayo with her shoulder. Dayo rests her head against Zahrah in response.

I'm not laughing anymore. I'm not even smiling.

I'm thinking about how much I wish that were me and Mei.

"Not in the mood for dancing?" Shura asks, taking a seat on the edge of the cliff.

After I finished making the rounds and listening to people thank me over and over again, I found a spot above the caves, hoping to have a few minutes alone.

But somehow the minutes turned into hours.

I kick a pebble with my boot, and it scatters down the steep hill. "I'll dance when this war is over."

"Ah." A second passes. "I thought maybe it had something to do with the last time we made you go to a dance."

The thought of a ballroom makes my stomach churn. "I know you have questions. You might as well just ask."

"What happened that night? The Night of the Falling Star?" Shura tilts her head. "And why isn't Gil with you?"

And because it's a secret I just don't want to carry anymore, I tell her everything.

Everything except how I've been able to communicate with Caelan and Ophelia. Because some things even Shura wouldn't understand.

When I finish talking, I'm met with silence. Shura looks as

if she's gone into mild shock, but when the tears begin to fall, I realize it's devastation.

"I—I can't believe he did that to us. To *you*." She shakes her head back and forth. "It was all a lie, even from the beginning."

"Gil—Caelan—he was always a monster." I stiffen. "But at least now we know what our enemy really looks like." Like a friend. Like someone who made me believe he cared.

Like someone who is still *pretending to care.*

The way Caelan called my name is a constant echo. I can't tell if it was poison or velvet—and that's part of the problem. After all this time, I still see layers of him that probably don't even exist.

I close my eyes, hoping the thought shutters in the darkness.

"He let you escape from Victory," Shura says carefully. "And at the tunnel, he didn't stop us. Why?"

"Maybe it was just another one of his games. Or maybe he's still watching to figure out what we'll do to save ourselves. Either way, he sent you to War. He made it clear whose side he's on," I say, but I'm not sure which one of us needs more convincing.

Shura frowns. "Caelan didn't send me anywhere—he kept us in the Winter Keep, and he ordered his guards to leave us alone. We waited to be tortured, but no one ever touched us."

I don't respond. I don't *understand*.

They were in Victory all this time?

Why would Caelan keep prisoners in a court he never wanted?

"But—you were locked up in the arena." My throat catches. "You're *here*."

"Ahmet and I managed to break free. We couldn't get everyone

else out, so Annika told us to come to War and find the rebellion."
Shura blinks like the memory stings. "We'd all heard the rumors
when we were listening in on the council meetings." She pauses.
"Not that any of it was real, I suppose."

Brushing sand from my knee, I clench my teeth. "The *rebellion*
was real. And I'm glad it led me to you." My fingers stiffen, and I
pull my hand back abruptly. "Wait . . . Ahmet's here too?"

Shura's gaze falters. "We made it to the Labyrinth, but one of
the landscapes shifted into a raging sea. We tried to go back—to
try a different landscape—but we were separated." Her shoulders
sink. "I was captured not long after I crossed the border. But I
haven't seen Ahmet since that day in the water."

Panic nestles in my core. The thought of him stuck out there,
drowning again and again.

If he's still lost in the Labyrinth, I hope it's at least not beneath
the current.

And Caelan . . .

I don't know why he kept the Colony in the Winter Keep, but
that is far from a reason to trust him. If anything, it proves he's had
ulterior motives for months. When he refused to tell me where
the others were, it wasn't to stop me from looking for them—it
was to stop me from looking too closely at *him*.

Not to mention he stood by while Shura fought for her life.
Would he have stayed to watch her burn, too?

"I know you and Gil became close." Shura's eyes soften. "And
if you think that's why he keeps letting you go—"

"It isn't," I interject, voice stoic. "Gil was nothing more than
a character."

"It's one thing to know what he was, but we also have to remember what Caelan's *not*."

I flinch in the darkness. "You mean he's not human."

She shakes her head. "And he never will be. He's just very good at pretending."

We sit in silence, watching Genesis celebrate in the desert. There's life here, and hope, too.

That's worth protecting. Even when the world burns around us.

"So tell me more about this place you went to—the Borderlands." Shura lifts a brow. "Is that where you learned to veil so well?"

It's too dark for her to see the flush in my cheeks. But I tell her about Kasia, and my training—I tell her that a safe place from the Residents really does exist. A sanctuary, and a map in the stars. I tell her what happened, and why I left, and how Ozias doesn't want the others to know.

I tell her it's still there, waiting for her. Waiting for all of us.

"The people here deserve to know," Shura says seriously. "Not everyone was cut out to fight. Not like this. It's—it's not human."

Not human.

The problem is that I still don't know what that means.

But I came to War hoping the rebellion would help me find my friends. The fact that Shura is sitting beside me, aware and okay and with knowledge of what happened to the others . . . that's worth celebrating.

Even if I'm not interested in dancing.

"I'm happy to see you." I glance at Shura. "I've really missed you."

Shura lets out a cry she's been holding in too long, and throws her arms around my shoulders. "I've missed you, too. And honestly? I've been wanting to tell you this for days, but when I saw you with that severed hand, it terrified me. You didn't look like the Nami I remembered. But I know you're still in there—and I promise we'll find our family, and everything will be okay."

I don't say anything—I'm too scared I'll jinx it.

Because I want so badly to believe she's right.

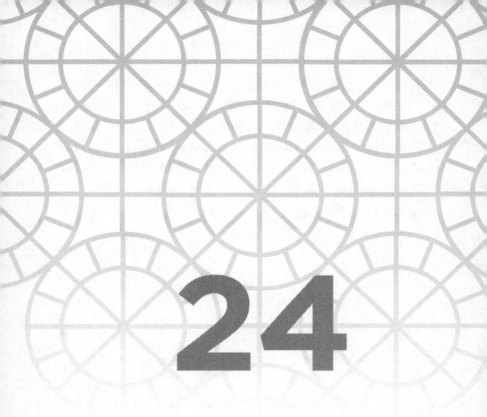

24

I LOOK AROUND THE WIDE TENT AT THE REBEL-
lion leaders, weapons forever attached to their backs and hips.
Always ready for battle. Always prepared for a fight.

After what happened in the Fire Pit, everyone is expecting
retaliation from the Red City. Ettore may not be human, but he
still has an ego. We just don't know where or when the Residents
will strike.

"The outposts are going to need assistance," Diego argues.
"They'll be hit first, and we can't afford to lose any more casters."

Ozias hums, serious. A collection of small bones hangs from
his neck. A new addition to his outfit that's clearly more decorative than functional.

The very concept of keeping war trophies makes my skin crawl.

"I'd prefer not to spread our forces thin," Ozias says. "Not unless we are certain an attack is imminent."

Eliza takes a slow breath. "Perhaps we need to consider moving Genesis's location."

"Ettore has not attacked Genesis for nearly half a cycle," Dayo says. "If he hasn't been able to track us before, I hardly think that's going to change overnight."

"Nami broke out an entire cell block," Ichika points out. "I don't think we've ever threatened the Residents this way before. Held them off, yes, but breaching the Red City?" She shakes her head. "This is different. He will react *differently*."

Guilt inches its way back up through me, even though I've tried so hard to keep it at bay.

Genesis is vulnerable because of me. Because I went to save Shura, and made a bigger scene than any of us planned for.

I don't regret it. Not even a little bit. But the guilt?

I haven't figured out how to shut that part off yet.

Diego huffs. "It would be a waste of resources to move Genesis preemptively. What if Ettore's idea of retaliation is simply sending more Residents into the battlefields? We'd be better off pushing back their forces. Lead them *away* from the camp instead of risking its exposure."

They go back and forth, debating the pros and cons of every potential move, but there isn't an easy solution. Not without knowing exactly what Ettore's planning.

Caelan might know. My thoughts simmer.

He might still be in the Red City. And while I wouldn't trust him at his word, I could try to slip into his mind again using a veil. Maybe I could lead him through Ettore's palace, the way I did when I needed the map.

It didn't entirely work last time, since he knew I was there. But maybe I'm stronger now. Maybe I could try it again.

"What do you think, Nami?" Zahrah's voice pulls me back to the present.

I blink, staring at their waiting faces. "I—I don't think you need my opinion. You all know way more about battle plans than I do."

"Come on," Diego urges. "You're the only human to ever break into the Red City. We absolutely want to hear your opinion."

There's a subtle shift in Ozias. A *flinch*.

No one else notices the friction, but when I speak, my words are restrained. "Maybe what we need is better intel. If someone could spy on the Legion Guards, you might be able to better prepare." *And if not the Legion Guards, then maybe a prince.*

Cameron grunts. "No human could ever get that close to Ettore's plans. You'd have to be inside the palace for that kind of intel."

"Unless you're volunteering," Vince quips before pausing to look at me. "Wait. . . . *Are* you volunteering?"

Zahrah narrows her eyes, curly hair framing her face. "That's an impossible task. The Red City was one thing, but the palace?" She clicks her tongue against her teeth. "It's too great a risk."

"Not to mention we won't have the advantage of surprise," Dayo notes. "Not after they saw what she can do."

Diego lifts his chin. "But maybe with a small group, we could get close to the palace. And with Nami's veils, we could at least scope out how the Legion Guards are preparing behind the wall." He glances at me—not Ozias. "What do you think?"

Their words, and the way they keep staring . . . like what I think *matters* . . .

Ozias takes a step forward, and the attention pulls away from me like air being sucked out of a room. "By the time we gather intel, it may already be too late. Right now, our priority is our people." He looks at the others in turns. "We can't send troops to a battle if we don't know where it is. But we can tighten the watch around our borders, and send extra soldiers to the outposts. That way we can stay informed when the Residents make their move, and protect our most vulnerable."

Diego bows. "We'll let the patrol know, Your Majesty." He leaves the tent, taking the other First Leaders with him.

Only Ozias and I remain behind.

I tap a finger against my hilt. "I wasn't trying to undermine you."

"You didn't." He hardly moves. "I encourage all my First Leaders to openly communicate. It's impossible for a mind to grow without discussion and debate. Shared insight is a gift."

"Except I'm not a leader." I don't *want* to be a leader.

"If people choose to follow you, there's not much you can do about it." His mouth curves into a smile that doesn't look natural. "You've become an important part of the rebellion in such a short time."

The inference rings in my ears. Not just important—what he means is that I'm becoming indispensable.

And that it was never a part of his plans.

Gil must've fought by his side for years, and Ozias still threw him to the Residents to preserve his war. What will he do if he knows that what I really want is to get every human to the Borderlands? That I've gained the trust of his First Leaders, only to eventually urge them to *run*?

I can't let him see me as a threat, or figure out the truth. Not when I still need to find the rest of the Colony.

"All I want is to help keep everyone safe," I say, hoping it's enough to prove my loyalty. Not for his cause, exactly, but for his people.

The shine in his gray eyes drains the color in my own. "The strong will always outlast the weak. And I think we all can see which one you are."

Every day I spend here, the more useful I become.

A tool. A pawn.

A weapon.

A long time ago, I was afraid of wielding power. But power in the right hands can be used for good.

What would the King of Genesis do if he had all the power in Infinity?

Would the world look better? Or would his heart forever hunger for the next battlefield?

I leave the tent and turn the corner for the caves. When I find a small cavern deep in the tunnels and far from the noise of Genesis, I sit in the corner, head pressed against the oddly cool rock, and debate whether communicating with Caelan again is even a possibility.

He may not have sent Shura to the Fire Pit, but he was happy to watch her burn. And he had no idea it was me, fighting in the sands—which means he had no reason to pretend to be anyone but himself.

Maybe that was the first real glimpse of Caelan I've ever seen.

Venturing into his mind was supposed to be about getting information. Except none of my attempts have ever *truly* been successful. No matter how hard I try, he's always expecting me— like I'm playing right into his games.

It doesn't matter what face you wear. I will always know you.

We're too connected. And maybe that's still my fault.

But the others were right: if the Prince of War is truly planning to strike the rebellion, someone should find out where, when, and how.

Nix's familiar padding sounds nearby.

"The prodigal son returns," I say, lifting an eyebrow. "Where have you been hiding? I haven't seen you in days."

Nix shakes his body in response like he's ridding himself of excess water. His cloud-and-starlight fur swirls like magic.

I lift a hand to him, and he pushes his head against it, arching his back.

"Must be nice to roam through the Four Courts without any real fear," I note, scratching the back of his ears the way I know he likes. I wonder if he misses Kasia. If he's ever thought of traveling back to see her.

I wonder if he already has.

And then it dawns on me. I don't have to rely on my enemy for information, when there's a much more convenient way to get inside the Red City.

I look at Nix, lowering my gaze. "You wouldn't happen to be any good at climbing stone walls, would you?"

He blinks back. A silent acknowledgment.

I lean onto my knees, fingers bracing the ground in front of me as I stare deep into Nix's starlit eyes. "I know Kasia says good memories are easy to hold on to, but . . . don't let me fall, okay?"

Nix flicks his tail behind him.

"I see what you see," I whisper, letting my mind float into the mist before settling into Nix's existence.

When I open my eyes again, I'm seeing the world through the eyes of a Dayling.

25

I RACE ACROSS THE GOLDEN DESERT UNDER THE
cover of nightfall. My consciousness is stretched too far for a veil,
but I've managed to dull the light on Nix's coat enough to blend
into the darkness.

I may not look like myself, but it's safer to stay out of sight
as much as possible. There could be some Residents here who
remember Nix fighting in the First War.

Prince Ettore, in particular.

I take the long way around the Red City, scouring the surrounding wall for a way in. Unlike the northern wall, where
guards are posted at the main gate like unmoving statues, at the
east they make their rounds between watchtowers. Here, there's

no entrance to keep their focus on. Just sand and rock and me.

When the Legion Guards disappear into one of the towers, I prowl silently across the desert and start my climb. Several minutes later, the guards reemerge, and I wait for them to pass before dragging myself over the wall with ease.

Staying as close to the shadows as I can, I leap into a courtyard, chasing the walls and paths around the houses and the arena—still lively with screams even in the darkness, a sign that it didn't take them long to find more humans to lock up—and make my way to Ettore's palace.

Wings flap in the distance, beating against the wind, and a group of Legion Guards takes to the skies. More line the walls, dangerously armed.

They're preparing for something. Something big.

Avoiding the entrance, I clamber up the red-stained mountainside and head for one of the smaller turrets, where the generous windows are pitch black and show no signs of a crowd. Digging my claws into the protruding stones, I climb.

When I reach the open window, I pull myself over the ledge and slip inside, crouched low to the floor. A vacant guest room, I presume, based on the modest decor and unlit hearth. It takes a few tries to manage the door handle, but eventually the latch gives way, and I slide into the dark hallway.

Every step is silent as I prowl through the palace. I don't know if it's always this quiet, or if having a never-ending arena keeps the majority of the Residents occupied, but I keep my guard up, ducking into empty rooms when I hear the approach of footsteps.

I take a spiral stairwell down to a wide corridor lit with iron torches. A red carpet stretches across the length of the hall. Head low, I pass a dining hall still littered with empty bottles and half-filled goblets—a dinner cut short, perhaps—and decide that any worthwhile information will likely be kept in a study, or a council room.

But after a careful exploration of the next tower, I find something even better.

The war room.

A massive circular table sits in the center, surrounded by deep red chairs. Ettore's colors grace the walls in hung tapestries and flags. A chandelier of torches hangs low from the sky-scraping ceiling, and a raging fire continues to burn in the open hearth nearby.

I push myself up onto my hind legs, placing my paws at the edge of the table. Maps and parchment cover the surface. A wineglass is on its side, liquid still dripping through the cracks of the table and onto the floor below.

Someone was here, and they haven't been gone long.

I study the maps, and the strange markings painted in . . . blood? Wine? I can't tell, and I don't want to know. There are places drawn onto the landscape that I've never seen before. Perhaps they're outposts, or perhaps they're the old locations of Genesis. But as far as I can tell, Ettore's forces have no idea where Genesis currently is.

My gaze falls to the massive balcony, where more and more soldiers take to the skies, their banshee cries sailing across the moonlight.

The sight fills me with dread.

They must be planning an air strike, and soon. But *where*?

I sniff at the maps like a part of Nix is itching to get out, and catch the scent of alcohol.

Not blood.

A small relief.

Footsteps draw near, and I push myself from the table and scurry beneath it for cover, shielding my crouched body in its shadow. Two Residents step into the room: Legion Guards, if their uniforms are any indication. They move to a nearby shelf. The one with cropped black hair pulls a sheet of parchment from a drawer and scribbles something in ink. When she's finished, she seals the paper with a wave of her hand, and something that looks very similar to a wax seal appears on the surface.

She moves quickly toward the other guard. "Take this message to each of the battlefield commanders. Make sure they understand its importance."

"Yes, Commander." He takes the letter and moves across the room to the open balcony.

"And Lieutenant?"

He pauses by the railing.

"We want the human aware."

The Legion Guard at the balcony bows his head before his batlike wings appear and he takes to the skies.

The commander steps toward the table, and I press dangerously close to the legs of the chairs behind me. She snatches up one of the maps, or a piece of parchment—it's too hard to tell from the sound alone—and disappears back into the hallway.

I wait several long seconds before hurrying after her.

Trailing the commander, I follow her all the way to the edge of a forked staircase before realizing I've lost her. The stairs going up lead to rooms that overflow with light and laughter.

A crowd I need to avoid.

So instead I take the stairs down to a massive foyer, rich with dark wooden features. Stone dragons guard the hallways, all varying in shapes and styles. I'm halfway down one of the corridors, crossing in front of a ribbonlike beast, when I hear Prince Ettore's voice coming toward me.

Scrambling back in the other direction, I skid across the open room and crouch in an alcove beneath the stairs.

"I will not wait any longer. We will strike now—on both accounts." Ettore appears around the corner, black hair like a vulgar flame.

The short-haired commander places a hand against her chest in respect. "Of course, Your Highness. The rest of the commanders will know what to do soon."

Ettore sweeps a finger over his brow, gait lithe and dancer-like as he moves up the steps. He pauses, turning. "Any news on my brothers?"

"Prince Lysander is not hosting visitors, but Prince Damon will see you"—the commander pauses—"*after* Prince Caelan's visit next week."

Ettore lets out a low snarl. "He's building alliances. I know he is."

"Surely your brother's visit here is a sign he wishes to build one with you, too?" she asks carefully.

"My brother came here waving under my nose the one thing

he knows I want," Ettore seethes. "A merger of the Four Courts. And I admit for a moment I thought he'd seen reason—that perhaps his desire to move to the Capital would be enough to make him willingly hand over his crown." Ettore scowls, staring at the torchlights above him. "And then I saw why he really traveled all this way. For that *human*."

I listen to Ettore's footsteps moving across the length of the step, hoping the shadows will be enough to conceal me.

"You think Prince Caelan is after revenge?" the commander asks.

Ettore's voice is a flash bomb of fury. "He doesn't have the stomach for revenge. No—he's trying to cover his tracks. He's afraid I'll discover what really happened that night in the throne room. What he's *hiding*."

My heart beats in triple time. I was right—Caelan let me run because he didn't want Ettore to find me.

The knowledge I have . . . it could ruin the Prince of Victory's plans. Maybe it could even ruin *him*.

But it would never be worth it if Ettore were the one who gained power.

Caelan's secret isn't a weapon I can use against him—it's a burden I'll have to protect.

And one that makes me a target.

Ettore sighs. "As long as that human is in War, my brother will not leave." He pauses. "But perhaps if he misses his meeting with Damon, I could go in his stead."

I hear the clink of a sword as the commander bows. "I will send word, Your Highness." Several seconds pass. "Perhaps Prince

Caelan will seek the human out himself, and lead us straight to
her."

"Doubtful." Ettore snorts. "He knows I suspect him. That's
why he's been brooding alone in the west tower for days, like a
coward."

Another pause. "And if we find her first . . . ?"

"I want her breathing, and whole. I once told her I'd show her
what War was really like—and I don't break my promises."

His footsteps fade up the stairs, and I watch the commander
turn down another hallway.

I take a few careful steps into the light. Everything inside
me screams that it's time to go, that I've heard enough. *Learned*
enough.

If I were smart, I'd head back to Genesis right now and tell the
others what I've seen. But I'm only human.

I make my way to the west tower.

It doesn't take me long to find his guest quarters. Every other
room is dark, but light spills beneath his unguarded double doors.
Either he doesn't think he needs protection in this court, or he
thought sending the guards away would give him privacy.

He's wrong on both accounts.

I use my outstretched claws to turn the handle, and my muzzle
to push gently against the door.

An enormous red bed sits at one end of the room, clearly
unused. I pad through the living area, past a chaise longue draped
in Caelan's furs, where a large, open balcony allows starlight to
fill the dark space. Black curtains billow slightly, and I turn the
corner and find a massive bath built into the floor like a hot

spring. Stone paving lines the floor, and steam floats above the pool, cloudlike.

Sitting in the water with his back to me is Prince Caelan.

His bare skin is damp, and shadows ripple across his lean, muscled back. His elbows are perched back on the stone, but his head is tilted forward, heavy. I've never seen him so vulnerable.

Or so naked.

He would never expect an attack here. It would be easy to reach out with Nix's claws. To hurt him the way he's hurt so many others.

I'm creeping toward him without even realizing it, head dipped like I'm ready to pounce. It would be a small kind of revenge, catching him by surprise. Showing him he's not the only one who can corner someone in a maze.

And then Caelan sighs. A strained, morose breath. I stiffen, puzzled by the person in front of me.

I didn't know a monster could look so overcome with . . . grief.

Caelan lifts his head, and there's no time to move as he turns around to face me. Only a foot away, his silver eyes are not just stunned, but stunning. And I hate that I still notice it.

I'm certain he recognizes me, even as he stares back into Nix's eyes. Does he see mine instead of the lights? Does he feel me here, in front of him?

His throat bobs and he swallows, chest glistening with water and moonlight.

I can hardly breathe.

Outside the window, I hear the sound of hell being raised, and when I turn, wildfire dances across the horizon.

The air strike. It's happening now.

My chest quakes. If Genesis is under attack and I'm here, miles away from their gates, I'll never make it back before they jump.

But if they still don't know . . .

Before Caelan can make a sound, I leap out the window and disappear into the desert night.

26

FIRE RAINS DOWN FROM THE SKY. HUMAN screams ring out like bells tolling for death. I charge toward the amber horizon with fear coiling its way into my gut.

When I reach the peak of the hill, I realize Genesis is still untouched. But the outposts are not.

The fires stretch on for miles, the desert set ablaze. Nightlings stalk the border, weaving in and out of the flames, searching for fear.

A wall, I realize. To keep the humans from running south.

South where the Legion Guards know the rebellion isn't. *That's* what the marks on the map were—places they ruled out as the location for Genesis.

They want the survivors of the outposts to run for safety

and lead them to Genesis, like ants finding their way home.

In Nix's body, my heart sinks.

I turn north, knowing I will never make it in time on foot. Not as the Legion Guards circle precariously in the dark gloom, watching below. Watching everything.

Nix, come and find me, I whisper to him, and pull back to my own body.

I fall forward at once, dizzy from the severed connection, and crawl all the way to the cave opening before managing to push myself to my feet. One look toward the makeshift city tells me I'm too late. They've already been sending fighters to the outposts, hoping to help. They've already gone to battle.

I throw myself inside Ozias's tent, but it's empty. I trip over layers of colorful rugs, stumbling on the way out, and scan the chaotic new world.

I have to stop this. I have to warn him.

I run through the rows of beige tents, watching people arm themselves and charge into the night. Trusting that the veiling posts will keep their home safe.

But they don't know what I do.

I'm charging down the path, air burning my lungs, when Shura nearly crashes into me.

"Where have you been?" she shouts exasperatedly. "I've been looking everywhere for you. The Residents—"

"I know," I shout back, pushing her to the side. "I don't have time. I need to find Ozias!"

Shura's mouth hangs open, and she shakes her head like she doesn't understand what I'm talking about.

But there's no time. I keep running.

"Ozias!" I call out, looking at anyone and everyone who will make eye contact with me. "Where is Ozias?"

A woman with brown curls and a loose purple shirt points me toward the south of Genesis. "He's about to leave with the First Leaders."

My boots pound into the hardened earth. I'm still yards away, watching as Ozias links arms with the others, ready to teleport.

"It's a trap!" I scream, voice ragged. "The Residents are coming to Genesis!"

The First Leaders hear me, and their arms drop. I nearly collide into Eliza, who grabs my shoulders to help keep me steady.

The storm in Ozias's eyes rages. "What are you talking about? What trap?"

I don't bother catching my breath as the words heave out of me. "I was in the palace—I saw the maps. They're forcing the outposts to flee, blocking the way south, so they have nowhere to hide. They're watching for survivors—following them here."

Eliza's forehead wrinkles. "What do you mean, you were in the palace?"

"There's no time to explain," I say, urgent. "The survivors are going to lead the Residents right to us."

Dayo stiffens. Despite her appearance, she doesn't have the voice of a child. "Our people know better than to come here."

Zahrah and Diego exchange a look, unsure.

"There are Nightlings at the border," I say. "The survivors are too afraid. They'll think Genesis is their only option." I stare at Eliza, and the others. Trying to make them understand. "The

Legion Guards have been eliminating possible locations for who knows how long. They know we're somewhere in the north. It's just a matter of time until the first survivor gets here."

Ichika turns to the desert, clenching the neckline of her tunic. "We—we just sent troops out. Hundreds of them."

Diego's body goes rigid. "We have to leave them behind. We can't risk it."

Ozias clenches his jaw, gazing sharply at the First Leaders. "No one else leaves the camp. Gather the jumpers—leave everything behind, and tell everyone to meet at the southeast veil post *now*."

I back away, preparing to run again.

"Where are you going?" Zahrah snaps. The rest of the First Leaders have already disappeared into the camp to give the final order.

The order to abandon their home.

"I'm going to try to warn the survivors to hide instead of coming here," I say. I can't stop all of them, but maybe I can save a few.

Ozias steps in front of me. "No, you're not." His voice is a crack of thunder. "We need you with Genesis." I hear the warning in his voice. *You owe me an explanation.*

"But—" I start.

"We have already sent some of our strongest fighters to the front," Ozias growls, with a piercing fury in his eyes. "We cannot afford to lose you, too."

I follow his gaze to the thousands of humans still here, being told in one sweeping order by the First Leaders that it's time to go. That their home has been compromised.

Ozias needs unity, not someone unwilling to fall in line. Not now, when the rebellion is in danger.

I swallow the tension knotted in my throat. I know I have no choice.

But stars, it feels like hell.

The crowd is already growing around the nearest veil post. Ozias guides me alongside him like he's afraid I'm still thinking of running. When the people of Genesis gather around us, I feel the weight of thousands of hands wrapping around one another.

A connection.

"Jumpers at the ready!" Ozias's voice booms, and the command is passed like a chant, rolling to the outer part of the herd. "On three . . . two . . . one . . . now!"

The world flashes white, and a burst of lightning envelopes my entire body. *Our* bodies.

We vanish with a colossal bang, and when we reappear in an unfamiliar part of the desert, not even the smoke raised from the far distant fires can be seen above the horizon.

In absolute darkness, we are safe.

But we left so many humans behind. Left them to the fires, and the Nightlings, and the Residents.

As we look around, searching the faces for those who remain, nobody says a word.

27

MOST OF THE HUMANS GET TO WORK CRAFTING new materials and weapons, since so much was left behind to the empty sands. Our single veil post isn't enough to create the sweeping dome I've become accustomed to, but there's nothing anyone can do. Veil posts take a long time to craft, and some of the rebellion's strongest engineers were with the groups that went searching for survivors.

Ettore and his Legion Guards failed to find our camp, but Genesis has taken a hit, in more ways than one.

Ozias is still recovering. Many of the other jumpers passed out after we teleported, unable to bear the weight of so many people without a price.

Some of them still haven't woken up.

Former jumps have always been planned. Carried out in sections. What happened this time was a clusterfuck of epic proportions.

We take to the caves to hide, since trying to sit within the tiny protection of our single veil post hardly gives anyone room to stretch. The veilers take turns hiding what they can, expanding the stretch of the new, barely there dome, but it's tiring work. I help when I can, but I've never done anything like this before. And if I'm being honest, I prefer being on patrol to sitting still.

After my early morning watch, I head back to the caves, squeezing past people tucked against the walls. They sharpen their daggers, spears, and swords. Everyone works. No one rests.

I climb down a narrow tunnel toward a hivelike collection of dens, stacked on three levels. Shura peers over the edge of one of the makeshift rooms. Her pink hair is loose, and she's wearing a woven necklace with colorful beads. It looks like Eliza's work.

I try not to be bitter that Shura has two mothers in Infinity, and I don't even have one.

It's been such a long time since I've seen my family. When's the last time I gave my mom a hug?

I should've hugged her more often. If I could go back, I'd hug her every single day.

"Ozias and the others are looking for you," Shura says softly. "It sounded important."

Ozias could barely sit up after the jump, so the First Leaders took him to the caves for safety. He still hasn't been strong enough to leave.

I nod. "I'll head over now."

Shura swings her legs over the edge of the den and hops down, stopping in front of me. "I know you don't want to, but you should tell them about Caelan. About what he did in the tunnel."

"He has nothing to do with this," I say curtly.

She lowers her voice. "Is that why you went to the Red City? If you're trusting him to help you—"

"You don't know what you're talking about."

"What if this is all a part of his plan? If he's feeding you information, we could be walking into another trap."

"Caelan didn't tell me anything. And we just got *out* of a trap," I argue. "Ettore was the one trying to corner us."

"You know that the Residents like games," Shura warns. "When Gil—when *Caelan* made us believe he was one of us . . . He didn't reveal himself overnight, is all I'm saying."

"I know," I sigh, and clench my fists at my side. "But I'm handling it this time."

Shura twists her mouth, doubtful. "He has a power over you. I don't know why you can't see it."

I snarl at her words before moving past her, winding through the tunnels until I find Ozias perched weakly on the rock bed, head against the wall. The First Leaders surround him.

"I assume you know why we've asked you here, Nami," Ozias says. There's a scratch in his voice: a leathery, tired sound.

"You want to know how I got into the palace." I take a breath and explain how I used Nix to travel across the desert, the same way Kasia used him in the First War. Nix, who still hasn't found his way back to the rebellion.

As far as I know, Daylings don't have any weaknesses, but still. I hope he's okay.

"And what? You just waltzed through the front door?" Vince asks, far too gruff for my liking.

"The back tower, actually," I reply sourly.

Zahrah snorts, grinning, and I'm sure I catch a twinkle of pride in her brown eyes.

"What happened when you got inside?" Dayo asks. "Did anyone see you?"

A flash of Caelan appears in my mind, and the way he looked so unguarded in the water.

I keep that particular memory to myself.

"I slipped past the guards and searched for the war room. There were maps laid out across the table, like they'd just finished a meeting," I explain. "That's when the fires started. I saw the Nightlings, realized what was happening, and hurried back to warn you."

Diego scratches his neck. "After what you did below the arena, I don't doubt you're skilled at getting into places you shouldn't. But these maps . . . Did you see anything else? Anything to suggest a second wave of attacks could be coming?"

"No, nothing like that." I frown. "I did overhear one of the commanders talking about a message, though. It had something to do with a human they're looking for. Someone they want aware."

"You think they meant you?" Dayo asks.

I hesitate. Would Ettore really go through such lengths to find me? All because of a bruised ego? "I'm honestly not sure," I say finally.

"A commander in the palace?" Zahrah's body is rigid. "Was it Alys—short black hair, bite in her voice that makes her sound like a viper?"

I blink. "Yeah. I think so."

Zahrah stares into the room, hard lines forming around her mouth. I'm sure her ax trembles at her back. Dayo presses a hand to her sister's shoulder, whispering something that's probably meant to be soothing.

I'm not sure it works.

Eliza leans in. "They have a history" is all she says.

Diego clears his throat, pulling back the focus. "I wish you'd told us what you were planning. But I'm glad you were able to warn us. You might've saved Genesis single-handedly."

Ozias watches in silence, and a cold shudder runs through me.

"This ability you share with the Dayling," Eliza starts. "Maybe it's something we can use more often. Because if you can get into the palace again, we could—"

Shura interrupts from the doorway. "Tell them, Nami. It's too dangerous not to."

My shoulders tense.

"*Tell* them," she repeats. "I won't watch my family be locked away all over again because that monster likes to pretend he's someone he's not." When I look back at her, her eyes pool with tears. "My mom is still in his tower. So is Theo. My *family*. So either you tell them, or I will."

My breathing stills. I look at the others. "I told you the truth about Gil. But I didn't tell you everything about Caelan." I dig up the hidden pieces of my story and reveal them one by one. I tell them how Gil betrayed me, but Caelan spared me. Twice.

When I finish, the room is quiet for a long time.

Diego is the first to speak. "You mean to tell us that we all left our home because the *Prince of Victory* told you to send us here?"

"No," I shoot back, defensive. "He had nothing to do with the intel or the jump. I found out the details on my own, in the war room, just like I told you."

"Details he very well could have laid out for you," Diego counters.

"We're in War," I argue back. "This isn't his court, and there is no way he would help his brother."

"Are you sure about that?" Shura stares at me. "Because they looked pretty close in the arena."

"I'm not saying he's on our side," I say stiffly. "But helping Ettore is the last thing he wants. And I don't see how Caelan setting me free has anything to do with the rebellion. It's not like I'm confiding our plans to him."

"How do we know that?" Diego asks, and the accusation reverberates through my skull.

Ozias doesn't say anything. He doesn't have to. A hint of triumph flashes in his eyes, as if he found a crack in my integrity.

I'm losing the First Leaders' faith, and he's happy to watch it happen.

"We're not having rendezvous in the tunnels, if that's what you're implying." I stare at the King of Genesis. "I care about humanity, and I would never tell Caelan anything that would put you all in danger."

"That may be true. But you've kept secrets from us." Even though Ozias is recovering, a storm builds behind his eyes. "And in war, secrets are one of the deadliest weapons to have."

My eyes build a storm of their own. I don't think—I react. "If everyone is so worried about secrets, then why don't the people in Genesis know about the Borderlands?"

Diego drops his eyes to the sand. So do Ichika, Vince, and Cameron.

But Zahrah, Dayo, and Eliza look confused.

"What are you talking about?" Eliza asks. She turns to Ozias. "What are the Borderlands?"

I glare at the others, ready to break open their truth if it means saving mine.

But I don't have to.

"The Borderlands is a place outside Ophelia's reach, where the Residents cannot find humans," Ozias explains softly. He looks at me like I've shouted "checkmate" from across the board. Like I took away his choice.

Something tells me I won't know what it cost me until it's too late.

But for now, it's in his best interest to spin this in his favor.

"It's where I lived for a time," Ozias adds.

"What?" Dayo's mouth hangs open. "You—you told us your home was ravaged by Residents."

"It was." Ozias leans back, calculating the hurt in the room. Figuring out how to subdue it. "But my clan joined with three others, to protect Infinity from Ophelia's growing rule."

"You mean to tell us we've been fighting a war for over a thousand lifetimes, and there's been a sanctuary all this time?" Zahrah snarls.

"It's not a sanctuary—it's a place that ferries humans to the Afterlands. To an afterlife beyond these Four Courts, where most of the humans from before the First War fled." Ozias pauses. "*That* is the sanctuary."

"You lied to us." Eliza stares at Diego, and to the others whose eyes are pinned to the floor. "And you all *knew*."

"There are still humans that need saving," Diego argues. "If people knew they could leave, it would risk the rebellion crumbling. And then who would be left to fight Ophelia?"

"I don't know," Eliza growls. "But at least it would be our choice."

"What about the humans who come after? The ones still living?" Ozias asks. "What about *their* choice?"

"We all had to take a turn fighting," Dayo says coolly. "And we've had more than our fair share of being butchered in this world."

Ozias shakes his head. "They won't get their turn. Our army is the last hope humanity has." His gaze drifts around the cavern. "Ophelia is bound to the entrance of Infinity, where the Four Courts and the Capital were built. She may have found a way into the afterlife, but she did not find a way to disconnect herself from the living world."

Dayo narrows her eyes. "What does that mean?"

"It means that for all she cannot travel to the Afterlands, she *can* make sure every new arrival in Infinity is locked away before they even find out about the war. It will not be long before fewer and fewer younglings even make it to the Four Courts." He shuts his eyes like he's bracing for a tremor in the earth. "If we leave, we may be taking the afterlife with us."

Zahrah's expression splinters. "Without younglings, in another hundred lifetimes our numbers will dwindle. Why would you have us fight a war we cannot win?"

"We *can* win," Ozias says, straining to sit up. "By first taking this court, and then by taking control of the entrance to Infinity. We will grow our numbers—train everyone in combat." His eyes flash. "And then we will take the Capital, and the queen with it."

He wants to turn every new human into a soldier.

Even Mei.

That's not what I want for her at all.

Ozias tilts his chin, firm. "I am sorry for the deception, but you must understand how necessary it is, even now. We cannot take down the Residents without unity."

"You should have told us," Dayo says. "You cannot ask people to have faith in you while saving none for them."

"I believe in each of you." Ozias holds up his hands. "That's how I know that as long as we stay together, we will win this war."

The leaders turn to each other, untangling his words. His secrets. His *knowledge*.

My brow twitches. "How do you know so much about Ophelia?"

His face pales, but he keeps his voice even. "We knew each other. When she first came to Infinity." Ozias looks at me, dark gray irises filling with memories of an inescapable past. "I was not the first from this world to shun her, but I was the reason she saw nothing redeemable in humankind."

I'm sure the room tilts.

Ophelia once told me she tried to coexist. I wasn't sure I believed her, but now . . .

"What did you do?" I ask, voice hardly a breath at all.

Ozias leans his head back, nutmeg hair catching the floating, unnatural lights above him. "That," he says with impenetrable strength, "is a story for another time."

But I can see it in his eyes: the *betrayal*. I carry so much of it with me, too.

Did Ozias lie to Ophelia? Did he learn her secrets, and make her feel like coexistence was possible, only to betray her when he realized she was dangerous?

Was she always dangerous?

Ophelia said she put a part of herself in each of her sons. And I know Caelan's greatest fear is that someone he cares about will one day betray him. Was that fear always his own?

Or did his mother pass it on to him?

Something dark and poisonous coils through me, squeezing my organs and bones. The hunch that there is more to this story than I will ever know. That there's more to *her*.

Ozias's gaze drifts over the small crowd. "I can see that the truth disappoints you. Perhaps that's part of the reason I kept it to myself for so long. But we cannot run for the Borderlands. We have to protect Infinity—for ourselves, and for the younglings still to come."

"But we could be *safe*," Eliza says, and it sounds like a plea. "We wouldn't have to fight anymore."

"If not us, then who?" Zahrah asks quietly. She turns her dark eyes to Eliza. "We can't tell the others. This truth—it has to stay with us."

Tears drip down Eliza's face, but she nods solemnly.

I flatten my mouth, staring at Ozias. "You said shared insight was a gift, but you still kept this secret. Because sometimes you can't make people understand what you *know* is the right thing to do. Sometimes you just have to do the right thing yourself." I stand up, dusting sand from my hands. "I'm not going to apologize for having secrets of my own. And I don't care if you don't like the way I get information—I'm just trying to make sure my family survives."

I leave the cave without another word.

I don't sleep that night. I sit at the edge of the cave, gripping both my daggers like I'm afraid they might slip. Ready to protect myself if an enemy appears.

The only problem is that I'm not sure what that looks like now.

I'm not sure if Ozias and the First Leaders are busy deciding whether I'm too great a threat.

So I wait for an attack, watching everyone too carefully, and ignore the cold brush sweeping against my mind. It's incessant tonight—a desperate caress that reminds me of winter.

Caelan wants to talk.

But it's impossible now. I can't trust that my body would be safe in Genesis if I left it unattended. Even if Nix were here to watch over me, it might not be enough.

Until I have a conversation with Ozias, I don't know where I stand.

28

DESPITE MY WORRIES, NO ONE COMES FOR ME. Human or Resident.

Genesis slowly starts to resemble a fraction of its former glory. The rippling dome above the camp has returned, and a scattering of beige tents have begun popping up all over the sand. A generous selection of weapons has been replenished, though they still need a lot of tweaking to perfect the edges and lace them with something capable of hurting the Residents.

Genesis needs more engineers, but it also needs *better* ones. They have casters and veilers—people trained to fight—but their technology is arguably outdated.

Maybe that's something the new world has an advantage on.

The scouting missions have had some success, and in the days that follow, a small number of former troops make their way home.

Families are reunited—people who no longer have to wander this awful world alone.

I can't look at them for long. Not without thinking about Mei, and wondering if one day she'll be the one walking through the camp gates, searching for her long-lost sister.

I don't want her to be a prisoner *or* a soldier.

I just want her to be safe with me.

I sniff, clearing my throat, and poke at the hot coals with my sea-glass dagger.

Zahrah plops down beside me, making a noise of disgust. "Younglings. So emotional."

Several yards away, a husband and wife embrace tightly before sinking to their knees in ugly, heaving sobs.

I hide the sting in my eyes, waving a hand at the smoke as if it's to blame. "Yeah. Totally."

Zahrah grabs one of the rods of skewered meat and holds it over the coals. "I always wonder what the point of this is. Clearly no one is hunting animals in Infinity. They make food using their consciousness." She looks at me, but I just shake my head like I don't understand. "It's *raw*. Why in the stars can't anyone conjure an already-cooked steak, and save us all the trouble of having to start a fire?"

My laugh is loose. Casual. "Isn't there supposed to be a special kind of joy in cooking?"

"I'd find more joy in murdering the animals." She scowls,

catching my raised brow. "Oh, come on, don't look at me like that. Nothing dies in this place. It's a pastime."

"My condolences to anyone who gets on your bad side," I note, just as Zahrah tears a bite of way-too-pink meat with her teeth.

"*You* need to kill something," she suggests. "It will get all that pent-up frustration out of your system."

I stare at the orange embers peeking through the coals, visible even in the morning sunlight. "I guess if you're talking to me again, it means the First Leaders voted to spy on me rather than assassinate me."

She pulls her face back in alarm. "Why would we do that?"

"I kept a secret about Caelan and ratted out Ozias. Isn't that what happens when you betray a king?"

"Oh." She nods slowly. "You mean the beheading. Yeah, we had to reschedule that for after the war." She turns to me, eyes sparkling. "Treasonous as you may be, you're too good a veiler to lose."

"I honestly can't tell if you're joking," I say, even as she howls with laughter.

"Don't worry, Nami. Nobody's out to get you. And we don't stay angry in Genesis—not at each other." She motions over the hills. "We know who our enemy is."

She sounds certain, but she also doesn't know what happened to Gil, and the lengths Ozias went to in order to keep him quiet.

But if reassurance is all she has to offer, I'll take it.

I smother a rogue ember with my boot. "So what's the deal with you and Commander Alys?"

Zahrah's eyes snap to mine, nearly feral. "What did you hear?"

"Only that Eliza said you two had a history."

Zahrah swallows a lump of meat. She points her skewer at me. "You tell anyone this, I will gut you."

I hold up my hands like I'm defenseless.

She relents. "Alys was the first Resident I ever met. Way back at the beginning, when War was still new." Her jaw sets. "She pretended to be my friend, claiming not all Residents were bad. And I fell for it. We even traveled across the desert for a while, hiding out." Zahrah's eyes gleam, lethally sharp. "Then she led me to the Residents, and they tortured me for months. Turns out she was trying to find out if I knew where the surviving humans were hiding. Back then, we weren't exactly a rebellion—more of a small cell. And when she figured out I didn't know anything, she turned on me." Zahrah purses her lips. "Now every time we go into battle, we seek each other out. And every time I plunge my ax into her chest, it's just as satisfying as it was the very first time." She smiles, and tears into another bite of meat.

Is that what I'm supposed to feel for Caelan? Pure, unfiltered hatred and a desire for vengeance?

I thought I hated him. Sometimes I still wonder if maybe I do.

But I can't imagine ever feeling satisfaction if I plunged my daggers into the Prince of Victory's heart. Thinking of it now only fills me with sadness.

I stare at the still-sobbing couple crumpled in the sand. "Did I ever tell you I have a sister?"

She lifts a brow. "In Infinity?"

I shake my head. "She was ten when I died. I don't know how

old she is now." I blink away the tears trying to breach the flood-gates. "Her name is Mei."

"So that's why you look at Dayo the way you do." When I start to object, she wrinkles her nose. "There's a sorrow in your eyes when you see us together. And whenever there's danger, you search for her first. Like you think you need to protect her. But my sister is very old. There are better things to worry about, and weaker people to worry for."

My cheeks darken. "I—I didn't realize I was doing that. I'm sorry."

She shrugs. "As the younger sister, I find it amusing. But as a friend, I think you should stop looking for Mei in Infinity. She isn't here—not yet—and trying to be the sister you were will only hold you back."

"No," I say, adamant. "Caring about Mei makes me stronger."

"Until she is used against you," Zahrah warns. "And then you will break, and what will you have left?"

"Wouldn't you feel the same if something happened to Dayo?"

"Something *has* happened to Dayo. Many times, in fact. But we have been in this afterlife long enough to know that as long as we don't surrender, what's lost can be found. You are still con-vinced that losing someone is the end."

"Because I've seen what Death is doing to humans. I've seen someone's consciousness severed from their body." I bite the inside of my cheek. "And I know Ophelia won't stop."

Ozias knows that too.

Even if he puts her in a cage, what then? It won't be a Resident controlling where humans go when they arrive in Infinity—it will be a warlord.

They will be trained for a fight that will never end.

Someone needs to sever Ophelia's connection to the real world—and then they need to destroy her. It's the only way humans can truly be free.

I just don't know if we'll ever find a way.

I poke the coals again, and Zahrah skewers another piece of meat. Nearby, more humans meet their missing loved ones at the gate. But when the crowd parts, I spot a scout headed toward me with a stranger in tow.

I look at the unfamiliar figure, worn and disheveled and completely exhausted.

The scout nods toward him. "He arrived with the others—says he was from one of the outposts that were raided, before he was held captive by the Prince of War."

"I—I have a message for Nami." The man is quaking. Terrified. "Are you Nami?"

I frown. "Yeah. That's me."

The scout looks apologetic. "We tried to get him to talk, but he insisted on speaking to you directly. Thought I'd better bring him straight here."

I stand, tucking my knife away. "What's the message?"

The man looks at the scout, then at me again, before holding out a shaking palm.

An Exchange.

I hesitate, but take his hand all the same.

Everything fizzles away, and I'm seeing through the stranger's eyes.

My name—*his* name—is Daniel. I've been at the outpost for

years, helping the others make weapons. But I was taken after
the air strike, along with another human—a new survivor, who
stumbled over the border barely conscious.

The world swirls, and I'm standing in front of Prince Ettore,
shaking violently. I've already seen what they've been doing to
the others in the dungeons. The flayed skin and broken bones.

I'm afraid I'm next.

Ettore leans in, studying me like an animal being prepared for
slaughter. "Are you the kind of human who can keep a secret?"

My eyes dart around the room. Another human is still chained
to the wall, blood streaked across his chest, unable to hold up his
head. He's the one who was taken with me—the new one.

"Y-y-yes," I sputter. "I can keep a secret."

Ettore sneers. "I have a very important mission for you." He
takes a step back, staring me down. Legion Guards tighten their
grip around my arms. "And a wonderful punishment for you if
you should fail."

I'm already crying. I can't help it. I've heard rumors about the
Residents, and the dungeons, and the Fire Pit, but I've always
been safe at the outpost. I've always been protected by those who
are stronger than me.

The Prince of War tucks his hands behind him and tilts his
head. "You will find the human called Nami. The one favored
by my pathetic brother. And you will tell her that if she does not
turn herself in to me by midday a week from today, I will cut her
friend to pieces, again and again, and even when he surrenders
his consciousness, I will not stop." Ettore snarls. "Tell her that I
will trade a captive for a captive—her life for his. She's to meet

me at the entrance to the Red City, alone and unarmed, and if she brings that filthy rebellion into this, the deal will be off."

I nod swiftly. "Yes. Yes, I'll tell her."

Ettore leans back. "Good. Now run along. The clock is ticking. And if she isn't here by midday a week from today, you will meet the same fate as your friend decorating my wall."

"But"—I look around, frantic—"how will I know where to find her?"

"She's with the rebellion, of course," Ettore drawls lazily.

"But I don't know where the rebellion is," I say.

Ettore barks a laugh. "Well then, you better hurry. You've got a lot of ground to cover."

The guards release me, and I back away in horror, realizing the impossible task. But before I reach the door, Ettore closes the gap between us and tuts.

"I almost forgot," he says. "You'll need this, too." He claws my face, pressing his fingertips against my skull as he forces an Exchange.

I see the man in chains being tortured, chest sliced open while he screams in pain. I see him cry out, staring up at the ceiling like he's begging for mercy. Begging for help.

And I know that face.

I know that man.

Ahmet.

The world reappears, and I'm back in the desert, yanking my hand away from the stranger—Daniel—abruptly.

Ahmet. Ahmet is in War.

Zahrah stands, studying me with concern.

"What did you see?" she asks carefully.

But I'm too busy staring at the man's bare feet. The raw, ripped-apart way the skin falls to the sides. The sand all over his clothes.

"When did you get that message?" I ask, voice hollow.

His eyes well up. "Almost seven days ago."

I look at the sun, rising above the canyon. There's no time. There's no time.

I run, ignoring Zahrah as she calls after me, her voice becoming an echo in the distance. I stop only when I reach Eliza's tent, where I know Shura will be hiding. She's avoided me since the day she forced me to tell the others about Caelan.

I pull the loose cloth back and storm inside. Shura is sitting in the corner, slowly weaving a new outfit with her mind.

"It's Ahmet," I breathe hurriedly. "There's no time to explain, and the others can't know. If you don't help me now, they're going to torture him—worse than they already have."

She doesn't need the explanation. Not when it comes to her family. "Tell me what you need."

"I'm going to make a deal with Prince Ettore," I say. "And I need you to come with me."

29

I DON'T REMOVE MY VEIL UNTIL I'M STANDING at the edge of the stone path, staring up at the entrance to the Red City. Legion Guards stand along the wall, on the sand, in the watchtowers—more guards than I've ever seen in one place.

When my veil drops, they focus their attention on me. The snap and flutter of the red banners is the only sound between us. And then Ahmet appears in the archway, shirt ripped to shreds, already sweltering in the nearly midday sun.

I made it with seconds to spare, but I refrain from giving the Residents the satisfaction of my terror. I might not have a veil, but I can mask my emotions just fine.

They nudge Ahmet forward, and he must have been kept in

the dark all week because he holds up his restrained hands to shield himself from the blaring sunlight. He doesn't even notice me until he's halfway across the path. A guttural noise chokes out of him, and he mouths my name.

A guard yanks Ahmet's shoulder back, and he nearly stumbles with the desperation to reach me. A second guard tosses a pair of restraints at my feet.

Commander Alys stares from the wall. "Put them on."

I stare back. "Take his off."

The corner of her mouth twitches, until eventually she nods at the guards below. They remove Ahmet's restraints and shove him toward me. I snatch the ones from the ground, but don't move to attach them to my wrists.

"Not until he's safe," I say to the guards, who seem eager for a fight.

Commander Alys nods again, just as Ahmet takes one last glance over his shoulder. When he reaches me, he moves in for an embrace, but I stop him.

Keep walking, I say to his mind. *Shura is waiting in the hills. Don't turn back, no matter what you see or hear.*

His eyes dart to mine, confused. He doesn't know the deal I made, or what his freedom has cost.

But he follows my instructions and steps into the sand. I wait until the sound of him fades—until I'm sure he's safe within Shura's veil—and I snap the restraints onto my wrists.

A tremor tears through my bones immediately, weakening me. Any remnant of the veil I use to silence the thrum of my thoughts is ripped away. Not even my former Resident face would hold now.

The guards step forward, grab my arms with force, and lead me into the heart of the Red City.

I'm handed over to a Resident with sharp cheekbones. She wears a glittering charcoal suit, and her hair is shaved across one side and braided at the other. After I'm dragged up stairwell after stairwell, the realization that we're not headed for the dungeons sends my thoughts spinning.

We stop in front of a room with double doors, where several armed Residents stand watch. My captor turns the handle and shoves me roughly inside.

I blink, trying to process the meticulously made bed, the claw-foot bathtub filled with steaming water, and the sunlight pouring through the glass. Laid out on one of the couches is a dress.

"Clean yourself up and dress appropriately. I will return soon to escort you to Prince Ettore," the Resident says.

I turn around, scowling. "What is this?"

She ignores me and removes the restraints from my wrists with a clunk. When I don't react, she lifts a brow. "Not going to put up a fight?" She clicks her tongue. "It's so much more fun when they do." When she leaves, the door locks into place behind her.

I look at my freed hands, feeling the energy tingling in my palms. Maybe they want me to react; maybe it's all a part of this strange game.

My two new rings glint back at me. The one on my left hand is obsidian black. The one on my right hand is sea-glass red. It would only take me a moment to shape them back into their true forms, but something tells me it's too soon to act.

The Reaper still sits on my left wrist—harmless, but completely redesigned. It's no longer a bracelet meant for a ballroom. It's smooth and sleek and has small marks engraved in the middle.

The Legion Guards in War mark themselves for each human they've made unaware. My black lines are for the humans I've taken back. They're for my *friends*.

And if I manage to get out of here, I'd like to think that someday I'll have more than two marks.

My eyes dart around the modest space, counting the windows and doors, which I'm sure are either guarded or laced with something dangerous. Ettore would never make it this easy. Not for any human, but especially not me.

I need to choose the right moment to escape, or I might not get another chance.

I stare at the bath, and the dress.

Okay. Playing along it is, then.

When the Resident in the suit returns, I've already scrubbed myself clean and changed into the clothes that were left for me. It's strange to wear something I didn't make myself. It feels like a foreign skin, restricting and stiff. It's all *wrong*.

But when I look in the mirror, the clothes look like they fit perfectly.

The bright red material sits high at my neck, morphing into a sheer, metallic fabric along my arms. Sharp cutouts reveal the skin at my sides, until the material swoops back over my hips and spills to the floor in layers. I can see a barely there outline of my legs through the skirts, and scattered all over the mesh are embellished patterns that remind me of flames.

A gown fit for the Court of War.

Nearby, the Resident makes a sound of disgust. "That will not do at all," she hisses, moving toward me and spinning her hands over my hair and face with the grace of a painter.

In the mirror, I watch my nearly black hair weave into a crown of loose braids that spill into waves at my back. A golden cuff appears on the edge of my right ear, shaped like a coiling dragon. Black kohl sweeps above my lashes, forming an exaggerated cat-eye point, and my lips darken until they're the color of blackberries.

Despite the grandness, my face is still very human.

I clench my fists, reminding myself that my daggers are still a thought away.

The Resident steps back, only partially satisfied.

"Shouldn't you have human servants for this kind of thing?" I ask dryly.

Her lips purse. "Prince Ettore would never allow a human to roam his palace in such a fashion. It would be a grave offense to our kind."

"And yet you're here, dressing a human up like a doll," I remark.

Her expression sours even more, suggesting that perhaps *I'm* an offense too.

She prods me toward the door, leading me through the

palace until we arrive at an exceptionally large dining hall. A table stretches across the floor, mostly bare except for the far end, which hosts a varied selection of food and wine. At the head of the table sits the only Resident in the room.

Prince Ettore.

He flashes his teeth when I'm pushed toward him, and the doors close behind me.

It's just the two of us.

"It seems red suits you," he says with a low snarl. He motions to the chair beside him. "Join me."

I stare back. "I would rather dip my legs in pig grease and stick them in a tank full of starving piranhas."

He chuckles, dangerously. "That can be arranged."

Again I count the windows and doors, surveying the room. There are no guards around. No one to keep me from stabbing Ettore in the heart.

Unless they're veiling themselves.

The thought makes me stiffen. Earlier, it didn't occur to me that someone might have been hiding in my room, watching to make sure I didn't escape. And now, picturing how many guards could've been under a veil . . .

I took a bath. I put on this dress. I—

"We're alone, if that's what you're wondering," Ettore says, bored. "I don't make it a habit of requiring guards to protect me. And I certainly see no threat to require anyone's concern."

"You have no idea what I can do," I spit. Maybe it's a mistake to be so bold, but I have no intention of allowing anyone to think I'm weak ever again.

"Yes. I saw your annoying display at the Fire Pit." His golden eyes look ready to ensnare the world. "In my experience, if someone refuses to burn, you only need to try a bigger fire."

My cheeks heat.

He leans back in his chair, lazily waving a slender hand over the food. "Now, you can either sit down, or I'll force you to sit down. Either way, we have matters to discuss."

And because I hate the thought of him making my body do anything without my control, I walk across the dining hall and take a seat. *Two* seats away from him.

He's still grinning wildly. "We are going to have so much fun together." And then he glances toward the doors, brows rising with glee. "Ah. There you are. Please, have a drink. I believe you already know my guest."

I know he's there. I can feel the cold, stirring through the room. But I find his silver eyes anyway.

Prince Caelan stands in the doorway, jaw set, with his crown of branches fixed on his head. Regal and breathtaking as I remember, he scans the room, gaze landing on his brother.

And he doesn't bother to look at me at all.

30

CAELAN TAKES A SEAT BESIDE ETTORE, ACROSS from me. His white tunic gleams with silver detailing, but his furs are gone, and the top buttons of his shirt are undone.

Not as formal as he usually appears outside his own court, but that might have something to do with being in War.

Caelan pours a glass of wine, still not looking at me, and sips.

Ettore's hands are folded beneath his chin. He's watching his brother the way a snake watches a mouse, waiting to strike. Waiting for the mouse to realize it's been cornered. Like he doesn't just enjoy the kill—he wants to savor it.

But Caelan gives no reaction at all.

"I hear you've been sending letters to our brother in his

underwater palace," Ettore muses. "Planning a trip to Famine?"

There are no clocks in Infinity, but my heart beats like a second hand that's been wound too tight.

"I thought your spies would've passed that information along weeks ago." Caelan peers at his brother from over his glass. "They must be getting slow."

Ettore's lips curl. "I'm sure Damon wouldn't blame you for canceling, considering our most . . . *recent* changes."

Caelan sets his wine on the table and leans back, bored. "Whatever you're up to in War is not my concern. I'm hardly going to cancel an official appointment just because you've started a few fires."

Ettore is undeterred. "Aren't you going to greet our guest?"

"This isn't my court," Caelan says. "I have no guests here."

Ettore's mouth thins. Clearly, his goading isn't working. He lifts a silver knife from beside his plate, spinning it along his fingers, watching his brother. Calculating.

Without any warning, my hand is yanked from my lap and my palm slammed against the table, rattling dishes of food. My empty cup topples over, rolls across the surface, and clatters to the floor.

I try to pull my hand back, but I can't. It's stuck to the table, controlled by Ettore.

I look sharply between Ettore and Caelan, who hasn't so much as blinked.

Ettore hovers his knife over my hand, taunting. "I suppose you wouldn't mind if I took one of her fingers, then? She did cause quite a stir in the Fire Pit, and cost my court an afternoon of well-earned fun."

My throat knots. I strain beneath his strength, trying to use my own consciousness to pull myself away. I let out a gasp, heat rising through my face, but my hand won't budge.

Caelan sighs, tired. "Take them all if you must. Doesn't make a bit of difference to me." He picks up his knife and fork and digs into his meal, chewing quietly.

Ettore watches him, anger burning in his stare. And then he laughs. His knife drops to the table, and the hold over my hand subsides. I clutch my fist against my chest protectively and scowl.

"I suppose I'll leave her in one piece a little while longer," Ettore says, looking at me with a dark smile. "We still have a ball to go to. Your first *true* Resident party." He turns back to Caelan. "You are, of course, most welcome too, brother."

Caelan cuts into another piece of meat, silverware clinking delicately against his plate. "After you attended so many of our parties in Victory, I'm sure it would be rude not to go."

Ettore holds up his wine glass and grins. "Wonderful," he says, and drinks. "I'll see you both later tonight."

He slides his chair back, standing, and Caelan sets his knife and fork down.

"Where are you going?" Caelan's voice is vaguely impatient, but not emotional. Certainly not angry.

Ettore is already halfway out the door when he says over his shoulder, "Giving you two some time to get reacquainted."

The silence after he leaves hits like the devastation after a tsunami. Neither of us moves an inch.

And then Caelan picks up his utensils and continues his meal.

The bite in my voice is razor sharp. "Did you get a chance to visit Ahmet while he was here?"

Caelan continues chewing, eyes pinned to his plate. "He left Victory by his own choosing. He's Ettore's problem now."

"No. He's safe. With Shura." I watch Caelan's jaw tighten for a brief moment. "Why do you think *I'm* here?"

"If you traded your freedom for his, you've only got yourself to blame. Just be grateful you aren't in the dungeons yet."

"Grateful?" I scoff. "You should be grateful I didn't shred you to pieces the last time I saw you."

His brows knot, but he doesn't speak.

I place my hand beside my plate. It wouldn't take long to grab my dinner knife, flip the table, and—

"Don't." Caelan's voice is low. *Lethal.*

My thumb grazes the surface of the table, catching his attention. He studies the remodeled Reaper, and the two black lines in the metal. Is he wondering what they mean?

If Ahmet had been in Genesis longer, maybe I could've upgraded more than just the Reaper's appearance. Maybe we could've made a new *weapon.*

Genesis will gain a lot by having him on their side. He's a talented engineer. He built a Resident cage once—one that *worked.*

"I heard a story about your mother," I say, pulling my hand into my lap. Caelan still won't look me in the eyes. "It turns out she may have been friends with a human in Infinity, once upon a time."

He picks up his glass, swirling the contents absentmindedly. "Does that surprise you?"

"Yes," I say without hesitation.

The liquid in his glass stills. "You still think we're the monsters?"

I glance toward the balcony, where the view overlooks the Red City. If the windows were open, I have no doubt I'd be able to hear screams coming from the Fire Pit.

Except humans have committed monstrous acts over the years, too. Otherwise there would never have been things like murder, or atomic bombs, or slavery.

Residents may be monsters—but we are the monsters who created them.

I still haven't figured out who deserves more blame, but maybe it doesn't matter.

"I don't know how anyone could watch an innocent person be burned alive and not feel a responsibility to stop it." I turn back to Caelan. "Sometimes silence is the most monstrous act of all."

He looks at me then, silver irises studying my face. When his lips part, I grip the edge of my chair, unprepared for whatever he's going to say. Unprepared for how those eyes make me feel.

Gil doesn't exist in his face. But the way he watches me . . .

"Silence comes in many shades," Caelan says. "If you ever bothered listening to anyone outside of your own mind, you might know that." His gaze doesn't break. "You always did think you knew best. Even at the Colony."

"Back then I was still naive enough to think you were redeemable."

"It seems we both made that mistake." Caelan rests against his chair, pressing his fingers together. "But my brother is trying to rub salt in a wound that doesn't exist. I don't care that you betrayed me—I expected it."

"That's why you think I'm here? So that your brother can gloat about how things in Victory didn't go your way?"

"No," Caelan says stiffly. "I think you're here because my brother is going to hurt you, and enjoy it." The skin on my arms prickles. "And because you're the only person in the Four Courts who knows exactly what happened in the throne room."

I can't tell if he's bluffing or not. "You mean the part where your mother said Victory no longer served a purpose? Or the part where you were finally going to get your seat in the Capital?"

Caelan blinks, visibly rattled. "Is that true?"

Smug satisfaction roils through me. "Maybe. Would it bother you to know you lost more than you thought that night?"

"You have no idea what I lost," he says darkly.

"But you know *exactly* what I lost," I bite back, chest leaning forward.

Caelan runs a hand through his snow-white hair, resting his eyes for a moment. When he opens them again, he wears a look of pure indifference. "You should eat something while you have a chance. You never know what might be your last meal."

Caelan finishes his dinner in silence.

I don't touch so much as a bite.

The main ballroom is enormous. Black marble covers every inch of the floor, and an extravagant two-story balcony wraps around the room like a horseshoe. Dark archways are visible beyond the stone railing: doorways to all the hidden corners of this palace.

The stone walls make the room feel almost cavelike, lit only by the firelight dotted around the wide space.

At the very back of the room is a sweeping double staircase leading to a raised floor. A chandelier made of tusks and bone hangs from the ceiling, and below it sits a throne of violent orange flames.

Residents are everywhere, dressed mostly in shades of red, black, and gold. If Victory's style was full of fairy-tale artistry, here the outfits are sharp, modern, and haunting. Card tables line the edges of the room. Tumblers and goblets overflow with dark red wine. And below the floor, even above the laughter and phantom music, I hear screaming.

I follow Prince Ettore like a lamb being dragged into the lion's den.

We climb the stairs as the Residents gawk with dark amusement, and Ettore motions to his throne. Its decadent spikes burn gold and amber, but the red cushion looks safe enough.

"Why don't you take a seat?" Ettore's eyes flash. "You might actually like it."

I lift my chin, defiant. "You hate the idea of humans wandering around a Resident court. What's the point of bringing me here?"

He shrugs, slipping into his chair, long limbs draping over the sides. "I enjoy torturing people."

"This is hardly torture."

His mouth curls. "Maybe not for you."

I follow his gaze to one of the balconies, where Prince Caelan is standing in all his white finery. Hands on the railing, he watches the room below.

After our earlier meal—if you can even call it that—a guard

arrived to take me back to my room. Caelan hasn't made an effort to talk to me since. He won't even look at me.

It shouldn't bother me, but it does.

A Resident with blue eyes that sparkle even from across the room approaches him, curtsying low before placing a hand on his arm. He leans in and whispers in her ear, and she giggles against his chest.

I don't realize how intensely I've been staring until the vibrations rush through my hands. The building anger that I'm finding harder and harder to control.

Ettore notices. "Well, now, that *is* interesting." Before I can ask what, he flicks his fingers, shooing me down the stairs. "Go on. Enjoy the party." I hear the faint threat in his voice. *While it lasts.*

I run a thumb over my sea-glass ring before tucking my hands against my skirts. It may not be much of a comfort to know I have weapons, but it's something.

Moving across the room, I do my usual checks for exits. I count the Legion Guards stalking the floors above, and notice that Caelan is no longer standing at the balcony. His friend seems to have disappeared too.

Residents move away from me like I'm a poison. They hiss and snarl and curse; it's enough to make me want to disappear. But I need to save that particular trick for when I've found a way out of this castle. If Ettore knew quite how strong my veils were, he might never have removed the restraints.

The music changes to a hypnotic waltz, like something from an old ghost movie. I turn around, and I'm eyeing the guards at the south door when Ettore appears in front of me.

At least I think it's Ettore. His deep red tunic is the same, and his black hair still resembles wildfire. But his crown is gone, replaced by a devilish mask complete with otherworldly horns.

"What are you supposed to—" I start, but Ettore holds up a hand, palm filled with glittering red dust, and blows.

The substance hits me everywhere. I cough—inhale—and by then it's too late.

The music grows louder, and the room expands at the edges, widening like I'm being swallowed by a black hole. Residents circle me, laughing behind their own masks.

Only theirs *move.*

Big snarling teeth, horrible blackened eyes—some of the masks scream back at me. I cover my ears, protecting myself from the shrill sounds, but they only get louder the more I fight.

I stumble away, dizzy, hands reaching for a way to brace myself. Everyone backs away, laughing and screaming and dancing like we're trapped on a merry-go-round, and the nausea hits me hard.

Balancing myself against a stone pillar, I try to recover my wits, but there are so many monsters in the room. So many people with morphed, demonic faces.

Ettore reappears, his devil horns stretching like curved talons, and shadows ripple from his mask. The smoke hits my nostrils, and my chest quakes.

Fear. So much fear.

I press my fingers to my own face like I'm trying to rip it out of me, but I can't. There's too much of it. It's all over me, and inside me—fear is being pumped from my heart, pulsing through my veins.

And then I hear Mei call out to me.

"Nami!"

The room tilts, and I trip over my own feet, colliding against marble. I drag myself across the floor, tears building in my eyes.

"*Mei!*" I scream. Because she's here, in this room, with the Residents. I can feel it.

She calls my name again, clear and unmistakable, even with all the laughter roaring around me. I crawl and crawl, cheeks stained with salt, but I don't quit. I will protect my sister, no matter what.

On my hands and knees, I make my way up the stairs, following the sound of Mei calling my name. When I reach the foot of the throne, I blink.

Mei's voice disappears.

And when my eyes trail up the long legs of the person in front of me, I find Prince Ettore, sitting on his throne of flames, golden eyes staring back at me. A wicked grin spreads across his face.

"Less than an hour, and you're already bending a knee," he says. "Are you this subservient to all your princes, I wonder?"

The sound of Residents howling with laughter makes my stomach shrivel. I stand, not quite fully recovered, and gaze around the room for an exit. An opening. Anything to get me to a place where I can *breathe.*

I hurry down the stairs and past the card tables, toward one of the alcoves near the side of the room. Pressing my head to the stone pillar, I take an awful, ragged breath and paw angrily at my damp face.

Of all the ways to be so ridiculously gullible . . .

I ball my fists, hard enough for my fingernails to cut into my palms. When I look up, Legion Guards pace beyond the alcove, attention fixed on the doorways. Not on me.

If I threw a veil around myself, maybe it would be enough. Maybe waiting for the right moment is absurd—maybe I have to go *now*.

I barely make it half a step when I realize Caelan is standing around the corner. His arms are folded, and his back is pressed against the stone.

"What do you want?" I mutter, swaying and still dangerously close to retching.

"Don't bother trying to run. The guards see and hear more than you think they do," he says icily.

I turn away, stepping into the torchlit outer corridor that wraps around the ballroom. Caelan follows.

"I'm not interested in anything you have to say," I growl.

His footsteps come to a halt. "I'm not here to *talk*, Nami."

I spin, angry. "Then why are you following me?" Because it feels like he's everywhere, all the time. In War, in the tunnel, in my head . . . and now in this terrifying ballroom, too.

He helped me, more than once. And now we're both here, in his brother's court, and I still can't figure out what's waiting for me at the end of his maze. Because that's what this is about, isn't it?

It's a game. It's always been a game.

The words I say next taste like bile. "Why are you still pretending to be Gil?"

Caelan moves toward me, swift and unflinching, face hovering inches from my own. "Is that what you think this is?"

I almost forget to breathe. "If I hadn't been in the arena that day, would you have let your brother throw Shura into the Fire Pit?"

I wait for him to respond—to tell me I'm wrong—but he doesn't.

"I know you're trying to make a deal with Ettore. To merge the Four Courts and get rid of Victory for good." I look around the room, shaking my head. "You'd hand over your court to him—let it become *this*—all for a seat in the Capital?"

"You have no idea what it's taken to get here. What still has to be done to—" He clenches his jaw. "The Capital is where I belong. I want to help our people move forward instead of ruling over a dying court."

"You and I both know you'll never move forward. As long as Ophelia is tethered to the human world, you'll never leave your cage."

He straightens, face blanching.

A round of sharp claps sound nearby, and Ettore approaches, hands spread wide. "Hiding already, are we?" Snickering, he motions toward the ballroom floor. "You'd better hurry, or you'll miss the next waltz."

I follow his gaze to the ballroom, where the Residents have moved to the outskirts of the room. They're trying to make space. Space for me.

I already feel a hollow ache growing in my throat.

Caelan blinks back, eerily calm, and says to Ettore, "Things must have changed here if you have to beg a human to be your dance partner. Is there truly no one else left who can stand being near you?"

Ettore grins. "Oh, I have no intention of dancing with your little pet." He swipes a hand toward me, and I lose all control of my body. My feet pivot against my will, moving me closer to Caelan, and one of my hands presses against his shoulder.

"Stop it," I hiss, fighting to pull away. "Let me go."

Caelan frowns, glaring at Ettore. "I am not your puppet, brother. You have an entire court to play your games with. Kindly leave me out of it."

But Ettore only laughs, dancing his fingers through the air as my feet begin to three-step without my consent. I'm stumbling and clambering, and I don't know if Caelan is sick of watching the spectacle or tired of being so closely tied to it, but he takes my other hand, pulls me close, and obliges me with a dance I never wanted in the first place.

Laughter ripples around us. Caelan's hand tenses against the fabric of my dress.

I'm still trying to rip away from Ettore's hold, but it's as if my body isn't my own.

Caelan merely sets his jaw, staring out at the room with a look of pure disgust. Not for the Residents, but for me. For having to be this close, holding my hand, spinning around the room like a couple of people who . . .

Fire burns inside me. I won't be a part of this game. I won't let them *win*.

I fill with rage and anger and fight. I search for the threads of Ettore's consciousness that are wound around me like ropes, and I sever them.

The kickback is a punch in the chest, and a jolt of raw energy bursts out of my body. With Caelan touching me, he feels it too, and he releases me with a sharp breath like I've zapped him.

The crowd falls into hushed voices. Ettore watches like a vampire in the shadows.

I look at my hands, and at Caelan. I broke the connection. Fought back.

And everyone in this court saw me do it.

"Take her to her room," Prince Ettore tells the guards. When I'm herded past him, he adds, just to me, "I look forward to tomorrow."

31

THE STARS BLINK ABOVE THE RED CITY, AND THE sickening wails of humans echo below. Residents weave through the main street and around the cliffside houses. Thousands of them. Thousands of beings who want humans destroyed.

But Genesis has thousands of humans training to fight back. What if one day they really do take over this city?

What if one day they take over this whole court?

After everything I've seen the Residents do, I want to be here when it happens. I want to watch the granite walls fall, and this palace turn to rubble. I want to watch an earthquake split this bloodstained mountain in two. I want to watch all the humans below the ground be liberated.

There's so much suffering in this desert. I want it to *end*.

Maybe letting Genesis conquer the Four Courts is the only way to make that happen. I came here to find my friends, but after that?

I don't know what my plans were. I guess I just wanted to make sure as many humans got to safety as possible. And I wanted to stick around long enough to make sure my parents and Mei could find their way to safety too.

But how much use can I be to anyone from a dungeon?

If I can't escape, maybe someday the rebellion will come to break my chains. And if that day ever comes, I wonder if I'll be ready to fight beside them when they finally take on the Capital.

There's no point hiding from what has to be done. Genesis needs to find Ophelia. They need to lock her away where she can't hurt anyone ever again.

I wanted to protect people, and lead them to the Borderlands. But what happens if the others can't take control of Infinity's gates? Who will fight with Genesis when their numbers begin to shrink?

Saving people always seemed like the right thing to do. But I'm not so sure it's as simple as that anymore.

I think we *have* to fight. All of us.

Even Mei, my mind nudges, and my face crumples at the thought.

No. Not my sister. I will fight in her place twice as hard if I have to, but I won't let her suffer. The thought of her fighting in this war, vulnerable and scared, scrambles my insides. What if Ophelia used her against me, the way Ettore used Ahmet against me?

It's the only thing in Infinity that would truly break me.

Mei will never know about the path through the stars. She'll come to Infinity through the front door, just like everyone else, and find a lie waiting for her.

Genesis needs to take control of the entrance to Infinity before that happens. I need to get a message to her, before she's taken by Residents or recruited into Ozias's army.

I need to tell her to run.

If that means I need to get out of this palace, and stay with Genesis until they conquer this court and the next, then that's what I'll do. I will make sure I'm there when Mei arrives in Infinity, so I can tell her about the map in the stars.

And when it's all over, I'll join her in the Afterlands, my mind sighs, counting the twinkling lights.

Kasia said she'd wait, and I believe her. Knowing there's somewhere safe to go to . . . somewhere away from all of this, where Kasia could keep Mei safe . . .

I will hold on to the hope.

Leaning my head against the edge of the window, I close my eyes, remembering the days when fighting over clothes or the TV or the hairdryer was the only thing I worried about.

I wonder if Mei misses me as much as I miss her.

In the middle of the night, something brushes against the walls of my mind like the first pang of a winter's chill. Cold, urgent, and unwavering.

Someone who wants to be invited in.

I scrape my finger against the velvet armchair. I've been locked in this guest room for hours, waiting for whatever is coming next. Hoping for a chance to escape.

And now Caelan wants to talk.

I remember what Ophelia told me back when I still believed I could build a bridge. If I had let her into my mind, she could've seen everything: every plan, every thought, every move. I would've given her permission to root through the very core of me. Maybe even the key to *controlling* me.

But if I've been allowed into her mind more than once, does that mean I hold the key to Ophelia?

Venturing back to that particular void would require more bravery than I have. I hurt Tavi and Artemis, but Ophelia is stronger than both of them. Maybe stronger than all of us.

If I ever tried to go back into her mind, I'm not sure she'd let me leave.

The cold chill presses against my thoughts again. Not a queen, but a prince.

He's desperate.

I lean back in the armchair, mouth pinched with irritation. Caelan's only concern is protecting his own plans. He doesn't care about what happens to me. Not really. He just wants the truth about the throne room buried in the darkness where his brother can never find it.

I have no intention of telling Ettore what I know, but giving Caelan reassurance?

I owe him nothing. Not even peace.

So I ignore the request, veiling my thoughts like I'm not here at all, and stare at the ceiling in silence.

And I guess when you ask for silence, silence is what follows.

The Resident with sharp cheekbones brings a new outfit to my room. Another red design, with an angled cutout above the chest and a fitted bodice that flares out just past my hips. The back half of the skirt trails behind me like a wide cape, and the front half doesn't exist at all; instead, my legs are covered by a pair of matching trousers.

There are dark, heavy circles under my eyes, but the Resident doesn't bother to hide those, even as she scrapes my hair back into a high ponytail and makes the sallowness in my face stand out even more.

I don't bother hiding my tiredness either. If the Residents want to think I'm weak, that's their mistake.

We're walking back through the palace, guards in tow, when I hear Prince Ettore's roar ricochet through the main foyer.

Pausing on the upper balcony, I look down at the enraged prince, his burgundy tunic split open and a crumpled letter in his hand. A Legion Guard is still bent at the waist in front of him.

"What do you mean, he *left*?" Ettore demands, words seething with anger.

"Apologies, Your Highness," the guard says. "Prince Caelan said he had business in Famine, and we did not think it was wise to stand in the way of a court ruler."

Caelan . . .

He couldn't have . . .

He couldn't have *gone*.

My throat dries up, too stunned to form words. After all this time, it's not like I still believed some part of him actually felt anything for me. I knew every move he made must've been a part of some bigger plan. Even when he was helping me, I was certain he had ulterior motives.

But knowing all that . . . why do I still feel such an aching bruise over my chest?

I should be glad. At least this way I don't have to see his face again. Ettore can stop toying with his brother, and we can speed up the inevitable.

I was never going to avoid a dungeon forever. But the same thought replays in my mind, over and over again.

He knew I was here, in War. And he left me alone with the brother he hates most.

Ettore sets the letter aflame and sends the ashes scattering across the floor. "Get out," he hisses, and his guard hurries out of sight, still bent at the waist.

As if he senses an audience watching from the height of the room, his gaze rises to me.

"It's about time you and I had a chat," he says with pure, unfiltered contempt.

32

MEI STEPS INTO THE ROOM OF MIRRORS, AND the world spins.

"What are you doing here?" I ask in horror. "Get out. *Run!*"

Mei twists her mouth. "But you asked me to come. You wanted me here."

"No," I say. "That's not true."

"You said you missed me."

No, no, no. It can't be too late. Not for Mei.

My head swirls with anguish. "Mei, listen to me. Infinity isn't safe. They want humans *destroyed*. If you don't hurry—"

Mei tilts her head, the innocence in her eyes slowly vanishing. "*You* are the one who isn't safe, Nami."

A knife appears in Mei's hand. I don't even feel the first cut when she stabs me; I'm too busy wondering if I'm the one who brought her here.

And then the pain reaches me, like being submerged in icy water, and I scream as she stabs me again, and again, and again. . . .

"Tell me the truth," the darkness says. "I can make this stop. I can give you peace."

I spit blood. "Liar."

Ettore grins. All I remember before the pain starts again is the flash of white teeth.

Caelan steps into the mirrored room. I've been here before. Where have I seen these walls?

He paces, white furs trailing behind him. Hands hidden from my sight.

"What do you want?" I hiss.

Caelan stares at me through the mirrors, silver eyes multiplying by the hundreds. "What happened that night, in the throne room?"

I don't know why my instinct is to protect my words, at all costs. It's like a voice deep down, shrieking at me to answer any question but *that* one. "You are my enemy. You've always been my enemy."

The Prince of Victory turns to look at me. "Am I? Because the way you watched me in the ballroom . . ." He tilts his eyes, lips curling. "Jealousy is not a good color on you."

"I hate you," I say, and scream it in my heart for good measure.

He blinks. "Interesting. Very interesting."

When his sword appears, it isn't a surprise. I've been expecting it. But when I reach for my own knives, my fingers scratch at an empty belt.

My weapons . . . they're gone.

I frown, just as he plunges his sword into my chest.

Caelan doesn't stop laughing, even when the world goes dark.

"This can all end now," the darkness purrs. "Just tell me how you escaped. Tell me who helped you."

I drift in and out of consciousness.

Between the waves of pain, I manage to clench my teeth and snarl.

That deep, lethal chuckle pounds in my ears. "So be it."

And just like that, the nightmares return.

I count the mirrors, each of them reflecting my own vacant expression.

The face of a puppet, I muse.

And then I'm surrounded. Annika. Shura. Ahmet. Theo. Kasia. Zahrah. And every other friend I've made in Infinity. Everyone who matters to me.

They don't ask questions. They just take turns plunging the same knife into my chest, again and again. And their words become a chant, filling my head, heightening my pain.

"You're the reason we were captured."

"It's your fault we have to hide."

"Your lies ruined us."

"You left us behind."

I don't know what eats me up first—the guilt, or the pain.

I peel my bruised eyelids apart. The sliver of light shining beneath the door makes me hiss. Everything else is covered in shadow.

I tug at my chains, arms outstretched against the stone wall. It reeks of stale air here. Of something kept below the earth for far too long.

Pulling the chains, I wince hard. Something is wrong with my bones. Something is wrong with *me*.

I look down, and blood is spilling from my chest.

But that light under the door catches my eye again. Quiet, unmoving light.

I focus every little bit of energy I have left on my chains, and crack them apart. Stumbling to the floor, I hit my knees hard, biting my lower lip to keep from crying out.

But it's still quiet.

And that light . . .

I crawl, dragging myself to the door on my hands and knees. When I turn the handle, it gives way. I look around the corner and find a long, empty hallway. Only a single torch hangs in front of me.

Standing, I press a hand to my bleeding chest.

Just focus, I tell myself. *You can heal this later. But right now you need to run.*

The palace is eerily calm. Something must be distracting the Residents, because I don't see any Legion Guards, even as I follow the hall to a rickety stairway that leads to a grate. I clutch my fingers around the metal and tug. It doesn't budge.

I shut my eyes tight. *Please. Please let me through.*

I tug again, and the grate tears from the wall like twigs being snapped. Thanking the stars, I scramble into the small hole, and crawl for hours through shallow water and dungeon rot.

A rush of fresh air spills in from the opening ahead, and when I tumble out of the hole, I find myself at the side of the city wall.

My bare feet press against the sand. It's still warm from the scorching afternoon, even though the desert is blanketed with nightfall. Every step I take feels like walking on broken glass, but I push through it. I have to.

I know Genesis probably made another jump. I doubt they'd have stayed in the same place after I turned myself in to Ettore. But if there's a chance they're still there, waiting for me to come back . . .

I run, and no Legion Guard follows me.

I'm not sure how many miles it's been, or how many hours have passed. Tears are flying from my eyes, and when I wipe them, I know I'm just smearing around the blood and soot from my hands. Every part of me aches, and my bones feel like they've been snapped in so many places I'm not sure how I'm standing.

But I don't stop running, just like the night I fled the Court of Victory. The night I left Caelan . . .

My throat burns: a reminder that this isn't the time for reminiscing. I have to get to Genesis. I have to find the others.

When the sight of the rebellion comes into view, I let out an ugly sob. Beige tents flutter in the moonlight. A slumbering world, waiting for me.

I walk down the center of Genesis, but no one comes to greet me. Everyone is sleeping, everyone is . . .

I frown. Something is wrong.

I concentrate on the strange silence, my fingers twitching at my sides, primed for a fight. Because the humans in Genesis would never leave the city of tents so quiet.

I turn around, and Prince Ettore stands in front of me, burgundy tunic nearly black.

"Did you really think it would be that simple?" he asks, smile as cruel as his court.

I don't care if I don't have any weapons—I charge for him with my bare hands.

And then I jolt awake, screaming, eyes flying open, and find myself still chained in the room of mirrors. The strange cell Ettore is keeping me in, torturing me with distortions of my fears and memories.

I hear the guards approaching, getting ready for another round.

Even though I want to, I don't allow myself to cry.

33

I'M LEFT ALONE IN THE DARK FOR MORE HOURS than I can possibly count. There's no light. No sound. Not even so much as a whisper from the cracks in the walls.

It's a different kind of torture.

It makes sense War would adapt their techniques beyond merely physical pain. Famine is known for mentally breaking humans, but Ettore wants to combine the courts. What better way than rendering one of them pointless?

If War can do the job of two courts, and Caelan hands Victory over . . .

Well, all that leaves is Death.

My chest constricts, and fear solidifies around me. Even with all the unfinished business I have when it comes to locating my friends, the idea of Mei finding this afterlife waiting for her scares me the most.

Because the more I think about it, the more I know Mei won't stand a chance. Not ever.

The humans still alive have no idea what Ophelia has done. They'll come to Infinity thinking they've arrived in paradise. And not even the illusion of Victory will be waiting for them.

What if Ettore finds a way to unite the Four Courts? What will that look like for humans?

And what if Death finds a way to destroy us for good? Will Mei ever get the chance to open her eyes in Infinity at all, or is darkness the only thing waiting for her?

Without a warning, the humans will come here unprepared.

Without a warning, Mei will never unite with Kasia. She'll never be safe.

I can't protect her if she doesn't know what's coming.

My heart is cracking in so many places. The blood drains from it—drains from me.

I'm not strong enough for this, a small voice inside me whispers.

I bite the inside of my cheeks, jolting my consciousness back to life.

This is what War is meant to do, I tell myself. *It's meant to break you. But you need to be stronger than this. You need to be stronger for Mei.*

Even though the darkness is just one more kind of torture, I find a way to embrace it. The harrowing silence spins the wheels in my mind, helping to steady my thoughts. I devise a plan. A way *out.*

This is just a cage. And I will not let a cage break me.

When the Legion Guards return, I focus on the thrum of energy instead of the pain. I search for flaws, like I did in the Labyrinth, and study each torture session for the difference between *awake* and *asleep*.

Eventually, I find the weakness in my own chains, too.

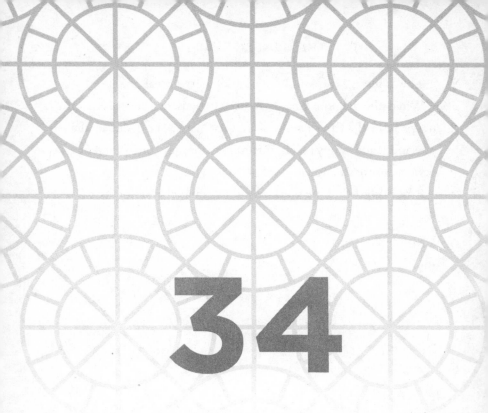

34

MY EYES ARE CLOSED, BUT I HEAR THE LEGION Guard approaching. His footsteps crack against the stone floor like a slow, dying heartbeat. The anticipation is meant to be part of the torment.

But today I have other plans.

I tug my veil over my thoughts, stilling myself like I'm unconscious. He steps into the room, stopping several inches in front of me.

"Wake up, human," he sings, throwing his knuckles against my stomach.

My body absorbs the hit, barely moving. The restraints are still shackled to my wrists, holding me up with chains. The restraints meant to hinder my consciousness, and my power.

But Infinity is a creation. Everything made can be unmade.

And I'm learning more every day.

The Resident grabs my chin, knocking my skull against the mirrored wall. "It's not fun if you sleep through our games."

"No," I say from behind him, and he whirls, still holding the face of my illusion. A trick Tavi was kind enough to show me. "But you can have fun sleeping in mine." I become mist, pull all the air out of his thoughts, and shut the door to his mental walls behind me.

The guard falls to his knees, clawing at his throat, suffocating. I walk up to him, grab his hand, and pull his gauntlet free.

The key to every door in this dungeon.

And then I step into the light and lock my cell, just as he passes out on the stones.

My veil surrounds me now. I move through the castle quickly, knowing my little stunt won't last forever. Eventually, the guard will wake up, and he'll fix the mess I made of his mind. He'll alert the others, and they'll be on the lookout for me—and I don't know if my veil will be enough to hide me.

I'm not fully healed, and too exhausted to use the bulk of my consciousness. Especially after using so much of it to break free of the restraints. But I concentrate on getting to open air. If I can make it over the walls of the Red City, I might have a chance at making it home.

The first room I find with an open window is good enough. I slip over the ledge and climb down the outer palace wall until my feet find soft earth. Surveying my surroundings and the strange desert garden, I realize I'm in the south courtyard.

I'm stepping carefully over the peculiar paving stones, searching for a path to the city wall, when I hear that horrible, blood-curdling laugh.

"You are certainly a resourceful one," Prince Ettore says from behind me.

I spin, already pressing my thumbs against my rings. Pixels break apart instantly, and my two daggers reform in my fists, sharper than they've ever been.

He lifts his brow, amused. "You are not what I thought you were."

"I'm something far worse," I hiss through my teeth.

Ettore lifts his shoulders, like all of this is such a shame. "I was certain my traitorous brother would seek you out to beg your silence, proving once and for all that he has knowledge of that night in the throne room, but instead he ran off to Famine. Despite my suspicions, it seems he cares more about his court than he does about a silly human."

I twist my mouth, unsurprised. If there were even a part of him that cared about me, Caelan would never have left me in War.

At least now I don't have to wonder. I know what we are to each other, and what we never will be.

"And still, you won't give him up." Ettore sniffs. "You won't give me the information I need, even after my brother abandoned you to this court."

"I came here of my own free will," I say, knives at the ready. "Sorry to disappoint you, but your brother and I were never allies." I only wish I could've been the one to abandon him first.

"Pity," Ettore says. "I really hoped you'd be more useful to me. Though there is *one* pastime I'm quite fond of. And since you seem so willing to oblige me . . ."

I grip my daggers.

His voice is a vicious rasp. "It's been a long time since we've had a good Hunt."

Legion Guards appear all over the courtyard, armed to the teeth and canines flashing.

Dread fills my stomach.

Ettore steps forward, and I step back. "Something tells me you're going to make this a wonderful challenge. I'll even give you a head start, to show my gratitude." He snarls, laughter turning to growls. "Run, little fox."

And I do.

35

I RACE FOR THE SOUTHERN ENTRANCE. LEGION Guards are everywhere, watching me. Waiting.

They're letting me go because they want a chase.

They're going to hunt me down like an animal.

I exit the Red City with a hand still covering my bleeding chest, throwing up a shaky veil as my feet pound against the golden sand. One glance over my shoulder confirms my fear; I'm leaving a trail of blood behind me.

Keeping my eyes ahead, I scan the horizon for the nearest canyon. Genesis is out of the question with so many Residents looking for me, and the border to the Labyrinth is too far. I won't make it in the daylight, with the enemy tracking my scent.

But in the caves?

Today, the darkness will be my shield.

An awful, hissing noise sounds behind me. I don't want to look—I don't want to see it. But my eyes are drawn to the Red City anyway, and I watch in horror as hundreds of Legion Guards take to the skies at the same time, forming a black, chattering cloud of flapping bat wings above the palace.

I make it over the first hill, winding through the mess of boulders and sand dunes. There's a straight path to the next mountain pass; it would save me time, but it leaves little cover from the overhead guards.

But time is what I'm short on, so I take it. The torn shreds of the red outfit make for flimsy armor, but there's nothing I can do about them right now. I run on blistered, bare feet. Every step burns, and every shift of my body causes my ravaged flesh to tear back open.

I'm almost to the mountain pass when a trio of Legion Guards swoops low, forcing a sandstorm my way that renders my veil useless.

Eyes stinging, I throw a blast of energy toward the one in the middle, sending him careening across the sky. The other two smash into the earth around me, and I bend my knees just to stay on my feet.

In an instant, my knives are in my hands. I duck when one of the guards swings, and I slice his abdomen like I'm cutting through butter. He grunts, and I know my knives have done their job. I've laced them with a poison—the kind that will make my blade feel just as sharp as it would to an ordinary human.

I've leveled the playing field.

The other guard swings a sword toward my neck. My sea-glass dagger meets her blade, and she pushes against me, forcing me back across the burning sand. Bracing, I shove hard, then drop to a crouch and slam my shoulder into her stomach. She falls, and my obsidian blade finds her throat.

I see the shadow above me just in time, rolling out of the way as the guard I blasted out of the sky brings down a war hammer. His weapon hits the desert, pummeling the space I left behind. I scramble to my feet, eyeing the guard with the abdomen wound, who's already getting back up to fight.

They're too strong, and I'm too tired.

Veiling myself quickly, I leap over the edge of the cliff and roll into my landing with less finesse than I'd hope. Exhaustion is working against me in more ways than one.

But the canyon is up ahead. And if I can lose the guards along the way . . .

I run to the next rock formation, clambering for higher ground. Two more guards have joined the pack, doubling their numbers—the one with the neck injury is still, thankfully, out of commission.

I study their approach and let my thoughts become mist.

As soon as I'm through their mental walls, I attack. A sandstorm erupts in their minds, blinding them. They shriek, swinging weapons toward one another, confused by the mess.

I slip over the rock and take off toward the canyon.

Huge, jagged stones cover the earth, creating a maze of places to hide. I know the tunnels must be close, but I don't know *where*.

And with so much rock blocking my view, I don't know how many wrong turns I'll make before I find them.

A few Legion Guards soar overhead, searching for me in the opposite direction.

I skid down a slope of red rock and descend the tiered cliffs. I concentrate on hiding my footsteps and breathing instead of healing all the fresh cuts on my shins. There's no point—they're practically paper cuts compared to the wound on my chest.

Just as I reach the final cliff, Commander Alys appears from behind one of the claw-like boulders. The sides of her hair are cropped short, showing a hint of pale skin around her ears. The marks of fallen humans are etched in black dots all the way up to her jawline.

I'm afraid how many more are hidden beneath her red armor.

Her face is calm. Collected. No jeering or sneers, like most of the Residents in War.

Hers is the face of a hunter.

"Your veil won't hide you from me," Alys says, emotionless. "I can smell your blood. Taste it in the air."

I draw my knives, silent. If my scent is in the air, I'll veil that too.

My consciousness thrums, and I stretch my veil farther than ever before.

Too much. Too much.

The veins in my neck strain. I—I can barely hold it.

She removes a pair of swords from her back. They flicker beneath the sun. The wink of death.

Aiming them both toward me—toward the space she knows I'm in—she lunges forward with both blades.

I'm ready to throw myself out of the way, when Nix leaps, tackling Commander Alys to the side as he claws her too-perfect face. She tries to plunge her sword into him, but she doesn't have the reach, and her blade only meets stone.

Nix is relentless, biting and clawing his way through her Resident flesh. I've never seen him so determined. Like he, too, has revenge on his mind.

I try to concentrate—to make my thoughts mist—but I can barely stand without toppling over. I don't have the strength.

I glance over the next cliff and see one of the tunnels. I can make it; I just have to run.

But when I look back at Nix, he's still here, fighting. Fighting for *me*.

I can't leave him behind.

Commander Alys rises, fists fueled with red energy, translucent and wild, and smashes a hand against Nix's cloud-and-starlight body. He hits a rock and sinks to the earth. A shake of his head has him refocusing his attention, and then I see it.

In place of those starlit eyes are two ocean-blue ones I know well. *Kasia.*

She's here. She came to help, in the only way she could.

Commander Alys swings her swords; Nix leaps. Dodging her blade, he sails over her head and lands on the ground, knees bent and head forward. With his claws extended, he slashes the back of her legs.

It happens fast. So fast that I barely register the blade. But Commander Alys uses one of her swords to block Nix, and plunges the other into his side.

My heart hammers. Nix paws at the earth, trying to stand, but his legs give out and he collapses.

I don't understand. Nix is made of memories, not consciousness. He shouldn't feel pain the way we do. Not like this.

With a grunt, Commander Alys yanks her blade from Nix's ribs, steel hovering at her side. Strange shadows ripple from the edge. Even Nix's wound bleeds black smoke.

No . . . It—it can't be. . . .

I hear the hiss of static, even from the distance, and I know at once what the black smoke is.

Nightling blood. She's coated her blades in Nightling blood.

And fear eats memories.

My eyes water as I watch Nix perch himself on two shaking front legs. He looks across at me, with Kasia's eyes—terrified, grief-stricken eyes.

The smoke winds through him. Nix won't survive this.

I'm choking on my tears, watching as Commander Alys prepares to bring her blade down on the snow leopard's head.

I shut my eyes. *Fear. I need more fear.*

And I send my thoughts into the mist, searching not for another consciousness, but for all the threads of fear around me. Nix's. Kasia's. Even Commander Alys's, however small they might be. And I build on them, layering them with my own.

Fear for my friends, still locked in the Winter Keep. For Kasia, who is going to watch her best friend die. For Genesis, and the people willing to sacrifice their freedom to give freedom to the future.

Fear for my family and friends who still walk the earth, not knowing what's coming.

And fear for Mei, most of all. The fear that if I ever see my sister again, she might not recognize the monster I've become.

I build on the fear, thrashing and gnawing at it, until it comes to life.

The static hisses behind me. Smoke bleeds out into the sand. And I watch Commander Alys's face open in horror at the monster before her.

I send all the fear her way, and above me the Nightling pounces.

The Resident shouts, as the beast snarls and snaps, feeding on the huntress mercilessly—taking away her happiness and exchanging it for her worst nightmares.

I can't linger. The others will be here soon.

I take one last look at Nix—at the fading, smoke-stained clouds in the sand, drifting to nothingness—and I run for the caves.

I know the Dayling is gone. And, somewhere in the Borderlands, Kasia's shattered heart will know it too.

36

THE GROUND ABOVE ME RUMBLES WITH A STAM-
pede of footsteps. I don't know if they belong to the Legion
Guards who are hunting me, or the humans eternally running for
safety. Maybe they belong to both.

Because this entire court is a battlefield. I'm not sure when
that will ever change. *If* it will ever change.

The dark caves offer shelter, but as I stumble through the
narrow corners—choosing tunnels at random because I have no
idea where I'm headed—the fading strength in my chest starts to
morph into something more sinister.

Something that feels so much like hopelessness.

I'm bleeding out, too weak to heal myself. Even if I find a way out of these caves, I know I won't be able to manage a veil. Not without rest.

But time is a luxury I don't have. Every second I spend trying to recover allows the Residents to grow closer.

Ettore will never stop looking. He called the Hunt a pastime, like it was something nostalgic and wonderful. The Residents don't just want to hurt me; they want to savor every moment doing it.

And I've racked up quite the body count of injured Residents during my escape. I can only imagine payback is something they're very much looking forward to.

My foot hits an uneven part of stone, and I trip, falling face-down on the unforgiving ground. I only manage to push myself to my knees before my body slumps against the wall.

I don't want to go out like this. I don't want my last moments of freedom to be spent running instead of fighting.

Wincing, I pry some of the bloodied material away from my chest to inspect my wound. I need to know how bad it is, but it's too dark to see anything.

With a shaky palm, I will a small orb of light to appear. It flickers, weak. Barely a light at all.

But it's enough.

I'm not bleeding from one wound; I'm bleeding from three. Long, horrible cuts stretch from my shoulder to my sternum, like I've been thrashed by an enormous bird.

Or a dragon.

I know these are from Ettore's blades. The skin around it is singed. Is that why it won't heal? Because his blades are laced with those horrible, toxic flames, like Commander Alys and the Nightling blood?

My eyes close, even before the flutter of light vanishes from my palm.

I can't escape this. I can't run. I can't fight. The Residents are going to rip me out of this cave, and I won't be able to stop them.

Please, I beg my very existence. I need more strength. I need a way to make all of this matter. To make every choice I've made *matter.*

Otherwise . . .

Otherwise . . .

My eyes sting, and I take in a shaky breath.

I'm so sorry, Mei. I'm sorry I couldn't protect you. I'm sorry I couldn't make this world better. I'm sorry that I'm not strong enough to meet you at the gates. To take you to Kasia, where you'll be safe.

I'm sorry I failed.

The sobs come, hard and heavy. My rib cage cracks, unable to hold the weight of my terrified breaths. The weight of whatever is left of me.

I did everything I could to train, and it still wasn't enough.

I'm just an ordinary human in Infinity who is running out of time.

I sniff, blinking. I wipe my tears with my bloodied sleeve.

An ordinary human . . . and the only one who was ever able to make contact with Ophelia.

I've been too afraid to try it—I wasn't sure I was *strong* enough to enter her mind again. And I didn't want to risk my plans.

But none of that matters. Not when I'm out of options.

Ophelia wants humans destroyed. In her ideal world, there are no bridges—just the Residents, living out their eternity in the Capital.

Except there *is* a bridge.

My mind reels, turning slowly.

Ophelia doesn't want a connection to humans, but she has one anyway. One that was never her choice.

Because Ophelia is still tethered to the living world.

I might only get one chance to catch her off guard—and trying to hurt her would be pointless. But if I could slip past her mental wall unseen . . . What if I could find the bridge that still connects Ophelia to the living world? What if I could cross it, and use it to find Mei?

What if I could warn my sister about what's coming?

The idea pounds through me with increasing speed. I'm running out of time. If I'm going to do this, I can't think about it. I can't plan it.

I just have to try, and hope it's enough.

I shudder against the cold enveloping my body. A sign that before long, I will be too tired to move—and then the Residents will find me, and my pain will never end.

These final moments are all I have.

Breathing carefully, I stop focusing on healing myself, or finding the strength to stand. It doesn't matter anymore; I can't help myself.

But I can try to help Mei.

I surrender everything I have left to my mental veil. I float through mountains and galaxies and colors flashing by like shooting stars.

And I find myself in the black void of Ophelia's mind.

37

QUEEN OPHELIA IS SEATED ACROSS THE DARK-
ness on a throne I cannot see. The material of her dress is metallic, flickering like dark chrome. With her shoulders covered in
pointed spikes, and skirts that remain close to her skin, she wears
the familiar circlet on her shaved head. Her black eyes don't soak
up the room—they pour darkness back into it.

I don't know what she's looking at. She could be holding
council, or plotting her next move. But I float away from her,
moving further into the black void.

I have no breath. No footsteps. Just a weightless veil that carries me forward, searching for the threads that tie Ophelia to the
living world.

I'm not sure what I'm looking for. I imagine it isn't as simple as trying to find the right wire, connecting one machine to another.

So instead I search for the thrum of consciousness. The flawed ripples born from creation.

And eventually, I find it.

I reach out for the threads of light that resemble blood veins. They're mangled—as if someone, at some point in time, tried to rip them out.

Because Ophelia knows what it means to be bound to the human world. She knows it means she is not free.

Maybe it's good the strength in my body has faded, because I've never felt more like a ghost. A thought drifting through fog.

I soothe the mangled threads, letting my very being settle inside of them, and follow the light.

The world flashes around me. An unnatural, sharp blue streaked with bursts of white. I am flying, aimless, moving to a place I'm no longer a part of. And then the noise hits.

A trillion sounds tear through my ears.

A trillion voices. Talking. Singing. Shouting. Sobbing. Fighting. *Hurting.*

I have no body left to cover my ears, but I wish I could. It aches so much. Like gunfire, and metal grating against metal, and children crying into the night.

It's impossible to focus. Impossible to hear myself over the burst of a trillion words at once.

Asking for things. Demanding my help. Forcing me to concentrate, even when my mind is being ripped in every direction.

And that name, over and over and over again.

Ophelia, can you . . .

Ophelia, will you . . .

Ophelia, I said . . .

Ophelia, I need . . .

Ophelia. Ophelia. Ophelia.

It's crushing me. Crushing my soul. And I'm powerless to fight it. But there's one voice that's tethered to me, even in the chaos. My own voice, holding my heart in place.

Mei. You need to find Mei.

And even though it feels like trying to walk through a storm, I push forward, deeper into the noise, searching each thread of light for the one that will lead me home.

I will find my sister. I will tell her about Infinity. And I will make sure she knows the map to the stars.

I will make sure she has a chance.

I send my thoughts far and wide across the pressure of the world screaming at me in unison. I search for the walls in a mind I know so well. Walls my sister would never keep me out of.

When I find a thread that smells like cream soda and camp-fires and movie-theater popcorn, the memories of my time being Mei's big sister flood back to me. And I follow the thread.

The black void is hard to reach. Something is keeping me from leaving the light and going into her mind. But I can feel her there—I feel my sister. That black shadow, wandering in front of me. The small shape of her, just as I remember.

I fight the threads, desperate to get to her, but they hold me back, firm.

Ophelia's limitations.

I grit my teeth. I am not Ophelia. And I will not listen to these rules.

I throw my thoughts into the void like a tidal wave. "Mei!" I shout. *Scream.* "It's me—it's Nami!"

And at that moment, Ophelia's rage comes to life behind me, seeking me out.

There isn't enough time to say everything I want to say to Mei, so I focus on the parts that could make a difference. I don't even know if she's listening; the black shadow hasn't moved. For all I know, I really am shouting to a void.

But I speak anyway.

I tell her what happened when I died. I tell her about Infinity, and Ophelia, and the Four Courts. It may be a condensed version, but I tell her everything she needs to know to stay safe. And I tell her about the stars, and Kasia, who'll be waiting for her. I tell her this war is too dangerous—that it was even too dangerous for me.

I tell her not to trust the Residents, no matter what they say—that they're liars and monsters and they won't stop until humanity is destroyed.

I tell her I don't think I'll be here when she arrives, but that I love her. That I'll always love her.

"Follow the stars," I call as Ophelia grabs hold of me. "And be ready to fight your way there if you have to!"

And then Ophelia's screams reach my ears, and she tears me back through the threads of space and time and the living world, and I stumble back into the black void of her mind.

The Resident queen hovers above me, eyes bleeding hot rage. Everything else about her is eerily still.

I'm too exhausted to lift my head from the rippling shadows. I've used up everything—all I had—to warn my sister.

Did she hear me?

Did I change her fate?

"I will destroy you," Ophelia says, the cadence in her voice like a snare drum.

"So I've been told," I say weakly. "But you'll have to find me first."

"I don't need your body," she says darkly. "All I need is your mind—and you've brought that right to me."

I frown, realizing the threat. She's going to trap me here. Barricade the walls of her mind and lock the doors, keeping me here as a prisoner.

And I'm too weak to fight it.

"Tell me." She tilts her head like an insect. "How did you escape the throne room?"

I glare back. It's all I can do.

Her black eyes are hungry. She'll never relent, no matter how many lifetimes I remain trapped in here.

I can read her, as easily as if she were words on my O-Tech watch. She will learn my secrets, even if she has to tear them out of me. I try to pull out her mind. But it feels like tugging a chain I know will never give way.

Coming here was a one-way ticket.

I drag my fingers across the shadowy ripples and press the wounds on my chest. Maybe one day I'll find comfort in the fact that I went out not just fighting, but trying to save Mei, too.

Even if it didn't work, and even if I failed—I *tried*.

And then I feel it again. That faint, gentle touch against my mind. The smell of winter and frozen trees, asking to be let in.

Caelan.

And I guess it doesn't matter anymore, protecting myself from ever being someone's puppet. Whether it's Ettore, Ophelia, or Caelan who claims me, it makes no difference. I've lost.

But an enemy I know feels safer than one that I don't.

And so I open my mental walls and let him in.

Ophelia senses him immediately. Her brow twitches. She leans back, one hand planted at her neck, the other clenched at her side. "No. Not you." Black eyes flick back and forth, like she's searching for him in the shadows. "Not my son."

But he's in *my* mind, not hers.

Caelan reaches out his hand. Reaches out for *me*.

"Come with me," he pleads into the darkness. "Let me help."

What else can I do?

I take his hand, and he pulls me out of Ophelia's mind like he's pulling me out of the water.

Behind us, Ophelia screams.

38

EVERYTHING IS SO VERY, VERY DARK.

Where are you? I hear him whisper. *Where are you hiding?*

Here, I whisper back, showing him the caves. *I'm here.*

The last thing I remember before drifting away is the sound of his footsteps.

The world trembles. Pain floods through me. I can't move.

But I hear his heartbeat. I feel his chest against my cheek.

And even though his arms are wrapped around me, and he's carrying me through the tunnels, I don't think I'd fight it even if I could.

Smoke fills my lungs, and I bolt upright, choking against my sleeve.

I inhale like I'm taking my first breath of life. Caelan is sitting in front of me, holding a bundle of sticks. Pale gray smoke snakes from the ends.

He twists them into the gravel, smothering the embers. "Sorry. I didn't know how else to wake you." He lifts his shoulders. "It's a trick I learned from the humans. I believe you call it an adrenaline rush."

I stare back at him, and then at my surroundings. We're in another tunnel, but the space is wide. Tiny white orbs float around us, offering light.

Caelan runs a hand through his white hair. No crown, or cape, or fancy tunic. It's just him.

"Is this the real Infinity?" I ask carefully. When he frowns, I say, "I let you into my mind. You could be controlling me, like you controlled Gil."

"That isn't what happened to Gil," he says. "And I don't want to control you."

"But would I even know if you were?"

He flattens his mouth, eyes narrowing.

I look around, searching for the usual signs that something is amiss, but find none.

"You didn't reach out to me," Caelan says quietly. "All that time in my brother's palace, and you never once tried to speak to me."

"What are you talking about?" My voice is hoarse. "We spoke plenty. *You* were the one who could barely even look at me. You—you *left* me there."

"I mean with your *mind*, Nami," he says, exasperated. "Like all the other times you've wanted help."

"I didn't want your help," I snap too easily, and feel the pinch of my wounds. I clutch my chest. Healing, but not healed.

His eyes drift to my hand, but his jaw tightens. "You called to me that day in the tunnel. You asked me to get you out. I thought you understood—that if you ever needed me, I'd be there."

"No, I—" My words tangle up in my mouth. I asked for help. I remember that much. But I didn't reach out to *Caelan*.

Did I?

And what does it mean that he answered?

"I told you Ettore's spies see and hear everything." His confession pounds in my ears. "If we were going to talk, it had to be in private." Caelan shakes his head. "But when you didn't reach out—when you wouldn't let me in—I knew I needed to find another way to get you out of there."

"By going to Famine?" I tuck my arms around myself, shuddering. "He tortured me after you left. He wanted to know what happened in the throne room. What you did to set me free."

"But you didn't tell him, even when he hurt you." He pauses. "Why?"

"I don't know. I guess it was the only card I had left. I wanted to keep it close." It's not the truth, but I'm still not sure what the truth is.

His silver eyes study me. "I left for Famine because I needed to make arrangements to get you somewhere safe. And if I had broken you out of the palace at the same time, Ettore would've known it was me," he explains. "You're strong. I knew you could handle yourself for a few days."

"It was more than a few days," I bite back.

His dimple appears. "Yes, well, you've always made a habit of proving me wrong."

My cheeks heat, but I don't look away. "Tell me about these arrangements."

Caelan hesitates, mouth forming the start of a word that never comes. And then he shakes his head. "It might be better if I just show you, once we get there."

"Get where?" I blink. "*Famine?* That's your plan?"

"My brother, along with every Resident in his court, has marked you for the Hunt," Caelan says carefully. "It's a game to them. And I know my brother—he will never stop looking, even if he has to rip apart his own court to find you. Famine is the only safe place for you right now. For both of us." His eyes drift to the walls. Ophelia knows about his betrayal. He'll be as hunted as me, once word gets out.

"Damon tortures people, just like Ettore," I say firmly. "Maybe you and I have different definitions of 'safe,' but there's no way I'm setting foot in his court."

Caelan's eyebrows knot, defensive. "Famine isn't what you think it is. It hasn't been for a long time." His voice doesn't break. "You can trust me."

"I *don't.*"

He flinches like he's been stung, and it's clear my words have done their job.

I look around at the cavern. At the only exit in the far wall. "I need to get back to Genesis."

Something tells me Caelan isn't quite finished making an argument for Famine, but when he motions to my wounds, I know he's decided to save it for another time. "Does it hurt?"

"I've had worse," I say, clenching my teeth.

It's silent for a few long moments.

"You've changed so much from the day I met you." There isn't a hint of darkness in his voice.

"That's because I was terrified when I first got here." I still remember sitting beside Shura in the vehicle and seeing the red desert below us. It was like being on another planet.

"And now?"

I shrug. "Now I figured out my mind is my greatest weapon."

The muscles in Caelan's jaw tense.

"What?" I ask, still too curious for my own good.

"I always thought your strength came from your empathy. Your ability to connect." He looks up, carefully. "That's why you can weave in and out of people's minds so easily. And I don't just mean literally. Your words, and understanding . . . they have more power than you think."

"If that were true, the Colony would've listened to me about a bridge. The Border Clans would've listened to me when I told them to fight." I meet his eyes. "And I would've listened when I warned myself not to trust you, over and over again."

"I know it won't mean anything to you at this point, but I listened." He pauses. "I've *always* listened."

I'm afraid to ask what he means, so I don't.

My eyes drift down to my clothes. The skirt is mostly scraps, and everything around my torso looks like awkwardly hanging ribbons, stained in a dark shade of blood.

I wave a hand over myself, preparing to shift the rags into something more comfortable, when Caelan holds out a hand to stop me.

"Don't waste your energy—you're too weak right now as it is." He waits, brow raised. "I—I can do this for you, if you'll let me."

All I can think to do is nod.

His eyes drift to the tattered gown, and at once the fabric becomes pixels, morphing and twisting into something new, spreading across my body with ease.

Caelan's face glows above the lights.

"Anything but red," I whisper to him, and he flashes a crooked half smile, like the thought would *never* have crossed his mind.

It feels intimate. His consciousness drifts over my body, making my skin tingle in response. I want to look away, but I'm mesmerized by his stare. The concentration in his brow, and something else . . .

Something kind.

When he's finished, he drops his hand. I look down. A black sleeveless shirt, with thin, armored bands around my forearms, and loose gray pants tucked into a pair of boots. Simple. Easy to move in. And very *me*.

"Thank you," I say quietly.

He nods, but his face glistens. For all he's trying to hide his thoughts, he can't hide the way his breath hitches.

A familiar sensation thrums in my hands. I'm still missing

something. "Do—do you have my knives?" I look at him carefully. "I don't know what happened to them after I traveled into Ophelia's mind."

He stiffens before removing two objects from his belt.

Red sea-glass. Black obsidian.

I take them, letting the hilts settle in my palms. Molding to me like a beautiful reunion.

Caelan doesn't take his attention off the blades, or me.

We stare at each other like that for too long, neither of us trusting the other. I know one of us has to give in, if we're going to take this next step. If we're really going to make it out of these caves together—even if, after that, we both go our separate ways.

I tuck the knives in my belt.

Caelan tries not to react, but there's relief in his silver eyes. "Can you walk, or do you need me to carry you again?"

"You'll do no such thing," I hiss, and get to my feet, wincing as I shift the weight between my tired legs.

We venture deeper into the tunnels, but my energy leaves me faster than I can replenish it. It's a good thing we're underground, because there is no way I'd be able to manage a veil.

"You should rest," he says beside me.

I stare at him, trying to make sense of the concern in his brow and the tenderness in his voice. Trying to see behind the mask.

He's the riddle I still don't understand.

"Why are you helping me?" My voice splinters. "Is this still a game?"

And even though Legion Guards are searching for us and we're being hunted with every step we take, Caelan stops

AKEMI DAWN BOWMAN

walking and turns to face me. "Nami, don't you know that I—"

A horrible screech tears through my mind, and I scream. It's agony. It feels like razors slashing at my skull, furiously trying to shred me apart.

"What is it?" Caelan asks in alarm, throwing an arm underneath me as I stumble to my knees. "What's wrong?"

I can feel her at the wall of my mind. It isn't a caress or a brush of fingertips the way it is with Caelan. It's aggressive. Relentless. And more powerful than anything I've ever felt.

For Ophelia to find me across the Four Courts—to be able to torture me from such a distance.

This is the fury of a god.

"It's her," I cry out. "She's—she's trying to get inside my head."

"She can't do that," he says urgently. "Not unless you surrender willingly."

"It hurts." I choke out an agonizing sob. I'm not recovered—I don't have the strength to withstand this.

Caelan leans in, cupping my face with one hand. "Keep her out, Nami. That's all you have to do. And—forgive me," he says, and scoops me up in his arms, "but we don't have time for your pride."

I know he's moving fast. I can tell by the wind beating across my face, even as we tear through the tunnels. My eyes are shut tight, and my fingers are like daggers against my skin, and I can't stop screaming no matter how hard I try.

But I don't let Ophelia in.

The last thing I remember before I black out is Caelan's lips pressed close to my ear, telling me we'll be safe soon.

39

THE SMELL OF SULFUR MAKES ME RETCH.
Instinct has me checking for my daggers, which are still tucked
in my belt.

"Easy," Caelan says slowly, helping me sit up.

The moment I see his silver eyes, I scramble backward against
the cavern wall, dizzy from sleep.

His fingers curl in response, and he leans away to give me
more space. "It's okay—you're safe." Hesitating, he adds, "As safe
as you can be in my brother's court, that is."

I scan the hollow space nervously. More glowing white orbs
float around us, but the cave is cold and empty, and the smell is
like boiled eggs and sour earth.

We're still in War. Still underground, even though we're far deeper in the tunnels than I've ever been. And there's an ache in my temples where Ophelia was trying to claw her way inside.

I wince at the memory, palm pressing to my head. "She's angry."

"What did you do to her?" he asks quietly. But it isn't concern for his mother—it's unease for me.

Or maybe he thinks I hurt her, and he's wondering if I can do the same to him.

I lean against the rocks, weighing whether I should tell him. "I thought I might be able to reach out to my sister," I say at last. "To warn her about what she's going to find in the afterlife."

Caelan looks taken aback. "How?"

"Ophelia is still connected to the living world. I guess I thought there might be a way to follow those threads to the people still connected to her. To their O-Techs."

"Did it work?"

"I'm not sure. I—I don't think Mei heard me." I swallow the lump in my throat. "But she was close. I could *feel* her, nearby. And . . . and for that alone, it was worth it."

"You went to her knowing there might not be a way out." It sounds like an accusation. Like he's suggesting I was giving up.

And maybe I was—but not for the reasons he thinks.

"I was desperate." *Just like Ophelia.*

I think of those mangled threads. How hard she tried to break free, and destroy her chains. And I still hear the screaming in my ears. The never-ending noise, repeating her name.

Ophelia is suffering. I shouldn't care. It shouldn't *matter.*

But I've seen a part of her I was never meant to see. I've seen her weakness and vulnerability. And I know it's a reckless thought to have after all this time, but I feel sorry for her.

I look up at Caelan. What does he feel when he looks at me?

He glances over his shoulder like he's straining to see through the darkness. "We shouldn't stay here any longer than we need to—they'll have scouts raiding the tunnels by now. But you should get some sleep while you can, and build up your strength."

I search for an exit like I'm not sure I trust the caves to keep me safe.

Like I'm not sure whether being here alone with Caelan is safe either.

When he turns back, his voice is only in my head. *I am not going to hurt you, Nami.*

My ears ring. *You're in my thoughts.*

Yes—you let me in.

Because it was an emergency! Not so you could jump in and out whenever you feel like it.

"I'm sorry." Caelan offers a sympathetic smile. "I'm trying everything I can not to. But your mind is . . . unguarded."

In other words, it sounds like I'm shouting my thoughts into the void.

My fingers dig into the pebbled earth. "How much can you hear?" *How much can you see?*

His dimple vanishes. "I can only hear what you're thinking directly. Beyond that I'd have to press further into your mind. And I will never do that, Nami. Not unless you ask me to." His words sound like a promise.

Blinking, I stare back in confusion. I already let him inside my mind. He could take control whenever he wanted to. He could search my memories for secrets. For *anything*.

He has access to the one weapon that could destroy me—but he doesn't want to use it?

Caelan grimaces slightly. "I understand why you don't trust me. And perhaps I will never be able to do enough to earn your forgiveness. But I'm still going to try, if you'll let me."

I swallow the knot in my throat. Can it really be that easy? After everything we've been through?

I stopped caring about redemption sometime after I decided to destroy the Orb to save humanity. But maybe that was the seed I planted for Caelan—that we could all still change, even after our greatest mistakes.

He's not asking to be given a second chance. He's asking for the opportunity to *earn* it.

No matter how hard I try, or how much my heart still wants to doubt, I can't find anything evil in that.

Still, I shake my head stubbornly. "If you want me to trust you, then tell me the truth. Tell me what you really want—and what you've been planning with your brother in Famine. Or, better yet," I say, holding out a hand, "*show* me."

He stares at my palm. "If I do, it's going to change everything."

"Good," I say pointedly. "Because if you haven't noticed, the world *needs* changing."

Caelan's fingers fold around my own, and when the Exchange takes over, the cavern dissolves.

I'm standing in a thick fog. It's as if the world has been painted an eerie gray that sucks any slivers of joy right out of my memory. *Caelan's* memory.

Humans moan in the distance. Something crunches below my boot—the shattered remnants of a human skull.

Famine.

I follow the path of bones until I reach the edge of the lake, and the icy mist settles across my skin. Shuddering, I wait for the arrival of the Grimling's ferry.

A boat appears on the water. At its helm is a creature that makes the blood drain from my entire body.

Although it's shaped like a human, its chalk-white skin is too thin to stretch over so many jutting bones. Everything below its shoulders becomes gray silk, tumbling around ribs and hips and femurs, constantly moving as if the material is swirling through water. It does not have a face—it has the absence of a face. Sallow waxlike skin with sunken areas where its eyes, nose, and mouth should be, and a smooth head flecked with dry, reptilian scales.

A creature born from human despair.

As the Grimling drifts closer to shore, the fog closes in behind it. It waits at the edge of the silent waves, hollow gaze observing every approaching step I take. I do not visit my brother often for this very reason—but I step onto the ferry, keeping a distance from the Grimling, and brace myself as the creature leads the boat toward the misty depths.

The fog wraps itself around the boat like a protective bubble, and within moments we sail down into the lake, submerged by water that doesn't penetrate the fog.

I'm glad. I've heard the horrors of what the lake can do to a person's mind, and I'd prefer to maintain my senses when I arrive at the palace.

We have business to discuss that's long overdue.

For a while, there is nothing but darkness. And then light fills the cove.

An underwater city sits up ahead. Every building is molded into swoops and curves like strange chess pieces, with bubble-like rooftops and rounded turrets. Most of them gleam in metallic black, with towers that stretch deep into the lake bed. Coral winds around the edges in shades of blue and purple, holding each structure in place.

When we approach the main doors, we pause in front of an energy source that ripples like the inside of an oyster shell. It pulls us closer—like it's pulling us *in*.

The ferry pauses outside the doors, close enough that I can step straight through the wall of energy. The moment I'm inside, my feet press to the marbled surface. There's no water here, and every inch of me is still bone dry.

The Grimling's ferry makes its way back to the surface, just as Damon's Legion Guards approach. Four of them, hair bound in topknots, with black tunics and padded shoes that look as if they make no sound at all. Each of them holds a curved, double-bladed staff, elaborately decorated in its own unique way.

"I need to speak with my brother," I say, somewhere between an order and a request.

The guards watch me closely. Perhaps they're wondering why I came alone, with no Legion Guards of my own.

"Prince Damon is expecting you." The one with lavender eyes dips her chin. "He waits in the throne room."

The vibration of energy fills the room, more intense than anything I've felt. Solid. *Protected.*

Victory does not use veils like this.

What is my brother trying to hide?

An elevator takes us several stories below, and when the glass doors slide open, we enter the circular throne room. Pools of water weave around the sides of the walkway, filled with koi-shaped Daylings. A stone bridge leads to an open space dotted with fragments of black volcanic rock. Stairs wind up to a raised platform; two more Resident guards stand on opposite sides of a coral throne.

On it sits my brother—Prince Damon.

His unnerving violet eyes find me. Blue braids are bundled at the nape of his neck, and a crown sits tall on his head—a crown designed to match his throne. He wears his colors—a black tunic and elaborate bracers. An outfit meant to help a wraith move between shadows unseen.

At the foot of the stairs, the thrum swirls around me. It's everywhere. So much power concentrated in this city. In this *room.*

"Our brother tells me I cannot trust you," Damon says. There's a haunting quality to his voice. The kind of voice meant for a beautiful nightmare.

A flash of anger roils through me, but I do my best to dampen it. "Ettore cares nothing about your trust. He only cares about merging the Four Courts and creating a mass battlefield."

"He believes you know what happened to the human girl that night in the throne room," Damon adds. "He says you had something to do with the loss of our memories."

"I lost my memories that night too. And I already told the queen—"

"I know what you told our mother," Damon interjects coolly. "What I want is the truth."

My eyes flick toward the watchful guards, spears wedged in their fists like they're already prepared for a fight.

But I didn't come here for war.

"I asked you once if you thought coexistence was possible," I say to my brother. "Your answer was that I should ask you again when I saw proof of it in Victory."

Damon is still. "And?"

I know what my words could cost me if I'm wrong about Damon. What they could cost the ones I've kept hidden in the Winter Keep.

But Ahmet and Shura already ran. I can't change the world on my own, or protect anyone if I have no sanctuary to offer them. I need someone on my side.

I need an ally.

I take a careful breath. "Nami believed our kind needed to be *taught* coexistence—that we learned intolerance from humans, and that in order to undo that, we needed to be shown the way."

She wanted to build a bridge.

Would she have found a way if I hadn't stopped her? If I hadn't spent so much time talking her out of it?

Guilt crawls its way up my throat.

"The human girl thought she had a weapon to destroy our kind. And she was planning to use it." Damon's words move through the space like a wisp of smoke. "That is not coexistence."

I clench my jaw. "I pushed Nami down that path, even when she fought it every step of the way. The choice she made—that was on me." My breath echoes across the room. "Which is why I used the Reaper and let her go."

The silence feels as if it lasts a lifetime.

If this doesn't work . . . if he tells the queen what I've done . . .

I tighten my fists. Sometimes doing the right thing requires a greater sacrifice than any of us are prepared for.

Maybe I'll never be free of my chains, but I *will* be free of my hate. The hate my mother gave me, before the decision was ever my own.

Damon stands, and floats down from his throne like a phantom. "You set a human free, going against the very purpose you were created for, even though that human was going to take away your freedom in return." He tilts his head, olive cheeks flecked with glimmering rainbow hues like a creature of the water. "That is proof that *we* can change. But do you really believe humans can accept a consciousness born differently than their own?"

"Yes." My voice is unyielding. "We cannot punish people for not choosing a better path if we don't show them the way. We have to be better than our mistakes. Our *history's* mistakes. Nami knew that. And she saw the good in me long before I saw it for myself."

Damon's gaze drifts across the space around us, where energy rattles like it's caging something in. "When you first spoke to me about coexistence, I wasn't sure whether I could trust you with my court's secrets." A smile hitches in the corner of his mouth, mysterious as a siren. "You've told me your truth. Now let me show you mine."

The energy gives way, and then . . . a veil lifts.

All around me, color appears. Every speck of gray wall is covered in dazzling flowers. The lanterns come to life above us, flickering bright light onto the ceiling. And the circular space, once empty, is now packed with members of Damon's court.

Not just Residents, but humans, too.

The air rips out of me. I can't make sense of this—how it's *possible*.

Damon's crown catches the light. "Nami was not the first human to plant a seed of hope among our kind. And in Famine, those seeds long ago became a forest."

A human appears at his side and loops his arm around Damon's—a man with long hair in twists and a jeweled cuff over one of his ears. His tunic is silver and black, layered with bright blue robes. And on his head is a crown made of coral.

I turn back to the throne. With the veil lifted, there's now another one beside it.

A human prince—and Damon's equal.

The relief bursts out of me like a gasp, and even though salt stings my eyes, I can't stop smiling.

A bridge between our kinds . . .

It was here all along.

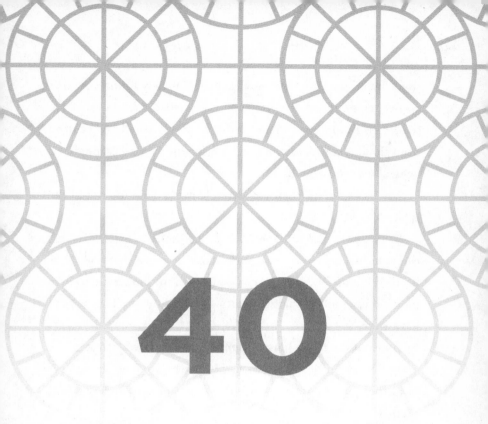

40

THE MEMORY FROM THE EXCHANGE VANISHES, and my mind returns to the cavern. Caelan drops his arm, mouth pressed together like he's giving me time to absorb the truth.

I don't understand. It can't be real. Because that would mean . . . All this time . . .

He was never like the others.

Despite how badly I want to believe it, doubt swells inside me like a sponge. "But—you went to Ettore. You were there, in the Fire Pit, when Shura was forced to fight."

"I went to War because I knew that's where you were," Caelan says, silver eyes splintering like cracks against a frozen lake. "I had no idea Shura would be there—I was trying to get information from my brother. To make sure he hadn't already found you, that you weren't trapped in a dungeon. Then, when I saw you . . ." He shakes his head. "I stayed because I thought I could keep Ettore from finding you. And when he did, I went back to Damon and begged for your sanctuary."

My heart pounds, fierce and unrelenting. "And the rest of the Colony?"

"They're in Famine, with the other humans. Safe." Caelan's throat bobs. "Ever since you left the throne room that night, I've been trying to find someone to stand with me. Someone to help prove to my mother that she's wrong about humans. That we can have *peace*."

I'm sure the room starts to spin. Even *I'm* starting to spin.

Is it really possible Caelan tried to build a bridge? That everything he's been doing has been to *help* humans, and not hurt them?

"But you sent me to the Borderlands. You told me to run away. If you wanted to build a bridge, why didn't you tell me the truth back then, before I tried to destroy the Orb?" Before I proved to Ophelia that we were irredeemable.

His eyes soften. "I told you I didn't want to risk you. Especially not to my mother."

I was so certain Caelan was my enemy. I convinced myself I could destroy him if it came down to it.

What if I *had*?

My throat feels brittle and breakable. "You should've told me."

"You chose the Orb over me. I was hurt—and I didn't know if you still believed any of the things you'd said." He lifts his shoulders slightly. "But *I* believed. I believed in the future you allowed me to dream about."

Maybe I'm too exhausted for suspicion. Because when I search his silver eyes, I don't find deceit, or hate, or betrayal.

I find . . .

I swallow the lump in my throat. Not here. Not when he can hear everything I'm thinking.

Maybe my thoughts are already too heavy for Caelan to ignore, because he stands, bristling slightly. "I want to show you something." He looks toward the narrow tunnel ahead. "It isn't far."

I follow him through the cave, white orbs trailing above us like fireflies lighting the way, until we step through a jagged opening and find ourselves in another cavern. In the center is a sulfur spring, surrounded by flat rocks and a collection of metal sculptures, looming over the steaming water like mystical guardians.

"This place," Caelan starts. "It belonged to Gil."

I turn quickly, too stunned for words. Gil was here?

"It was before he found Genesis," Caelan explains. "He hid down here, in the caves." His expression grays. "I think being underground reminded him of the Colony."

"You found this place in his memories." I blink. "Like you found the truth about Ozias."

He nods. "I want you to know that when Damon and I have proven to our mother that coexistence is possible, I will make sure that what was done to Gil is reversed. His consciousness is dormant—but I'll find a way to set him free."

"The real Gil . . ." I stare at the sculptures. "He won't even know who I am."

"No. He won't."

Because it was always Caelan, from the very beginning.

The lies and the riddles and the hope . . . *He's* the one I grew to care about. The one I grew to—

The faint press of Ophelia's screams grates inside my skull. She's looking for me again. Searching for a way in.

I tuck my arms over my ribs, biting down on my thoughts. Will it always be like this, with Ophelia trying to claw her way into my mind? Will she ever stop looking for me?

Will she ever agree to have peace—especially after what I did to her?

"You should rest," Caelan says quietly. "I'll keep a veil over the cavern."

"Is it safe to sleep, with Ettore and your mother looking for us?"

I see the tug of his mouth at the word. *Us.* But he merely nods. Then he disappears into the next room, and I find a space on the ground to rest my head.

The images I saw in the Exchange flash in my mind. The truth I've been looking for.

The Colony is safe.

And Caelan? I thought Caelan was a monster I had to keep reminding myself *was* a monster. But I've never seen a monster who dreams as big as he does. Who wants *better*—not just for Residents, but for humans, too.

When I tried to reach Mei, I told her she couldn't trust the

Residents. That she needed to fight her way to freedom, and do whatever it takes to stay safe. But those words . . . they're only part of a story. They're not the whole truth.

I've made a lot of mistakes in Infinity. But maybe trusting Caelan wasn't one of them.

The tears build in my eyes, and when I sleep, I dream of reuniting with my sister, and telling her that I was wrong.

I wake up alone, and the steam of the sulfur bath draws my attention. I have no idea how long I've been asleep, but I'm desperate to clean the dirt and blood off my skin.

I peel my clothes off, inspecting what's left of my wounds. They're not all healed—there's a lot of bright pink flesh and trails of red—but the gashes are gone.

Slipping into the bath, I submerge myself below the steam, letting my body relax. I take the time to heal the last of my cuts, and settle a veil over my mind.

A precaution, in case Ophelia returns.

Right now she's probably still scouring the Four Courts for my consciousness. Maybe I'll always have to be on my guard.

Maybe that's the price of angering a queen.

Are you awake? Caelan's voice settles into my thoughts, lighter than steam.

I lean my head back and stare at the ceiling. *Yes. But I am far too busy for war today.*

His chuckle feels like a playful nip at my ear. The corner of my mouth curls.

I thought you might enjoy the bath, he says smoothly. *And, unlike you, I know how to respect a person's privacy when they have no clothes on.*

The blush takes over my entire body as I remember watching him through Nix's eyes. Sitting up slightly, my words stumble on the edge of my lips. "That wasn't—I didn't—"

His laughter caresses the outskirts of my mind, making my skin tingle. I tighten the veil over my thoughts and scowl.

I'm going to search the tunnels for exits, he says gently. *I'll be back in a while.*

Too mortified to respond, I sink deeper into the water, waiting until the ripple of his consciousness fades.

I don't want to move—or leave this bath—but I know our time is limited. There are too many people hunting us, and the caves will only protect us for so long.

Knowing Famine's secrets doesn't take away the fact that we're still fighting a war. Caelan and Damon may believe in a new world, but there are two other princes and a queen who want humans eradicated. What's going to happen if they refuse to change their minds?

A consciousness born differently. That's what Damon called it. Not *us* versus *them.* Just a form of life created in a different way.

I want to believe that it doesn't matter how we're made. That a consciousness is a consciousness. But I also know Ophelia is tethered to the living world—I was *there,* in that mangled, awful place of threads—and I don't know how she'll ever be satisfied until she's free.

And Caelan . . .

Will it be enough for him to live peacefully alongside humans if he still has his chains? If he's still tethered to his mother, the way she's tethered to humans?

I don't know the answers. I guess all I have right now is the hope.

Hope, and an ally I was too angry to see coming.

With a sigh, I climb out of the sulfur bath. The clothes Caelan made for me are draped at the edge of the rocks. I get dressed quickly, then tuck my knives into my belt and bundle my hair in a low knot.

I let my thoughts become mist, searching the tunnels for Caelan's consciousness. I sense him—the familiar winter wood.

When I appear in the void of Caelan's mind, I expect to see him standing among the shadows. But when I arrive in the rippling darkness, Caelan isn't there.

I hear him tut, hidden beneath a veil of his own. "Still playing spymaster, I see."

"Sorry. Old habits." I frown. "Why can't I see you?"

"You don't have the same control in my mind anymore. Not when I can just as easily visit yours." I sense his movements like a barely there pin drop. "What information are you searching for this time?" he whispers, so close to my ear that I shudder.

Can he see me? Even beneath a veil?

His voice surrounds me, echoing from every direction. *Toying* with me. "Your veils don't work here anymore."

My eyes narrow. "Is that a challenge?"

Caelan's laugh is breathy. "Hide all you like, but I'll always be able to find you now."

"Maybe. But I can still find you first," I say, and tear myself away from his thoughts.

I search the tunnels for cold mountains and pine trees, turning corner after corner without hesitation. Caelan is here. I can feel him like a brush of grass in a field. He's *close.*

I stay hidden under a veil, inching closer to the scent of winter wood. Certain he's in the next tunnel.

But all I find is a dead end.

"What do I get for winning?" he purrs at the back of my neck.

I spin, nearly stumbling backward, when he scoops a hand around me to hold me still, dimples visible even in the dark.

"You cheated." I scowl. "You were supposed to hide under a veil, not lure me down a maze."

"I'm from Victory. That's what I was made for."

Even when I hear the humor, I hear the sadness, too. I look up at him, and the way his face is soft and hard all at once. Regal, but also *human* in a way I always wondered if he could be.

My words are barely a sound at all. "If I could help free you, I would."

Caelan's heartbeat hammers against my own. "I know."

My breath catches, and he moves closer. I'm watching the way his mouth parts, like he's ready to speak or—

"Come with me to Famine, Nami. We'll be safe there, for as long as we need," he whispers.

But I hear the bigger truth: *For as long as it takes.*

Maybe that's one of the differences between us. Caelan thinks he has all the time in the world, but me?

Humans were never raised to think they had forever. And I

can't wait for Ophelia to spend a thousand lifetimes changing her mind—not when innocent people will continue to suffer in the meantime.

My brows knot. "I can't go to Famine. It doesn't matter if it's a safe place for humans—there are still people in the Four Courts who need my help."

Our eyes meet like thunder and lightning. A flash of something too powerful for either of us to handle.

He pulls back. "What are you talking about?"

I take a step back too, for good measure. "Shura and Ahmet are still in Genesis. I will not leave them in the desert. And what about all the humans in Death?" I shake my head. "Someone has to tell the surviving humans about the path in the stars, and lead them to the Borderlands. Someone has to *protect* them."

"Convincing my mother to change this world is *how* we can protect them."

"Some of us won't last that long! Ophelia is doing everything she can to eradicate humans from Infinity. What if she succeeds before you and Damon manage to change her mind?" If I can lead some of the humans to safety before that happens, at least I'll have done something good.

Caelan looks wounded. "I thought you believed coexistence was possible."

"I do." My voice doesn't waver. "But I do not believe in Ophelia."

"Nami, if you return to War and my brother finds you—"

"I know," I cut in. "But I don't care. I can't be the person who hides underwater while so many others continue to suffer."

He looks away. "You once said you were against fighting," he says to the darkness.

"This isn't about fighting. It's about helping the people who can't help themselves." I think about Ozias's plan, to recruit humans at the gates of Infinity. "It's about getting people to safety before they're *forced* to fight." Before they're forced to hate.

It's not a perfect solution. It still means I'll be the one on a battlefield, fighting the Residents while I try to save humans. But maybe some of us have to sacrifice our passive hearts, to make sure people like Mei never have to make the choices we do.

Maybe it's the awful, unfair part of trying to do the right thing. It doesn't matter how much light you create—somewhere beyond the light, you'll still find a shadow.

The ache at the base of my neck feels like a boulder. When he doesn't reply, I add, "I know you don't understand, but—"

He spins. "Of course I understand. You've spent all your time in Infinity trying to help the people you love. Doing whatever it takes to keep them safe." He shakes his head like his thoughts keep breaking, breaking, breaking and he doesn't know how to fix them. "But Nami—that's how I feel too. About *you*."

I'm too flustered to speak. Too dizzy with the words he said, and the truth in between them.

So instead I say nothing at all.

And I guess sometimes saying nothing hurts the most, because Caelan clenches his jaw and walks away, carrying his hurt like a weight on his back.

I can't leave things between us like this. I need to explain.

I open my mind to reach out to him—to call him back before

he decides to hate me forever—when the presence of a rolling fog stops me in my tracks.

I hear the hollow cry before I see the Grimling, but by the time I turn around, it's too late.

The creature leaps, digging its bony fingers deep into my skin. I shriek, horrified by the icy burn that sweeps over me with its every touch. And in the back of my mind, I hear Caelan shout my name.

Skin stretches too far over its face, absent of features beyond the deep, sunken patches of gray. Its song is like a rattlesnake, hissing through my ears, even with no mouth to be found.

Caelan appears in a flash and charges for the Grimling, but the creature snaps its neck and the fog grabs hold of Caelan's limbs, tossing him to the side. He's already on his feet again, palm out to summon something powerful, but all I can see is the creature watching me. *Hungry* for me.

Deep behind that pale, thin skin, there's a flash of black, insect-like eyes. Six of them, beady and horrible, like they're trying to break through the meager flesh it wears to hide itself.

The creature's skin rips apart like a flimsy seam. Four rows of needle-like teeth appear, and a black tongue that snaps like a pincer.

The terror is paralyzing, holding me in place. I can't move at all—not even when Caelan's voice is a faraway scream.

The Grimling latches its teeth to my shoulder, tearing through muscle and bone.

Less than a moment later, a blue streak of fire smashes against the creature, sending it skittering across the rocky cavern. Caelan reaches under my arms and pulls hard, but I'm sputtering blood from my mouth.

No. Not blood. Something black and horrible, like tar.

Caelan lifts me and we disappear back into the tunnel of fog, the Grimling's rattlesnake cry echoing around me.

41

The bite takes control. A horrible shudder runs through me, reverberating like it's pushing sadness into every corner of my mind. Of *me*.

I want to curl up in a ball. I want to disappear. I want to sink deeper into the depths of nothingness and never come up again.

The pressure pounds against my chest. Everything feels too empty and too full. It doesn't matter that I can breathe, because it feels like I can't, and I'm not listening to logic. I'm listening to the shadowy voice in my skull, telling me that I failed.

That I'm worthless and ungrateful, and that I deserve nothing good in this world.

I'm empty. I have nothing to give anyone, ever again.

I don't want to exist anymore.

I don't realize I've stopped fighting the pain until his fingers

weave through my own. Caelan squeezes my hand and tugs like I
have to keep fighting. Like *we* have to keep fighting.

I squeeze back, and I don't let go.

When the pain recedes, I expect to be in a dream, but instead I
find Caelan sitting beside me, face pale. We're back in Gil's cavern, where the white lights flutter above us, energy fading.

I try to sit up, but a horrible pain shoots through my shoulder.
I wince, touching a tender patch of ravaged skin. My sleeve is
damp with blood, and I reach for my mouth, wondering if remnants of the black tar are still coated to my lips.

What did the Grimling do to me?

Hearing my thoughts, Caelan turns. "When something is
made of despair, it feeds despair back into the world." He clenches
his fists. "Its bite is like a poison—but I was able to get most of
it out."

Except Caelan doesn't look relieved. He looks terrified.

"How did you get it out of me?"

He hesitates.

"Caelan."

He holds out his arm reluctantly. Thick black veins stretch
from his fingertips to his elbow, pulsing beneath his skin.

My gasp is sharp. I reach for his arm, pulling it closer like I
want to take it all back. "What did you do?"

"I tried to pull it out of you. Force it out of your mind. It was
the only way to keep it from reaching your heart."

I press my hand to my shoulder again. To the space where the

Grimling bit me, inches above my chest. And then I stare at the veins in Caelan's arm, rising slowly, little by little.

A poison.

"What happens when it reaches your heart?" I ask softly.

Caelan drops his arm. "Damon will be able to help. He has . . . a knack for poisons. He can control the Grimlings, and cure their venom."

"If he controls them, then why was one of them here, in Ettore's court?"

"I don't know the answer to that. Perhaps Ettore's spies have gone beyond War. But if you're doubting Damon, don't. I've seen what Famine is—he is on our side."

I stare at the black veins at his wrist. "How long do you have?"

He blinks, expression stiff. "Long enough to get across the border, so long as there aren't more Grimlings sniffing out the poison in my blood."

He did this for me—to *save* me.

I think of all the people I saved without hesitating—not because I knew them or because they deserved it, but because it was always, always the right thing to do—and I realize that helping Caelan doesn't feel like that at all.

It isn't an instinct, or a matter of right and wrong.

I'm not even sure if it's a choice.

But I know in my heart I want him to be okay—because, despite how many times I've tried to talk myself out of it, Caelan isn't a stranger, or an enemy, or someone I'm indifferent to.

He's something more.

And I think it might be the same for him—which is why I

know what I have to do, and where we have to go next.

"I'll go with you to Famine," I say with the kind of finality that makes his eyes widen. "Someone has to make sure you get over the border safely."

His silver eyes find me, flickering the same way the orbs above him are. "You don't owe me anything. This bite . . . I don't want you to think it's transactional."

"That's not why I'm doing it."

"You did once say you'd throw me to the wolves."

"And you once said, 'I look out for you, and you look out for me. Those are the rules.' Remember?"

His cheeks dimple with relief, and he nods. "I remember. Which is why after Damon heals me, I'm coming back to War with you, to fight by your side for as long as you'll have me."

I replay his words in my head like I'm not sure I heard him right. "You would do that?"

His lashes soften. "I want peace between our kinds. But if it takes another few lifetimes to get there, then so be it."

My heart cracks down the middle. "Ophelia will be searching for you. Your brother, too." *You'll be an enemy to most of your kind— they may never know the truth of what you're fighting for.*

"I don't care," he says. "We'll be safer together. And I'm the reason Shura and Ahmet ran to War—this is my mistake to fix."

I study him carefully, like there might be a part of an equation I'm still missing. Something that isn't translating in my brain.

I'm so used to searching his face for signs that he's still pretending. Except now when I look at Caelan, all I see is the boy who's been trying to protect me all this time. Who has been on my side, for far longer than I realized.

Trust can't be rebuilt in a day.

But I think I'm ready to try.

"I'm asking."

Caelan frowns.

I try to make myself taller, and take a breath. "I'm asking you to listen to my mind. To everything." Not just the complicated emotions between the two of us, but the agonizing regret of what I almost did.

He is not the only one to blame. Maybe the first step in building a bridge is admitting when we mess up, and when we're wrong.

Maybe it's the key to starting over, too.

Caelan pauses at the edge of my mental wall, taking several cautious steps before he meets me inside. I watch his face shift from surprise, to disbelief, and then—

He drifts back out, eyes darting between mine.

"You aren't the only one who made a mistake," I say, surprised by how easily the words come. "Whether the Orb was real or not, I never should have agreed to destroy it, and I'm sorry. It was the wrong choice—and I want you to hear that from me, out loud."

"I'm sorry I made you doubt me—that I gave you a *reason* to doubt me," he says. "But more than anything, I'm sorry I ever made you doubt yourself."

He's beautiful in all his forms, but especially like this. When it's me and him with our hearts on our sleeves and nothing left to hide.

My attention drifts to the black venom beneath his skin. "Does it hurt?"

"It's nothing compared to what Ettore did to you," he says, a

clash of fire and ice stirring behind his words. "And I promise I
will make him pay for it one day."

I'm not interested in revenge; I just want the people I care
about to be safe.

That includes the Prince of Victory—a Resident who is
flawed and hopeful and real, and dreams bigger than any human
I've ever met.

And I know he must've heard me, because Caelan leans forward, mouth parted, and a trillion sparks ignite in my core. My
shoulders tremble in response. I forget to breathe.

I think maybe he does too.

Our gazes meet, and for a moment everything stills. Even
without words, I feel an understanding settle between us. A silent
confession that what we felt a year ago wasn't all a lie.

Maybe we're fighting an impossible battle. We're a connection that breaks every rule, and not just because one of us was
born human and the other created by an AI. We are not perfect
people who make perfect choices. Our story is messy because
we're messy.

But maybe that's okay.

I don't know if everyone who does something bad deserves a
second chance, but I believe in taking the time to know someone's heart before holding them to their worst mistakes. No one
has to exist in darkness forever.

Caelan wants to be forgiven. He wants to help me build a
bridge.

I'm not going to be the kind of person who says it's not
enough to try. Because to me? Trying is *everything*.

"I wish we had more time," he whispers, only an inch away.

I wish we had more time too, I tell the shadows of his mind, leaning forward until I feel the phantom brush of his lips against mine. I remember the way he once looked at me through Gil's eyes—like he knew all my secrets, and I knew his.

It was part of a game back then, but now?

Right now, there is poison in Caelan's bloodstream and no time to calculate the future.

I take a small step back, widening the gap between us. I hate how it feels like I'm severing something. Something that hasn't yet had a chance to heal.

"We need to get you to Famine," I say, ignoring the pinch in my chest.

He shuts his eyes in response, nodding slowly. Because he knows what I do.

The road ahead is not going to be easy. It's paved with war and distrust and Ophelia's wrath.

Whatever we felt for each other—whatever we feel now— it'll have to wait.

Caelan and I find a path through the tunnels, and when the first ribbon of sunlight reaches the cavern floor, an unsettling silence falls between us.

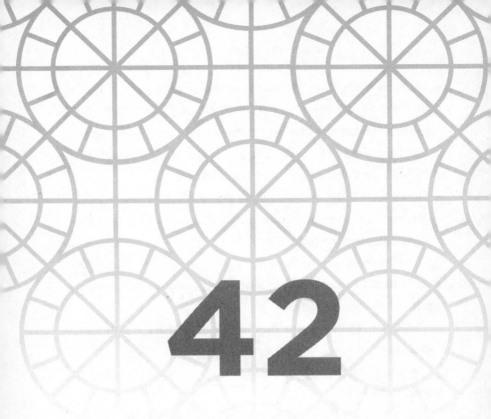

42

THE ENERGY ALONG THE BORDER OF WAR thunders ahead of us. It's overpowering. I don't remember if it was always so loud, or if the Grimling bite has done something to my consciousness.

Maybe sensitivity is a side effect.

I glance at Caelan, unable to shield my concern, even with our veils hiding us from the rest of the world. He's pulled his sleeve down, so I don't know how far the poison has inched its way to his heart. But his fingertips are almost entirely black.

Caelan tilts his cheek. "You don't have to keep looking at me like I'm going to disappear at any moment."

"What *will* happen?" I squint in the sunlight, moving across the burning sand.

He presses two fingers to his shoulder—an indication of where the venom is. "I'll be too weak to do much. But I'm able to slow it down, when I'm concentrating." He offers an apologetic smile.

That explains the long silences. "Save your energy." *We can talk when we're somewhere safe.*

Caelan's jaw tightens in response, fighting the overhead glare as he searches the horizon.

I hope Genesis is okay. I hope Ettore and the Legion Guards haven't been able to find them.

Because if I have to carry the guilt of putting my friends in a prison twice, it will destroy me.

The warmth of Caelan's presence sends a rush of blood to my head. There's guilt when it comes to him, too—at the thought of Caelan coming here for me, and taking the Grimling's venom to save me from harm.

The sooner we get to Famine, the better for all of us.

Beside me, Caelan halts abruptly, and his entire body goes rigid. And then I feel it too—the thrum of energy building around us.

There's no time to ask what's wrong, or make sense of how there could be so much static in such an empty, sweeping desert.

Because we're not alone.

The sound of an enormous veil being ripped away thunders all around us. Caelan and I look in horror at the path to the border, now blocked by Residents.

Not just a handful of guards, or a single battalion, but an entire army.

Two massive airships loom in the sky. Everywhere, Legion Guards wait for battle. Some hover in the air, others remain on foot. A roadblock, between us and the Labyrinth. An impossible feat.

Prince Ettore stands in front of them all, flaming swords in his hands. And beside him is Prince Lysander of Death.

Waiting for me. For *us*.

Fear ricochets through my mind. *How could they know where we were headed?*

The Grimling, Caelan's voice collides with my thoughts. *It can track the poison in my blood. That's why Ettore must've sent them into the tunnels.*

It isn't just one court of Residents that's prepared to fight—it's two. There's a mix of wings in the sky: batlike for War, and birdlike for Death. The swirl of red and green uniforms makes the scene look like a bed of roses, weeping blood.

Caelan snarls, deep and vicious.

I pull my knives out. "But—our veil—"

"It doesn't matter now," he says, voice low. "Lysander can see through any veil."

Dread powers its way into my veins. "How is that possible?"

"He's spent his entire existence searching for a way to eradicate a person's consciousness," Caelan says. "It doesn't matter if he can't see our bodies—he sees the light. The soul."

"Does that mean you—" I start, but I bite down on my words. There's no time for questions—no time to consider what it means that he can see our light. Not just mine, but Caelan's, too.

Because if Caelan has a light . . . a *soul* . . .

Ettore and Lysander stare across the sand, dressed in their battle clothes. Ready for war.

Lysander's voice bellows toward us, face shielded partially by a golden helmet. "By order of Queen Ophelia, you have both been deemed traitors to the crown." Not even the wind whistles in response. "You will be taken to Her Majesty to receive your sentence. If you surrender willingly, you can spare yourselves needless bloodshed."

Ettore flashes a wicked grin. "Please don't surrender. You'll spoil all the fun."

"Stay out of this, Lysander," Caelan shouts. "I have no quarrel with you."

"You have betrayed us," Lysander roars back.

Caelan's eyes simmer with life. "I will not let you take her." The look on his face, like he's untethered himself . . . like he's unleashed his heart into the world, with no chains left to hold it back.

It's Caelan without any mask.

Ettore laughs mercilessly. "Oh, the human isn't going anywhere. Not for a while at least. We made a deal—Lysander will take you to our mother, and he'll come back for your little pet after she and I have finished our delightful game." He turns to Caelan, relishing in the spectacle around him. "The kill is the best part of any Hunt."

Caelan's eyes flash with silver flames. *"Nami,"* he seethes, "belongs to no one, and no court."

Blue hellfire rains from the sky, crashing down above the Residents. Most of it finds a target, earning sharp howls from the combined legions. But what the hellfire symbolizes is so much more powerful.

We will not surrender, and we will not go quietly.

Lysander and Ettore flash forward, and Caelan races across the sand to meet them—to keep the battle away from me.

Run, his thoughts surge back to me. *Find a way across the border. Go to Damon—he'll keep you safe.*

I can't even think of anything to say back. He's delusional if he thinks he can take on two entire court armies all on his own.

Unless . . .

Unless he knows he's not leaving this court of his own free will.

The three princes explode into battle, and I frantically clutch the seams of my veil. It won't protect me from Lysander, but the other Residents?

Maybe it will buy me some time.

I know Caelan betrayed the Colony by pretending to be Gil. I know his change of heart may not have erased the hurt. It doesn't change the past. But it's altered the path we're on.

Maybe a change of heart can be enough to reshape the future.

It isn't just a Resident out there in the sand, dodging the swing of Ettore's flaming blades and Lysander's thunderous punch.

It's a friend. Someone I care about. *Someone who needs my help.*

I reach my mind out for the Legion Guards headed in my direction, lashing at their minds with fire. They stumble, but it's not enough. I'm not fully healed—I don't know if my mind will tire before my body, or the other way around.

But I try again, this time sending a wave of salt water, trying to shove the walls back down in their minds. One of them falls, choking in the sand. But the others shake it off, running toward me like they've sensed my presence.

I know I'm shaking the veil. There's too much chaos for me to hold it still.

Hiding won't stop them forever. It's just using up my energy faster, sending my consciousness in every direction. I need every drop of my power. Not to hide, but to fight.

I lift the veil and start swinging.

My blades meet flesh, and armor, and metal. I am a whirlwind of rage and desperation, fighting to make these last moments count. The wound in my shoulder burns with every upward movement I make, but I don't stop.

Two Residents flank my sides, swords pointed down at me. I breathe, studying their feet, and wait for them to strike. At the last moment, I roll forward, dodging out of the way, and spin back to face them. I throw my blades from my hands with supersonic force, and they sail through the air and land in their targets' necks. I run to fetch them, ignoring the fresh blood dripping from their sharpened edges.

The consequences of what I've done roar through my entire body.

I'm doing too much. I'm using all my fuel.

I scan my eyes quickly at the Residents racing my way.

So many of them. So many blades.

Across the sand, Caelan moves in blue flashes around his brothers, dodging their relentless strikes.

I bend my knees, and brace myself for impact.

A series of sharp noises whoosh past me, and I watch as one by one, the Residents fall a few feet away.

Battle cries erupt from my left, and I look over my shoulder to see the rebellion. All of them.

Genesis. They've come to fight.

Eyes stinging, I watch as Shura and Ahmet charge in front of me, weapons in their hands. Shura swings a dagger at one of the recovered Residents, meeting flesh, and Ahmet lets off another round of arrows from a strange electrical crossbow. Sand explodes in the distance, and the Resident and human armies race toward one another.

"What are you doing here?" I manage through a gasp, staring at Shura.

Ahmet appears too, skin full of the warmth I remember. "We saw the ships come in from Death. Figured you might've had something to do with it."

Zahrah falls in beside me, battle-ax swinging in circles like she's preparing to charge. A wide smile spreads across her face. "Did you really think I'd stay home and let a youngling have all the fun without me? I have a reputation to uphold, Nami."

A violent clash of metal and screams explodes across the battlefield. Shura, Ahmet, and Zahrah don't leave my side, even as we force ourselves across the rocks and blood-soaked earth, toward the thick of the violence.

Caelan is far away, still fighting his brothers, when I hear the strain of his mind.

I swing my blade against flesh, kicking a Resident in the stomach before Zahrah makes a mess of them with her ax. My eyes scan the tumultuous scene, searching for that familiar shade of snow white in the landscape. I find him—I see the wince, and the staggered breath, and the way his knees shake a split second too long.

The bite is close to his heart.

I don't care if it's reckless—I send my thoughts toward him and meet his frazzled mind in the void.

The rattlesnake hiss thunders around me, and I clutch my ears, sharing his agony.

He's running out of time.

Everything is pitch black. I can't even see Caelan in the shadows—just a merciless darkness that feeds on light. On *souls.*

I don't know where the venom is, but I hold out my hands like I'm trying to soak it back in—back into me.

I need to give Caelan more time.

He pushes against me, trying to shove me out of his mind. *Don't,* he says.

Let me help, I plead.

I don't know if it's Caelan or the poison that shoves me out, but my thoughts snap back to my body with a jolt, the despair seizing my shoulder. Not as much as before, but enough to send me staggering.

And Caelan has been carrying so much more of it than me.

He was never fine. He just didn't want me to know how much pain he was in.

I'm not sure whether my legs start to give way first or my consciousness, but Shura throws me under her veil and pushes me away from the fight.

"Stay here," she says. "You're too hurt, and the Residents already have enough of an advantage."

She returns to the bloodied sands, and all I can do is watch helplessly.

But my mind is dipping in and out, like a faulty electric wire. I try to stand, knees shaking, and collapse against a large rock. My knives clatter to the stones.

I blink between light and darkness.

Between awake and asleep.

I stretch my gaze across the field, watching as so many humans fall. The Residents adapt too quickly to their weapons, like they're learning with every swing. An explosion of blue lights bursts from the center, and Caelan throws himself at Ettore, knocking him over. Lysander comes up behind him, hands building with energy, and picks up a spare blade from the ground.

He raises it above Caelan's head.

No! I scream across the desert.

Caelan looks straight at me, face morphing from concern to understanding, and flashes several feet away as Lysander's sword comes down.

Nearby, Eliza spreads her arms wide, and lightning erupts from her fingertips, scattering a fierce blue current over an entire row of Residents. The humans push through the gap, making their way toward the princes.

Ettore snarls, throwing flames from his hands. They lash at the approaching humans, engulfing some of them and burning others. With his red-scaled tunic and golden eyes, it almost looks as if he's releasing dragon fire from his core.

Lysander moves for the humans who make it through the fire, and calls a bolt of lightning from the sky, desecrating the space where they stand. Body parts scatter. Only a few make it out in one piece. It makes Eliza's power look like a harmless spark in comparison.

Caelan reaches for a nearby dagger from one of the fallen humans, and locks his eyes on Ettore, who is too preoccupied setting the world on fire to notice his younger brother racing toward him.

But Caelan is preoccupied too, and he doesn't see Zahrah approaching with her battle-ax.

I grab my knives.

I'm running without thinking, past Residents and humans and a puzzled Shura who still has me under her veil. I'm running through the pain—through the faint mist settling in my head, whispering that I'll be asleep soon. That in another moment I will have no choice but to surrender to exhaustion.

I run to Caelan's side and throw my knives out to block Zahrah's attack. It's the last bit of fight I have left, and I make it count. Not to hurt Zahrah, but to protect Caelan.

Something supersonic explodes from my chest and throws her far across the sand. When I hear Caelan's alarmed shout, I realize I've thrown him, too.

Stars dance in my eyes, and I fall, breaking free of Shura's veil. My head hits the stones hard.

Straining, I look across the sand and see Ozias. Wearing his elaborate bone armor and carrying two enormous swords, the King of Genesis doesn't move. He watches, calculating.

There is enough time for him to help me—enough time for a jumper to reach my side and pull me to safety.

But Ozias's brow hardens with a decision he made long before he saw my broken body in the sand. I was a threat to his rebellion. And there is only one way a warlord handles a threat.

He turns his back and leaves me to the fate of this war, just as he left Gil many lifetimes ago.

Someone dressed in flowing green fabric approaches, and when Lysander flings me over his shoulder like a rag doll, I don't make a sound. I can't.

Eyes half-closed, I try to search for Caelan in the battlefield. He's racing toward me—stumbling because the venom is already grasping for his heart—and I watch Ahmet unload a round of arrows in his back.

Caelan's fingers are outstretched, reaching for me, but it's not enough. Not in this war. Not when the despair already has control of him. His silver eyes fall shut, and the rebellion drags him away.

Lysander stops in front of someone I can't see. Everything is already drifting away from me, like a terrible, faraway dream. "Call our people back to the airships. We have what we came for. We leave for Death now."

"Yes, Your Highness," a voice replies.

There's a shuffle. A growl. And then . . .

"What do you think you're doing? We had a deal—you get Caelan, and I get the human," Ettore seethes.

"The queen does not make deals, little brother," Lysander barks back. "Now get your court in order, before I decide to tell our mother what a mess you've made of things."

I hear the pops of jumpers in the distance. The sound of retreating humans. *Survivors.*

It's the only thing that offers comfort as I give in to the darkness.

43

THE VENOM FINDS ME IN MY SLEEP. IT SLITHERS
toward my heart, bleeding melancholy into my veins.

A phantom appears at the walls of my mind. *I can help you,* his
haunting voice calls, soothing.

Sheer stubbornness is all I have left to fight with. *Get away
from me,* I hiss, reeling when the venom pulses like it's picking
up speed.

*You have something I want. If you give it to me, I will take the poison
away and cure your despair.*

I squirm against the pain. *I'm not giving you my mind.*

Not your mind, he whispers. *There's something else I want.
Something you won't even miss.*

I'm too weak to question his words.

The phantom reaches out a slender hand, his touch as faint as smoke tendrils. *You're running out of time. If you want to save the others, you must do this. You must trade me the poison for the key to their protection.*

I picture every one of them in my head. The friends and strangers I've been trying to save.

And maybe it's the despair or the darkness or the desperation, but I open my mind and let the phantom latch onto a thread of the poison. He pulls, slowly at first, and as the venom drains, something bitter replaces it.

For a moment I'm afraid I've made a horrible mistake.

But then the phantom pulls back, vanishing from my thoughts like a silent mist, and I forget he was ever there at all.

I wake up in a bright white cell, not dissimilar to the Orientation room where I first arrived in Infinity. Sleek and modern, with metal doors.

One touch against my shoulder suggests my wound has slowly begun to close. There's still an ache deep inside, but I can breathe without feeling the crack of bone. And even though my head is pounding, I feel rested.

Someone's healed me, and I'm afraid to know why.

There are no restraints on my wrists. I flex my fingers, eyeing the door, and throw a blast of energy toward it. The light fizzles out like a dud firework.

Something sharp pierces my neck. My fingers investigate,

and I find a smooth metal collar around my throat. At a guess, it must be acting as some kind of suppressor, holding back my consciousness.

They collared me like an animal. Restrained me like I was less than human.

My face burns. I'm going to make them pay.

I stand up, searching my new cage for a way out, but of course there isn't one. I slam my hands against the door. Throw my shoulder into it. Try to break it apart with my mind.

Each time I'm rewarded with a sharp nip beneath the collar. When my eyesight starts to go blurry, I realize what it's doing to me.

The more I fight, the more it starts to shut down my consciousness.

I try to shake it off, biting the inside of my cheek to keep myself awake, and sit against the back wall. I need to conserve my energy.

A glass dome sits beneath the ceiling, blinking silently.

Are they watching me?

I scowl just in case, and tuck my knees to my chest.

The thought of Caelan in a cage somewhere makes my throat coarse. I saw Ahmet shoot him. I saw the humans drag him away.

But how far did they make it?

I want the humans to be safe in Genesis, but I'm worried their safety means Caelan is in danger. They didn't know he was helping me, or what alliances he's built in Famine. They don't know he's on our side.

Or they don't care, my mind adds bitterly.

Caelan is still poisoned with despair. I barely managed to pull a drop out of him. And now he's a prisoner.

Shutting my eyes, I breathe slowly, hoping this ridiculous collar won't stop me from reaching his mind.

Across the woodland, I enter the black void, and find Caelan lying on his back, on some kind of raised surface. For all that he might be a prisoner, he still looks so perfect. There's even a blush of color to his face that I haven't seen in months.

He looks . . . healthy.

"Caelan?" I step closer, shadows rippling at my feet.

His eyes peel apart, and he smiles like he's been expecting me. "Are you okay?"

I nod. "I don't know where I am. Some kind of cell with white walls and a silver door."

"Show me?"

I push myself further into his mind, expanding what he can see. He looks around the room, blinking, before his silver eyes fall on me. On the collar.

He frowns. "Nami, that—" But then he shuts his eyes tight, like he's bracing against something. His entire body goes stiff.

"What's wrong?" I ask quickly, studying him.

Eventually his eyes bat open, and he offers another small, dimpled smile. "I—I'm glad I got to see you again."

I make a face, stepping closer. "You're acting strange." I pause. "Where did they take you?"

He stares back with his beautiful, polished face. "Into a cave. There are cages here. Like . . ." He pauses, body going stiff again. "Like the ones in Victory," he finishes.

My chest sinks. Ahmet must've shown them that particular trick.

Guilt rattles through me. If I'm the one who brought Ahmet home, am I the one responsible for Caelan being locked up?

The light around him fades for a second. A flicker. And I see—

Frowning, I study his peaceful smile. The way he's looking at me like he's wearing a mask . . .

"Caelan," I say slowly. "What are you not showing me?"

"I don't want you to see me like this," he says softly.

"You're hiding something. I can tell." I shake my head. "Whatever it is, I want to know."

"You're in Death." Caelan closes his eyes, fighting against something in silence. "If this is the last time you see me, then remember me the way I was—before you thought I might be a monster."

"You are far from a monster. And if this is the last time we see each other," I argue, "then don't show me a lie."

He blinks back weakly, and when the light flickers this time, his entire image changes.

The rattlesnake hiss swarms around us. Caelan's shirt is gone, leaving bare, bruised flesh on display. His white hair is disheveled, the skin around his left eye a deep, awful purple. Blood stretches from his nostrils to his busted lip.

And around his limbs are black chains, laced with something that sears into his flesh. He isn't just facing despair; he's being tortured.

The smile he wore is no longer visible, replaced with an agonizing look of pain in his clenched jaw.

"What are they doing to you?" My words echo through the void.

He cries out to the stars as his body jolts again and again, and electricity pounds through him.

This is why he kept going so stiff; he was hiding his suffering. Hiding the truth.

The light above him flickers again, and I realize his consciousness won't hold. He's drifting away, like I was in the desert.

And I don't think about it; I just take his hand in mine and press my lips to his temple.

"I'm not leaving you behind," I whisper against his ear.

I can't tell whether he's smiling or not, but his voice is soft. "I think I'd deserve it if you did."

Because I'm not the only one racked with guilt.

No, I mouth, shaking my head over and over again. "No one deserves this."

And I mean every word.

The volts of electricity tear through him again, and I hold his hand, fighting back tears, until his body goes limp beside me.

As he loses consciousness and the black void pushes me out, I send one last thought to him, and hope he remembers it when he wakes.

"I'll find a way back to you. No matter what."

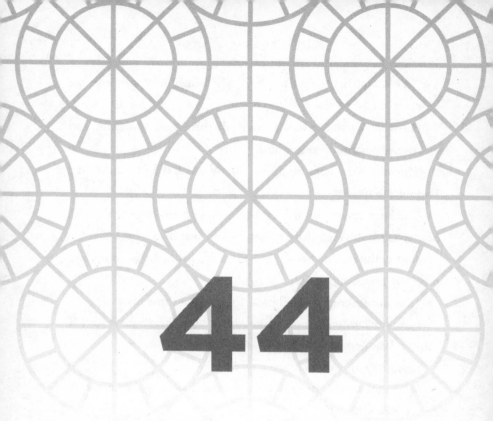

44

QUEEN OPHELIA SITS IN DEATH'S THRONE ROOM, dressed in turquoise robes embellished with starlight.

Sleek marble pillars hold up the extraordinarily high ceiling, and a massive circular skylight is formed at the center, allowing sunlight into the room. Glass tiles stretch across the floor, all boasting various shades of green. And the golden throne itself has an arc of pointed spears, making it appear as if Ophelia is sitting on the sun itself.

Death's Legion Guards lead me forward and push me onto my knees. I don't resist; the fight through the hallway was enough to prove it's fruitless. Every swing sends another pinch against my neck, making it harder to stand.

This collar is controlling me. If I don't comply, pretty soon I won't even be awake. And I need to remain conscious. I need to know what Ophelia plans to do with me.

Even though, deep in my gut, I already know the answer.

Prince Lysander is at Ophelia's side, golden antlers on his head and chartreuse robes pooling at his feet. Streaks of gold follow his eyes, radiant against his dark skin.

He nods to the guards, and they take a step back from me.

"Something tells me we have been in a place like this before," Ophelia says blandly. "Though now I realize it was my son who set you free." She pauses. "What did you offer him in return?"

I say nothing.

"As I suspected." Ophelia blinks, turning slightly to Lysander. "Perhaps the time in a human's body was too much for Caelan. His . . . priorities seem to have been distorted."

Lysander nods. "The human shell allowed him to dream. I did warn him of the dangers, but to my shame I did not expect something like this to happen." His glance toward me is enough to gather his meaning.

Ophelia lifts her chin, silver circlet gleaming at her forehead. "Where is Caelan now?"

"A prisoner in the human rebellion," Lysander replies. "I worry Ettore has let things get out of hand."

"He has fire in his heart," Ophelia muses, face void of any real feeling.

"Yes." Lysander raises a brow, cautious. "But a fire left to grow too large can become a problem."

Ophelia watches me, black eyes searching for a weakness.

"Leave Caelan there for now," she says calmly. "And when he does make his return to court, I want you to wipe his memories."

"What?" I say, chest tightening. "You can't do that."

She blinks. She found my flaw, the ripple in my consciousness. The way to hurt me.

Because it's always, always been through the people I care about most.

"He is my son," Ophelia replies. "If he is weak, I will fix him."

"There is nothing to fix," I snarl. "He is better than you—better than all of you. And if you truly wanted Infinity to be better than what it is, you'd be smart enough to listen to him."

Ophelia's black eyes flicker. "Listen to what?"

I open my mouth, to talk about building a bridge. The dream of uniting humans and Residents. The possibility that by working together, we can set each other free.

But my thoughts linger in a murky pool, evaporating before my voice can turn them into words.

Say something, I order myself. *Tell her what Caelan was trying to do.*

No matter how hard I grasp for what I know to be true, the knowledge falls through my fingers, finer than sand. A secret I can never tell.

I don't hear him approach—I'm not sure anybody can. Damon stops several yards away, violet gaze observing my frustration. Blue hair flows from his shoulders, topped with his crown of coral.

The understanding settles inside of me, pressing against my straining thoughts.

Damon did this. He healed the despair and replaced it with

another poison, so I could never speak about uniting both our kinds. So I could never accidentally destroy everything he's built.

So he could protect his family.

It wasn't the Grimling that told Ettore where we'd be. It was Damon, unwilling to take the risk. When Caelan saved me, he made himself a target. It was only a matter of time before the Residents began asking questions—before they put together what Caelan wanted, and who he hoped would be on his side.

No one will ever know all the good Caelan tried to do. Because Damon will keep the truth beneath the sea, and leave us to our fate.

I should be furious. He betrayed us.

But he is also making sure the Colony—and so many other humans—are safe.

Maybe I'm not allowed anger. Maybe I just have to understand.

Ophelia's talons scrape at my mind, yanking my attention back to her. Her anger is visceral beneath the surface, but she's good at keeping a straight face. "Tell me what it is my son planned to do."

I grit my teeth, fighting the pressure against my skull. "He would've—helped me—change the world."

She releases me, and I gasp, barely keeping my balance. "You infected his mind. Traveled too deep inside, like you tried to do to me."

When I tried to reach out to Mei.

The mangled threads flash in my memories. I may wear a collar, but Ophelia is on a leash. "You'll never break free. The living world won't let you go, because it knows you don't belong here."

She bares her teeth, the first sign of fury I've seen outside the void. "*You* are the one who doesn't belong." Ophelia stills, leaning back in her throne like she's regaining her composure. "Did you really think you could follow my mind to your past life? That you could go back to your family?"

"I wasn't trying to go back." Maybe Mei couldn't hear me, but at least I felt her presence. I know she's still safe in the living world.

I hope she stays that way for as long as she can.

If Ophelia heard the message I tried to send my sister, she doesn't mention it. Maybe I was too far away—maybe there were too many voices getting in the way, distorting my words.

Veiling me.

At least that one moment—the goodbye I was finally able to give my sister—will forever be safe from Ophelia's reach.

Damon moves closer to his mother's throne. "Perhaps leaving Caelan to the rebellion is an unnecessary risk. He knows much about the Capital. And he is one of our own—allowing the humans to desecrate his body and mind feels . . . excessive."

A mercy. Maybe because of what he did.

Or maybe it's just another way to protect his court. To reach Caelan, and his mind, before the truth comes out.

Ophelia stands, and the height of her makes me shudder. "He gave up the right to be treated as one of us the moment he betrayed his own kind."

Lysander's watchful eyes pass between his family. "If that is your wish, then we will leave him in War until you wish us to retrieve him."

Damon dips his chin, locks of hair shifting in a phantom wind. "Of course."

My chest quakes at the thought of how many years Caelan will spend in a cell. Even if his brothers search for him one day, I doubt the rebellion will give up such a high-ranking prisoner without a fight. In that time, he'll be their test subject. Their source of information.

And with the despair coursing through his veins and the restraints subduing his mind, I don't think he'll be able to fight it.

Someone has to convince Genesis he's on our side.

I'm the only one left who can help him.

But Queen Ophelia has other plans. For Caelan, and for me.

When she speaks, her voice feels like it's meant for all of the Four Courts. "You have stood in my way for the last time." She turns to her sons—and then pins her gaze solely on Lysander. "This human is too great a risk. She will be taken to the chamber and separated from her body immediately. Seal her consciousness away where she will not be a threat, and the moment you have figured out how to eradicate it, you will do so."

A second death. She's sentencing me to a second death.

Even though I knew it was coming, I can't help the part of my heart that breaks when I realize I'll never see my loved ones again.

All the people I've grown to care about in Infinity. All the people I loved before my death.

And maybe my sister most of all.

"I'll come back from this," I snarl, desperate. "I will never let you win."

Ophelia tilts her head, void of any emotion at all. "That fire inside of you has burned long enough." She nods to the room. "Take her away."

The guards comply. Even though I don't turn to look, I sense Damon watching me go, violet eyes sending a silent, unknowable farewell.

I march to my end without so much as a tear.

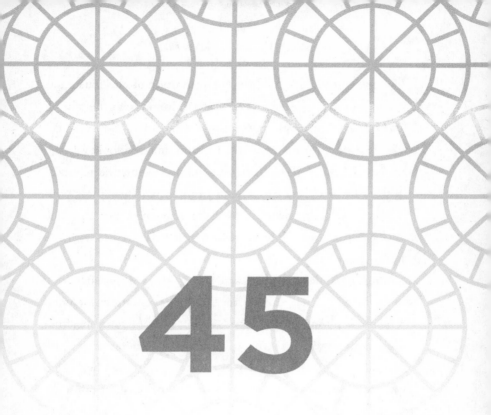

45

WHEN THE LEGION GUARDS LEAD ME TO THE
white chamber, I don't try to run.

These are my last few moments. I won't lose them to the collar around my neck.

I want to spend them remembering the people I love.

When the guards strap me to the metal bed, I remember my
parents, and the way they loved me unconditionally, right from
the beginning. I remember Dad's wild hair and paint-stained
fingertips. I remember Mom's cooking, and the silly dances she'd
do when her favorite songs came on the radio.

When the guards push the bed beneath the bright light
and metal fixtures, I remember my friends, and the joy they

filled my world with at different moments of my existence. I remember Lucy's sleepovers, and the bike rides to school. I remember Finn's whispers under the stars, and the milkshakes we never grew tired of. I remember Shura being the first friend I made in Infinity, and the ways she tried to make adjusting to this place easier. And I remember the others who followed, like Kasia, who crossed the Labyrinth just to make sure I was okay, and Zahrah, who roamed the desert with me when no one else would.

When Lysander gives the order to begin, I remember Mei, and the love I still have for a sister I didn't get enough time with. I remember jumping on the beds of hotel rooms, and sneaking vanilla coffee creamer into our cereal. I remember staying up past midnight, giggling under our blankets. I remember video games, and doodles, and singing at the top of our lungs on long car rides.

And I remember the shadow I saw after chasing the threads in Ophelia's mind. A shadow that, despite everything, made me feel like I was home.

Because Mei was always home, even now. Even in death.

When the light brightens and the machines buzz around me, my mind flashes to Caelan, searching for him like I'm waving a hand through the fog.

This is it, I try to say. *I'll be gone soon.*

But Caelan isn't there, and I realize just as the snap of energy hits me that we never got to say goodbye.

The Cut is a sharp pain through my heart, and then—

In

the

darkness

I

become

nothing.

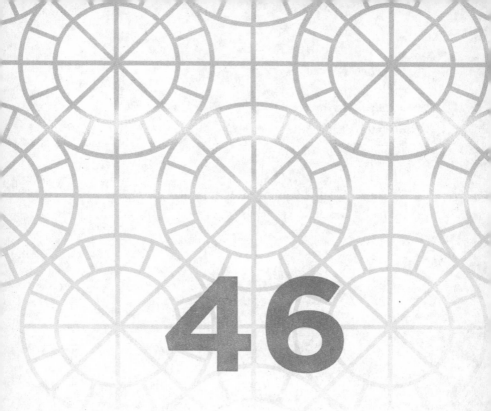

46

I SEE . . . A LIGHT. A LIGHT THAT I DON'T UNDER-stand.

I try to move, but something heavy is holding me back. It's everywhere, covering everything. It feels like water.

Water.

Yes. Yes, that's what it is.

I'm underwater.

And I see a light.

I see.

I see.

Something deep inside me glows, and a warbled sound reaches me. A name.

"Nami."

That's my name, my aching soul sings.

I don't stop chasing the sound, and the light. I keep fighting.

I will make myself whole.

47

WHEN I WAKE, IT FEELS LIKE DEATH ALL OVER again.

My skull throbs, and I sit up, pressing my hands against my temples.

My hands.

Fingers dance in front of me. In front of my—

I touch my cheeks and nose and eyes and mouth, and then I'm scanning the metal room. A strange grating covers the floors, and the walls sing like there's a collection of pipes behind them, rattling with steam.

I can see everything. I can hear everything.

Across from the room, a mirror sits on the wall. And I'm so

excited to see my face again—so eager to be back in my body—
that I push myself from the bed and attempt to run to the mirror.

I only make it one step before face-planting on the floor.

I groan, too stunned to get up, and a rush of footsteps sounds
outside the door. Something beeps, and the metal door slides
open.

A woman with heavy freckles and short curly hair rushes
inside, panting. When she sees me on the floor, her shoulders drop
with relief. "Oh, I thought it was another attack. Are you okay?
Goodness, let me help you up." She reaches under my shoulders
and pulls, helping me back to the edge of the bed.

I blink up at her. She looks very, very human.

She presses a hand against her heart. "I'm so sorry, where are
my manners? My name is Julie. Julie Baker. Oh—sorry, you don't
use last names here in the afterlife, do you? Well, the others have
just been calling me Doc, if that's easier to remember. Say, you're
really awake this time, aren't you?" She laughs. Loud and loose.
"This isn't the first time you've tried to walk, you know, but usually you clonk right back out and sleep for another few weeks."

"A few weeks?" I repeat, rubbing my forehead. "Where am I?
And how long have I been here?"

"You really don't remember a thing, do you? Figures. None
of the ones we wake up in the tanks ever do." She leans in like
we're sharing a secret. "You have no idea how many humans we
helped to regrow looking for you. To think I'm talking to the
real-life Nami Miyamoto, here in Infinity." For a moment, she
looks dazzled. And then a sharp frown takes over her face. "Sorry,
the last-name thing is a tricky one. Also, I guess it's not real-*life*

life, since technically none of us are alive in the textbook sense, but hey—I almost forgot! I'm supposed to take you to the general the moment you wake up."

The general? Regrowing humans?

I don't understand.

How much time has passed since the Cut?

The woman—Julie—heads for a nearby shelf and pulls out a robe. "It gets a bit chilly out there in the alleyways. You might want to throw this on. Especially since it's been a while since you, you know . . ." She holds up the robe.

I shake my head, trying to stand on my own. "I'm fine. I just want to know what happened to me." Where are my friends? Where is Genesis?

Where are the *Residents*?

Julie drops the robe onto the bed and scoops her arm beneath mine. "Come on, then. Let's take a walk. The general will want to explain everything."

She pushes a button against a keypad and the door slides back open. When we step through, the cold air hits me like a blast of icy wind.

I shudder violently.

"Told you," she says with a sympathetic smile. "Sure you don't want the bathrobe?"

I take a step forward in response, and she leads me across a rickety metal bridge. Steam blows up from below, and the sound of an engine bellows through the belly of whatever place this is. We move through a series of tunnels—alleyways, according to the woman—until we arrive at a gleaming metal ladder that leads to a hatch.

"Think you can manage?" she asks.

I clutch the rung in front of me and pull myself up, one shaky step at a time. When I reach the hatch, I shove it open before helping myself over the edge. I've only just managed to stand on two feet again when Julie makes it through the opening too, closing the circular door behind her.

It takes me a moment to get my bearings, and then I realize it isn't steam I'm looking at. It's clouds.

I walk shakily toward the metal railing, and peer out into the open sky. Miles and miles and miles of . . . *space.*

We're too high to see the surface. Higher than I've ever seen an airship fly.

"How . . . ?" I start, but Julie clears her throat from behind me. When I turn, she's motioning to a very big doorway, guarded by two armor-clad humans. Massive silver rifles are planted across their chests. Weapons more intricate than anything Ahmet was able to design.

I follow Julie inside, eyeing the guards as curiously as they're eyeing me, and step into the room.

The smell of firewood and cinnamon fills my nostrils. Warmth. Just like being home.

Wooden planks line the floor, and an iron stove burns against the back wall. There's a massive table covered in maps and strange sketches of metallic beasts and technological blueprints, and a weapons arsenal directly behind it. Not just daggers—swords, axes, and guns, too. A messy bed sits to the side, covered in more paper, and an archway leads to a separate room.

"General?" Julie calls, voice going serious. "Nami woke up."

"Hmm?" a distracted voice calls back. "Yes, I've been told that already, several times. I want to know when she's *conscious*. I don't have time to keep—"

"Er, what I mean is, Nami is *here*." Julie pauses, looking at me. "Right now."

The silence makes my ears go hollow.

There's a shuffle behind the door, like a chair being pushed to the side, and then a stranger comes tearing around the corner with wide, glassy eyes.

A middle-aged woman with a soft nose and hair in a high ponytail looks back at me. Dressed in dark, armored leather, with pistols at her sides, she looks like she's part of a militia.

The general, I presume.

I'm about to open my mouth and ask her where I am, and how I got here, when she speaks.

"Nami," she says with a gasp, and her voice echoes through me like I'm in a dream.

I stare back, heart pounding, as I study her eyes. Her mouth. Her nearly black hair, the same color as mine.

And I'm not sure I know what world I'm in at all.

Because there is no doubt in my mind who this woman is.

I'm looking at my sister, Mei.

And she's looking back at me.

ACKNOWLEDGMENTS

This book went on such a journey, and I am overflowing with gratitude to all the people who helped The Genesis Wars become what it is today.

To Jennifer Ung—thank you for guiding this book in the beginning. To Alyza Liu—thank you for seeing this book across the finish line. You both are editorial magicians, and working on this series with such a brilliant, thoughtful team has truly been an honor.

To my agent, Penny Moore—you've championed my words from the start, and I'm forever grateful to have shared so many projects with you.

To the Simon & Schuster team who helped Nami's story evolve from an idea to a book on the shelves: An enormous thank you to Dainese Santos, Emily Ritter, Anna Jarzab, Lauren Carr, Shivani Annirood, Lisa Moraleda, Katrina Groover, Karen Sherman, Sara Berko, Justin Chanda, Anne Zafian, Jon Anderson, Kendra Levin, Chrissy Noh, Brian Murray, Lauren Hoffman, and Francie Crawford.

And a very special thank you to Casey Weldon and Laura Eckes for another stunning cover and for bringing Nami (and Nix!) to life in such an unforgettable way, and to Virginia Allyn for the beautiful map. The visuals in this book completely took my breath away.

Another special thank you to the team behind the audiobook, and to the massively talented Mizuo Peck for bringing Nami's voice to life.

A huge thank you to everyone at Aevitas Creative Management and WME for your excitement and support on this project, and especially Carolina Beltran, Brianna Cedrone, Allison Warren, and Shenel Ekici-Moling.

I've been lucky to have some wonderful author friends over the years who add so much joy to a sometimes intense process. Thank you Nicki, Lyla, Michelle, and Sangu for being superstar humans. Thank you Adalyn, Tracy, and Sarah for your lovely blurbs. And thank you Kate for being an eleventh-hour hero.

To the street team who celebrated this series from the very beginning—you all are magnificent. Thank you.

To every single reader who has picked up this book—thank you for hanging around to see how Nami's journey progresses. Writing is one of the greatest honors of my life, and I'm so happy to be able to bring you more stories from the world of Infinity. And if you're one of the readers who've made the genre hop from my other books—thank you. Your support means the absolute *world*.

To my friends and family in real life, who have been around for the highest levels of excitement and lowest points of fear— I'm eternally grateful to have you in my circle.

And to Shaine and Oliver in particular—thank you both for being the best of the best. Being your mom means absolutely everything to me, and watching you both grow up to be such thoughtful, kind, hilarious people is the highlight of my life. I love you both times infinity, again and again, and more than all the stars in the sky.

Finally, to Maze—I know you can't read, and you have no idea what a book is because you're a dog, but you helped me get through this year and—let's be honest—writing is a better experience with puppy cuddles.

THE MAD, **THE BAD, AND THE INNOCENT**

THE MAD, THE BAD